KT-524-505

# Speaking in Tongues

## Language at Play in the Theatre

*Marvin Carlson*

The University of Michigan Press
*Ann Arbor*

Copyright © by the University of Michigan 2006
All rights reserved
Published in the United States of America by
The University of Michigan Press
Manufactured in the United States of America
♾ Printed on acid-free paper

BATH SPA UNIVERSITY
NEWTON PARK LIBRARY
Class No.
792.01 CAR
Dawson  17/11/06
DISCARD

2009   2008   2007   2006     4   3   2   1

No part of this publication may be reproduced, stored in a retrieval system, or transmitted in any form or by any means, electronic, mechanical, or otherwise, without the written permission of the publisher.

*A CIP catalog record for this book is available from the British Library.*

Library of Congress Cataloging-in-Publication Data

Carlson, Marvin A., 1935–
  Speaking in tongues : language at play in the theatre / Marvin
Carlson.
      p.   cm.
  Includes bibliographical references and index.
  ISBN-13: 978-0-472-11547-1 (cloth : alk. paper)
  ISBN-10: 0-472-11547-2 (cloth : alk. paper)
    1. Drama—History and criticism.    2. Language and languages in literature.
3. Dialect drama—History and criticism.    4. Dialect drama, Italian—History
and criticism.    5. Experimental theater—History—20th century.
6. Experimental drama—History and criticism.    7. Theater—Developing
countries—History—20th century.    8. Interpreters for the deaf.
I. Title.
PN650.L34C37      2006
809.2—dc22                                                     2005031391

*Acknowledgments*

Under different titles and in earlier versions, portions of the chapters in this book originally appeared in the following publications: Material from "The Macaronic Stage," "Postcolonial Heteroglossia," and "Postmodern Language Play" appeared in *East of West: Cross-cultural Performance and the Staging of Difference,* edited by Claire Sponsler and Xiaomei Chen (Palgrave, 2000) and in *Text and Presentation* 22:1–21. Material from "The Contribution of Side Texts to Heteroglossia" appeared in *Assaph* C, 16 (2000): 77–90.

# Contents

# Introduction

THE RISE OF PERFORMANCE studies at the end of the twentieth century encouraged many theatre scholars to take a broader view of their discipline, and to consider models other than the one long dominant in the West. Ever since Aristotle, Western writers have primarily considered theatre as closely tied to the written text, essentially the physical enactment of such a preexisting text. With tools provided by semiotics, reception theory, cultural studies, and other theoretical approaches, current research in theatre and performance has vastly extended its areas of interest, greatly enriching the field.

In the excitement and stimulation of this new orientation, however, certain more traditional areas of concern have been relatively neglected. Traditional theatre was from time to time almost forgotten in the early days of performance studies, as attention was given to a wide variety of other cultural performance and to nonliterary celebrative occasions. The long-standing theoretical privileging of the dramatic text was largely replaced by an attention to nonlinguistic and especially nonliterary phenomena. Language in the theatre, once a central theoretical concern, was generally relegated to a distinctly minor position. At the same time, changes in linguistic theory and theatre practice at the close of the century provided a challenge for a rethinking of theatrical language and of the various ways that language can function in the theatre. The purpose of this book is to suggest how the new perspectives opened by these changes can enrich our understanding of both present and past theatrical activity.

When semiotic analysis began to be applied to theatre, in one of the major theoretical developments of theatre studies in the last century, it tied modern theatre theory close to modern linguistic theory, and encouraged the use of a communication model for analysis. This model, developed from the pioneering work of Ferdinand de Saussure early in the century, sought to develop an objective, scientific means of analyzing human discourse. Perhaps the best concise expression of this model of linguistic performance was provided by linguist Noam Chomsky, as a situation in which an "ideal speaker-listener" operates "in a completely homogeneous speech-community," and "knows its language perfectly."[1] One can recognize in this formulation the regularizing and abstracting qualities, the search for an essential core, that characterizes much modernist thought in the arts, and dominated the thinking not only of linguists, but of theorists throughout the social sciences in the early twentieth century as they sought to ground their disciplines on solid "scientific" principles.

A central manifestation of late-twentieth-century thought, however, has been to challenge these abstract and totalizing constructions, through postmodernism in the arts, poststructuralism in language and cultural studies, and the new performative emphasis in the social sciences, particularly in anthropology and ethnography. Interestingly enough, performance theorists of the late twentieth century once again found significant inspiration in linguistic theory, this time in the work of J. L. Austin and John Searle, just as theatre theorists a generation earlier had found inspiration in the linguistic theory of Saussure and his immediate followers. A new generation of linguistic theory has moved even further away from the model Chomsky describes, but is a natural development from Austin's emphasis on the total speech situation and is closely tied to the tendency in modern performance analysis to pay attention to the individual performance event, rather than to some generic abstraction. This contemporary approach to linguistics has been called "integrational linguistics" by Roy Harris, one of its leading proponents. The term was first used in Harris's *The Language Myth* in 1981 and became extensively employed to suggest this new orientation by the end of the century.[2] This approach stresses the improvisatory and indeterminate nature of every speech act: "language is continuously created by the interaction of individuals in specific communication situations."[3]

Such an approach fits very well with recent developments in performance studies and performance analysis, but its possible relevance to the theatre as it has been traditionally conceived and studied has been much less explored. There still exists a widespread assumption that the vast majority of theatre through history has operated fairly closely according to the model of orthodox linguistics. That is, the dramatist can be looked at as functioning in the role of Chomsky's "ideal speaker-listener," and his audience as the "completely homogeneous speech-community, who knows its language perfectly." This view of theatre would not be so widespread, of course, if theatre did not possess a number of features, at least as a communication system, that offer support for such a view. Because of its close ties with the specific conditions of performance, theatre has in all times and places been strongly aware of its responsibility to relate to a particular audience. Indeed, it may be said on these grounds to be the most local of the arts. The great majority of the world's drama has been created by dramatists who were working with a specific audience in mind, and not uncommonly dramatist and audience shared not only a common language, but often a highly specialized language unique to theatrical communication. They not only shared a common language in this standard sense of the word, but a wide variety of the other "languages of the stage" that semiotic theory has brought to our attention—particular theatrical conventions, acting styles, and the potential meanings of each aspect of production, from the theatre building itself to the smallest particular gesture. This general characteristic of theatre is intensified by its close relationship with language (indeed with spoken language), making the matters of locality and specificity clearly more central than they are in a more abstract art like dance. One can surely assume that the first dramatic productions to use language, whatever and wherever they may have been, used their audience's common tongue or at least a tongue whose general features could be understood by all or most of that audience.

This feature is reinforced by the fact that, although a society may possess considerable cultural diversity, the audiences that have attended particular theatres have generally been distinctly less heterogeneous than the society that surrounds them. Moreover the theatre has often, consciously or less consciously, been seen and employed as an instrument of cultural and linguistic solidification As a public art devoted to cultural self-reflexivity, theatre has not only reflected but often helped to reinforce and to crystallize norms of social action. Lessing, Goethe, and Schiller saw the theatre very much in these terms, and during the ensuing romantic period, an almost invariable component of the rise of nationalism in Europe was the establishment of a national theatre, contributing to the formation of a unified and univocal people by presenting the history and myths of that people in their own language.[4] Alongside the building of these modern nations developed the modern colonial empires, and if theatre was perhaps not so central to these, the importance of the great national dramatists, Shakespeare in England, Racine, Corneille, and Molière in France, indisputably played a major role in the construction of the subaltern's worldview in the colonies of these nations.

One of the strongest statements concerning the proclivity of theatre toward this totalized and monolithic communication model was developed by Mikhail Bakhtin, who argued that the drama, in contrast to the novel, was an essentially monologic form. In his discussion of dialogue in Dostoyevsky he specifically took issue with Leonid Grossman, an earlier commentator, who had called Dostoevsky's dialogues "dramatic." Bakhtin insisted, on the contrary, that "the rejoinders in a dramatic dialogue do not rip apart the represented world, do not make it multi-leveled; on the contrary, if they are to be authentically dramatic, these rejoinders necessitate the utmost monolithic quality of that world." Although the characters may come together "dialogically," they do so within "the unified field of vision of author, director, and audience, against the clearly defined background of a single-tiered world."[5] This view of drama bears, I would note, a striking similarity to the orthodox view of language, the "unified field of vision of author, director and audience" and the "single-tiered world" they share corresponding closely to the "completely homogeneous speech-community" of classic linguistic theory.

Elsewhere I have taken issue with Bakhtin's view of the operations of the drama, with examples drawn from such major classic authors as Calderón, Shakespeare, Ibsen, and Shaw,[6] but more recent developments both in dramatic practice and in cultural theory have raised significant new questions about Bakhtin's attempt to deny heteroglossia to the theatre. A useful intertext for indicating the way that Bakhtin's original concept has been productively appropriated and expanded in more recent cultural analysis is James Clifford's influential 1988 study of the interrelationships of contemporary ethnography, literature, and art, *The Predicament of Culture.* The opening chapter of Clifford's book.

"On Ethnographic Authority," makes extensive use of Bakhtin's idea of heteroglossia, but also remarks that in Bakhtin the idea of polyphonic discourse is "too narrowly identified with the novel."[7]

The major concern of Clifford's opening chapter is to trace "the formation and breakup of ethnographic authority in twentieth-century social anthropology." In the wake of the breakup of colonial power, the development of the radical cultural theories of the 1960s and 1970s, and the increasing exposure of varied cultures to one another in the late twentieth century, the monologic Western "voice" of ethnographic authority has given way, in more recent cultural theory, to a consciousness of the varied "voices" that this monologist view silenced or suppressed. Clifford invokes Bakhtin to express this new concern: "With expanded communication and intercultural influence, people interpret others, and themselves, in a bewildering diversity of idioms—a global condition of what Mikhail Bakhtin called "heteroglossia." In citing this usage, Clifford quotes Bakhtin's comment that heteroglossia assumes that "languages do not *exclude* each other, but rather intersect with each other in many different ways," adding that "what is said of languages applies equally to 'cultures' and 'subcultures.'"[8]

Clifford, like Bakhtin, speaks very little about theatre and drama specifically, but many of his observations about the cultural complexity and the workings of heteroglossia in the plastic arts and in literature have clear relevance to the world of theatre, especially postcolonial theatre, as in his discussion of the work of Aimé Césaire. Césaire's writing Clifford sees as emblematic of the "hybrid and heteroglot" intersection of language that characterizes some of the most interesting and powerful postcolonial expression. Later in this book I will consider some of the operations and implications of heteroglossia in the linguistic intersections and negotiations that are central to an understanding of postcolonial artistic expression.

More broadly, however, I would like to extend Bakhtin's concept of heteroglossia somewhat in the way Clifford has done, to explore certain theatre and performance manifestations rather than more general cultural and ethnographic ones. I propose to examine some of the many ways that languages, in Clifford's phrase, have intersected with each other in a wide variety of different theatrical contexts, and some of the implications of these intersections in terms of reception, mimesis, and the social, political, and cultural investments of theatrical presentation. I hope to demonstrate that "playing with language" in the theatre is not simply a postcolonial or postmodern strategy (although linguistic play has become of major or even central importance in both postcolonial and postmodern theatre) but an activity found very widely in theatrical cultures past and present, around the world, and that such "playing," as is the case with much "play" in theatre, has often involved very serious social and artistic concerns.

Before laying out the general plan of this study, however, it is important that I offer some introduction to the very vexed question of what is meant by *language*. Like many general terms (such as *performance*) that a generation ago seemed more or less clear and unambiguous, language is now a term that conjures up a wide and in some cases quite contradictory range of meaning. This situation has been largely the result of two developments. On the one hand, semiotic theory worked to extend the term to cover any sort of communication system that could be described in codified terms, so that, for example, one of the first books on theatre semiotics published in English was entitled *Languages of the Stage*,[9] and semioticians often spoke of the "language" of gesture, costume, makeup, scenery, or architecture. On the other hand, the integrational linguists dismissed the very concept of "language" as a misleading myth, and argued for the replacement of the language study, so central to traditional linguistics, with a study of contextualized communication situations.[10]

David Crystal's *Dictionary of Linguistics and Phonetics,* the standard guide to terms in the field, provides a useful starting point. Its entry on *language* begins with the caution that even "everyday use of this term involves several different senses, which LINGUISTICS is careful to distinguish." One of these senses, although of major importance to the theatre, will be little considered in this book. Crystal describes it as the sense of a "particular VARIETY, or LEVEL, of speech/writing" such as "scientific language" or "bad language." Since the theatre reflects the linguistic world around it as it does the cultural world in general, the varieties of language can naturally be found there as well, but the theatre also offers many examples of its own sort of "scientific language," of what might be called "stage language." This is not a particularly familiar expression in English, although the Germans use the term *Bühnensprache*. Since the

*Homebody/Kabul*). Nevertheless, both characters and audiences are aware that several languages are involved in such works. Certainly the question of understanding is a major one, and cannot be avoided when one is speaking of multilanguage theatre, but on a pragmatic level it does not provide a clear and unambiguous way of distinguishing polylinguistic from monolinguistic theatre.

A more workable approach is to recognize that each language, like the concept of language itself, is a social construction, and that languages on the stage as elsewhere are recognized and coded as languages by their employment of features culturally related to that construction rather than by comprehension or noncomprehension. This same process of social construction continues to apply in the separation of languages from dialects. For the most part what is popularly spoken of as a "language" is one of many competing dialects that for a variety of reasons—commercial, political, and cultural—emerged as the "standard" language of a geographical area. The most familiar Western examples are the languages that worked in tandem with the development of the modern nation-states, and contributed significantly to consolidating and establishing the authority of those states. So effective was this process that a major project in contemporary sociolinguistics has been explaining that existing languages are not superior in any objective way to their various alternative dialects past and present, but have gained their prominence by a concrete historical process.[14] The fact that, as Crystal notes, separation of dialects is encouraged both by "geographical barriers" and "divisions of social class" has naturally meant that in addition to dialects being generally somewhat looked down upon by speakers of the "official" language, dialect speakers have often suffered the additional stigma of being marked by their speech as coming from a subordinate or inferior geographical area or social class. I recall several years ago being somewhat surprised by the gales of laughter from a Berlin audience at almost every speech of Polonius in a production of *Hamlet,* including lines that seemed to me to have no comic content whatever. Finally I asked a German friend what was so funny and he patiently explained that the actor was used a Swabian accent, a source of much amusement to the sophisticated Berliners.

Naturally all of these linguistic social dynamics are reflected in theatrical presentations, which inevitably reflect the social operations of their culture. From classic times onward language differences have been utilized not only to place characters within multilanguage or multidialect cultures, but almost always also to reflect the power relationships embedded in language usage.[15] Although there is no tradition of comparative linguistics in classical Greek writing, there is certainly an awareness of different languages and different dialects in such authors as Herodotus, although no very clear distinction between the two.[16] Homer characterizes the Carians, a people of Asia Minor who spoke a language quite distinct from Greek, as *barbarophonos*, "of barbaric speech,"[17] a coinage that stimulated extensive discussion among subsequent authors. The geographer Strabo summarizes this discussion and adds comments of his own that are quite relevant both to the Greek theatrical use of alien language as well as to such usage in later theatrical cultures. Strabo suggested that the term *barbarophonos* was first used onomatopoetically, "in reference to people who enunciated words only with difficulty and talked harshly and raucously," as in the sound of the Greek word for stutter, *battarizein*. Strabo notes that this descriptive term gradually took on social and cultural significance. Non-Greek speakers were called barbarians

> in the special sense of the term at first derisively, meaning that they pronounced words thickly or harshly; and then we misused the word as a general ethnic term, thus making a logical distinction between the Greeks and the others. The fact is, however, that through our long acquaintance and intercourse with the barbarians this effect was at last seen to be the result, not of a thick pronunciation or any natural defect in the vocal organs, but of the peculiarities of their dialects. . . . So, therefore, we must interpret the terms "speaking barbarously" and "barbarously-speaking" as applying to those who speak Greek badly.[18]

When we turn in the following chapter to the specific depictions of "barbarian" speakers in the Greek drama, we will find that on the whole the speaker of the foreign language or dialect is marked as a figure of ridicule, or at least condescension, a feature that will characterize much subsequent theatrical use of foreign speakers, especially in the comic theatre.

Within the Greek theatre itself, some "barbarian" speakers did not in fact utilize words or phrases from any specific foreign language, or even from any specific dialect, but rather were depicted with an accent, suggesting such languages or dialects to an audience who had likely only a limited acquaintance with these alterative voices. In linguistic terms an accent is distinct from a dialect in that accent refers only to pronunciation, while dialect also involves grammar and vocabulary,[19] but in more general usage the boundaries between accents and dialects, like those between dialects and languages, are extremely fluid. General usage also associates accents as departures from some generally accepted "normal" speech, speech "without an accent," although anyone with an ear trained to notice verbal distinctions is aware of what linguistic theory stresses, that no one speaks without an accent, even if that accent (as is almost never the case) is perfectly attuned to the standard speech of the surrounding culture.

In this light, one can readily see that the much-admired "standard stage English" of the early-twentieth-century English Shakespearian actors was also an accent, although traditionally the term *stage accent* or *stage dialect* has referred to a particular pattern of intonation and pronunciation designed to give the impression of a character coming from an alien linguistic background. The stage dialect is best understood as a particular form of stage language. Although it is meant to suggest actual dialects and languages in the world outside the theatre and therefore borrows certain of their features, these features are exaggerated or simplified for theatrical purposes. As Jerry Blunt explains in the introduction to his *Stage Dialects,* "A *stage dialect* is a normal dialect altered as needed to fit the requirements of theatrical clarity and dramatic interpretation."[20]

Obviously the primary function of the stage accent is related to that of scenery and costume in the standard Western theatre. It is one of the codes employed to provide audience members with a sense of the physical and temporal location of the imaginary world being constructed on stage. In what is, to the best of my knowledge, the only study to pursue the cultural and social implications of stage dialects,[21] Angela Pao has stressed that the tradition of the stage dialect, developed on a basis of technical skill without significant engagement with the culture behind the dialect, "carries the potential for ethnic stereotyping as much as performing in blackface or yellowface perpetuates racial stereotyping."[22] So far the visual and behavioral aspects of performing race, such as black-face performance, have attracted far more attention than the vocal aspects, such as dialect, of performing ethnicity, but the same tendency toward stereotyping, and the embedded cultural bases connected with stereotyping, exists. Pao's essay is a major first step toward engaging these vocal aspects, with telling examples from the major textbooks for stage dialect learning of the past half-century.

The history and importance of the stage accent, but also its linguistic ambiguity, suggest a number of tensions fundamental to the theatrical experience, in particular the tension between self and other and that between reality and convention. Although one can argue that with modern international touring, international festivals, international audiences, and international companies, a significant heteroglossic theatrical tradition is developing, but it is nevertheless true that in most locations and in most historical periods theatre has been a predominantly local phenomenon. In the case of most traditional theatre audiences, essentially drawn from the surrounding community, there was normally a very close relationship between the cultural practices and assumptions of theatre and the audience for which it is created. Throughout most of theatre history, a dramatist and the audience for which that dramatist created almost invariably spoke essentially the same language, both literally and figuratively, even if that language was colored, in the theatre, by such agreed-upon artistic conventions as alexandrines or iambic pentameters. Bakhtin's example of Racine is a particularly clear case of a dramatist and audience not only essentially homogeneous in terms of cultural assumptions but also in the way that these assumptions were expressed theatrically.

Important as this centripetal dynamic has been, it is also true that a culture's concept of itself, like a concept of individual identity, inevitably involves on some level a recognition of what lies outside that concept, of the other who provides a defining contrast to the self. As an art form centrally concerned with cultural self-reflection, then, the theatre could hardly escape bringing into its considerations the other that supported and provided a necessary counterpart to the concept of self. A great variety of strategies have been employed over the centuries to mark the other in theatre, but surely one of the most striking has been the actual employment of the other's language.

The problem of just how this language is to be represented theatrically has elicited a very wide range of responses, the variation in which is closely related to the ever-present struggle in theatre between reality and artifice. Many of the arts are involved to a greater or lesser degree with the imitation of life, but none is so extensively involved as theatre with using the raw material of life, bodies, objects, sounds, even on occasion smells, as the specific means of this imitation. In semiotic terms, theatre is the most iconic of all arts, often extending iconicity beyond mere perceptual resemblance to what I have elsewhere described as "iconic identity," in which an object on stage actually *is* what it represents.[23] In somewhat different terms, Bert States remarked that theatre was dedicated to the constant "colonization" of reality, to consuming "the real in its most real forms."[24] At the same time the theatre, like all arts, operates by conventions that qualify and modify the material it utilizes according to the codes developed within each culture according to which art is both created and received. There is thus a continuing tension in theatre between this art form's ongoing commitment to the utilization of extratheatrical material and the often artificial codes and operations of the form itself that facilitate reception.

A character speaking an alien language is a particularly clear example of this ongoing struggle in theatre between verisimilitude, the actual or apparent utilization of the real, and artistic convention, which adjusts and qualifies reality in the interests of consensual strategies of reception. The force of verisimilitude encourages the use of actual foreign languages on stage, while the necessity of adopting the raw material of life to the theatrical and social conventions of a particular public, here including the language they speak, has resulted in a variety of substitutions for or supplements to actual foreign speech. The major substitution has been various forms of stage dialects, an artificial "stage speech" that one may consider a kind of artificial dialect; the major supplement, in modern times, has been the supertitled translation, about which more will be said in my concluding section.

The chapters that follow will consider various aspects of heteroglossia in the theatre, how and why it has been used in different theatrical contexts, and what it reveals about some of the social and cultural dynamics of this highly reflexive artistic form. The first chapter takes up what might be considered the "purest" form of theatrical heteroglossia, the appearance in a play of speeches or even whole scenes in an actual language different from that of the main action of the play. Although this might seem a rather odd phenomenon, it has in fact been utilized throughout the history of the theatre and around the world. Often verisimilitude is the major structural motivation for such linguistic mixing, but no cultural activity, and certainly not language, is devoid of associations and values, and so beyond the rather simple and straightforward concern of verisimilitude, theatrical heteroglossia almost always involves a wide variety of social and cultural issues.

The second chapter turns from a consideration of language to that of dialect. As I have already noted, I will be primarily using dialect in the common meaning of a subdivision of language. This meaning involves two widely held but not in fact accurate assumptions that will be engaged within the chapter. The first and more important is that there is a superior "regular" language that provides the norm, with various dialects as variations from it. Although this assumption accurately describes a cultural fact, it is important to realize that from a linguistic point of view, the dominant language is simply one dialect among many, which by social and historical forces has achieved a position of centrality. One of the major concerns of this chapter will be tracing how these forces operate in theatrical terms. The second assumption is less central, but necessary to note because it also has specific theatrical implications. This is the assumption that speakers of different dialects can understand each other (in common usage indeed this is what distinguishes a dialect from an independent language).

The idea that dialects can presumably be understood by speakers of other dialects would seem to suggest that they would be much more commonly utilized in the theatre than alternate languages, which present greater problems of communication. At first glance this seems to be the case, since dialect speech is far more widely encountered in the theatre than the sort of mixed language production discussed in chapter 1. The situation is more complicated than that, however. To begin with, the great majority of characters presented on stage as dialect speakers are not in fact speaking a "natural" dialect, but a "stage" dialect, a very different matter, as Pao has suggested. A typical and famous example is the Welsh, Irish, and Scots soldiers that gather under the banner of Henry V in Shakespeare's play or the "stage Irishman" of the nineteenth-century American theatre. As Pao has noted, these stage representations of dialect speakers have often represented little more than ethnic stereotyping, as far removed from the actual dialects they evoke as blackface or yellowface entertainment was from the actual race it represented. Or, to keep the question in a linguistic framework, this tradition of stage dialect bears essentially the same relationship to real dialect as a stage French or German accent ("Come wiz me to zee Casbah" or "Ve haff vays of makink you talk") have to those actual languages.

What then of real dialects as they actually occur in the world? How have these been utilized on the stage? In fact the dynamic is rather different from that of separate languages. There are certainly examples of what might call heteroglossic dialect theatre, especially in the theatre of the past century, but on the whole the dynamic of the dialect theatre has been rather different, attempting to maintain itself within a culture as an alternative to and often in opposition to the regularizing mainstream theatre. The heteroglossia it provides has traditionally been maintained more within the theatrical culture as a whole than in individual plays, and therefore it has been often treated with disdain or outright hostility by the dominant language theatre, as when the Italian fascists tried, unsuccessfully, to stamp it out. The question of the status of dialect theatre and the negotiations between dialect and mainstream theatre has been particularly important in the history of the Italian theatre, and so the second chapter takes a different approach than the first, looking not at dialect in the theatre in a wide range of theatrical cultures, but rather examining the single example of Italy as a particular case study of the ongoing negotiations of dialect in the play of theatrical language.

The third chapter moves back to a more global perspective, to consider some of the many ways that multiple languages are negotiated in the postcolonial world. Nothing was more central to the colonialist process than the imposition of the colonizer's language, but this imposition resulted in an almost infinite variety of linguistic negations and the emergence of all manner of hybridizations of language. Not surprisingly, both of the first two major critical studies of postcolonial theatre in English, Helen Gilbert and Joanne Tompkins's *Post-Colonial Drama*

*Theory, Practice, Politics* (1996) and Christopher Balme's *Decolonizing the Stage: Theatrical Syncretism and Post-Colonial Drama* (1999) devote a major section to language in the postcolonial theatre, and both emphasize its heteroglossia. Indeed, as Balme points out, the European colonial languages were for the most part introduced into cultures that were already bilingual or multilingual, thus creating an even more complicated mixture that, in turn, came to be reflected in the theatre produced by these cultures. Postcolonial examples of heteroglossic theatre will be examined, concentrating upon work in the Caribbean, Africa, Australia, and New Zealand, and suggesting the varied uses of native languages and colonial variations, including pidgin and creole. The chapter will conclude with a discussion of recent heteroglossic monodrama, and especially of its relationship to immigrant and "border" voices, an increasingly important element in postcolonial dramatic expression.

The fourth chapter turns to a quite different sort of heteroglossia in the theatre, but one that has become steadily more significant in recent years, with the rise of postmodernism, an aesthetic with which it has much in common. Normally in art that has been characterized as postmodern, various elements are assembled without either the totalizing aesthetic vision that was used to justify previous formal and abstract experimentation in the theatre and other arts, or the appeal to verisimilitude that grounded traditional realistic theatre. This chapter considers the largely experimental tradition that developed in the international theatre of the late twentieth century to assemble actors from different cultural and linguistic backgrounds and allow them to collectively create consciously disparate and open-ended work. Although Peter Brook's international company in Paris was in some senses a pioneer in such work, Brook himself remained committed to a more modernist totalizing artistic vision at odds, to some extent, with the heteroglossic company he assembled. This tension within the Brook aesthetic is discussed along with the work of subsequent artists who carried Brook's intercultural experimentation in more truly heteroglossic directions. Particular attention is given to such experimentation in the contemporary German spoken theatre and in the modern Tanztheater.

The question that haunts all heteroglossic experimentation in the theatre is of course that of reception. There is no question that the burgeoning of heteroglossic theatre at the end of the twentieth century reflected an increasing heteroglossia in communities around the world. This is the result both of the increasing mixture of cultural populations and of the decline of both the nationalist and the colonialist projects in their attempt to delegitimize and silence minority voices that challenged and potentially subverted their hegemony. Heteroglossic cultures in the modern world are more common, more complex in their linguistic mixing, and more visible politically and theatrically than at any time in the past. This means that the theatre, for centuries essentially monoglossic in both production and reception, can in many cases assume a heteroglossic audience for heteroglossic theatre, or, as in the case of much postcolonial theatre, an audience that is at least partially heteroglossic, allowing plays to send different messages to different sectors of the audience. For much mixed language theatre, however, the problem of communication remains a significant one, and in a closing chapter I consider some of the strategies of translation that have been developed to deal with this challenge.

The translation device most associated with the rapid expansion of heteroglossic theatre at the end of the twentieth century is the supertitle, created to provide a readily accessible, if necessarily abbreviated gloss on the language spoken on the stage for those in the audience to whom it was not otherwise accessible. It thus served (like its close relative, the oral simultaneous translation) as a presumably neutral extra channel that operated outside the actual aesthetics of the stage production itself. In his analysis of dramatic text, Ingarden employs the useful term *side text* to refer to what is more commonly called the stage directions, or the didascalia of the printed play, indicating such matters as the attribution of lines and suggested physical movement or vocal delivery. The twentieth century has developed more literal "side texts," operating not in the printed form of the playscript but during its physical staging. These are actually quasi-independent texts "on the side" of the production, above or below the stage in the case of subtitles or supertitles, or literally at its side when a person stands in this position and provides a simultaneous sign language "translation" of the play for deaf spectators to whom the language of the play proper is not accessible. Such signing offers another sort of presumably neutral "side text" for the actual performance, of which it is not an integral part.

What gives these "side texts" particular relevance to the present study, however, is not their function as devices to provide access to otherwise inaccessible language on stage, but rather the fact that in the later years of the twentieth century, such translation tools have begun to be utilized not simply as transparent conveyors of other stage languages, but as languages in their own right, capable of conveying their own messages that could supplement or enter into dialogue with other languages on the stage. My final chapter therefore opens with a brief discussion of the role of the translator in the heteroglossic theatre, and then goes on to consider how sign language and supertitles, each utilized at one time only as a translation device in the theatre, both evolved into fully operative theatre languages. This meant evolving from tools for supporting a monoglossic experience, to new voices of their own, and thus contributors to the theatre's increasing heteroglossia. Interestingly, both supertitles and sign language have achieved important success as contributors to heteroglossic production not simply on experimental stages, but in the major theatres of modern Broadway.

From the local township theatres of South Africa to the major commercial theatres of London and New York, from expressions of the aboriginal experience in Australia and New Zealand to avant-garde experimentation in Belgium and France, from Berber/Arabic monologists in North Africa to Chinese/English monologists in Canada, heteroglossia has become one of the most striking new developments in the global theatre, reflecting a world that is itself becoming increasingly heteroglossic. In her essay "From Pastiche to Macaroni," published in 1999, Celeste Olaquiaga begins with an encounter with a New York friend, Imàn, with whom she normally spoke in a mixture of English, Spanish, and the combined New York pidgin Spanglish, she being a Latin American trained in English, he the son of Spanish-speaking immigrants. He suddenly confused her by adding "another layer to his Spanglish, that of black and Latino drag balls." This "newfound patter," she suggests, "is the product of a time when the artificial boundaries of nations and cities have collapsed under the weight of a diversity that could no longer be bond by uniform languages or monological discourses. It is the oral equivalent of the polysemantic clutteredness of Chinatown, Fourteenth Street, and Times Square, whose shrewd merchants, Chinese, Arab, or Jewish, transit fluidly between English, Spanish, Chinese, Hebrew, and Arabic—a macaronic verbality perfectly suited to a pastiched visuality."[25] Tom Lanoye, with whose *Schlachten!,* a postmodern reworking of Shakespeare's history plays, I conclude my discussion of contemporary heteroglossic theatre, comments that his play reflects "the confusion of languages that totally surround us today." We live, he suggest, in a kind of "speech aquarium, which seems, depending on how you view it, extremely rich and varied or extremely polluted."[26] The ease of international travel, the remnants of colonialism, the global impact of the media, and the enormous shifts of populations, from the freely chosen path of the emigrant to the enforced dislocation of the refugee, have resulted in a more complex and more widely distributed mixture of languages today than the world has ever seen. This may be particularly apparent in the polysemantic clutteredness of a global crossroads like Times Square, but there is scarcely a corner of the world today so remote that interlinguistic interaction is not a common fact of life. It would be strange indeed if this global phenomenon were not reflected in the global theatre, an art particularly concerned with social and cultural reflection. The tradition of a theatre closely tied to a particular nation and a particular language still may dominate a generally held idea of how theatre operates, but the new theatre that is most oriented toward the contemporary world no longer is restricted to this model, and one of the most important challenges it faces is the presentation of a newly interdependent world that speaks with many different voices. The heteroglossic stage, for centuries an interesting but marginal part of the dramatic tradition, became in the late twentieth century a truly important international phenomenon. The background and the features of that stage are the concern of this book.

# 1 *The Macaronic Stage*

THE THEORY AND PRACTICE of postmodern and postcolonial theatre and performance has given new prominence to heteroglossia, but it is not a new phenomenon. Despite Bakhtin's attempt to deny its operations in the drama, examples of multiple voices can be found throughout theatre history, not only in the limited and abstract sense of voices taking positions at odds with those of the author, but also in the literal sense of voices that speak a language not that of the author or the presumed audience. The practice and motives for this most extreme form of theatrical heteroglossia are the concern of this chapter.

The very idea of a drama utilizing an alien language seems to run counter to a normal communications model of theatre, such as that put forward by classic semiotic theory. According to this model, based like classic linguistic theory upon the work of Saussure and his followers, the primary operations of theatre depend upon a model speaker (the author, or in the case of production, the entire production apparatus) creating the complex "message" of the play or production in a "code" (or a language) that is shared in its entirety by the model receiver (the audience). In such a monoglossic or monologistic system, the introduction of any heteroglossic code or language element must be viewed as distracting or, worse, seriously disruptive, threatening a breakdown of the entire system. However, just as more recent linguistic theory and cultural practice has unsettled the Saussurian model of monolithic communication, so the study of postcolonial and other recent theatre and performance practice has unsettled the related monologistic semiotic model in these fields.

Modern cultural theory recognizes that few cultures or languages have ever been as monologistic as the formal and abstract linguistic and anthropological analyses of the earlier twentieth century depicted them. Neither theatre communities nor the larger cultural communities that surround and include them are ever totally isolated from intercourse with other communities. Thus the theatre, committed to reflecting mimetically upon the culture of which it is a part, has had to find, in all times and periods, strategies for depicting not only the perceived social operations of its audience but also the impact of external forces that invariably affected that audience, however homogeneous it may have been.

## The Speech of the Outsider

Surely nothing so immediately marks an outsider as representing another culture than the fact that he speaks an alien language, and the alien voice of the outsider has always been a major contributor to heteroglossia in the theatre. As I have already remarked, however, there is an inevitable theatre tension between the often cited goal of "truth to nature" and the demands of meeting audience expectations, including, of course, comprehensibility. An excellent example of this tension at work can be seen in one of the most famous documents of Western theatrical theory, Victor Hugo's *Preface to Cromwell,* the central manifesto of French romanticism in theatre. The main thrust of Hugo's argument is that the artists of the future should no longer be content to follow academic rules and to copy previous artists, but should seek their inspiration directly from nature and from truth. Approximately half way through this lengthy essay, however, he introduces an important qualification: that at least in his opinion there is an "impassable limit" that must always separate "reality according to art from reality according to nature," a limit unrecognized by "certain ill-informed partisans of romanticism."[1] He then proceeds to illustrate the foolishness of such "unreflective advocates of absolute nature" by imagining the reactions of one of them attending a performance of Corneille's *Le Cid.* Interestingly enough, he begins with the matter of verisimilitude in language:

> "What's that?" he will say at the first word. The Cid is speaking in verse! It is not *natural* to speak in verse!—How then would you have him speak?—In prose. So be it. Then, an instant later:—"What," he will continue if he is consistent, "The Cid is speaking French!"—"And so?"—"*Nature* requires that he speak his own language; he

can't speak anything but Spanish." We will not understand anything he is saying, but once more, so be it. But you think that is all? By no means. Before the tenth sentence in Castilian, he is certain to get up and ask if this Cid who is speaking is the real Cid, in flesh and blood. What right has this actor, whose name is Pierre or Jacques, to assume the name of The Cid? That is *false*. And there is no reason why he should not go on to demand that the sun should be substituted for the footlights, *real* trees and *real* houses for those deceitful wings. For, once you have started down that path logic has you by the collar, and you are unable to stop.[2]

From a twenty-first-century perspective, Hugo's straw man, the "ill-informed" advocate of romanticism, turns out to have been far more prescient than Hugo imagined. The assumption that a tragic hero must speak in verse, virtually inviolate since the crystallization of French classicism two centuries before Hugo wrote, was given up during Hugo's own lifetime, a once universally accepted "stage language" that fell before the demands of realism. Later still, the growing incorporation of real materials into stage fictions and the conscious mixing of art and life in twentieth-century experimental theatre saw copious examples of actors from Buffalo Bill to Spalding Gray appearing on stage as their flesh-and-blood selves, not to mention the sun being substituted for footlights and real trees and real houses for deceitful wings.

Of course the demands of comprehensibility made the speaking of an actual foreign language one of the most intractable of the "natural" manifestations Hugo would ban from the stage, but had he looked beyond the specific classical tradition in which he was seeking to place his own work, he could have found examples, even in the contemporary French theatre, of characters shown speaking languages other than French in the interest of truth to nature. These could be found in the work of writers of melodrama like Guilbert de Pixérécourt and other pioneers, whose works inspired French romantic drama and who were even more dedicated to verisimilitude than Hugo and his colleagues. Pixérécourt accompanied his dramatic scripts with extensive notes and incorporated historical documents and recorded conversations as obsessively as any subsequent naturalist. Writing for a popular theatre and a popular audience, he had even less need to accommodate the formal conventions of the classic drama than did Hugo, who was attempting to storm the citadel of high art, the Comédie Française. Hugo took liberties with the alexandrine, the traditional poetic line of French classic tragedy, that caused near riots by the conservative Comédie audiences, but he kept the form itself, and even defended it (to "speak in verse") in the passage just quoted. Pixérécourt felt free, in the name of verisimilitude, to abandon the alexandrine altogether. Even more radically, Pixérécourt, again in the interests of authenticity, created non-French-speaking characters, to whom he attempted to give an accurate representative voice. Just as he consulted memoirs and accounts of battles to guarantee the facts in his historical spectacles, he utilized a recently published dictionary of "Caribbean" language to create the quite extensive speeches of the natives Columbus encounters in the New World in the final acts of his melodrama *Christoph Colomb*. His preface to that play, "The Author to His Public," concludes with a paragraph that takes precisely the opposite position from Hugo, but with equal conviction and appeal to logic:

> The public will no doubt think, as I do, that it would be completely ridiculous to use our own language, even corrupted, for men who are seeing Europeans for the first time. Fully confident that my innovation could not fail to be approved by persons of taste, I made the inhabitants of Guanahani speak the language of the Antilles, which I have taken from the *Dictionnaire Caribe* created by R. P. Raymond Breton and published in Auxerre in 1665. Within the play will be found the translation of all those words which I felt, in any case, I ought to use in moderation.[3]

Indeed, had Hugo looked in any detail at dramatic traditions outside the monologic classic French serious theatre, he could have found examples of heteroglossia in almost every previous period. Bert States's astute observation about the theatre's drive to absorb external reality is not of course directed at the realist movement in particular, but points to a general characteristic of the art form, and since cultural contact (or conflict) has been a part of the human experience at least as long as the drama, it is hardly surprising that there is a long tradition of theatrical attempts to negotiate with, if not absorb, this contact, often by means of contrasting languages.

The first extant Western drama, Aeschylus's *The Persians,* is in fact a drama dealing with such cultural confrontation. Here, at the very beginning of the tradition, we find an attempt, modest but significant, to give dramatic expression to the voice of the Other. The chorus, made up of Persians, speaks (or sings) primarily in Greek, but Aeschylus also provides them with specific exotic words and with mourning laments in at least an approximation of Persian, providing his audience with the impression of a distinct confrontation with that alien language.[4] Persian being the non-Greek language best known to the Greeks, it was the one most likely to appear, even if corrupted in form, in the plays. Thus Pseudartabas in Aristophanes' *The Acharnians* speaks in what J. M. Starkie identified as "perfect Old Persian,"[5] but which most commentators have more cautiously identified as an imitation of Persian. The Scythian archer in *Thesmophoriazusae* speaks in an artificial nonsense supposedly representing this Persian-related language. One of the most famous "barbaric" speakers in Aristophanes is the Triballian god in *The Birds,* whose barbaric speech is not in fact that of the Thracian Triballi, but an incomprehensible corrupt Greek that Heracles interprets according to his own interests. These comic uses of "other" languages may be said be inspired by verisimilitude, or perhaps more accurately, by exoticism (a later example would be the mock Turkish in Molière's *Bourgeois Gentilhomme*), but they serve other functions as well. Chief among these is the particular type of humor they involve. An important element of humor has always been laughter at the expense of an outsider, whose actions, assumptions, or in this case language, mark him as someone who does not understand or follow the cultural codes of the dramatist and his presumed audience and is therefore offered as a fit subject for laughter. Aristophanes' barbarian Triballian god and Scythian archer are very early but quite clear examples of this dynamic at work.

It was not until the late twentieth century that language scholars began to study what came to be known as sociolinguistics, investigating how variations in language not only mark their speakers as belonging to particular social groups but also participate in the process of privileging or subordinating their members. A recent work in the field explains:

Often, people want to be considered a part of a particular social group as opposed to other groups, and so they project their identity with this group in a number of ways, including "talking like" other members of the group. Sometimes, group membership is voluntary and sometimes it is rooted in consignment to a particular social group without choice. In either case, though, group membership may end up carrying connotations of pride and loyalty.[6]

The first major work in this area was William Labov's *The Social Stratification of English in New York City* (1966), which considered the relationship between language and social class, studying how language variables reflect class and style stratification, as well as gender and ethnicity.[7] These relationships were the subject of an outpouring of studies in Europe and America in the 1970s, and the new attention to the relationship between language and social power received particularly powerful expression in Pierre Bourdieu's 1982 book, *Ce que parler veut dire: L'économie des échanges linguistiques,* translated (in a somewhat different form) into English in 1991 as *Language and Symbolic Action.*[8] Although Bourdieu does not, in this collection of writings, address theatre, his discussion of language and power is obviously relevant to the theatrical use of a foreign language, already present in the Greek drama, to mark and often to disparage the "outsider." Bourdieu focuses, as most sociolinguists have done, not upon the interplay of languages but upon that of dialects, where the social dynamics are more clearly in play. I will therefore consider his observations in more detail later when I turn to dialect theatre. Here I wish only to indicate that the "connotations of pride and loyalty," of group membership "as opposed to members of other groups," has in the theatre been often involved whenever the speaker of an alien language is depicted.

An early clear example of the use of language to express social stratification is the classic Sanskrit theatre of India, in which Sanskrit is spoken by noble or upper-class characters while the local vernacular languages (the *pakrits*) are spoken by common characters. This tradition is carried on in much Eastern folk theatre, especially in India, where if the drama is serious in tone, it is likely to draw upon ancient epic verse, while a clown, master of ceremonies, or other intermediary character provides a running translation or commentary in the vernacular for the audience.

This use of multiple languages has been developed in far more elaborate fashion in both the puppet theatre and dance-drama of Southeast Asia, whose traditions go back at least to the fourteen century, but which are still performed today. Both the Topeng dance-drama of Bali and the Wayang shadow theatre employ a wide variety of languages, some still in active use, others once active but now heard only in performance, and still others entirely artificial, never living languages, but existing only in poetic texts.

In an analysis of the Topeng drama *Jelantik Goes to Blambangan,* ethnographer J. Stephen Lansing describes the operations of seven different languages or registers operating in this single text: Sanskrit, Old Javanese, Middle Javanese, High Balinese, Middle Balinese, Low Balinese, and modern Indonesian.[9] The first three are ancient languages, now spoken only in performance. These have a semimystical and incantatory quality, and are used evocatively, in the words of A. L. Becker, to "speak the past."[10] To "speak the present" one uses Balinese or Indonesian, which still provide a wide linguistic choice. "High Balinese is courtly language; Middle Balinese is formal speech between equals; Low Balinese, the vernacular of the villages." Modern Indonesian provides yet other associations, invoking "a modern urban context."[11] It may seem that what is involved here is less verisimilitude to actual language uses than the following of an extremely elaborate performance code, but in fact the operation of a variety of linguistic levels within normal social discourse is one of the features of the culture, as ethnographer Linda Conner explains:

> The stratification of Balinese speech structure into various high and low forms imposes a highly patterned mode of interaction between inferiors and superiors, both in this and the other world, based on relations of ascribed authority and unquestioning subservience, of willfulness and restraint. . . . In everyday interactions, ignorance or violation of the elaborate formulas governing polite discourse is interpreted not merely as a breach of good manners, but as a transgression against cosmological order, and in more extreme cases, as a statement of one's political opinion vis-à-vis the holders of power.[12]

Normally, different characters speak different languages, appropriate to their station and their relationships, but a longer speech by a single character may also display very great linguistic variety. Thus the opening speech of Pensar Kelihan, the clown-narrator of *Jelantik Goes to Blambangan,* begins in formal Middle Javanese as the story is introduced, switches to Old Javanese with a descriptive passage from the *Mahabharata,* switches to Middle Balinese to speak formally to the audience, then to High Balinese to ask the approval of the king whose story is being told, then to Middle Balinese to speak to the audience, then to Old Javanese for a short descriptive passage from the *Ramayana,* then to Low Balinese (the local dialect of Klungkung, where this performance was being held) for the actor to complain about his working conditions, and so on.[13] Matters are complicated still further by the frequent use of Kawi, an artificial language composed of ancient and medieval material from Old and Middle Javanese combined with Balinese elements. In her study of language in the Wayang, Mary Zurbuchen describes Kawi as a language "never learned as a mother tongue, which is always learned with the help of writing." In Bali Kawi is used primarily "to relate epic tales in dynastic chronicles studied by learned men, in esoteric philosophy, and in drama."[14]

### Latin and the Vernaculars

The late medieval theatre in the West provides a somewhat similar though less elaborately stratified dynamic, when Latin at first reigned supreme, and remained the language of power and authority, while the emerging vernacular languages provided countervoices from below. Works, dramatic and nondramatic, that incorporated Latin and the vernaculars in varying combinations came to be called macaronic. As in classic usage, one motivation for such mixing was verisimilitude, but the play of language was far more complicated than anything represented on the stages of the classic era. During the fourteenth and early fifteenth centuries the emergence of the vernacular languages and, perhaps even more significantly, the vast economic and demographic changes that were involved in population shifting from country to cities and from town to town created a intermingling and contestation of languages and dialects. As a result, there was a widespread consciousness of the operations of language and an openness to experimentation with the cultural implications of linguistic mixing. In a major recent article on language play in the late medieval drama, Matthew Boyd Collins argues that the complex play of language and dialect choices in the drama of this period can be best understood by the kind of analysis developed in postcolonial studies. Just as postcolonial authors "may choose to write in the language of the colonizing center" (in this case Latin), "deny its influence for an indigenous identity" (here the emerging vernaculars with their various dialogues), or "appropriate and mimic its discourses," so fifteenth-century writers made elaborate use of "the possibility and problematics of writing in one language or another," sharing with modern postcolonial authors an ability "to address the conflict in a variety of ways."[15] The strategies of language mixing in postcolonial theory present a special case of such complexity and importance that I will return to them in a later chapter.

At one time European medieval theatre was conceived of according to an evolutionary model, beginning with liturgical plays staged entirely in Latin within the church, and then gradually introducing secular elements, including pieces of vernacular language, and moving outside the church into a more public realm. More recent work has revealed that at least as early as the twelfth century, Latin liturgical plays within the church coexisted with Latin and vernacular plays outside it and that the two doubtless exerted influence on each other.[16] It is also becoming increasingly clear that the old model of quite different authors, actors, and audiences for liturgical and secular theatre is not supported by either external evidence or the surviving playtexts, but that a wide variety of combinations existed in different communities.[17] It seems generally clear that there was in most cases a significant overlapping of audiences and audience experience in different theatrical contexts, with members of the laity and clerics alike having a certain familiarity with both the purely Latin liturgical drama and its more secular macaronic parallel. As an English sermon as early as the mid–thirteenth century remarks, plays were performed for "bothe this lewed and this clerkes."[18]

There is an interesting similarity between the use of Latin in the macaronic cycle plays and that of Kawi or Old Javanese in traditional Balinese theatre. Janette Dillon has argued that in the cycle dramas, and particularly in the N-Town cycle, Latin, as the language of tradition, religious insight, and philosophical speculation, directly represents "the brighter light of God's presence."[19] She quotes in this context the comments of Catherine Dunn on Latin and Latinate language (which she proposes as the voice of the church—*la voix de l'Église*) in the Towneley cycle. This "voice"

> denotes an authoritative commentator, recognized by medieval men for the interpretation of Scripture. It denotes also the wisdom of a collective entity existing through many ages and penetrating the great human problems of all times with a philosophical awareness. It implies also a detachment from the immediate dramatic event, that serves to distance the turmoil or conflict or even comic action and envelop these things in a luminous veil.[20]

In short, one of the most common and important uses of Latin in the cycle plays is to serve a function almost identical to "speaking the past" in the literary and antique languages utilized by the Balinese theatre.

As in the Balinese drama this literary or philosophical function may supersede that of verisimilitude, but the latter is also a frequent justification for linguistic mixing. Not surprisingly, God, Jesus, angelic figures, and churchmen may speak in Latin or use Latin tags, but there are also more complex and more surprising intrusions of the "language of the past" into the normally present-inflected world and vernacular speech that dominates the cycle plays. One of the most striking and revealing examples is also one of the best-known cases of the voice of the divine breaking into the voices of the secular world, the appearance of the angels to the shepherds by the authors of the N-Town and the Wakefield cycles, providing a clear example of very different possibilities of the dynamics of linguistic encounters. In the N-Town cycle, when the angelic "Gloria in Excelsis Deo" is heard, the non-Latin-speaking shepherds immediately fall into a quarrel over what they have heard. The first asserts that he heard "Gle, glo, glory." The second disagrees, saying that it plainly was "Gle, glos, glas, glum." The third, however, is granted the grace of understanding:

> The songe methought it was "Glory"
> And aftyrwarde he seyd us to
> Ther is a chylde born xal be a prynce mighty.
> For to seke that chylde I rede we go.[21]

Immediately the others recognize the accuracy of this understanding, and they depart to seek the child, singing in the language they can now miraculously use as song: "Stella celi exitrpavit." Janette Dillon perceptively characterizes this as a "Pentecostal moment, a celebratory recognition of divine grace intervening in human affairs," and relates it to a tradition of medieval miracles in which the gift of a foreign language was divinely bestowed.[22]

The parallel sequence in the Chester cycle provides a significant variation on this approach. There also the English-speaking shepherds are quite confounded by the alien tongue of the angels, and they argue about it in a manner similar to and even more extended than the debate among the N-Town shepherds. More than a dozen exchanges (compared to the three in N-Town) are devoted to the meaning of the opening word, proceeding, in part:

> 3RD SHEPHERD: . . . it was "grorus glorus" with a "glee."
> It was neither more nor lass.
> TROWLE: Nay, it was "glorus, glarus, glorius";
> methink that note went over the house . . .
> 1ST SHEPHERD: Nay, it was "glorus, glarus," with a "glo,"
> and much of "celsis" was thereto.
> As ever I have rest or woe,
> much he spake of "glass."

After this extended N-Town-like interchange, however, the shepherds begin to respond to the power of the Latin words, sensing the "luminosity" claimed for this language by Dillon. Although it is not quite a Pentecostal moment of total discursive understanding, Latin nevertheless breaks through to communicate with the shepherds on a deeper spiritual and emotional level:

> 3RD SHEPHERD: Yet, yet he sang more than all this,
> for some word is worthy a fother.
> For he sang, "bonae voluntatis":
> that is a crop that passeth all other.
> TROWLE: Yet, and yet, he sang more to;

from my mind it shall not start.
He sang also of a "Deo."
Methought that healed my heart.[23]


The Wakefield cycle's treatment of Latin and the vernacular in the parallel *Second Shepherd's Play* is strikingly different from either of these, and suggests something of the range of possibilities of language mixing in the cycle dramas. The angels' Latin Gloria is immediately followed, not by a conversation among the shepherds, but by an angel explaining to them, in English, that the Savior has been born, and how he is to be found. No Pentecostal breakthrough is necessary, therefore, and when the angels depart, the shepherds do not debate the meaning of their words, but rather discuss the musical setting and execution. Clearly it is not the Latin that impresses them, but the beauty and complexity of the angelic music.[24] This orientation is quite in keeping with the style of the Wakefield master, who, as Martin Stevens observes, is an adept linguist who nevertheless finally "distrusts all foreign languages and dialects." Latin, for him, does not have the numinous, iconic quality found in many medieval works, as in the N-Town cycle, but it, along with French, appears "consistently in the rants of tyrants for the purpose of intimidating their listeners."[25] In the Wakefield cycle macaronic Latin and English verse appears almost exclusively in those stanzas attributed to the Wakefield author, and usually in such passages as the long opening rant in the *Processus Talentorum* or the Latin proverbs spoken by the villainous priests Caiphas and Annas in the *Flagellacio*. The Wakefield Herod, a character whose tyrannical ranting became proverbial, ends his play significantly with "I can no more French." A bit of corrupt macaronic discourse is found in the *Second Shepherd's Play* in the lines of one of the shepherds who apparently has intellectual pretensions, expressed, for example, in a garbled macaronic prayer:

Iesus onozaorus
Crucyefixus,
Morcus Andreus
God be oure spede.
  (Lines 422–25)

His foolish use of "Laton," is however, dismissed with abuse and contempt by his fellows. In short, macaronic speech proves an important dramatic technique in both the N-Town and Wakefield plays, but the flexibility of the technique is indicated by its employment here in almost diametrically opposing ways. As Dillon succinctly puts it: "Whereas Latin and Latinate English are normally part of the language of holy speakers in N-Town, so that any deviant use of these dialects is seen as a parody or appropriation of that norm, in Wakefield a more vernacular norm turns Latin into a frequent marker of blasphemous speech."[26]

These three parallel scenes negotiate the bilingual operations of Latin and the vernacular in quite different ways, but the important linguistic attitude that they share is a common concern that these operations must in some way be negotiated. Sarah Beckwith has commented on the ideological changes taking place in religious thought at this time. Before the rise of vernacular, suggests Beckwith,

> It matters little that the mystical text, like any other text, is dialogic, because it was thought to be the monologue, the *one voice* of God Himself. But in fact the increasing use of the vernacular has a crucial effect, a simple but powerful one, for it means precisely that there is a renewed attention to the way that language actually affects what is being expressed. And once this relationship is acknowledged, the monolithic claims to speak for an oracular authority become markedly less convincing.[27]

Significantly, Beckwith in this context evokes the "central insight" of Bakhtin on the contrasting pulls in language between monoglossia and heteroglossia. The establishment of Latin as the language of scriptural truth, Beckwith remarks, was "closely tied up with the centralizing, ecclesiastic ambitions of the ecclesiasts of the central Middle Ages," while the arrival of the competing vernaculars relativized the dominant language and its attendant claims to truth.[28] As Bakhtin noted, specifically in reference to the breakdown of monoglossic expression in the late Middle Ages, "Two myths perish simultaneously: the myth of a language that presumes to be the only language, and the myth of a language that presumes to be completely unified."[29] As we shall see, this dynamic of heteroglossia becomes central in the development of postcolonial drama. Within each of these pastoral scenes, however, can be seen an attempt not perhaps to restore the lost monoglossia of the sacred texts, but in the face of a heteroglossia created by the establishment of vernacular expression, to claim an authoritative primacy and particular spiritual clarity for the sacred tongue.

Latin continued to play a major, though increasingly contested, role in the theatre of Renaissance Europe, but its intellectual dominance was steadily declining and a boisterous clamor of modern languages were jostling for attention and offering exciting new expressive challenges. Not surprisingly, many authors were fascinated, not only by exploring the new possibilities offered by these alternative tongues, but also in placing them in performative dialogue, making Renaissance Europe richer in heteroglossic drama than any period before modern times. Nothing could better illustrate the Renaissance delight in such multilinguistic playfulness than the famous passage in Rabelais's *Gargantua and Pantagruel* when Pantagruel first meets his lifelong companion, Panurge. When hailed, Panurge addresses Pantagruel with passages in German, Italian, Basque, Dutch, Danish, Spanish, Hebrew, Greek, Latin, and three invented languages before discovering that he and Pantagruel share the same mother tongue, which is French.[30]

This famous encounter is anticipated by a less famous one three chapters earlier, which recounts Pantagruel's first adventure after completing his studies. He and his friends encounter on the Paris road a young Limousin scholar who, ashamed of his native dialect, attempts to pass himself off as a Parisian by speaking an affected macaronic blend of French and Latin. When asked his origins, for example, he responds that he is "From the alme, inclite, aned celebrated academy that is vocitated Lutetia." After several such pronouncements Pantagruel suggests that the young man is "coining some new devilish language," but one of his followers asserts that in fact the fellow is "trying to imitate the Parisian's language, but all he is doing is murdering Latin." Threatened by Pantagruel, the terrified Limousin soils himself and lapses into his own dialect. His story, concludes the narrator, proves "the truth of the Philosopher Aulus Gellius's observation, that we ought to speak the language in common use."[31]

A similar delight in multilinguistic playfulness may be seen in the popular comedies of Andrea Calmo in sixteenth-century Venice, whose linguistic complexity has clearly hampered critical study and appreciation of his work. In the preface to his *Il Travaglia* (1556), Calmo asserts that a pure literary style may be appropriate for the printed page, but in the theatre, and especially in comedy, the goal should be to capture the way people actually speak, including all the variety of such discourse.[32] Thus in Calmo's *La Rhodiana* (1553), for example, the Venetian merchant Cornelio (played by the author himself) has a bravura scene somewhat reminiscent of Panurge's self-introduction, delivered in a wide variety of different languages and dialects (act 4, scene 14), while Cornelio's Paduan servant Truffa pretends (act 2, scene 8) to be possessed by a series of spirits, each of which, when conjured up, speaks in a different tongue: Neapolitan, French, Milanese, Ragusan, Spanish, Florentine, and Albanian.

*Renaissance Variations*

There is clearly a close connection between this interest in linguistic verisimilitude and the dramatic potential of alternative modes of speaking in early authors of literary comedy like Calmo and in the commedia dell'arte, which was developing in Italy at about this same time. In the following chapter I will discuss in more detail the most prominent linguistic feature of the commedia dell'arte, its widespread conventionalized use of particular dialects and their close association with particular characters or character types. The primary motivation for such accents was surely not to increase the realistic illusion of this highly patterned and contrived form, but to take advantage, as comic theatre has always done, of particular recognizable character types, whose predictable and stereotyped accents became, like their costumes, properties, and preoccupations, part of the infinitely repeated mechanical quality that Bergson pointed out as one of the traditional bases of comedy.[33] Nevertheless a certain concern for verisimilitude was clearly present even in dialect choices; the learned Dottore's Bolognese accent associated him with one of the most ancient and honored university cities in Europe, Pantalone's Venetian dialect related him to one of Europe's greatest commercial and trading centers, and so on.

When we turn from the use of dialect in the commedia to the use of actual alternative languages, the primary topic of the present chapter, the concern for a degree of verisimilitude becomes even clearer. The Dottore frequently salted his speeches with Latin phrases, doubtless incomprehensible to most of the public, whose knowledge of Latin was surely restricted largely to church services, but familiar enough to be recognized as Latin. Indeed, by its very incomprehensibility and association with obscure learning it was a perfect sign for the intellectual pretensions of this character, the same device that Rabelais uses to make fun of his pretentious Limousin and that was already in use, as we have seen, in the late medieval drama. In fact the use of Latin (and occasional Greek) words and phrases as a mark of the stage pedant is found throughout Renaissance Europe, and is carried on as a common device in the work of Shakespeare, Molière, and later writers into seventeenth- and eighteenth-century comedy.

Spanish presents a particularly interesting case in the commedia tradition, since the southern half of the Italian peninsula, the Kingdom of Naples, was under Spanish control in early modern times, and thus Spanish functioned there in a manner somewhat similar to later colonialist languages. The Spanish imperialist enterprise gave a militaristic edge to what was already the language of the ruling power, intensified by the conscription of many inhabitants of southern Italy to fight under the Spanish flag in far-off imperial struggles, particularly in the Netherlands. Well before the rise of the commedia dell'arte, one of its most popular characters had appeared in Italian literary comedy, the flamboyant, bellicose Spanish captain, a clear physical and linguistic reflection of these political and social realities. He is first encountered in one of the most appreciated and widely read of the Italian Renaissance comedies, the anonymous *Gli ingannati,* presented in Siena in 1532, when that city was under occupation by Spanish troops. Here the vain and boastful Captain Giglio speaks Spanish throughout and is made a fool of by Pasquella, the clever maidservant. A similar, if somewhat less grotesque Spanish captain appears in Alessandro Piccolomini's Siennese comedy *L'amor costante* (1536), and by the end of the century he had become a ubiquitous commedia figure. Fittingly enough, when he spoke Italian, it was normally in a dialect from one of the southern regions under Spanish controls, Neapolitan or Sicilian, but Spanish was his favored language, a phenomenon Riccoboni credits to political realities:

> The domination of the Spanish in Italy drew certain actors from that
> nation to this country and these gave to the theatre the Captains, who
> spoke only Spanish or a mixture of the two languages.[34]

Although Latin and Spanish were the foreign languages most accessible
to Italian audiences and therefore most common in the commedia, there
are scattered examples of Jewish and Greek merchants speaking their
own languages, and at least pidgin attempts at both French and German. There was even a traditional lazzo of learning to speak French,
with comic and often obscene misunderstandings,[35] a device taken over
by Shakespeare in his famous "learning to speak English" scene in
*Henry V.*

Shakespeare and the Elizabethans, not surprisingly, offer their own
often elaborate examples of multilanguage theatre, precisely the sort of
triumph of realism over neoclassic purity and clarity that one might
expect of the open theatrical culture of Renaissance England. As M. C.
Bradbrook notes of this period,

> There was widespread interest in modern languages, and this is
> shown in the drama by a frequent introduction of foreigners who talk
> either broken English or their own tongue. The groundlings might
> not be able to understand them, but they were interested to hear the
> sound of a strange language.[36]

Dillon argues that English dramas of the 1580s and 1590s still frequently
used Latin in the manner she suggested was operative in medieval
works, as an emblematic language of the past, not primarily to be understood discursively but "to invoke deep responses that bypassed any
engagement with the sense of the words and allowed particular
moments to develop a presence that took them beyond the limits of the
playworld."[37] Latin operates "to freeze a single moment" so that it
"stands out in high relief against the vernacular world which makes
space for it."[38] So, for example, Ate, the goddess of revenge, opens each
act of *The Lamentable Tragedy of Locrine* (ca. 1594) with a emblematic
dumbshow and line or two of Latin, which she then explains in English.[39] A similar extranarrative abstract character, Genius, appears in
Thomas Lodge's *The Wounds of Civil War* to announce, in Latin, Scilla's

impending death.[40] There may also be an attempt to place Scilla in an appropriately "classic" frame by this usage, which seems also the reason for the Latin interchange between the classic lovers Dido and Aeneas at their moment of parting in Christopher Marlowe and Thomas Nashe's *Dido, Queen of Carthage* (ca. 1585).[41]

John Marston's love tragedy *Antonio and Mellida,* fifteen years later (1599–1600), shows a more contemporary and ironic treatment of this same device. In this play, not in classic times, but in a more contemporary Venice, the lovers also move to the heightened plane of another language at a moment of meeting, here Italian. Whatever this device might gain in either elevation or verisimilitude is, however, immediately challenged by the comic deflation of the page immediately following and beginning "I think confusion of Babel is fallen upon these lovers, that they change their language," an error, he suggests, "easier to be pardoned by the auditors than excused by the authors."[42] An even odder shift to Italian occurs in George Peele's *Edward I* (1590–93) when Joan, Edward's presumed daughter, discovers she is in fact the illegitimate daughter of a friar. She falls to the ground and, apparently taking leave of her senses, begins to speak in Italian. Dillon suggests a parallel with Robert Greene's *Orlando Furioso* (1591), whose hero's madness is heralded by an Italian passage denouncing women taken directly from the Italian original.[43] Since Peele's Joan also quotes the Ariosto epic,[44] it seems clear that this moment is indeed being linguistically coded to recall that central literary expression of the onset of madness, but the usage in Peele is much more complex than in Greene. Joan's quote does not refer to the onset of madness but to a seemingly arbitrary passage about horsemanship, almost as if *any* passage from Ariosto could suggest madness. Yet Edward responds to her outburst by his own Italian quotation, also from Ariosto, but in his case totally appropriate to the situation: "Almighty God! How fallible and vain / is Human Judgement, dimmed by clouds obscure."[45] It seems that Peele expected at least some of his audience to understand enough Italian, if not to recognize the voice of Ariosto, at least to understand the gist of Edward's reaction.

The widespread knowledge of Ariosto allowed an association of Italian with mental instability, but an even stronger association was with Machiavelli and the sort of secret and duplicitous villainy he represented to the Elizabethan mind. Often Italian is conflated in this respect with

Spanish, since the tensions of the years just before and after the defeat of the Spanish Armada in 1588 made Spain the primary political threat. This gave it (and its language) a role somewhat similar to that of Persian in the classic Greek drama. So the villains Barabas and Ithamore in Marlowe's *The Jew of Malta* often employ Spanish, and Hieronimo in Kyd's *The Spanish Tragedy* uses Spanish when he begins to practice deception (act 3, scene 14), and he subsequently exchanges Italian couplets with the play's central Machiavellian villain, Lorenzo. The Spanish-English conflict is played out in linguistic terms with particular clarity in the late morality *Three Lords and Three Ladies of London* by Robert Wilson. The three ladies, Love, Lucre, and Conscience, are wooed by the three lords, Policy, Pomp, and Pleasure, but are challenged by three rival lords from Spain, Pride, Ambition, and Tyranny, which they handily defeat. As a prelude to the final confrontation, a mock tournament, the two sides engage in a battle of languages. The section is introduced by Pride announcing (in Latin) that the English may feel free to speak their own language, since the Spaniards understand it, though normally do not deign to speak it.[46] In fact a linguistic potpourri ensues, in which the Spanish and their interpreter, Shealty (glossed in the play as "an Irish word" signifying "looseness"), speak in a mixture of English, Latin, and Spanish, while the English indeed respond in their own language except occasionally, when they show that they also could speak the "other" language if they deigned to do so:

PRIDE: Buena buena per los Lutheranos Angleses.
FEALTY [his page]: Mala, mala per Catholicos Castillianos.[47]

Contemporary vernacular languages play a much more important heteroglossic role in the work of Shakespeare and his contemporaries than they do in the Elizabethan drama of the previous generation. Such linguistic mixing is most fully developed in *Henry IV, Parts I and II* and in *Henry V,* where it moves to the very center of the dramatic action. The most extensively developed "other" language is French, although there is also an extensive use of English dialects (Welsh, Irish, and Scotch) and actual passages in *Henry IV, Part I* where both Owen Glendower and his daughter, Mortimer's wife, speak in Welsh, though

Shakespeare here merely indicates where the lines appear and does not write them out, as he does the later French passages.

Both languages and dialects in this trilogy contribute to the overall celebration of Englishness and the political and military triumphs of the English state over alien (foreign-speaking) enemies both at home and abroad. The difference in the use of Welsh in *Henry IV, Part I* and *Henry V* suggests the evolution of this process. In the former play, the Welsh are allied with the king's enemies, the Percys, but the refusal of either side to assimilate (despite Mortimer's marriage) stands as a symbol of the disunity that will eventually contribute to their downfall. Henry V, on the other hand, has the power and the skill to bring together such disparate forces, first by bringing the various strands of British culture, Irish, English, Scotch, and Welsh (now, significantly, reduced from an alien language to an English dialect) together in the representatives of these various factions gathering to support Henry in battle, and second, in the gradual colonization of French by English that continues throughout the play.

Surely the best-known foreign-language scene in Shakespeare is the comic "learning to speak English" scene between the French queen Katherine and her servant Alice in *Henry V*.[48] Once passed over by most commentators as a trivial, even intrusive scene of comic relief, it has more recently attracted the attention of feminist and cultural critics as of major symbolic importance. Lisa Jardine, for example, has commented,

> Long before it is certain that Henry will be victorious, Katherine has apparently transferred her allegiance to the English cause. What else is her enthusiastic attempt to learn the rudiments of English but a capitulation in advance of the fact? The sexual innuendo of the "English lesson" transposes the impending "conquest" of France into a "conquest" of France's women.[49]

The scene in fact establishes both linguistic and thematic concerns that are developed through the rest of the play. The scene immediately following shows the French court already contaminated both linguistically and sexually, bemoaning in mixed French and English their weakness at the hands of the English "bastards," Norman products of mixing

English and French blood. A masculine echo of the Katherine scene is found on the battlefield in act 4, scene 4, where the rough Pistol with his dogged English takes prisoner a terrified and somewhat affected French-speaking soldier, but the most complete development of the themes introduced in the "English lesson" scene is found in the final scene of the play, where Henry both politically and linguistically assumes control of Katherine and the nation she represents. It is clear that Katherine is the one who must submit linguistically, from Henry's opening observation: "O fair Katherine, if you will love me soundly with your French heart, I will be glad to hear you confess it brokenly with your English tongue," to his closing request-command: "Come, your answer in broken music—for thy voice is music and thy English broken; therefore, Queen of all, Katherine, break thy mind to me in broken English, wilt thou have me?" The almost obsessive repetition of "broken" emphasizes with particular clarity that not only a language is being broken here, but the individuality and independence represented by the royal speaker of that language.

It is true that Henry, always the politician, makes a few attempts himself to speak some French to Katherine, but they are half-hearted at best, and he soon draws back from them with the oath: "Now, fie upon my false French! By mine honour, in true English, I love thee, Kate," privileging English (as the Pistol scene prefigured) as the language of direct, honest expression, best suited to the rough, plain-speaking soldier that Henry presents himself to be in this scene. It is most fitting that this climactic scene, which so heavily relies upon heteroglossia, should reach its political climax with the Duke of Exeter's request to the French king that he acknowledge Henry's sovereignty in three languages, English, French, and, with a nod to political and ecclesiastical history, Latin.

Shakespeare's use of French in *Henry V* is unusually extensive, but French, Spanish, Italian, and occasionally Latin were frequently utilized by his fellow dramatists. His contemporary Thomas Dekker was particularly enamored of linguistic mixing, with substantial non-English passages in six of his plays, spoken by four Dutchmen, four Welshmen, and one Irishman. The Welsh scenes in his *Patient Grissil* are in fact so detailed and accurate that it has been suggested that Dekker may have utilized a Welsh-speaking collaborator for them.[50] In Dekker, as in Shakespeare, real foreign speech is used, with real content that often contributes, sometimes quite significantly, to the content of the play. It would be dangerous to assert that audience members with no knowledge whatever of Spanish or French or Dutch would find a scene conducted entirely or largely in one of these languages wholly meaningless. The ingenuity of actors and the multiplicity of theatre's communication channels would naturally offer them at least some insight into the content, even though a full enjoyment of the scenes, and especially of the jokes, does require such knowledge. Although the precise makeup of historical audiences is notoriously difficult to determine, Shakespeare could reasonably rely on at least a rudimentary knowledge of French among his more well-educated patrons and Dekker on some knowledge of Dutch among the not inconsiderable part of the Elizabethan public engaged in shipping and trade, while at least some Spanish, Italian, and Latin were readily accessible to a significant part of the educated public. For these patrons, not necessarily a minority, the macaronic references would be reasonably transparent, while the rest would have to follow the shape of the scenes by context and nonverbal clues, by no means an insurmountable task.

A certain amount of the problem that macaronic theatre presents to reception analysis disappears when we recognize that in many periods, including the modern one, audiences were themselves macaronic, at least in part. Certainly, to return to the original meaning of this term, the creators of vernacular texts in the late Middle Ages and early Renaissance that included Latin passages could obviously assume that they would be accessible at least to the learned among their audiences. This has remained true, to a limited extent, in subsequent Western drama, even in dramatists generally associated with realism and monoglossic theatre. Moreover Latin, when used, almost always suggests the numinous, otherworldly, mystical echoes that recall its use in certain medieval drama and the Sanskrit "voice of the past" in Asian theatre. Thus Ibsen, the father of modern drama, ends his epic *Brand* with the haunting and mysterious voice calling out of the avalanche: "He is *deus caritas.*" Strindberg often utilizes Latin phrases and whole passages to reinforce the impression of quasi-religious allegory in works like *To Damascus* or *There Are Crimes and Crimes,* and the climax of Edward Albee's *Who's Afraid of Virginia Woolf?* involves George's recitation of an extended Latin passage from the Catholic Mass for the Dead.[51]

From the seventeenth through the nineteenth centuries the cultural dominance of France meant that European dramatists from England to Russia and from Denmark to Italian could include phrases, or even whole scenes, in French with the expectation that a reasonable percentage of their audience would find this language quite accessible. Affected or pretentious characters in the English theatre, such as the Lade Melantha in Dryden's *Marriage à la Mode* often use French rather in the way that Renaissance pedants used Latin, as a sign of their presumably superior cultural background. A passage in George Villiers's 1671 parody-drama *The Rehearsal* shows his parody dramatist, the pompous Bayes, bragging specifically of his use of this device:

> 1 KING: You must begin, *Mon foy.*
> 2 KING: Sweet sir, *Pardonnes moy.*
> BAYES: Mark that: I makes 'em both speak *French,* to shew their breeding.[52]

Goldoni's *Una delle Ultime Sere di Carnovale,* his last play written in Venice before his departure for France in 1762, appropriately includes a major character, Madama Gatteau, who speaks almost entirely in French. Throughout the play she is urged by others to speak Italian, and indeed she enthusiastically responds, "Allons, toujours italiano; parlare sempre italiano," but her efforts are in vain. Most of her speeches are entirely in French, and when she is pressed to speak Italian, she can at best come up with such modern macaronic utterances as "Si tour è vero quell che voi dite; si monsieur Anjoletto è amoroso di un'alta giovine, je ferai le diable à quatre."[53] Failing in her hope to marry Anjolette, she nevertheless ultimately finds a Venetian husband, who, rather in the manner of Henry V, connects the matrimonial agreement to a linguistic request: "Voleu, o no veleu, in buon Italian?" But the stout Madame Gatteau is no yielding Katherine. She gives up her hand, but not her language: "Voici la main, mon petit Coeur."[54]

The rise of nationalism and of national theatres devoted to the promotion of a particular language, culture, and history during the nineteenth century provided a powerful disincentive for the sort of dramatic mixing of languages often found in the Renaissance, and to a lesser extent in the baroque theatre. During the nineteenth century, as modern national consciousness developed, it was often closely tied to the celebration of a national language, which in turn was connected to the development of a new national theatre. Thus a Czech language theatre was established in Prague as a national alternative to the earlier German language theatre, a Norwegian theatre in Christiana (today Oslo) as an alternative to the earlier Danish language theatre, a Gaelic theatre in Dublin as an alternative to the earlier English language theatre, and so on. Conversely, linguistic minorities in alien lands often founded theatres speaking their own language to give them a cultural and social center, as we can see in the many ethnic theatres in nineteenth-century America. Another encouragement for monologism in the nineteenth-century theatre was the trend of dramatic writing, strongly favoring domestic and indeed local realism in both comic and serious drama. Characters like Dekker's Dutch sailors, Shakespeare's Welsh soldiers, even Goldoni's French-speaking tourists were highly unlikely to appear in the bourgeois living rooms that dominated the mid- and late-nineteenth-century stages of Europe and the many countries that followed the European dramatic fashions.

*International Touring*

Probably the most important mixed-language productions of the late nineteenth century were created not out of an interest in verisimilitude but rather as a means of cross-cultural communication, in the phenomenon of international touring. This, with the increasing ease of travel, became a major part of the theatrical culture of the late nineteenth century, stimulating a variety of experiments with linguistic mixing. One should not, of course, underestimate the ability of trained actors to communicate meanings across language barriers by expression and gesture, as we see, for example, in Fyrres Moryson's account of the Elizabethan actors performing with success before a German-speaking public in Frankfurt:

> I remember when some of our cast despised Stage players came out of England into Germany, and played at Frankford in the tyme of the Mart, having nether a complete number of Actours, nor any good Apparell, nor any ornament of the Stage, yet the Germans, not under-

standing a worde they sayde, both men and women, flocked wonder-
fully to see theire gesture and Action, rather than heare them, speaking English which they understood not.[55]

Not many years before this, English audiences had their own experience
of the possibility of "understanding" performances in another language
with the visits of Italian commedia players in the 1570s.[56] Nevertheless,
as soon as touring companies began to travel regularly outside their own
language community, they clearly discovered the power of mixing even
a few foreign words or phrases into their offerings. This sort of adjustment came particularly easily to the loosely scripted and occasion-driven
performances of groups like the commedia dell'arte companies as they
traveled about Europe. The gradual replacement of Italian by French as
the Italian actors settled in Paris and became an established part of the
theatre world there provides a particularly interesting example of mixed
language production as a transitional operation between one language
community and other. Commedia companies first appeared in Paris as
early as 1571, but did not establish a permanent theatre there until 1662,
after which they performed there regularly until 1697. The first
recorded use of French by the company is a drinking song in *Le regal des
dames* of 1668, the first production by the new company to depart from
the traditional Italian repertory.[57] Following this innovation, French
was more and more utilized, especially in the memorized set speeches of
Arlequin. The old tradition of multilanguage playfulness was not aban-
doned, however, as we see in a traditional routine from a 1670 piece by
Angelo Agostino Lolli called *Le gentilhomme campagnard*. Arlequin
enters "dressed one half as a Frenchman, one half as a Spaniard,
wrapped in a long, black cloak and with two hats on," and, meeting the
Doctor, first speaks to him in French:

> Bonjour, monsieur, are you not a M. Baloard? He answers that that is
> his name, I make him a ridiculous comment, then I reveal the other
> side, I speak to him in Spanish and ask if he is the Docteur Baloard,
> he says yes, and me, I continue gravely that I am Don Diego, of those
> Diegos as noble as the sun, and I have come here to marry well, etc.
> Then I again reveal the other side and ask him in French, who is that

man who was speaking to you. Do you know he had the bad manners to turn his back on me?[58]

Although the evolution of the Comédie Italienne from a polyglot Italian-based company in the late seventeenth century to a monologistic French-speaking company in the next century provides a particularly extensive record of linguistic adaptation, the records of international touring are full of more modest examples of the linguistic accommodation to shifting audience languages. Nor is this restricted to new and occasional plays, but affects even the comparatively fixed texts of the literary tradition. The great international stars of the late nineteenth century very often performed the works of Shakespeare, for example, in their own original language while all or most of the supporting cast, often recruited locally, spoke the language of whatever community the international star was visiting. Some productions were also bilingual even in their leading roles, as when Tomasso Salvini and Bogumil Dawison each appeared with Edwin Booth in *Othello,* the former speaking Italian, the second German, with Booth in both cases responding in English. Certain stars carried this mixing even into their own roles. Ernesto Rossi, speaking primarily in Italian, presented first individual speeches, then scenes, and finally the entire last act in English while touring nineteenth-century America with his *King Lear,* an innovation that was cheered by enthusiastic audiences. The *New York Herald* of January 18, 1882, reported that the shift to English late in the play met with "hearty and admiring response" from an audience "fairly electrified by a patriotic of egotistical enthusiasm."[59] In the mid–twentieth century as Vakhtangov's company toured to countries outside or Russia with their famous *Turandot,* one feature of the production was improvised sequences between the clowns and the audience in whatever the local language happened to be.[60] This process still continues in touring companies around the world. South African director Robert Mshengu Kavanagh provides an excellent example from the tours of a musical called *ZZZIP!* by his Workshop '71 in the late 1970s. Kavanagh reports, "The company performed first in the Witwatersrand [the area around Johannesburg], and then took the play on tour to the Transkei and the Cape, where Xhosa is homogeneously spoken and Zulu, Sotho, and tsotsitaal are imperfectly understood, if at all."[61] In 1996 I witnessed in New York a recent example of this traditional practice. In a production visiting the United States from the Vaidilos Ainai Theatre of Vilnius, Lithuania, called *Mirages,* the actors had learned scattered lines in English for this occasion, and planned, like Rossi, to keep adding English lines so long as the tour continued.

Traditionally the phenomenon of bilingual touring has been based upon an originating artist or company bringing their language into another linguistic field and to some extent incorporating material from that target field, but many variations are possible. An interesting example of double origination and targeting was undertaken in 1990 by the Salon Theatre of St. Petersburg in Russia and the Irondale Ensemble, a New York–based company that has a particular interest in the reworking of traditional texts in the light of contemporary social and political concerns. The two joined together to create a joint Russian-English experimental production of Chekhov's *Uncle Vanya.* Generally speaking the St. Petersburg actors performed scenes and sequences in Russian and the Irondale actors in English, but occasional sequences or lines were also given in the "other" language in a highly complex structure that, in the Irondale tradition, mixed scenes from the original text with new material growing out of rehearsal improvisation. The goal was apparently both to develop a better understanding between artists as each language group began to experience something of the feeling of the other, but also to develop a production that would provide access to both Russian- and English-speaking audiences, since it was presented in both the United States and in Russia.

In the long historical tradition of this kind of linguistic mixing the essential goal remains the same, to establish a closer rapport with the audience, a goal that has probably been more important historically than the more obvious one of improving comprehension of the play. One can hardly argue that Rossi's delivery of the single line "Every inch a king" in English, his first experiment in this direction, added much to the comprehension of the play by his American audiences, but the extended cheering and applause that inevitably followed this line demonstrated clearly that the audience appreciated it as a international gesture of friendship. In terms of linguistic theory, it is not so much an example of a content-bearing message as of what linguistic theorists have called "phatic communion," defined by Charles Hockett as "minimal communicative activity which has no obvious consequences save to inform all concerned that the channels are in good working order."[62]

Phatic communion aside, however, offering material in the language of the host culture obviously does improve communication for international touring artists. A related strategy has been the use of a third language, not necessarily the primary tongue of either performer or audience, but a lingua franca accessible to both, Latin in the late classic and early modern period, the colonial languages in the nineteenth century, and in much of the world, English today. In May 2000 I attended in Berlin a new dance-theatre piece called *Körper,* by one of Germany's leading choreographers, Sasha Waltz. I was not surprised to find that the piece contained a good deal of spoken material, since this is typical of today's German Tanztheater, but I was surprised that the majority of this spoken material was English. When I asked Waltz about this after the performance, she explained that the production was planned for international touring and that English was now the most generally accessible international language, as well as the only one common to her international company. One naturally wonders if this motivation—in addition to his stated reason that the life of the play is contained in the music of its words—encouraged Peter Brook in his unusual decision to present his 2000 version of *Hamlet,* destined for extensive international touring, primarily in English for its premiere showings to a Parisian audience.

The reception process of bilingualism in international touring during the nineteenth century was complicated, especially in America, by the existence in many large cities of sizable foreign-language-speaking populations. Although many of the audiences who attended the performances of a Bernhardt, a Salvini, a Modjeska, or a Dawison had little or no knowledge of the language the star was speaking, newspaper reports of the time often mention the enthusiastic response these artists received from the immigrant communities whose language and culture they represented. In at least certain cities, the audiences for these bilingual tours were clearly significantly bilingual as well. The international touring star thus provided a unique occasion for the gathering of a theatrical culture that, although it might live in a highly polyglot urban center, remained almost totally monologistic in its theatre experience.

Although communities of linguistic minorities have always been a part of the population of many large cities, these have tended historically to remain in ghettoized enclaves. During the nineteenth and early twentieth centuries many of these communities, especially in America and possibly under the influence of the national theatre movement in Europe, developed theatres created by and for themselves. Although they have until recently been generally neglected by traditional totalizing American theatre histories, America possesses a long and significant tradition of non-English-speaking theatres: German, Polish, Yiddish, Norwegian, Italian, Spanish, and Chinese among many others. The world premiere of Ibsen's *Ghosts* took place not in Scandinavia but in a Norwegian-speaking theatre in Chicago.

Even in urban centers where many inhabitants speak, or at least somewhat understand, more than one language, individual theatres have traditionally catered to a single language as they have to a single type of drama, such as boulevard comedy, musicals, or experimental theatre. Although the major urban (and theatrical) centers of the modern world are becoming increasingly multilingual, the major theatres in many of these cities remain essentially monolingual, reflecting the dominant or official language of the city. Alongside these, most large international cities today will also offer a number of monolingual minority theatres, such as the Turkish Stage in Berlin, the Swedish theatre in Helsinki, or the Repertorio Español in New York.

Another, somewhat utopian model for minority language theatres was offered as a tribute to such theatres in 1998 by New York's experimental En Garde Arts company. *The Secret History of the Lower East Side* was written by dramatists from three different ethnic minorities and focused on the popular nineteenth-century immigrant theatres of the Lower East Side, a traditional destination of newly arrived immigrants in New York as well as a center of theatres created by these varied immigrant populations. *The Secret History* includes a playful re-creation of a performance in one of these theatres which presupposed actors drawn from Italian, German, and Yiddish backgrounds working together to create a melodramatic spectacle in which each actor spoke his own language and acted in his own conventionalized style. Of course, although the nineteenth-century Lower East Side offered a rich performance tradition in each of these languages, cultural and linguistic mixing in any one location would in fact have been unthinkable at that time. The languages of the surrounding communities were as unknown to the audiences of these theatres as their own language was to the stages of the majority population in the city center.

## Modern Multiculturalism

Nevertheless, the multilanguage production displayed in the *Secret History of the Lower East Side,* if unthinkable in its own time, has striking parallels to many theatrical manifestations in the world today. In this multicultural world many theatres mount multilanguage productions, recognizing that the culture that surrounds them is no longer, if it ever was, truly monolingual, and seeking to appeal to and accurately reflect the concerns and interests of a multilingual society. Thus, along with its traditional monolinguistic theatres, New York toward the end of the twentieth century saw the appearance of groups that considered mixed language productions central to their mission. The so-called Thalia Spanish Theatre of Queens, for example, despite its title, began in 2000 regularly offering a modern multicultural form named for the traditional Spanish *zarzuela,* but in fact mixing basically English libretti with musical numbers in Spanish. In speaking of the 2001 production of *La Gran Via/Broadway.* Thalia's director, Angel Gil Orrios, observed: "If there's any place in the world that demands bilingual theatre, it would be Queens."[63]

In fact the number of places in the world that demand bilingual or indeed multilingual theatre seems to be constantly increasing. Not surprisingly, some of the most important work of this kind has appeared in communities that are officially bilingual, such as eastern Canada. Until fairly recently the theatrical traditions and productions of French-speaking and English-speaking Canada were totally distinct, but in the late twentieth century a significant body of bilingual drama and tradition of bilingual production appeared and is constantly growing in importance. Perhaps the best-known example is David Fennario's 1979 play *Balconville,* which dealt with two neighboring families, one primarily French-speaking, the other primarily English-speaking, and with the relationships between them and to the larger political system. It was performed with great success in Montreal, Toronto, and Ottawa and won the Chalmers Award for the Best Canadian Play of the year. As an officially bilingual city, Montreal seems a particularly appropriate location for use of multiple languages in the service of verisimilitude, but in today's constantly shifting linguistic communities almost any urban center could provide dramatic encounters of this sort. One of the first productions, for example, of the experimental group Stoka in Bratislava, Slovakia, the *Sentimental Journal* of 1991, concerned a young couple trying to understand each other, he speaking English, she Slovak.

In a later chapter, on postmodern heteroglossia, I will speak about the growing importance, especially in Europe, of multicultural and multilinguistic companies from that of Peter Brook onward, in which multiple languages have been normally used, not in the interests of verisimilitude, as is the case of most of the examples in this chapter, but for more distinctly formal or symbolic ends, as part of the play of signification in postmodern work. Some contemporary international companies use heteroglossia in a manner more like these modern bilingual companies, with actors speaking their native language, in character or as themselves, in the interests of verisimilitude. An outstanding current example of such work is the International WOW company, primarily based in New York but founded in Thailand in 1966 by theatre artists from Thailand, Indonesia, Japan, and the United States. Since that time it has added actors from Austria, Canada, England, France, Pakistan, the Philippines, Puerto Rico, Taiwan, and Venezuela. Although the company's basic language is English, their productions regularly contain characters allowing cast members to speak other languages. For example, in the 2004 production, *The Comfort and Safety of Your Own Home,* a major scene near the end is an extended dialogue between company members from Indonesia and Palestine, conducted entirely in their native languages, Bhasa and Arabic. Despite this barrier, they manage to communicate in some measure with the audience in the process of learning to communicate with each other, thus providing a model study of intercultural communication and understanding.

Obviously the issue of communication is central to any such production, but in almost any community with competing languages, this competition involves other political, social, economic, and class tensions as well. Heteroglossic drama thus almost always uses various languages as a powerful symbolic shorthand for these matters. This is certainly what

Fennario does in *Balconville* or what Brian Friel does in *Translations,* dealing with an Irish teacher of Latin and speaker of Gaelic who is confronted with the literal and figurative encroachment of English into his domain. These concerns are almost invariably present in one of the most fascinating and complex areas of heteroglossic theatre today, the drama of postcolonialism, which I will consider more specifically in a later chapter.

The amount of multilanguage theatre being produced around the world today is considerable and seems to be growing, just as exposure to a variety of languages is everywhere increasing. There are a wide variety of reasons for this. Certainly one is the growing ease of international travel. Before the twentieth-century touring performers, from the traveling actor-diplomats of the late Roman Empire to the international stars of the late nineteenth century, performers normally took their productions and their languages to foreign audiences. During the twentieth century more and more audiences were able and willing to travel abroad to experience foreign theatre in its home. Foreign travelers, occasionally seen in premodern drama, have become far more common figures in modern theatre, as they have on the streets of any large modern city. In Europe, the English-speaking tourist has become particularly common both on the streets and in the theatre, and since English is now so widely spoken in continental Europe, he very frequently appears speaking his own language. This sort of character seems to be particularly favored in the contemporary German-speaking theatre, where passages in English are regularly found in the work of most younger directors. A particularly amusing and unusual "English" tourist was a major character in *Hotel Angst,* the production with which Christoph Marthaler opened his administration of the Zurich Schauspiel in November 2000. This character not only spoke English throughout, but English with a thick and to my ears impeccable Scottish accent, much to the delight and apparent complete understanding of the cosmopolitan Swiss audience.

Marthaler's Scotsman is distinctly in the tradition of the colorful "barbarian" who brings his or her language into the linguistic world of the play and its audience, like Goldoni's Madame Gatteau or Shakespeare's Katherine, and for most audiences in most historical periods, the experience of the linguistic outsider was something they knew about objectively, but not subjectively. Today, with international travel comparatively easy and common, the Scotsman may also become the protagonist of a drama, moving in a linguistic culture alien both to himself and to the watching audience, an experience today much more likely to be shared by members of that audience than at most periods in the past. Priscilla Ceiling in the second, "Kabul" act of Tony Kushner's diptych *Homebody/Kabul* is an excellent example, first appearing in precisely the role of the disoriented tourist. According to the opening stage direction, she is "in her burqa, trying to read the guidebook's small map through the burqa's grill."[64] She first tries to question a woman, who speaks to her in Dari, the Afghan dialect of Farsi (Persian), and then to a man, who responds in Pashtun, the other, more tribal language of Afghanistan, with disastrous results. Only when she makes contact with the multilinguistic guide Khwaja is she (and her English-speaking audience) able to enter into the discourse of the play. Translation, and its difficulties and inadequacies, is a recurring concern in this play, and not only between English and the Afghani tongues. In a later scene, Priscilla encounters Mahala, a former librarian, forced by the Taliban to give up her job. Mahala bemoans the fate of Afghan women in a mixture of English (a few words), German (one passage), French, and Dari. Since Priscilla can understand only English, Khwaja attempts to translate the rest, but he does so only selectively, cutting longer passages and more offensive material, as is apparent to any audience members with some knowledge of French. This disjuncture between the actual content of an onstage foreign language and the translation (if any) provided of course reflects the real-life experience of anyone who has ever been involved in the process of translation (perhaps especially political or diplomatic translation, which is close to the case here). It also opens up a space for dramaturgical intervention, not much used by Kushner but more important in other works, as I will explain later.

Although Kushner's play is set against a very dark sociopolitical background, the tourist experience with alien languages evokes on the whole positive, even humorous associations. A much less benign force for the mixing of languages in contemporary society and thus for the exploration of this mixing on contemporary stages has been the ongoing economic and political dislocation of language populations. A reflection of this latter process clearly marks the multiple language productions of the great experimental director Tadeusz Kantor, who evoked the linguistic mélange of Poland in his youth by including speeches in Polish, Yiddish, Hebrew, and German in *The Dead Class* and of Polish, French, German, and Russian in *Today is My Birthday.* While the situation of the outsider, whether tourist, military occupier, or refugee, attempting to learn and speak the language of a new environment, still provides grist for comic authors, as it did for Dekker, Shakespeare, and Molière, this dynamic is often wedded in more modern drama to the all-too-familiar tensions of cultural displacement and the breakdown of communication between and within cultures. Ionesco's *The Bald Soprano* is not, strictly speaking, a multilanguage play, but the cultural tensions of learning a foreign language provide its foundation, as it was inspired, its author asserts, by a French primer for learning English. The linguistic subtext of Ionesco's play comes to the surface in two more recent dramas also built upon language learning, Caryl Churchill's *Mad Forest,* whose first act is built around the learning of basic sentences in Romanian, or Marie Irene Fornes's *The Danube,* which builds each scene around a passage from a language-learning tape for the study of Hungarian. In each of these works, the tension of language learning opens the way to deeply disturbing studies of cultural conflict.

One of the central concerns of David Edgar's *Pentecost,* presented at London's Young Vic in 1995, subsequently at the Yale Repertory Theatre, and in 2004 in both New York and California, was the difficulty of contemporary global communication, strikingly illustrated with actors speaking a variety of languages, among them English, Arabic, Russian, Turkish, Polish, and Sinhalese. Even in international cities like London or New York, there was little chance that any audience would contain spectators who could understand the majority of this linguistic potpourri, and most audiences have initially been taken aback by the linguistic barrage. Most of the characters in the play, however, are no better equipped to understand the others, and as they seek for ways to communicate with each other, the audience itself becomes engaged in this process. Each character finds his or her own way into the play's discourse with whatever language skills are available, and each spectator learns to do the same. The process reveals what international travelers have always known: that despite language barriers a surprising amount of communication can take place based upon context, nonverbal signs, and the goodwill and imagination of the would-be communicants. The play thus provides a powerful metaphor for a process that is being played out today not only on the national level in all parts of the world, from New Zealand to Nigeria to Canada, but also in the international world of the modern global village, where traditionally isolated language communities are increasingly confronted with the need to interact more directly and to find ways of understanding each other. Whether one takes one's own language, as a tourist, a guest worker, an emigrant, or a refugee, into another language community, or whether one remains linguistically at home where one more and more encounters such outsiders, the traditional isolation of language communities is more and more giving way to the polyglot world of Edgar's drama.

Charles L. Mee's *Time to Burn,* a reworking of Maxim Gorki's *The Lower Depths* created in 2004, almost an even century after its model (premiered in 1902), strikingly draws the down-and-out inhabitants of the grim cellar from a linguistic community much like the homeless vagrants of Edgar's drama. The play thus offers some Hispanic characters, a couple who speak to each other in Polish, some scraps of Turkish, and two extended passages in Greek, one a scene from Aristophanes' *The Birds,* performed for the entertainment of her fellow sufferers by an indigent Greek actress.

An interesting parallel to these multilanguage Western dramas could be found at almost the same time on the opposite side of the world, in Taiwan, where several theatre companies in the late 1990s began to create plays reflecting the linguistic diversity actually heard on Taiwan's streets. Xu Ruifang's *The Phoenix Trees are in Blossom* (1995) was a part of the author's ongoing project to develop a Taiwanese theatre, to supplement the "official" language, Mandarin, which is taught in the schools and dominates the theatres. Mandarin was brought to Taiwan by the "Mainlanders," members of the ruling Nationalist Party who retreated there after their defeat by the Communists in 1949, but there is still a large population speaking the previously dominant language of the island. Although set in the 1940s and 1950s, the play is rather like Fennario's more contemporary *Balconville* in that it reflects actual language negotiations within a bilingual community at a particular point in time. The main plot of *Phoenix Trees* concerns a Taiwanese family and is spoken almost entirely in the local Taiwanese dialect. A secondary plot concerns an actual historical figure of that period, the movie star Li

Xianglan, who was born to Japanese parents, but raised in China. Her story is told primarily in Mandarin, except for a scene in which the actress imagines a conversation with her mother in Japanese.[65]

Even more complex was the heteroglossia in another Taiwanese script of the same period, Li Guoxiu's 1997 *Play Hard,* the fourth in a series of plays by this author begun ten years earlier and devoted to the depiction of life in contemporary Taiwan. Each play in this series has used both Mandarin- and Taiwanese-speaking characters, with some Cantonese, but the most recent work adds Hakka, the language of a significant minority group, Sichuanese and Shangainese, reflecting the diversity of those who immigrated from the mainland in 1949, and English. The eighteen characters in the play have different primary and secondary languages, and most speak different languages to different characters. Xiao Shumei, the head of publicity for the Ping-Chong Acting Company, founded by Li Guoxiu and for whom his pieces are created, justifies this linguistic complexity on the grounds of verisimilitude. He notes that it is quite natural in Taiwan to speak one language with one person and another with someone else, and that audiences accept this in the theatre because it mirrors their own experience.[66] It also serves as a continual reminder of the background of each character and how they wish to present themselves to others, since each language conjures up memories of current and past political and social events and tensions. Given the current linguistic plurality of Taiwan, Li Guoxiu can assume that almost all of his audience will understand to some extent several of the languages he employs, more than Edgar can assume for the majority of audiences for *Pentecost.* Even so, both of these Taiwanese plays, unlike *Pentecost,* provide subtitles to help audiences through the linguistic maze. The subtitles are characterized by Weinstein as a necessary compromise. Since no audience member can be expected to understand all eight languages, "for the meaning to come across, the play must sacrifice some of the 'natural' effect."[67] From the point of view of reception, the subtitle is clearly a useful tool, but phenomenologically it increases the complexity of the reception process at the same time that it facilitates discursive comprehension. In a very real way it adds yet another "language" to the multiple languages of the performance, a phenomenon that I will address specifically in the final chapter of this study.

Despite the considerable variety in cultural context and in apparent intended effect of the multilanguage theatre so far discussed, all of these examples, from classic to contemporary times, share one very important characteristic. They all involve dramatic texts created, for whatever purpose, from linguistic elements borrowed across cultures. A quite different and rather more surprising sort of macaronic theatre has, however, become more and more common in recent years, productions in which a text originally written in a single language is given a modern production in which more than one language is utilized, often involving the introduction of new material or a greater or lesser reworking of the original material. A fascinating experiment of this kind was the production in May 1985 of Beckett's *Waiting for Godot* by the Haifa Municipal Theatre in Israel. Haifa, like Montreal, is a bicultural and bilinguistic city, but with deep cultural tensions and with very little cultural cooperation between the two communities. Arab characters have appeared fairly frequently in Israeli dramas since the 1930s, but until fairly recently the language of these characters was presented only suggestively, in the manner of "outsider" languages ever since the Greeks. Yaakov Yaffe's *The Spring* was in 1932 an early example of an approach followed by most dramatists of the next generation. Its Arab characters spoke a rough, corrupt Hebrew, accompanied by curses, a few short expressions in Arabic, and Arab-sounding exclamations, such as "yah" or "eh," that appeared in the text as independent words.[68] Even dramas written by Arab dramatists, such as Muhammad Watab's *Coexistence,* staged by the Haifa Municipal Theatre in 1970 using only Jewish actors, presented great difficulties for those actors in creating anything like an authentic Arabic pronunciation of Hebrew. In 1979 Nola Chilton's *Na'im,* attempting to present a sympathetic Arab title character, nevertheless employed for this character such conventional "stage Arabic" that it produced unintentionally, the comic effect associated with that language practice.[69]

Gradually, however, Israeli companies moved away from this conventional stage use of language, significantly mixing Hebrew and Arabic, and, most importantly, often performing with linguistically mixed companies. An important example was the Haifa company, sociopolitically oriented and much concerned with questions of Jewish-Israeli identity and with the Arab-Jewish conflict. It had for some time included Arab actors and technicians in its company and produced plays, like *Coexistence,* by Arab dramatists, and in 1985 it decided to open a new auditorium in the center of the Arab section of the city, with *Waiting for Godot,* directed by Ilan Ronen, as the opening production. The play was presented in two versions. In the new Arabic auditorium, for Arabic audiences, Vladimir and Estragon were played in Arabic by leading Arab members of the Haifa company. In this version, Pozzo spoke Hebrew to them, and a distorted, limited Arabic to Lucky, while Lucky's monologue was in an accented Arabic, with some of its phrases suggesting the classic Arabic of the Koran. In the version presented to Haifa's Jewish audiences, Vladimir and Estragon spoke Hebrew with a marked Arabic accent. In both cases, the symbolic use of the macaronic production was clear, and provoked much uproar and controversy. In the words of one reviewer:

> Vladimir and Estragon appear to be two Arab construction workers of the group who come daily from the occupied territories and wait at the "slave markets" on the outskirts of Israeli cities for somebody to hire them for a one-day job. When Master Pozzo passes their way . . . he speaks Hebrew, the masters' language.[70]

For this reviewer, at least, the indexical use of language to encourage a current political reading of the play proved successful. Somewhat surprisingly, however, an analysis of the actual audience of this production found the reviewer's reaction to be uncommon. In this analysis, some three hundred audience members from both theatres were questioned about their interpretation of this innovative production. Jewish audience members, who were more familiar with *Godot* before seeing this production, not surprisingly tended to view it within a larger context, as presenting an existential and universal problem. Rather more surprisingly, however, Arab audiences, for most of whom the play was unfamiliar, also reported seeing it in general terms. Some saw it as a general social parable, with Pozzo representing any conqueror or oppressive force; others viewed it in class terms, with Vladimir and Estragon as exploited workers, Pozzo as a bourgeois capitalist. Almost none spoke of its possible specific local relevance.

Shoshana Weitz, from whose excellent article I have gained most of my information about this production and the subsequent audience analysis, concludes from the latter a semiotic problem, a "wide gap between the sender's intentions and what the spectators . . . received," that the majority of those surveyed "did not respond to the rhetorical devices," including languages used, which were "meant to guide them towards a local political interpretation of the play."[71] Although the responses apparently support this conclusion, I am not entirely convinced. In the highly charged cultural climate of Israel in the 1980s, it seems to me equally likely that many audience members, especially Arab ones, might be reluctant to admit to seeing too clear a reference to their current problems, especially if asked, as I assume they were, by an Israeli interviewer.

In any case, in a world where almost any major city now possesses sizable populations speaking different languages, we can no longer think of bilingual cities like Haifa or Montreal, or indeed multilingual cities like Tainan in Taiwan, as being exceptional. Since the social tensions and concerns aroused by this development can be easily and powerfully signified in the theatre by the use of different languages, it is inevitable that such cities will see many more experiments in multilingual theatre, created specifically to comment in theatrical terms upon these tensions, whatever the difficulties multiple languages may present to conventional ideas of reception. In 1996, for example, I witnessed in Mulheim an experiment with certain interesting similarities to the Haifa *Godot*. Roberto Ciulli, the director of the Mulheim state theatre, created a fascinating production of Brecht's *In the Jungle of Cities* with a cast drawn partly from Ciulli's own company and partly from a sister company in Turkey. The primary announced goal was to develop international cooperation in theatre production. However, the particular choice of Turkish, a language commonly spoken by the immigrant workers who form a significant minority of the population of Mulheim, and the further choice to cast the Turkish-speaking actors in the "Oriental" roles in Brecht's play, a play that is driven by economic, class, and social conflict between Oriental and Occidental characters, seemed to me inevitably to place the use of language, as in Haifa, among the production's clear political referents.

The Onafhankelijk Toneel in Rotterdam has for the past several years been involved in a project similar to that of Ciulli in Mulheim. Rotterdam has a significant minority of Moroccan immigrant workers, whose social position is similar to that of the Turkish immigrants in Mulheim. Gerrit Timmers, the director of the Rotterdam theatre, has staged three productions mixing Dutch and Moroccan actors, all speaking their own language and each production calling attention, in some way, to the social tensions between these two language communities in that city. The most successful of these productions was his staging of *Othello* in 2000. Othello was portrayed as a white mercenary, a Dutch general in the service of a rich Gulf emirate. He spoke Dutch with his confidants and French with his employers, while they converse in Arabic when he is not present, a situation similar to the shifting linguistic positions of the Taiwanese plays already discussed. Just as Li Guoxiu and Xu Ruifang wanted to bring into their respective theatres a Taiwanese-speaking public that did not attend the majority Mandarin-speaking houses, Timmers sought to attract the nontheatregoing Dutch Moroccan community. This may also have been a concern of Ciulli; in any case the production seems to have had that effect. I was surprised to hear a good deal of Turkish conversation in the lobby during the intermission of *In the Jungle of Cities,* something I had never before experienced here or anywhere else in Germany (except, of course, at the Turkish Theatre in Berlin). Even so, each of these productions also inevitably evoked the social tensions within their cultures represented by the conflicting languages.

Macaronic productions of this kind, strange as they may seem at first, can be viewed as a recent and culturally powerful variation upon a long-standing practice of changing visual referents in the work of a classic dramatist like Shakespeare to reflect local concerns. So Romeo and Juliet, for example, have been recast as representing every sort of socially, politically, or culturally divided families, and today one can find examples of them linguistically divided as well. Bernstein's *West Side Story* comes close to such a division, one that was fully articulated in a famous late-twentieth-century production at the Lilla Teatern, a leading experimental theatre in Helsinki. Like Quebec, Finland is officially bilingual, with a substantial Swedish-speaking population. Here also each linguistic group traditionally had its own theatres, but recent years have seen more and more explorations of bilingual productions, and the Lilla Teatern in particular has specialized in mixed language productions, like this bilingual *Romeo and Juliet,* with the gap between social groups emphasized both by language and by national clichés. One could readily imagine Shakespeare's doomed lovers appearing (if indeed they have not already done so) in a Haifa production, one speaking Arabic, the other Hebrew.[72]

One of the most powerful examples of the introduction of heteroglossia into a classic text to stress contemporary sociopolitical concerns was the 2003 revival of Aeschylus's *Oresteia* staged by Andreas Kriegenberg in Munich. From the beginning of the production Kriegenberg visually stressed connections between the cycle of vengeance at the center of the classic Greek trilogy and the events of September 11 and their international aftermath. The opening setting is a huge city wall, to which, after a prologue citing a history of murders and atrocities, a bedraggled and crippled chorus staples pictures of missing friends and family members like those that covered public spaces in New York in the weeks following 9/11. The Herald appears covered in white ashes, visually evoking the survivors who fled the collapsing towers.

The production's most daring innovation came when Kriegenberg inserted a series of comic interludes, clearly a reference to the missing satyr play of the original, placed not at the end of the trilogy, but inserted into the *Agamemnon*. These scenes are played, until their own climax, entirely in English, and feature actors wearing cartoon masks of George Bush (who speaks with a very convincing Texan accent), Donald Rumsfeld (whose accent is more neutral but clearly American) and Angela Merkel, leader of the German Christian Democratic Policy, who strongly supported Bush's "war on terror." Until the last of these interpolated scenes, they are kept entirely separated from the main action, rather like the clown scenes in Shakespeare, and are composed essentially of comic routines based on Bush's grandiose visions of world domination. In the last, truly heteroglossic scene, however, this modern satyr play chillingly merges with the main action.

When Agamemnon enters the palace, the chorus leaves the stage and Cassandra is left alone, in a metal refuse barrel among the spoils of war. Here she is discovered by the English-speaking clown figures. Bush and Rumsfeld, finding her in what they take to be an oil barrel and speaking a (to them) incomprehensible language, take her to be a terrorist. Merkle helpfully offers to translate, saying the woman can foretell the future. Encouraged, Cassandra pours forth a stream of mixed Greek and German, predicting ruin for the house of Atreus, for the house of Bush, and for all conquerors swollen by pride and arrogance. Merkle, the faithful diplomat, translates this into a bland, but negative message, which is still too much for Bush and Rumsfeld, who beat the prophetess to death with baseball bats as Merkle flees. Cassandra's body is then left for the returning Chorus to find, as the play resumes. Thus such standard features of Cassandra's story as her ability to prophesy but not to be understood, her status as war victim, and her destruction as an innocent sacrifice to a politics of revenge are all reconfigured with reference to fearfully contemporary events, with the use of multiple languages a central part of this complex intertextual structure. Although the idea of each character speaking his or her "appropriate" language, American English for Bush and Rumsfeld, German for Merkle, Greek for Cassandra, recalls the traditional force of verisimilitude behind this mixture of language, the effect, as has often been the case in heteroglossic theatre, goes far beyond this surface concern, with language mixture being used to reinforce a wide range of social, political and cultural matters, not the least of which is the relationship between language and power. All of these concerns will appear again, in a rather different configuration, as we turn from the heteroglossia of language in theatre to that of dialects, which will be the concern of the next chapter.

# 2 *Dialect Theatre: The Case of Italy*

Dialects, like foreign languages, except normally in a less extreme form, provide a potential disruption of the normal assumption that a theatre will utilize the same language as its surrounding culture. Thus dialect in the theatre can offer another aspect of heteroglossic production. By way of introducing the concept of dialogue I will again quote Crystal's standard work, the *Dictionary of Linguistics and Phonetics*. The entry on *dialect* begins:

> A regionally or socially distinctive variety of language, identified by a particular set of words and grammatical structures. Spoken dialects are usually also associated with a distinctive pronunciation, or accent. Any language with a reasonably large number of speakers will develop dialects, especially if there are geographical barriers separating groups of people from each other, or if there are divisions of social class. One dialect may predominate as the official or standard form of the language, and this is the variety which may come to be written down. The distinction between "dialect" and "language" seems obvious: dialects are subdivisions of languages.[1]

A number of elements in this definition deserve special attention. First, while it is clearly true that established languages will inevitably develop dialects, this dynamic must be balanced by the following statement, which is often given less attention. Dialects do not only evolve as offshoots of an official "language"; any such language itself began as a dialect. A variety of social forces, cultural, economic, and geographical, determined which of a variety of competing dialects would become recognized as a "language." The less successful dialects are then necessarily relegated to inferior positions in the cultural hierarchy, which of course includes their use in the theatre. This same dynamic continues to operate as the inevitable new dialects appear, encouraged, as Crystal notes, by both "geographical barriers" and "divisions of social class." This of course has meant that in addition to dialects being generally somewhat looked down upon by speakers of the "official" language, dialect speakers have often suffered the additional stigma of being marked by their speech as coming from a subordinate or inferior geographical area or social class.

It is generally assumed that speakers of different dialects of the same language can basically understand each other, although this is in fact much more true of the written forms of the dialects than their spoken forms, which is of course the primary concern of the theatre. Almost any language with a substantial number of dialects—English, French, German, Italian, Arabic, Chinese, to mention only some of the most obvious examples—possess many dialects that are essentially unintelligible to each other, especially in their spoken form. What really distinguishes a dialect from a language is less a matter of intelligibility or any particular features it possesses, than the matter of whether it has established a kind of recognized cultural sovereignty over a body of speakers. Italian, Spanish, and French were once dialects of Latin, but have now become established as independent languages with dialects of their own. The necessary subservient or derived status of the dialect means that the heteroglossia it may introduce to the theatre is among its most important features.

*Types of Dialect Theatre*

Normally when the term *dialect theatre* is used, the reference is to a theatre created for a particular dialect community, and plays in this tradition will normally utilize that dialect throughout. In this they are parallel to plays written in standard and conventional languages such as French, English, or Italian, and the language itself is not normally a central concern of the play (except of course for its importance in grounding the play firmly in the community of its audience). Once one dialect emerges as the "standard" dialect, and eventually the official national "language" (Castilian in Spain, Tuscan in Italy, the dialect of the Paris region in France, East Midland in England), the rival dialects that survive are increasingly relegated to subservient and marginalized positions, their speakers provided with less and less of what Bourdieu calls "linguistic capital" for trade outside the narrow confines of their dialect community. The tension-filled power relationship between the "official" language and its weaker rivals can then provide the grounding for the most common use of dialect in the theatre, the dialect character or characters, whose utilization invariably evokes this unequal power relationship. In plays created by and for the speakers of the official language, the dialect character appears as a site of otherness, to provide exotic coloring, or a threat, or comic entertainment. In plays created by and for speakers of the dialect, an outsider speaking the official language reverses this dynamic, offering, either as a threat or the subject of ridicule, a site of resistance to officialdom, which almost invariably involves political as well as linguistic dominance. In the contemporary world, where both language and dialect groups are coming into increasing contact, elements of both of these dynamics may be found within a single performance situation, due to the mixture of audience elements. This is particularly a feature of postcolonial theatre and will be discussed in a subsequent chapter.

A third form of dialect theatre, more common in earlier times and today than in the eighteenth and nineteenth centuries, is more directly heteroglossic in the sense of most of the language examples of the previous chapter. Here characters in the same play speak a variety of different dialects. In the more recent examples of such mixing, the power relationship of the dominant and the subservient language is often foregrounded, as in the Swiss production of *An Enemy of the People* that I will discuss presently. In earlier periods, competing dialects were more commonly used as a kind of theatrical shorthand to suggest or reinforce particular character types, usually for comic purposes (although sometimes also to suggest people from varied backgrounds united in a common cause, like the Irish, Welsh, and Scottish dialect characters assembled to support the British cause in Shakespeare's *Henry V* or, in the same tradition, the Texan, African American, New York Italian or Jew, and so on assembled on the front lines of American war movies).

Generally speaking, both the dominant theatre with possible dialect elements and the dialect theatre with possible dominant elements is, predictably, oriented toward an audience that shares its majority language, dominant language theatre toward a general or dominant language public and dialect theatre toward a public speaking that dialect, with one important qualification. The social dynamics of linguistic power normally result in members of dominated language groups knowing the language of the dominant power but not vice versa (an important part of the operations of language in the postcolonial theatre, which will be addressed in that chapter). This means that while plays in the dominant language may circulate freely (or be imposed by the dominant culture) on dialect communities, dialect plays have very little circulation outside their home communities.

The dynamics of moving a production, especially a heteroglossic one, from its home linguistic community to a different one are substantial, and in terms of audience relationships to the characters, as important in a theatre that mixes dialects as in one that mixes languages. I was particularly struck by difference in a noted Swiss production, the version of Ibsen's *An Enemy of the People* mounted by Lars-Ole Warburg, head of the Theater Basel, in 2000. The production was presented, as is common throughout the German-speaking theatre world, in the standard stage dialect of High German, although the actual dialect spoken in Basel is quite different, indeed almost incomprehensible to speakers of standard German. Warburg's production was unconventional in many ways, but its most radical change was in the climactic public meeting scene, where Stockmann reveals his discovery that the contaminated baths are in fact symbolic of a general corruption of the whole society, whereupon he is prevented from speaking and driven from the hall as an "enemy of the people." In this production, the actor playing Stockmann (Michael Neuenschwander), instead of giving the speech Ibsen wrote, stepped to the footlights, called for the house to be illuminated, and stepped out of the world of the play to address the theatre audience directly. Just as Ibsen's character suddenly realizes and bursts forth with a condemnation of his own society, Neuenschwander announces his own vision of the corruption of his own society. The free Switzerland of legend has become an ersatz escapist world devoted to tourism, blind to its current deep involvement with the global concerns of late capitalism, and in denial about its past involvement with Nazi gold. Like the mineral springs in Ibsen's play, or like today's Rhine with its chemical runoffs, its pure mountain springs have been poisoned by these involvements.

As in Ibsen's play, the other actors are appalled by this outburst, but here their concern is not only social, but also theatrical, and indeed linguistic. "Is this Ibsen?" one of them cries, since Neuenschwander has not only departed from the traditional text, but from the traditional stage language of the text, and is addressing the audience in the Swiss-German dialect they share, further emphasizing the connection to their shared experience of a real social context. Eventually the actor is drowned out by the shouts of his colleagues and the frantic playing of patriotic Swiss music over the theatre's loudspeakers, but the impact of the scene was enormous, giving its Basel audience a feeling of the shocking immediacy and radical message of Ibsen's work when it first appeared.

I saw this same production later, in the annual Berlin spring Theatre Festival, under totally different linguistic and theatrical circumstances. Neuenschwander's Swiss-German was almost as impenetrable to Berlin audiences as it was to me, and so Stockmann was joined at the footlights by Mrs. Stockmann, who held the microphone and translated his work into standard German. This is not out of keeping with the dynamics of the play, since Mrs. Stockmann does in fact rally to support her visionary mate, but it emphasized that this move in dialect, a device for direct audience contact in Basel, was necessarily a distancing device in Berlin. Linguistically, the Berlin audience remained on the side of the conservatives in the play, who of course continued to speak in High German, even when trying to silence Stockmann. Obviously the social and political concerns of the production remained clear, but however Berlin audiences might have sympathized with these concerns, their primary response to the production was as an artistic artifact, not a political one, a response encouraged of course by the context of the Theatre Festival (which is limited to what critics have selected as the ten best German-language plays of the past year) but also by the conversion of the dialect from a strategy for encouraging deeper audience identification and involvement with the action to a sequence more coded as a theatrical or metatheatrical device.[2]

Clearly, with the aid of some such device as Mrs. Stockmann providing simultaneous translation, or, in today's theatre, more likely with supertitles, dialect theatre can potentially circulate as freely as any theatre into other linguistic communities. There is some such circulation, particularly in Italy, where the dialect theatre tradition is strong, but even there it is not common. The reason, I think, is not that dialect theatre is more local and special in its concerns than other theatre, but that dominant cultures remain generally indifferent to the theatre of cultures they consider socially or linguistically inferior to their own. This remains quite clear in the ongoing indifference, by no means overcome today, of the old colonial powers (as well as the newer ones, most notably the United States) to almost any drama produced by anyone in the old colonies.

The continuing indifference of theatre historians to dialect theatre is quite striking. Even today, when modern performance studies have focused attention on a huge range of popular and folk entertainments and performances, the rich history of dialect theatre in Europe from the eighteenth century onward is still studied only by a few specialists. It is perhaps a phenomenon too close to conventional theatre to interest scholars in performance studies and too close to popular culture to interest more traditional theatre scholars. Most theatre histories and encyclopedias ignore it completely, and even the monumental *Enciclopedia della Spettacolo,* with its extensive information on film, ballet, even puppets and circus, devotes to it a scant four paragraphs, providing only a brief definition of the form and noting that although it can no longer be considered a "minor" form, it will be treated in the encyclopedia only within the entries of various national theatres, a promise in fact not fulfilled.[3]

The correction of this historical oversight is beyond the scope of the present study, but the particular relationship of the European dialect theatre tradition to theatrical heteroglossia is so important in terms of linguistic negotiation that a certain amount of space must be devoted to it. Rather than take examples and illustrations from a broad range of material, as I did in discussing language play in the opening chapter, I will in the case of dialect theatre draw my illustrations essentially from a single tradition, that of Italy. This is in part because, due to the lack of historical attention to dialect theatre, it will be necessary to provide the examples with more context, and in part because the Italian dialect theatre tradition, one of the most successful and best documented in Europe, provides a particularly good range of examples of the ways in which language and power have been negotiated in that tradition.

Never (until the late nineteenth century) subjected to a strong centralizing government (as were Renaissance England, France, and Spain), Italy remained particularly open to cultural, linguistic, and theatrical diversity. As a result its tradition of specifically dialectal theatre is among the strongest in Europe, from the Venetian plays of Ruzante in the Renaissance, through the eighteenth-century Venetian comedies of Goldoni, to the twentieth-century Neapolitan plays of Eduardo De Filippo and Sicilian dramas of Luigi Pirandello. At the same time, Italian theatre has remained particularly open to dramatic productions that have mixed a variety of dialects within a single work. Plurilingualism has from the beginning been an important feature of the Italian theatre tradition, from Ruzante and Calmo to Dario Fo, appearing in a wide variety of forms, from the coexistence of different languages or dialects in the same text (sometimes called horizontal plurilingualism) to that of different stylistic registers of the same dialect (sometimes called vertical plurilingualism).

## Florentine Dominance

The preeminence of the great trio of Florentine authors Dante, Petrarch, and Boccaccio, along with the relative closeness of the Florentine dialect to Latin, made Florentine an attractive choice for those seeking a unifying literary language for Italy. The Venetian Pietro Bembo in the early sixteenth century began the campaign to make the Florentine language of these three canonical authors the standard tongue of Italy, a campaign carried on mostly by Florentine authors later in the century. This campaign achieved a fair degree of success with literary texts following the tradition of these authors, works of prose and poetry intended for reading. The number of people who could read was limited, and most were willing to develop a skill in a dialect somewhat different from their own (this was necessary even for educated Florentines, as the Tuscan they used in everyday life was two centuries removed from that of these literary models). Even the educated classes, however, showed little enthusiasm for adopting some variation of the Florentine dialect for spoken communication.

The nature of theatre, as both a literary and performed art, placed it, as is so often the case, precisely on the fault line of this linguistic conflict.

To the extent that theatre was considered literature, it reflected the pressure toward the developing "high" literary language of Florence, but as a performed art and moreover one grounded in mimesis, it was subject to the combined pressures of communication and verisimilitude, both of which pressed it to utilize the actual everyday speech of its audience. Before the sixteenth century all popular theatre in Italy, even religious popular theatre, was created in the local dialect. When the first Italian literary dramas, based on Latin models, were created, their public was a limited, courtly, educated one, and the artificiality of literary Tuscan was rarely seen as a problem; indeed it was regarded as a mark of elegance and refinement. Tragedy in particular benefited from this attitude, since the standard authorities, Horace and Aristotle, agreed that the language of tragedy should be elevated above that of everyday speech, and the ancient models Sophocles, Seneca, and Euripides were recognized as among the most elegant of the world's poets. Leading tragic writers such as Giangiorgio Trissino, Giraldi Cinthio, and Sperone Speroni might disagree about whether Greek or Roman tragedy provided a better model, whether plots should be drawn from history, and whether happy endings were acceptable, but they were united in the conviction that this genre demanded an elevated poetic style. Comedy, however, dealing with matters of everyday life, could not easily avoid the problem of everyday speech. It was thus primarily in the works and the theoretical statements of would-be comic dramatists that the struggle over dialect was carried out in the Italian theatre until the rise of modern realism made the question inescapable in the serious drama as well.

Since Italian Renaissance drama began with and was dominated by comedies, this made the matter of the language to be used of central concern. The first Renaissance drama to be performed in Italian was an anonymous translation of Plautus's *Menaechmi,* presented in Ferrara in 1486. Its language followed the general literary taste of the court, a rather neutral elevated style, essentially Tuscan, in rhymed poetic lines. Among the audience members was the young Ludovico Ariosto, who, under the inspiration of the Ferrarese theatricals, became the first significant dramatist of the Italian Renaissance. Linguistic tensions were present from the very beginning of his enterprise. The prologue to his first original play, *La Cassaria* (1508), begs its audience to be tolerant of this new experiment, a play created in the vernacular, acknowledging that "neither our vulgar prose nor our verse can be compared with those of the ancients," and that "our vernacular, which is mixed with Latin, is barbarous and uncultured."[4]

Ariosto soon discovered that the lower esteem held by the "barbarous and uncultured" vernacular was only part of the difficulty in attempting to write in that style. His *Cassaria* and, in the following year, *I Suppositi* were enthusiastically received, but nevertheless drew criticism from those who were attempting to establish literary Tuscan as the privileged Italian vernacular idiom and who found Ariosto too much under the influence of Ferrara courtly style and expression. The most specific criticism came from Machiavelli, in one of the most important statements on theatre language written during this period, his *Discorso intorno alla nostra lingua*. Scholars date the *Discorso* to 1515 or 1516, making its remarks on language and comedy especially significant, since they serve as a kind of preface to the best-known Italian comedy of the period, Machiavelli's own *Mandragola,* published in 1518. The imagined dialogue is with the spirit of Dante, and concludes with a celebration of Tuscan as the source of and hope for a significant Italian literature. Interestingly enough, Machiavelli allows comedy the most flexibility in grounding itself not in Tuscan but in the native expressions of the community of its author and its audience. The aim of comedy being "to hold up a mirror to domestic life . . . with a certain urbanity and with expressions which incite laughter," it is therefore necessary, asserts Machiavelli,

> to use words and expressions which have such an effect, which they do not and cannot do unless they are local, popular, and understood by everybody. This means that a non-Tuscan will never do this well; if he wants to use the phrases of his own country he will produce a patchwork coat, half Tuscan, half foreign, and this will reveal what sort of language he uses, whether it be local or understood by everyone. And if he does not want to use them, and does not know Tuscan, his work will be maimed and will not achieve its proper form.

For both Dante and Machiavelli, natives of Florence, this program of course would present no problem, but for non-Florentines who attempted to aspire to Florentine unity and elegance, the verisimilitude and specificity Machiavelli sees as necessary to the stimulation of comedy's socially oriented laughter would be muted and compromised. This, Machiavelli argues, was a shortcoming in the comedies of Ariosto:

> To prove this, I would have you read one of the comedies written by Ariosto of Ferrara. You will find an attractive work in a correct and graceful style, an intrigue well set out and still more cleverly resolved, but you will find it without any of the salt that such a comedy demands, and precisely because he did not like the Ferrarese expressions and did not know the Florentine ones, so did without.[5]

For Florentine dramatists, like Machiavelli, the major challenge of comedy was to find a flexible realistic dramatic language based upon Tuscan, but with a variety of styles reflecting everyday speech in Florence, a goal Machiavelli achieved with great success in his major drama *Mandragola*. Machiavelli's follower Giovan Battista Gelli also successfully pursued this ambition, commenting in the dedication to his most popular work, *La Sporta* (1543),

> As for the language, I respond that I have used such words as I have heard spoken every day by the sort of characters I have introduced, and, if they are not to be found in Dante or Petrarch, this is because one language is used for written material involving elevated and literary matters, and quite another when one speaks familiarly, and that everyone knows that what Tully writes is not that which is spoken every day.[6]

For non-Florentine writers, who accepted the privileging of Florentine speech by Machiavelli and others, the problem was more difficult. There is a distinctly apologetic tone in Ariosto's prologue to *Il Negromante,* written in 1520. While the previous work had been set in Ferrara, this was set in the Lombard city of Cremona, and since the play was written at the request of Pope Leo X for performance in Rome, Ariosto suggested that a somewhat decentered linguistic background was appropriate to the physical displacement of the action itself:

If you don't seem to hear the proper and accustomed idiom of Cremona, you can attribute it to the fact that she picked up a few terms
while passing through Bologna, where there's a university. She liked
them and remembered them. Then she tried to make them as elegant
as possible while passing through Florence, Siena, and all of Tuscany;
but, in so short a time, she has not been able to learn enough to hide
completely her Lombard accent.[7]

In other parts of Italy the pressure to create a Tuscan-based literary
comedy parallel to the more formal literary tragedy was much less.
Rome was notorious as a melting pot of languages and dialects, and
Tuscan was remoter still politically and culturally from the regions to
the south. It was in Venice, however, that the most significant dialect
theatre developed, and since this city not only profoundly influenced the
development of the improvised theatre, the commedia dell'arte, but
later, through the work of Goldoni, the development of the Italian literary comedy as well, its fascination with dialect guaranteed that this
would remain central in the development of the Italian drama.

Crucial figures in the development of dialect comedy and indeed in
the development of the Italian theatre as a whole are the early-six-
teenth-century artists Andrea Calmo, Gigio Giancarli, and Angelo
Beolco, the latter better remembered for the character he created,
Ruzante. Although Venice was relatively slow in welcoming the new
literary comedy based on Latin models, perhaps due to the absence of
the usual princely court, it had a long and rich tradition of popular
drama and spectacle, and it was out of this background that Ruzante
and his fellows came. Particularly important for the subsequent love of
linguistic experiment were the entertainments of the comic entertainers *(bufoni)* and the wandering jesters *(giullare)*, whose activities have
been brilliantly re-created and reinterpreted in modern times by Dario
Fo. Central to the performances of such entertainers were displays of
verbal dexterity: patter songs *(frottole)*, boasts *(vanti)*, satirical verses,
and dramatized debates or quarrels *(contrasti)*, allowing a single performer to demonstrate a variety of voices.[8] Not surprisingly, the comic
mimicry of non-Venetian dialogues and accents was an important part
of such entertainment.[9] The rather strange and distinctive up-country
dialect of the hills behind Bergamo was a particular favorite of the

*bufoni,* since the region of Bergamo appears to have provided menial laborers to many parts of Italy during the sixteenth century. Even as far away as Rome, a Bergamask porter makes a brief appearance in Bibbiena's *Calandra,*[10] but the dialect was particularly popular in Venetian comedy, Bergamo at this time being a part of the Venetian republic and the capital being a natural mecca for the migrant workers of that region. The effect of this particular class-related dialect humor on subsequent theatre was enormous, since the Bergamese-speaking servant pervades not only the world of the early Venetian comedies of Ruzante and others, but also the subsequent commedia, to the extent that Bergamo has often been cited as the original home of this major comedic tradition.

Ruzante, the best known of Venice's early comic authors, relied heavily in his plays upon the one-act form of the *commedia buffonesca,* often a two-person skit between characters speaking contrasting dialects. His probable first play, *La Pastoral* (1521), begins with a shepherd wooing a nymph in the familiar stilted rhetoric of literary Tuscan. Just as this situation is developing to a tragic climax, Ruzante wanders in with his bird nets, his down-to-earth peasant concerns, and a broad rustic Paduan accent. Although Ruzante, following Venetian comic traditions, often used Bergamask, here in the speeches of the quack doctor Mastro Francesco,[11] Paduan, his own native dialect, became a standard part of his trademark character. There were theoretical and well as practical reasons for this choice. The preface to his second play, *La Betìa* (1523), begins with a defense of "the natural" as the basis of all honest art: "When you remove anything from the natural," he asserts, "it becomes confused." The major implication of this credo for Ruzante is, interestingly, linguistic, and variations on these comments may be found in a number of subsequent prologues:

> Do not think that I wish to behave like certain opportunists who want to appear literary or scientific and in portraying shepherds in what are called pastorals have them speak in the Florentine manner, which, by the blood of the Antichrist, causes me to shit myself laughing. Being a good Paduan, I wouldn't exchange my tongue for that of two hundred Florentines, nor give up being Paduan even to be born in Bethlehem, where was born Jesus Christ himself.[12]

The affectation of Florentine speech was for Ruzante a clear example of the artificiality that he felt corrupted both life and art, and he returns to this theme again and again, as in the preface to *La Fiorina* (1529), which responds to those who would have him write in Tuscan: "Should I, who am a Paduan and from Italy, turn German or French? A pox on these empty-headed fools! I understand instead that only by honestly following nature can I give pleasure."[13]

The three dialects of Venetian, Paduan, and Bergamask formed Ruzante's basic linguistic triangle, as in the *Interlocutori beltrame fachin, Tuognio villan et Rancho bravo* (The farce of Beltrame the porter, Tuognio the peasant, and Ranco the bravo, ca. 1529) in which each character speaks their "traditional" tongue: Bergamask for the porter, Paduan for the Ruzantian peasant, and Venetian for the bravo. Florentine is almost always used, as in *La Pastoral,* with parodic intent, inevitably mocking the pretensions of this stilted upper-class speech from the viewpoint of the more "natural" peasants. Typical is a scene in *La Vaccaria* (1533) where the Paduan servants Truffo (Ruzante) and Vezzo eavesdrop and comment upon the mannered Florentine love dialogue of Flavio and Fiorinetta:

> VEZZO (aside): Ah, words like honey poured on honey. . . . They get me so stirred up that I get all shivery.
> TRUFFO: Yes, it's like putting your ass down into a bucket of hot milk.[14]

One Ruzante play, *La Moscheta* (1529), even takes the affected speaking of Tuscan as its announced subject. Here Ruzante fears losing his wife Betja to the wiles of Tonin, a lustful Bergamask neighbor, and so he disguises himself as a rival suitor who speaks *moscheto,* a Paduan word for the affected literary speech of Florence.

A kind of bridge, in terms both of dramatic style and linguistic experimentation, between Ruzante and the commedia dell'arte is provided by the work of Andrea Calmo and Gigio Artemio Giancarli, who turned, from Ruzante's continued dedication to linguistic realism, to multilingualism as "a device in its own right, in which simple realism was constantly giving way to linguistic experiment and sheer comic fantasy."[15]

A later chapter will consider a similar development in today's international postmodern theatre.

Most of the work of these two dramatists appeared in the 1540s and 1550s, just after the death of Ruzante (in 1542) and exactly during the period when Aristotle's *Poetics* was exerting its first major impact on theatre theory and practice in Italy. Everywhere the taste for rules and order associated with classic practice had to struggle against the turbulent and carnivalesque tradition of popular entertainment, but in Venice the popular side of this struggle was more successful than in many other cities both because of the lack of a central court theatre to impose rules and because of the strong tradition of popular entertainment established by Ruzante and others.

In the preface to his *Il Travaglia* (1556), Calmo directly confronts the partisans of literary purity and high style, asserting proudly, "Whoever is looking for the elegance of the Tuscan language should not seek it in these plays, but should look to Bembo, Trissino, Sperone, and other worthy poets," interestingly enough citing a lyric poet and two leading tragic dramatists, but no writers of comedy. High literary speech, he argues, belongs on the printed page, while in the theatre, and especially in comedy, the artist must try to represent the real variety of spoken discourse.[16] In this argument Calmo sounds much like Ruzante, but in his work he is much less interested in capturing the reality of spoken discourse than in displays of linguistic virtuosity for their own sake. All of Calmo's six comedies contain a bewildering variety of languages and dialects. Venetian, Paduan, Tuscan, and Bergamask are, as in Ruzante, the most common, but Calmo also has a strong affection for Greghesco, corrupt Venetian spoken by Greeks, a common dialect in a city with many Greek colonists, and touches of Neapolitan, Ragusan and Milanese also occur, not to mention fragments of many other languages, among them German, French, Spanish, Albanian, and even Saracen. Despite his theoretical defense of realism, Calmo is much less careful than Ruzante to justify this linguistic mélange on those grounds. He is much more interested in bravura display, as when a Venetian merchant (played by himself) suddenly does an imitation of a wide variety of languages and dialects that he has no real reason to know (in *La Rhodiana,* act 4, scene 4) or in comic effect, as when (in

*Saltuzza*), a lame and ugly maidservant speaks the refined and elegant Tuscan.

Giancarli, from whom only two plays survive, does not seem himself to have specialized in a dialect character, but his plays show much the same multilinguistic playfulness. Giancarli made no claim whatever upon realism as a justification for this activity since most of his characters, no matter what their social position, spoke more or less standard Italian. Against this linguistic backdrop, however, he displayed a colorful array of eccentric exceptions. *La Zingana* (1545) includes the familiar Paduan peasant, Bergamask porter, and Greek traveler, but the linguistic star of the show is the title character, the gypsy, whose pyrotechnic language, which has never been fully analyzed, ranges from elements of various Italian dialects to bits of Berber and Semitic tongues.

## *The Commedia dell'arte and Goldoni*

The date of publication of *La Zingana,* 1545, is also that of the first surviving notarial document recording the formation of a professional commedia dell'arte company, in Padua.[17] During the rest of the century such companies rapidly developed and spread throughout Italy, and then throughout Europe. Increasingly, as the improvised comedy developed, it became more and more distinct from the literary comedy of Italy, although *commedia dell'arte* and *commedia erudita* were not yet used as distinctly contrasting terms. Calmo and Giancarli were the last bridging figures. On the one hand, they were professional actors, leaders of their own companies, and on the other, playwrights whose works were published and made a claim to literary status, often supported by theoretical prefaces. In the next generation, these two orientations became clearly divided, with professional actors developing the new, largely improvised commedia dell'arte, leaving the literary comedy in the hands of learned gentleman amateurs. Thus developed the split between the literary drama and the act of performance that has haunted much Western theatre ever since. This split also had important implications for linguistic practice. The composers of literary drama, under a pressure that has often been felt in the West to make the potentially unruly and carnivalesque art of theatre more respectable, more like lyric and epic poetry, accepted the growing pressure among literary scholars and theorists to cast their work in a standardized and elevated literary language.[18] The professional actors, seeking to appeal to a public largely uninterested in such literary manners, continued to utilize the long-established and much loved tradition of dialect humor, partly for verisimilitude, but much more often to reinforce familiar comic stereotypes, to play upon class and regional differences and misunderstandings, or simply for the display of verbal dexterity, as important to the commedia as physical skills. Linguistic versatility was one of the essential requirements for an actor, according to Tommaso Garzoni's *Piazza universale di tutte le professioni del mondo* (1585). The actor must "mimic every type of speech," notes Garzoni. While Bergamask is essential, he must also be able to use "Florentine for poetic passages, Neapolitan for flourishes, Modesese for playing the fool, Piedmontese for languishing." Moreover he must imitate the professional jargon of the law, medicine, and scholarship, and all classes from the highest to the lowest.[19]

One of the most striking features of the traditional Italian commedia was its multilingual character, amply documented in the surviving texts. The obvious problem that this would pose for reception has been considered by every writer who has dealt with these texts linguistically, and their conclusions are perhaps best summarized by Gianrenzo Clivio in a 1989 essay on the subject.[20] Clivio notes that during the sixteenth and seventeenth centuries "all social classes in Italy, regardless of wealth or education, spoke dialect at all times" and "the inhabitants of the Peninsula must have been accustomed to hearing dialects other than their own to a much greater extent than is the case nowadays," a situation particularly likely in large cities and the various courts, "where persons of different regional origins lived together" and where, also, dramatic performances were most likely to occur.[21] One might note, in anticipation of my later comments on modern multilanguage performances, that this situation is today being replicated on a global scale, where in modern international cities multilanguage performances can find publics who are also accustomed to hearing (and in many cases speaking) languages not their own.

In addition to the surviving commedia texts, a 1699 treatise by Andrea Perrucci entitled *Dell'arte rappresentative premeditata ed all'improvviso* provides the most comprehensive guide to the dialects normally employed by the major commedia characters from a period when the form had achieved a high level of linguistic standardization. Only the lovers, the *innamorati,* were to speak official "literary" Italian, and that not the actual spoken dialect of Tuscany, but the distinctly artificial speech found in "the best Tuscan books."[22] Except for the lovers, all commedia characters both wore masks and spoke in dialect, and this linguistic potpourri was clearly part of the expectations and attractiveness of the genre. Perhaps the most familiar and popular of the masked characters was the avaricious old man, Pantalone, who spoke invariably a Venetian dialect. According to Perrucci, the actor who performed this role "must have a perfect command of the Venetian tongue, with its variations, proverbs, and vocabulary."[23] Another familiar masked character was the pompous pedant, the Dottore, whose accent invariably marked him as a resident of the great university city of Bologna. Again Perrucci advises that the performer of this mask must speak a dialect that is "perfect Bolognese," but in this case, unlike that of Pantalone, he is willing to allow some concessions for a dialect considerably more difficult for other Italians than Tuscan or even Venetian.[24] In "Naples, Palermo, and other cities far from Bologna it is not necessary to be so strict, because the speech cannot be understood without a bit of moderating, for which Tuscan can be used, not that of the commoners but of the nobility of that illustrious city, which will not detract from the story."[25] The other most familiar older character mask, the Captain, was the only common commedia character particularly associated with a non-Italian language, but even he, when speaking Italian, utilized dialects associated, like Spanish, with the south of Italy, Neapolitan, Sicilian, or Calabrian. Clearly these southern dialects would have been as difficult for northern Italian audiences to understand as was Bolognese in the south, but Perrucci does not show a similar concern for accommodating the Captain's Calabrian. Indeed the strangeness and at times virtual incomprehensibility was apparently an accepted part of his character, like the Latin passages of the Dottore.[26]

The other major element of the traditional commedia was the servant roles, particularly those of the male servants. These as a rule came in pairs, the traditional male pair, one clever and manipulative, the other slow and dull, or the matched male and female pair. In both cases, the form's fascination with linguistic variation was again illustrated by the common practice of having each pair utilize contrasting dialects. Perrucci notes that a variety of different dialects could be used for the servants, but those particularly favored for the clever servant were Milanese, Bergamask, Neapolitan, or Sicilian. Paduan, the alternative servant language favored in mid-sixteenth-century Venetian comedy, doubtless due in significant measure to the impact of Ruzante, seems to have fallen out of favor as soon as the commedia began to spread to a wider geographical area, while Bergamask, whose lower-class speakers were themselves much more widely spread geographically, remained in much of Italy the preferred dialect for the second servant.[27] Not surprisingly, this was less true in the more remote south. In Naples, for example, the second servant was almost invariably the popular Pulcinella, who spoke a local dialect.[28] Riccoboni in his report on the commedia, goes into much less detail on dialects, but does emphasize their importance. "No Italian Company ever contains more then eleven Actors or Actresses," he asserts, "of whom five, including the Scaramouch, speak only the Bolognese, Venetian, Lombard, and Neapolitan dialects."[29]

As the examples of Perrucci demonstrate, the elevation of Tuscan to literary preeminence during the sixteenth century by no means cleared its way for theatrical dominance, in the way that a national theatrical language developed in Renaissance and baroque France and England, doubtless due in large part to the fact that Italy was far later in developing the centralized political system that could encourage or impose such standardized usage. Literary Tuscan, a fairly accessible dialect, especially in the north, could serve as a kind of lingua franca, and was generally utilized by writers of the rather sterile and now largely forgotten literary comedies, but for the vast majority of Italian artists and audiences, this remained (and in some parts of Italy still remains today), a remote and rather alien dialect, at worst incomprehensible and at best stilted and artificial. Not a few dramatists in other regions used it, as did Ruzante, as the object of ridicule, the tongue of foolish affectation. Speakers of Tuscan are also invariably figures of ridicule in the early-seventeenth-century plurilingual comedies of the Bolognese author Adriano Banchieri, who even published a treatise arguing for the superiority of Bolognese over Tuscan, the *Discorso della lingua bolognese,* in 1629. Later in the same century, the popular Carlo Maria Maggi in Milan created a series of comedies using dialects much in the commedia manner. His *Il barone di Birbanza* (1696) offers characters speaking

Milanese, Bolognese, Venetian, and Genoese, with touches of Latin, Greek, and Hebrew. As in other Maggi plays, representatives of the snobbish and corrupt aristocracy communicate in Tuscan and are (or pretend to be) quite incapable of understanding the simple and straight-forward dialect of the more honest and sympathetic representatives of the people.[30] One of the strongest traditions of dialect theatre in Italy developed in Naples during the seventeenth century, though its most popular variations developed in the early 1700s. This was the musical comedy, the *commedia de musica,* which challenged the elaborate baroque opera of the north with much more realistic plots and charac-ters, all speaking the local dialect. During the eighteenth century the Neapolitan opera buffa spread throughout Italy, where it became both more melodramatic and, not surprisingly, more Tuscan, with only the lower-class characters speaking in dialect. The use of Tuscan was not unknown in Naples, but it was generally used there ideologically, as in the work of Ruzante in Venice and Maggi in Milan. Often the only Tus-can-speaking characters are both outsiders and villains, like the pander-ing nun Fersina in Pietro Trinchera's *La moneca fauza* (1726) or the cor-rupt lawyer Masillo in Gennaro D'Avino's *Annella tavernara* (1775?).

For these artists and their audiences, even tragedy, with its traditional association with a high and somewhat abstract style, presented certain problems when written in Tuscan, and the necessarily more accessible comedy (and later, drama) could hardly be imagined in this alien tongue. This dilemma has troubled every generation of Italian drama-tists from the Renaissance onward, from Ariosto through Goldoni, to Verga, Pirandello, Betti, and Fo. When Goldoni, in the mid–eighteenth century, sought to bring the life and theatrical power of the commedia into the literary comedy, one of his most serious problems was that of language. "One of the matters upon which I was most strongly attacked," he reports in his *Memoires,* "was that of the purity of lan-guage."

> I was Venetian, and thus had the disadvantage of having absorbed with my mother's milk the habit of a dialect which was very agree-able, most seductive, but which was not Tuscan. I studied the rules and I cultivated by reading the language of the best Italian authors, but my earliest impressions still occasionally reappeared despite the

efforts I made to avoid them. I made a trip to Tuscany, where I remained four years into order to familiarize myself with this language, and I had the first edition of my works published in Florence under the eyes and under the censure of the savants of that region, in order to purge them from my linguistic faults. Yet all my precautions were not enough to content the purists; I always lacked something; I was always reproached for the original sin of Venetianism.

Goldoni found some consolation in the experience of Tasso, who had similarly run into opposition from Florentine linguistic purists, particularly the powerful Accademia della Crusca. The Accademia, founded in Florence in 1540, served as a model for the later and more famous Académie Française, seeking to establish and promulgate proper linguistic usage, particularly through the creation of a standard dictionary. The *Crusca* of the title meant bran or chaff, and the emblem of the society was a sieve, sifting out linguistic impurities. Tasso's most famous work, *Jerusalem Delivered,* Goldoni notes, did not win the approval of the Accademia, which favored less successful work. Goldoni pragmatically concluded:

One must write in good Italian, but one must write to be understood throughout Italy. Tasso was wrong to adjust his poem to please the academicians of La Crusca; everyone reads his *Jerusalem Delivered* and no one reads his *Jerusalem Conquered.*[31]

Clearly an important part of the privileging of Tuscan was a desire by the literary elite to create and preserve a literary hegemony condemning such outsiders as Goldoni to an automatically inferior position. His desire to reach a broader popular public they dismissed, as the literary elite had done since the beginning of the Renaissance, as a strategy inevitably leading to the cheapening and coarsening of literature. Theatre remained positioned on this linguistic and theoretical fault line as an art looking, as it so often does, toward high art on its literary side, and popular entertainment on its performative side, a tension particularly clear in the case of comedy. In the theatre the disjuncture between the language actually used by the audience and that used by the writer was more striking and more troubling than in works created only to be read, partly because of literary convention, but more importantly because the reading public in Italy at this time was still relatively small and for the most part accustomed to the use of literary Tuscan, while the theatregoing public was more heterogeneous and accustomed to the linguistic fluidity and flexibility of the commedia and popular farce. Goldoni's dilemma was in many nations and many historical periods familiar to dramatists seeking to create a theatre with more literary depth and high cultural capital without losing the appeal to a popular audiences. Almost invariably, such authors have found, a careful adherence to the standards of the prevailing literary establishment may gain praise and honors from that establishment, but at the cost of creating dry and sterile dramas that neither attract a broad public in their own times, nor achieve a lasting reputation.

Among non-Italian students of theatre, Goldoni is primarily remembered for having "elevated" the traditional improvised comedy to a literary status, a critical development in the Western theatrical tradition, which has generally privileged the literary dimension of theatre. Goldoni's reform was, however, much more difficult than the shift from improvisation to set texts, since the generally recognized model for the latter was not workable either for him or for his public, and therefore he was forced literally to develop his own dialect, a creation unique to him but accessible to his public and an alternative model to literary Tuscan for the dramatists who followed him. The linguist Gianfranco Folena describes it in these terms:

> Goldoni's language is a use of Italian that is essentially a *Bühnensprache,* a theatrical language, a scenic phantom that often possesses the liveliness of the spoken language but is nourished rather by non-literary writing, warmly welcoming large numbers of Venitianisms, Lombard and French regionalisms alongside colloquial Tuscan and the stylized speech of romances and opera; it is a makeshift, a hypothesis that yet is often quite demonstrative of reality, based on the assumption of a communal intelligibility.[32]

Doubtless frustration over the academic restrictions on printed literature helped to inspire Goldoni's announcement in the preface to his 1748 tragedy, *Nerone,* "I have no wish to write for publication, but only for the theatre," but his desire to create a more sophisticated Italian comedy, his own growing reputation, and the potential financial rewards of publication soon led him to a different opinion, despite the inevitable conflicts he faced from the literary establishment as soon as his plays left the theatre for the page. At first the publications were under the control of Goldoni's impresario, Medebac, but in 1753 Goldoni split with Medebac and negotiated on his own for the first edition of his dramatic works, to be published by the house of Paperini in Florence. The ten-volume work appeared in 1757, and at the close of the final volume Goldoni printed an open letter to the Associates of the Press, one of his most important artistic manifestos. Needless to say, one of its central concerns was linguistic, and Goldoni took some care to anticipate attacks on these grounds:

> Certainly these works could be a bit more improved, especially in the matter of their language . . . but readers in other countries and the future should know that my books are not literary texts, but a Collection of my Comedies, and that I am no Academician of La Crusca, but a comic poet who has written to be understood in Tuscany, in Lombardy, and above all in Venice, and that everyone should be able to understand whatever Italian style I use; that the Florentines themselves do not observe all the rules . . . in familiar speech; and that comedy should be an imitation of people speaking rather than writing, so that I made use of the most common language in respect to Italian as a whole.[33]

A significant part of the famous conflict between Goldoni and his major rival, Carlo Gozzi, was fought out on linguistic grounds. Although Gozzi championed the freewheeling fancy and imagination of the traditional commedia against Goldoni's more realistic and nuanced modern comedy and in his own fanciful *fiabe* reintroduced the traditional characters complete with dialects, he nevertheless championed literary Italian as the ground of his work and roundly condemned Goldoni for not respecting it. As the leading spokesman of the conservative Venetian literary society, the Accademia Granellesca, he campaigned against Goldoni's corrupting influence. His comic almanac *Tartana degl' influssi per l'anno bisestile 1756* (The tartan of influxes for the leap year 1756) contained extensive attacks on the experiments of Goldoni and was itself written in octave verse that its author boasted was "strictly literary Tuscan," a "pure style purged of Lombard and Venetian slang," one "inspired by that of the ancient Tuscan authors."[34]

A battle of pamphlets and poetry ensued between Goldoni and Gozzi in which the former justifiably accused the latter of carrying on the hegemonic campaign of the Cruscans and arguing that his works, if not Florentine, were legitimately Italian and had been proven effective and pleasurable in the theatre. Gozzi haughtily replied that anyone who claims to write in Italian should take the trouble to learn "pure Tuscan," without which no one can make such a claim. After citing a list of literary authorities supporting this position from Bembo onward, Gozzi dismisses Goldoni's argument of popular success, insisting that a real artist strives to give pleasure to "a few cultivated persons" rather than the uneducated masses.[35]

As Gozzi's genealogy of critical support indicates, the linguistic quarrel between himself and Goldoni involved an unresolved and indeed unresolvable issue that had been argued in Italy since the beginning of the sixteenth century, and in which the theatre provided a particularly troubled example. On the one side stood the academicians, from Bembo to Gozzi, who argued for a pure and standardized language for Italian literature, and on the other practicing dramatists from Ruzante to Goldoni, who argued that drama must employ language as it is actually spoken, not only for verisimilitude, but to be understood by and appreciated by a more general public. The shifting literary and cultural world of late-eighteenth-century Europe, however, put this traditional opposition in quite a different light. The concern for purity of style and strict regulation of the arts so typical of the early Italian literary academies found fertile ground in France in the seventeenth century and, reconfigured as French neoclassicism, spread through Europe, including back into Italy, where, for example, the Arcadian Academy was founded in Rome for the express purpose of encouraging Italian neoclassic literary art based on French models. Its first president, Giovan Crescimbeni, condemned the increasingly popular opera for its mixing of genres, its indifference to classic rules, and its debased language.[36]

The academic traditions in France and Italy were thus closely interrelated, and shared a common uneasiness about the unruly and unrespectful art of theatre. Nevertheless, during the eighteenth century the increasing influence of the Enlightenment philosophy of the Encyclope-dists caused more and more concern among conservative Italian acade-micians, and the former harmony on artistic questions became dis-rupted by tensions on broader social and cultural matters. By midcentury an academician like Gozzi could also be deeply suspicious of contemporary French thought, seeing it as subversive and anti-Ital-ian. When the most prominent of the French intellectuals, Voltaire, praised Goldoni for his "faithfulness to nature," Gozzi saw this as a confirmation of Goldoni's close relationship with current French thought, a relationship stressed by Gozzi's close friend and staunch advocate, Giuseppe Baretti, one of the leading Italian theorists of this period. In his highly partisan literary journal, the *Frusta letteraria* (The literary scourge), founded in 1762, Baretti continually attacked both Goldoni and the French. Typical was a 1764 review of a recent literary study that had called French authors of the period of Louis XIV the greatest in the history of literature. Baretti sharply disagreed, praising Sophocles, Euripides, Plautus, and Terence, and for that matter Ariosto and Shakespeare as clearly superior to Corneille, Racine, and Molière, and arguing that a misplaced veneration of the French was used by authors like Goldoni to justify their "continual bastardization of our beautiful language."[37]

The critical pronouncements of Baretti, combined with the popular-ity of Gozzi's freewheeling dramatic fantasies and its interest in fairy and folk traditions, led many later French and German romantics to regard the Gozzi-Goldoni debates as a precursor of classic-romantic confrontations, a serious oversimplification that takes little account of the personal and cultural dimensions of the debate. This is particularly true in the matter of literary and theatrical language. The coming of romanticism, and the closely related political movement of nationalism, gave the language question in Italy both a new significance and a new orientation that would not at all have been pleasing to the presumed protoromantic Gozzi.

As Victor Hugo observed, romanticism politically was closely allied with liberalism, hardly an attractive position for the conservative Gozzi, and along with this, romanticism often sought a broad popular audi-ence, precisely the strategy Gozzi condemned in Goldoni. In Italy this

search led to a new concern with the gap between language and literature, since only a small and invariably privileged class composed the
reading public for literary Tuscan. Later in the century, as the movement for national independence and political unification gained force,
the creation of a living Italian language became no longer merely an
artistic concern, but a matter of immediate and essential political relevance. Until this time, the centuries-old campaign by artists and theorists to establish literary Tuscan had not in fact had any serious impact
on the Italian population as a whole. Indeed according to Bruno
Migliorini's classic *Storia della lingua italiana,* in 1861 only some 2.5 percent of the population was able to use Tuscan fluently.[38]

## *The Nineteenth Century*

The central figure both of Italian romanticism and of the attempt to find
an accessible and flexible literary language for Italy in the early nineteenth century was Alessandro Manzoni. Manzoni's lifelong interest in
language was stimulated by a winter he spent in Venice in 1803, at the
age of eighteen, when he became fascinated by performances of
Goldoni's plays and by the disjuncture between the supple Venetian
popular dialect and the artificiality of traditional written Italian. Five of
the next seven years of Manzoni's life were spent in Paris, where his
closest friend was the young Claude Fauriel, preeminent among whose
many interests was the history of languages. With him, Manzoni had
many discussions on the relationship between language and literature,
and as Manzoni pursued his first major literary project, the verse
tragedy *Il Conte di Carmagnola,* the search for a workable language
became one of his greatest concerns. He was fascinated by Shakespeare,
but could find no acceptable models among his own countrymen. "What
a lot of trouble is often taken to do things badly," he marveled in a letter
to Fauriel in the spring of 1816 discussing his progress on the new play.

> How much labor to make men talk neither as they talk ordinarily nor
> as they might talk, to set aside both prose and poetry and to substitute
> for them the language that is the coldest and the least well adapted to
> arouse any sympathetic response.[39]

The publication of *Il Conte di Carmagnola,* with its challenge to traditional tragic language and the neoclassic unities, placed Manzoni at the head of the then-emerging romantic movement in Italy, but he continued to be frustrated in his desire to discover a workable literary language. The question became even more central to his concerns as he began work on what would be his most famous creation, the novel *I Promessi Sposi.* An 1821 letter to Fauriel complains at length of the difficulties of creating any sort of literary work in Italian. The French writer, Manzoni noted, spoke the language he wrote, and both he and his audience were familiar with it in a great variety of modes. On the other hand, any Italian writer who is not Tuscan

> writes in a language that he has almost never spoken, and, even if he is born in that privileged region, writes in a language that is spoken only by a small number of the inhabitants of Italy, a language in which the great questions are never discussed, a language in which works dealing with the moral sciences are extremely rare and remote, a language that . . . has been corrupted and disfigured by the very authors who have in recent times used it to deal with the most important matters.[40]

In attempting to find a suitable natural speaking style for his characters, Manzoni, recalling his early love of Goldoni, first thought of Venetian, but soon realized that he, as a nonnative speaker, could not expect to achieve here the flexibility and naturalness he sought. His own dialect was Milanese, and the first draft of the book was oriented in this direction, until he was discouraged by Fauriel and others from creating so "local" a work. Finally he began to favor Tuscan, but with his literary tone softened by the introduction of more popular expressions, from spoken Tuscan, but also from Milanese, even from French. His research became an obsession that dominated the rest of his life, and it came at a critical period politically, since it corresponded with the creation of a united Italy in which a standard language became a matter of enormous importance. In 1868 the minister of public instruction of the new Italian kingdom appointed Manzoni to preside over a commission of language standardization. Largely due to the influence of Manzoni's writings and research, a modified and more flexible and more widely understood Tuscan-oriented literary language became widely if by no means universally used in Italy in the later nineteenth century.

By the middle of the nineteenth century the forces seemed in place in Italy to resolve the tension over theatre languages once and for all. Increased communication throughout the peninsula, standardized systems of social and political organization, many of them the result of French occupation, and most important of all, the rising pressures for political consolidation of the Italian state, all favored a similar linguistic consolidation, a common commercial, political, and literary tongue. Although Roman and Venetian had strong advocates, Tuscan clearly had the advantage, not only because of its historical dominance in literature, recently reinforced by Manzoni's demonstration that it could be developed in a more generally accessible direction, but also because the new kingdom of Italy first consolidated in the north, in Piedmont and Lombardy. In fact the Italian Risorgimento, the period of political consolidation, rather surprisingly saw a simultaneous encouragement of a national use of standard Italian and an unprecedented flourishing, especially in the theatre, of dialect literature. The new dialect theatre of this era had am organization, orientation, and motivation distinctly different from that of previous periods, but it was no less significant, and in many regions more significant, than ever before.

The flourishing of dialect theatre in Italy during the Risorgimento is actually much less surprising than it might at first glance appear. Although certainly not in line with the drive toward political consolidation, it was clearly responding to some of the same cultural concerns that were fueling that drive. Much of the emotional grounding for the nationalist movements throughout nineteenth-century Europe was provided by romanticism's strong interest in one's local and native culture, in the history, myths, legends, and folk practices of one's home territory. The use of local language was a significant part of this dynamic, and often was particularly involved with the theatre. The founding of a national theatre, presenting plays on national themes in the national language, was a highly visible part of romantic nationalism across Europe from Hungary to Norway and Ireland. Thus some of the same pressures that led toward unification, political, cultural, and linguistic, also encouraged throughout Italy a new interest in regional languages and traditions, hitherto taken for granted but now threatened with disappearance by assimilation. The same sense of national identity that was being felt throughout Europe at this time also operated throughout Italy on a more local level, encouraging a new interest in, and consciousness of, the culture of smaller regions and communities. Later in the century, the new literary aesthetic of realism, or verismo, provided another impetus toward an interest in accurate portrayals of regional dialects on the stage, both in depictions of the newly emerging petit bourgeois class and in the struggles and sufferings of the more disadvantaged laborers in the countryside or the growing cities.

A fascinating example of the close relationship in emotional appeal and the practical tension between a national and a local dialect theatre is provided by the popular patriotic author Vittoria Bersezio of Turin, who at different times championed both. Turin, as the capital of Piedmont, the grounding state of the new Italian kingdom, was at the center of this emerging national entity. It is therefore striking, and surely not coincidental, that the first important modern dialect theatre in Italy was also established in Turin, and in 1859, the same year that Milan, by joining Piedmont, provided the first major step toward national consolidation. Bersezio was at first astonished and indignant upon hearing of a project so seemingly at odds with the temper of the times, and he fulminated against the proposed new venture in the Turin paper, the *Gazzetta Ufficiale:*

> They want to set up what a dreadful anachronism! a Piedmontese theatre, with a Piedmontese repertoire, with Piedmontese actors, with Piedmontese jokes (help!), with Piedmontese dullness. While there has never been a greater need for us to become truly Italian, they want to go backward and revive the blissful times of the "Count Piolet!"[41]

For Bersezio, dialect theatre thus represented a regressive nostalgia for an outmoded practice. The late-seventeenth-century *Count Piolet* Bersezio cites with such scorn, written by Giovan Battista Tana, was an early but typical example of the plurilinguistic dialect theatre of that period, featuring a Pantalone-type merchant who spoke only Piedmontese interacting with other characters speaking both that dialect and more standard Italian. It anticipated the more elaborate and better-known plurilinguistic comedies of the Milanese Maggi at the end of the century, but did not inspire a significant tradition of dialect theatre in Piedmont itself. In fact, that remained for the generation of Bersezio, and particularly for the popular Piedmontese actor and director Giovanni Toselli, whose project to establish a dialect theatre in Piedmont in 1859 inspired Bersezio's article.

Toselli's opening productions brought Bersezio to realize that the dialect theatre could in fact be something very different from *Count Piolet,* and something far closer to his own concerns. The first of these was *La Cichin-a d' Moncal,* by Federico Garelli. The traditional Italian serious drama had been much more closely tied to literary Tuscan than the comedy, especially since the work of Vittorio Alfieri in the late eighteenth century. One of the most revered dramatic works in early-nineteenth-century Italy was the Alfierian tragedy *Francesca da Rimini* (1815) by Silvio Pellico, a major precursor of Italian romanticism. His work was also a landmark of patriotic expression from a writer who spent ten years in an Austrian prison for his patriotic sympathies. Garelli and Toselli realized that the sentiments of Pellico's drama would be particularly welcome in the atmosphere of heightened national pride of the Risorgimento, and sought to give the work a special power for their Piedmontese audiences by resetting it among farmers in that province, speaking the local dialect. Their experiment was an enormous success, achieving a significant run of thirty performances, and this encouraged them to follow it at once with a political allegory in dialect, *Guera o pas,* concerning the Austrian war against Piedmont.

The success of these works converted the highly patriotic Bersezio, who in fact became the leader of the group of dramatists writing dialect dramas for Toselli. His 1863 *Le miserie 'd monss—Travet* became a classic of the dialect theatre, and was even performed on major stages in other regions, including at the Royal Theatre of Milan, with Manzoni himself in attendance.[42] Later Bersezio works took the dialect comedies of Goldoni as their model, but his themes remained closely involved with the social problems and concerns of his own society, similar in this respect to the evolving social drama of contemporary playwrights like Augier and Dumas *fils* in France.

The political prominence of Piedmont in the early years of unification may have attracted attention of artists in other regions to the Toselli experiments. The works of Bersezio in particular were performed with success in Milan and Venice, and inspired local dialect work in both of those cities. Quite aside from the Piedmontese model, however, there was an almost simultaneous flowering of dialect theatre during the Risorgimento in many parts of Italy, clearly responding to much the same political, social, and cultural dynamic that fueled Toselli's work in Turin. The pattern everywhere was similar. While the earlier Italian dialect theatre had been largely developed by dramatists, the new dialect theatre of the Risorgimento was, as in Turin, often encouraged by local dialect companies. In Venice, the leading such company was that of Moro Lin, who before founding it had worked with Toselli in Piedmont. During the 1870s he restored Venetian drama to a prominence it had not enjoyed since the days of Goldoni with dramas set among the Venetian fisherman by Riccardo Selvatico and with the popular family crisis dramas of the prolific Giancinto Gallina. Despite its local orientation, the company toured successfully throughout Italy until it disbanded in 1883, and in turn inspired dialect theatre in both Venice and Milan. Even in far-off Sicily, *I mafiusi,* a powerful work anticipating the socially engaged theatre of Italian verismo, was premiered at Palermo in 1863. Its authors were two traveling Sicilian actors, Gaspare Mosca and Giuseppe Risotto, and its subject matter was the real-life experiences of prison inmates at the Carcere della Vicaria in Palermo.

Among the many dialect theatres that flourished throughout Italy during the Risorgimento, one of the most prominent and interesting was that of Naples, built, as was not the case in many other regions, upon a tradition going back at least to the early seventeenth century. Although this tradition turned from the earlier sailors and fisherman to the bourgeoisie in the later eighteenth century, marks of continuity remained clear, especially in the work of Antonio Petito, Naples's leading dialect actor-dramatist of the 1860s and 1870s. The traditional comic dialect servant Pulcinella, from his first work, *Pulcinella va truvanno la fortuna soia pe Napule* in 1863, was one of his most popular characters, although later Petito created a much more contemporary figure, the foolish bourgeois Sciosciammuocca. Petito died on stage in 1876, but his work was carried on with even greater success by another actor, dramatist, and director, Eduardo Scarpetta. Scarpetta gave up Pulcinella but retained the popular Sciosciammuocca, and turned the Neapolitan dialect theatre even more obviously in the direction of contemporary French social drama, both in the many works he created himself and plays he adapted directly from the French.

Even taking into account such traditional elements as Petito's Pulcinella, the dialect theatre of the Risorgimento, from Venice to Sicily, responding to a distinctly different and rapidly changing social climate, was in many respects quite unlike the dialect theatre of earlier periods. One of the most obvious changes was that the playful plurilingualism of earlier times almost entirely disappeared. The dialect dramas of the Risorgimento, like the evolving social drama of contemporary France, were normally set entirely within one social group, often a single family. Sometimes this group would be rural, but much more commonly it was drawn from the urban petit bourgeoisie, showing their financial and marital problems and their attempts to survive and prosper in an often cruel and manipulative new urban culture. An occasional bankrupt aristocrat or gossipy servant might appear, but they were almost always peripheral to the main action and no longer a center for dialect humor. Many of the new dialect dramas were comedies, or had comic passages, but the clear trend was toward the more serious drama. The role of dialect in the theatre had shifted from linguistic playfulness, comic juxtaposition, and social satire to an attempt to relate more directly and with greater verisimilitude to the social concerns of a dialect-speaking target audience.

One might assume, as some historians have done, that rise of modern literary realism in Italy was one of the major forces for this new interest in dialect theatre, but the relationship between the two phenomena is not that clear. The dialect theatres of the 1860s (coming in any case before the Italian verismo movement, centered in the 1880s) seemed much more to respond to cultural, social, and political movements than literary ones. As verismo developed, certainly a number of its leading dramatists interpreted its program of seeking the truth of everyday life to create dialect theatre, but this was by no means true of verismo dramatists as a whole. Perhaps the best known of them, Giovanni Verga, was strongly influenced in his youth by the cultural dominance of Manzoni. Like Manzoni, and for that matter, like Ariosto and Goldoni, he traveled to Florence, spending four years there to immerse himself in the Tuscan tongue, only to find his early works condemned (as Ariosto's and Goldoni's were) by literary purists as failed attempts by an outsider to capture the nuances of this venerated language. The passage of half a millennium had not removed the usefulness to the literary establishment of using this sanctioned tongue as a means of protecting their privilege.

When around 1880 Verga committed himself to the new school of realism, this could have provided him with a clear justification to renounce literary Tuscan, or even the more flexible but still literary variation of it developed by Manzoni, in favor of dialect literature based on the language actually spoken in his native Sicily, but instead he devoted himself, as Manzoni had, to developing a compromise language that would not depart too far from the expectations of the established literary language and yet would give the impression of realistic speech. His biographer Thomas Goddard Bergin describes his approach in these terms:

> His method is to arrange good Tuscan words in Sicilian word order and to make the reader aware of the rhythm of dialect under the Italian sentence. Outside of a few titles . . . a few nicknames . . . and a very occasional quotation of a proverb in the original, there are no words in his Sicilian stories which cannot be found in any standard Italian dictionary. But the arrangement of the words, the loose order of the sentence, and a certain rhythm in his prose: in brief, the style of these things is very far from Tuscan.[43]

This style, developed in Verga's short stories and novels, was also utilized when he adapted one of the former, *Cavalleria rusticana,* for the stage in 1883. Premiered in Turin with several of Italy's leading actors, including Eleanora Duse, it was an enormous success and became the best-known drama of the verist movement. Its contemporary setting and powerful emotions made it a landmark in the modern Italian theatre, but the power of the dramatic action was not strongly supported by the language, characterized by one of Verga's biographers as "amorphous and colorless," the language "of the bourgeois spectators rather than the characters."[44]

Like dialect dramatists of the previous generation, dramatists in the verist movement were almost invariably dedicated to dialect theatre under the influence, not so much of literary or cultural theory, but of specific acting companies eager to work with such material. Thus one of the most popular verist dramatists, Carlo Bertolazzi, turned to dialect theatre at the request of the Sbodio-Carnaghi company, which performed in Milan from 1890 to 1899 and premiered during that decade thirteen of Bertolazzi's works, including his still popular *El nost Milan* (1893).

## The Early Twentieth Century

The close relationship between verism and the flourishing of Italian dialect theatre in the late nineteenth and early twentieth centuries is nowhere clearer than in Sicily, whose growing importance and achievement attracted major dramatists like Capuana and Pirandello to dialect theatre. The power and imagination of their work in turn proved that dialect theatre could find enthusiastic audiences not only in its own community, but throughout Italy, and indeed around the world. A key figure in this development was the critic, playwright, and director Nino Martoglio, a champion of Sicilian dialect and culture. It was Martoglio who encouraged the dialect puppet performer Giovanni Grasso to turn to the live theatre, where he achieved great success with social dramas very similar to the socially committed dialect plays being created at this same time in Germany by Gerhart Hauptmann.

Grasso soon gained a reputation not only as a dramatist, but as an actor and director. He formed his own company, devoted to dialect theatre, which toured Sicily in 1901 and then moved beyond the region of its home dialect to prove its attractiveness on the national and then the international stage. In 1902 the Grasso troupe went to Rome, where lavish praise by the critic of the *Tribuna* filled the Teatro Argentina. The company then toured elsewhere in Italy, to growing enthusiasm, then in 1908 to Berlin, in 1911 to Paris and London (where they counted Edward VII and Henry Irving among their admirers), and finally to Russia, the United States, and South America. What impressed the critic Manca of the *Tribuna,* and most of the other enthusiastic supporters of Grasso's company, was the apparent naturalness and spontaneity of their performance, the convincing fire and passion, the lack of traditional theatrical artifice. In an era when a new, more "realistic" style was being sought throughout Europe, the largely untrained if impassioned actors of the dialect theatre clearly had a kind of appeal that more traditionally schooled actors lacked, and in Italy this distinction had a natural relationship to the long-standing tension between the more formal and somewhat abstract "literary" Italian and the living dialects. In this era Eleanora Duse was often spoken of (by Bernard Shaw for example) as different from (and superior to) her great rival Sarah Bernhardt because Duse relied more strongly upon "nature" and Bernhardt upon "technique," but in Italy, beloved as Duse was, her orientation was toward the "literary" theatre, and on those grounds she too could be challenged by the more "natural" actresses of the dialect theatre, as can be seen in a striking comparison of Duse with an unidentified Sicilian dialect actress by Luigi Capuana in their playing of Santuzza in Verga's *Cavalleria rusticana:*

> To my Sicilian eyes Santuzza-Duse appeared as a kind of falsification of Verga's passionate figure in her gestures, the expression of her voice, her dress (an unbelievable medley of Lombard and Roman costumes!), in spite of the passionate response which only Duse could elicit. The poor, regional actress, instead, her clothes borrowed from the peasant women of the town she was passing through—shoes, earrings, skirt, the blue cloth cloak—suggested a real, live "Santuzza," as there may have been one among her audience.[45]

This comparison appears in the preface to Capuana's *Teatro dialettale siciliano,* and the contrast in clothing stands as a clear metaphor for a linguistic contrast as well, Duse utilizing the "unbelievable" and artificial medley of "Lombard and Roman," with the regional actress borrowing directly and honestly "from the peasant women of the town she was passing through."

Nino Martoglio, who had drawn Grasso into the theatre, founded his own company, which, while lacking the international reputation of Grasso's, nevertheless was highly regarded. He was extremely sensitive to variations in language, and in his writings we find particularly clear evidence of the heteroglossia of the dialect drama of this period. He began his literary career as a poet, and was one of the leading authors of the movement known as *phonografismo,* a branch of verismo devoted to

dialect poetry that, as its name suggests, sought a highly accurate reproduction of colloquial speech.[46] This attempt to capture the speech of
everyday life created a dialect that was obviously not conventional Italian, but was also not conventional literary Sicilian, which had hitherto
served most of the island. When Martoglio turned from dialect poetry to
dialect drama, however, he began to employ, with considerable sophistication, a strategy that linguistic theorists of the later twentieth century
would refer to as code-switching.

Code-switching is based upon an important linguistic phenomenon
first described in detail in 1959 by Charles A. Ferguson, and called by
him "diglossia." According to Ferguson, diglossia occurs when "two or
more varieties of the same language are used by some speakers under
different conditions." The most common example is when members of
a community speak a local dialect at home or among friends and a "standard" dialect with people from other dialect communities or on public
occasions.[47] In Martoglio's Sicily, the standard dialect was the Sicilian
koine, but at the same time the newly unified Italian government was in
the process of imposing standard Italian as the language of prestige and
of the bureaucracy.[48] In such cases there is almost invariably a social and
cultural pressure to privilege the "standard" dialect, and to denigrate or
even deny the existence of the "local" variation. This dynamic, as we will
see in the next chapter, is extremely common in colonial situations, and
indeed after unification standard Italian operates in Sicily much in the
manner of an imposed colonial language.

Martoglio's dramatic use of language indeed anticipates that sort of
heteroglossia which is widely found in postcolonial dramatic expression.
That is, he employs code-switching, a common feature of diglossic communities, not only to differentiate characters but also, in the case of characters who have ability in a variety of registers within a dialect, to show
how they adjust their language for particular social effects. This heteroglossic process is clear from Martoglio's first play, *I Civitoti in Pretura*
(1901). Antonio Scuderi, who has made a close study of the code-switching in this play, notes that "the qualities of a particular code—falling
somewhere between dialect and standard—and of a particular register"
allows the dramatist to offer "a clear indication of the individual's social
position, education, wit or lack thereof, etc." Those characters like the
bailiff and the attorney who are diglossic speakers enjoy the prestige

offered by their access to the higher code, "while their code switching underscores the integrity of high and low functions, and the advantage to be gained by both."[49]

Despite his commitment to dialect drama, Martoglio as a director staged occasional works in literary Italian, most notably the first plays of the most famous Sicilian dramatist Luigi Pirandello. Interestingly, the young Pirandello felt the need to justify this language choice, which he did in an essay "Teatro siciliano?" published in 1909. A poet writes in dialect, Pirandello suggests in this essay, for a variety of reasons:

Either the poet does not have the knowledge of the widest means of communication, that is, standard language, or else he does, but feels that he cannot use it with the same liveliness, with that precisely appropriate spontaneity that is a principal, indispensable condition of art; or else the nature of his feelings and images is so deeply rooted in the earth whose voice he seeks to be, that any other means of communication except dialect would seem unsuitable or incoherent; or else what he want to represent is so local that it could not be expressed beyond the limits of a knowledge of the thing itself.[50]

A dialect theatre, Pirandello continues, is made to remain within the boundaries of that dialect, since it cannot be enjoyed or even understood by audiences who understand the whole cultural context represented by the dialect. Grasso's international success Pirandello condemns as "Sicily for export," his acting a "terrible, marvelous bestiality," which achieves its effects not by imparting any knowledge of Sicily but by a powerful violent mime, in its own way quite mannered and artificial.[51]

Despite these misgivings, Pirandello achieved his first major dramatic success in the dialect theatre, which he undertook under the combined influence of his friend and mentor Martoglio and the actor Angelo Musco, who was another artist brought into the dialect theatre by the indefatigable Martoglio. Musco worked for a time as a leading actor in Grasso's company, but the violent and passionate fare favored by Grasso was not to his taste, and so in 1915 he founded his own company, still devoted to theatre in the Sicilian dialect, but of a much lighter mood. Despite his different style, he was clearly as powerful and impressive a stage figure as his rival Grasso, and came to enjoy an equal national and international reputation. Gordon Craig called him "the greatest actor in the world," and André Antoine claimed never to have seen an actor of such power.[52] Antonio Gramsci, writing in the journal *Avanti* in 1919, used a review of Musco's work to champion dialect theatre as "alive and real, its language seizes every aspect of social activity," while condemning the standard literary theatre as a "provisional output of the Italian non-genius, a false and pretentious production by bombastic individuals."[53]

Musco, ever seeking new plays for his repertoire, approached Pirandello in 1915, and he agreed, with much reluctance, to complete in dialect a play he had proposed some years before to Martoglio. In the event, as Pirandello's interest waned, Martoglio wrote most of the play, *L'aria del continente,* which enjoyed an enormous success and remained a standard revival piece for Musco for years. It also offered a somewhat new variation on traditional theatrical bilingualism in keeping with the code-switching that Martoglio had made his particular specialty. While earlier dramatists writing both formal Italian and dialect in the same play normally used them to mark social tensions, utilizing formal speech for outsiders or those with somewhat foolish social pretensions, while turning to the dialect for sympathetic characters seeking common ground with the audience, most of the characters in *L'aria del continente* speak both Italian and Sicilian, as was becoming increasingly true of Martoglio's audience. There is a certain traditional mocking of social pretensions through language, but, interestingly, not by contrasting formal Italian with Sicilian. The foolish and wealthy protagonist Don Cola salts his speech with borrowed French to display his continental sophistication. The dialect is used instead to mark changes in intensity and formality. The normally Sicilian-speaking Don Lucinu turns to more formal Italian when he forbids his wife and son to visit Don Cola, and when Don Cola quarrels with his wife, his growing fury is expressed in a steadily increasing use of Sicilian. This use of dialect to reflect changes in mood and formality, central to the dramatic expression of Martoglio, would become a major characteristic of the mature art of the leading Italian dramatist of the next generation, Eduardo De Filippo.

The financial and popular success enjoyed by *L'aria del continente* encouraged Pirandello to create several more dialect plays for Musco in

1916 and 1917, among them *Liolà,* a classic of the dialect theatre, and two plays coauthored with Martoglio. Despite Musco's notorious tendency to improvise on his texts, Pirandello always spoke fondly of his first major interpreter, but deplored what he saw as Musco's willingness to present popular works that did not come up to Pirandello's standards. In a letter to Martoglio in January 1917 Pirandello complained that Musco could not "free himself from being the slave of his public." Pirandello firmly concludes:

> I might have been able to attempt some artistic revival of a new Sicilian comic theatre with you, but I just don't feel like cooperating in trying to prop up a shack full of puppets for farce makers. I can use my talent in other ways and get other kinds of satisfaction.[54]

Indeed, soon after, Pirandello turned away from the dialect theatre, the populist nature of which was quite alien to his literary commitments. His interest now turned toward a theatre committed to literature and high culture, the vision that gave birth in 1924 to his Teatro d'Arte in Rome. Not surprisingly, Gramsci felt that Pirandello, in turning from works "conceived in dialect where a rural 'dialectal' life is depicted," to those "conceived in literary language where a supradialectal life of national and even cosmopolitan bourgeois intellectuals is depicted," also moved from his most effective artistry to an abstract intellectualism.[55]

This same year Pirandello also very publicly joined the Fascist Party, attracted by its conservative and nationalist agenda. Thus politically as well as aesthetically he moved still further away from the dialect theatre, which was strongly opposed by the Fascists in their commitment to national unity. Dialect dramas (especially those that dealt, as many did, with the sufferings of the lower classes) were condemned as "un-Italian," as was the 1928 drama *I nullatenenti* by the popular interwar Neapolitan dramatist Raffaele Viviani, when a 1940 revival of it was attempted in Milan.[56] As Gramsci astutely observed:

> Every time the question of language surfaces, in one way or another, it means that a series of other problems are coming to the fore: the formation and enlargement of the governing class, the need to establish

more intimate and secure relationships between the governing groups and the national-popular mass, in other words, to reorganize the cultural hegemony.[57]

The defeat of the Fascist government in the Second World War removed official resistance to the dialect theatres, and the combined forces of nostalgia and regional pride reestablished them in the cultural life of many communities, a position they maintained, although somewhat tenuously, through the rest of the century. Pier Paolo Pasolini as late as 1968 could still complain about the arbitrariness and artificiality of a theatrical tradition based on "an Italian that does not exist. Upon such a convention, that is, upon nothing, upon what is nonexistent, dead, it has based the conventionality of diction. The result is repugnant."[58] Nevertheless, the growing ease of travel, the spread of mass communications, and the migration of workers from all parts of the peninsula to the cities created far greater pressures for standardization than had ever been achieved by Risorgimento spirits or Fascist decrees.

For generations most educated Italians were at least bilingual, using a standardized if somewhat abstract Italian in their intellectual or commercial pursuits and a dialect in more informal and local situations. More universal education and exposure to the media during the twentieth century both narrowed the division between these two languages and much increased such bilingualism. A dramatist could still, like Pirandello, specifically reject dialect for a more neutral "intellectual" style, or at the other extreme, provide largely local fare for the scattered regional dialect theatres. The tendency in much of modern Italy to associate dialect theatre with illiteracy, cultural deprivation, and isolationism has weakened the dialect theatre, although interestingly enough, at the end of the twentieth century a new interest in the artistic uses of dialect appeared, in recent Italian poetry, in the cinema (as in Troisi's much-acclaimed *Il Postino* or Martone's *Amore molesto*), as well as in the music of a number of recent Italian rock groups.[59]

## De Filippo and Fo

Italy's best-known dialect dramatist of the later twentieth century was surely Eduardo De Filippo, whose work provides a useful index to the changing role of dialect theatre during this turbulent era. De Filippo was the natural son of the great Neapolitan dialect actor and dramatist Eduardo Scarpetta, making his first stage appearance in Scarpetta's company at the age of four. As a young man he played leading roles in the same company, now directed by Scarpetta's son, Vicenzo. During the 1920s he so grew in popularity as an actor and then as a playwright that he established in 1931 his own company, the Compagnia del Teatro Umoristico De Filippo, so popular in its turn that it quite escaped the Fascist efforts to discourage dialect theatre in Italy.

After the war, however, De Filippo's art broadened and deepened, and his approach toward dialect began to more closely reflect that of his surrounding society. The "half-Neapolitan" already spoken by the middle class of that city was becoming more and more the vernacular of the lower classes as well. Indeed by the middle of the twentieth century most of southern Italy shared a more or less common spoken vernacular, with distinct local inflections in various regions, but still readily understood throughout the south and indeed throughout Italy. In short a kind of dialect was available much closer to the dialects familiar on the American and English stages, living dialects actually spoken by members of a particular social or geographical group and distinctive of that group, but still understandable to a more general public, who can respond to these dialects as dramatic signs, like costumes, that help situate individual actors.

Thus De Filippo did not need to seek, like Verga, a compromise between a living language and a widely comprehensible one. Nevertheless he developed his own distinct and flexible use of dialect in a new kind of bilingualism that was among the most distinctive and successful in the late-twentieth-century Italian theatre. In the work of De Filippo appeared the most sophisticated and successful development of the practice earlier seen in works by the Sicilian dramatist Martoglio and Neapolitan Viviani, both of whom created characters that spoke formal Italian and the local dialect with equal ease and moved from one register to another according to the formality or emotionality of the situation. A typical example of De Filippo's use of this technique may be seen in his most popular work, *Filumena Marturano* (1946), when Filumena has summoned her unacknowledged natural sons to her home. There they are greeted by the maid Lucia, who, totally confused by the unclarity of their social situation, addresses them in a speech that moves frantically back and forth between Italian and Neapolitan.

Eric Bentley has rightly praised De Filippo for his creation of a "popular" theater, as opposed to an "art theatre," an achievement Bentley attributes directly to its language: "It uses a popular spoken language and not an official, national, bourgeois language, in this respect resembling Synge and O'Casey rather than Pinero and Galsworthy."[60] The comparison is useful, but somewhat misleading. Certainly for a non-Neapolitan Italian theatregoer, the language of a play like *Filumena Marturano,* while understandable, unquestionably marks the play as Neapolitan and evokes all the associations of that culture, just as the language of an O'Casey play, while understandable, instantly evokes Ireland for a London theatregoer. It is, however, not true that *Filumena Marturano* does not employ "an official, national, bourgeois language." Indeed the lawyer Nocella speaks primarily in that language, and others slip in and out of it according to the circumstances. What De Filippo has done is what successful Italian dramatists have always done, taking the traditional linguistic flexibility of Italy in a direction particularly suited to his own historical moment and to his social and artistic concerns.

The popularity and success of De Filippo might suggest a gradual assimilation of the traditionally marginalized, boisterous, and irreverent dialect theatre, with its close ties to the socially and politically disenfranchised, into the mainstream of Italian theatrical culture, but one of the outstanding Italian theatre artists of the late twentieth century, Dario Fo, has championed a return to the playful language world of the wily Bergamask porters and clear-eyed Paduan peasants of the early Renaissance, or more accurately, to the wandering comic entertainers, the *bufoni* and the *giullare,* whose solo performances, often heavily based upon linguistic play, provided the ground for the more elaborate creations of artists like Ruzante and Calmo. In homage to this tradition, Fo has called his solo performances *giullarta,* and his central work *Mistero Buffo* (1970) offers both a history and a re-creation of *giullare* performance. Central to Fo's interest in this material was its popular origins. Before the *giullari* were appropriated for religious instruction by the church and entertainment by the court, they served, Fo has asserted, as popular and irreverent sites of resistance to the repressions of such cultural powers, and Fo has sought in their revival to again engage in the struggle of the oppressed by providing a liberating voice of resistance. One of Fo's leading Italian commentators, Lanfranco Binni, has observed:

> The "epic theatre" of the mediaeval *giullari,* in which the *giullare* became the choral, didactic expression of an entire community and the feelings, hopes and rebellion of exploited people to whom he performed in a piazza, projected their desire for liberation from the religious sphere set up by the authorities.[61]

Essential to the effectiveness of the original *giullare* was that they were performed in the language of the people, albeit enriched and enlivened by bits and pieces of all sorts of other linguistic material: the official Italian and church Latin of the oppressors, the dialects or languages of visiting merchants, soldiers, or travelers, and imaginary language arising from the fancy of the performer. For a combination of historical, social, political, and aesthetic reasons, Fo has chosen not to perform his *giullarta* in standard Italian (the language of his more traditional farces) but in a special language that evokes the popular languages of this tradition. Fo's own native dialect is Lombard, a variation of which is Bergamask, a standard *zanni* dialect of the classic commedia. Using this as a base, Fo has mixed in elements of Venetian, also of course closely associated with the early commedia, and other northern Italian dialects. The result, Antonio Scuderi has suggested, is in fact something rather close to generic Paduan, which was the dialect of the dramatist Fo has most often cited as his inspiration, Ruzante.[62] Hence the name of one of Fo's protagonists: Johan Padan in *The Discovery of the Americas* (1992).

Aside from his use of local dialects, Fo has developed another linguistic strategy extremely popular with early traveling entertainers, grammelot, a nonsense speech that closely imitates the sounds, rhythm, and intonations of actual language. Various motivations have been suggested for the development of grammelot, that it was simply a technique for a performer to display his verbal skills, agility, and imagination, that it was developed by itinerant players for use when they did not share a common language with their audiences, that it originated as a device in France in the seventeenth century when commedia players at the fairground theatres were forbidden to speak French on stage. Not surprisingly, Fo himself links grammelot to political concerns, claiming in his prologue to *Zanni's Grammelot,* with which he frequently opens performances of *Mistero Buffo,* that grammelot was originally utilized by the commedia actors to escape censorship.[63]

The skill and range of Fo's grammelot in his various monologues is dazzling. He has presented grammelot routines that were totally convincing but meaningless imitations of a wide variety of languages, from Polish to Native American, as well as dialects of other languages, such as British and American English, not to mention the more specialized discourse of bureaucrats, computer engineers, or space scientists. One can readily see the linguistic connection between Fo's grammelot deflation of a pompous modern authority figure, say a general or a scientist, and the foolish Spanish captains or learned *dottores* of the commedia, with their equally hilarious and meaningless linguistic turns.

The enormous success of Fo, nationally and internationally, provides clear evidence that despite the many pressures, political and cultural, toward a homogenization and standardization of the language, the performative power of dialect in the theatre is still great, and if this performance, like so much of postmodern culture, returns to the practices of the past in a highly self-conscious and reflexive manner, if Fo's dialect theatre and grammelot now appear as a kind of cultural quotation, that in no way diminishes their social or artistic effectiveness. He has clearly demonstrated their continuing usefulness in the hands of a skilled artist-performer.

# 3  Postcolonial Heteroglossia

Aₛ ᴛʜᴇ ᴘʀᴇᴠɪᴏᴜs ᴄʜᴀᴘᴛᴇʀs have sought to demonstrate, linguistic mixtures have, for a variety of reasons, been utilized in the theatre throughout its history. Nevertheless, serious critical attention to the phenomenon of heteroglossia on the stage has developed only recently, largely due to postcolonial theory. The operations of language are central to such theory because language itself was a basic tool of colonial authority. Bill Ashcroft, Gareth Griffiths, and Helen Tiffin, leaders in this emergent field of study, devote one section to their collection, *The Post-Colonial Studies Reader,* to language, explaining:

> Language is a fundamental site for the struggle for post-colonial discourse because the colonial process itself begins in language. The control over language by the imperial centre—whether achieved by displacing native languages, by installing itself as a "standard" against other variants which are constituted as "impurities," or by planting the language of empire in a new place—remains the most potent instrument of cultural control.[1]

## Language of Cultural Domination

This use of imposed language for cultural control, the essence of colonialism, is closely connected with a strong and long-established tendency in Western thought to make clear dividing lines between areas of human activity, to seek a kind of Platonic essence and to consider exemptions and irregularities as at best irrelevant, and at worst harmful, deviations to be suppressed or eradicated. Traditional ideas about language have been marked by this mode of thinking, as has already been noted in the traditional linguistic concept of the homogeneous language

community, with its "ideal" speakers and listeners, as well as in the privileging of "official" languages and the relegation of dialects to the status
of merely minor or deviant derivations of this basic tongue. From a postcolonial perspective, the power dynamics of establishing and maintaining these "official" languages has a distinctly colonial feel about it, as did,
even earlier, the establishment of Latin in the late classic period as the
language of a "colonizing center."[2]

One of the first important explorations of the use of language as an
instrument of cultural domination, especially within the colonial context, was Frantz Fanon's seminal 1952 study *Black Skin, White Masks*.
The book begins with a chapter called "The Negro and Language"
because, Fanon explains, language possesses a "basic importance" in the
definition of self and in the placement of oneself in a cultural context. By
way of illustration, he discusses the operations of language in French
colonialism and their psychic effects upon the colonized black within
that system. Here, the colonized black is denied human recognition by
the white colonizers unless he adopts their language and culture, thus
isolating him from his own. "The Antilles Negro who want to be white
will be the whiter as he gains greater mastery of the cultural tool that
language is," and since no cultural alternatives to that of the colonizing
power are recognized by that power, the Antilles Negro "will come
closer to being a real human being—in direct ratio to his mastery of the
French language."[3] Although Fanon was careful to note that there was
a wide variety of differences in how the negotiations between the language of the colonizers and those of the colonized developed in different
cultural contexts, he also insisted that essentially "the same behavior patterns obtain in every race that has been subjected to colonization."[4] In
the early days of postcolonial theory the unquestionable accuracy of
Fanon's observations in general encouraged in some a totalizing view of
this process, with colonial subjugation giving indigenous writers the
options of assuming the voice of the colonial other or being reduced to
silence. This simplistic view, however, was soon generally disregarded,
and attention given to the many and complex ways that on the one hand
the colonized voices modified and adapted the colonial language and on
the other how indigenous languages survived, sometimes in something
close to their precolonial form but more often in a wide variety of adap-

tations and blendings with the language or languages of colonization. In other words, the simple model of a dominant monoglossia replacing a subordinated one gave way to a model of two or more languages coming together in a particular power relationship, but producing a wide and by no means predictable variety of heteroglossic compromises.

This model was basic to much of what has come to be called post-colonial theory, a methodology that can be dated back to work from the late 1960s onward by a number of social scientists and literary critics in continental Europe and the former British empire. As a critical field of study, particularly in the English language, however, postcolonialism did not really become developed until the late 1980s. It was closely connected to the radical reshaping in the late twentieth century of the social sciences, particularly anthropology and ethnography. This change in turn was due in part to the breakup of the colonial empires of the preceding century, in part to radical new cultural theory influenced by post-structuralism, and in part to the increasing exposure of different cultures around the world to each other. One of the most important and influential of the early theoretical statements in the new field, *The Empire Writes Back,* by Bill Ashcroft, Gareth Griffiths, and Helen Tiffin, was published in 1989. Although this work dealt with a variety of approaches to postcolonial literature, its major emphasis was upon language. The introduction asserts that "one of the main features of imperial oppression is control over language," and that for that reason the discussion of postcolonial writing in it will be "largely a discussion of the process by which the language, with its power, and the writing, with its signification of authority, has been wrested from the dominant European culture."[5]

Within the field of cultural studies, a major work in articulating the new orientation was anthropologist James Clifford's *The Predicament of Culture* (1988). Here too language plays an important role, and Clifford's approach to cultural theory is of particular interest to the present study because its introduction is cast in linguistic terms, with a particular evocation of heteroglossia. In Clifford's terms, recent cultural theory has involved the traditional monologic voice of Western ethnographic authority giving way to a consciousness of and a respect for the varied cultural "voices" that this colonialist viewpoint suppressed. Monolithic cultural identities, like monolithic linguistic identities, give way to shifting, ambiguous, continually renegotiated practice. In a key passage, Clifford specifically invokes Bakhtin to suggest this situation:

> With expanded communication and intercultural influence, people interpret others, and themselves, in a bewildering diversity of idioms—a global condition of what Mikhail Bakhtin called "heteroglossia." This ambiguous, multivocal world makes it increasingly hard to conceive of human diversity as inscribed in bounded independent cultures. Difference is an effect of inventive syncretism.[6]

During the 1990s, postcolonialism became a widely accepted critical approach, especially to works, literary and nonliterary, involved with discourse. The first three major books in English to consider theatre and drama from a postcolonial perspective were Brian Crow and Chris Banfield's *An Introduction to Post-Colonial Theatre,* Helen Gilbert and Joanne Tompkins's *Post-Colonial Drama Theory, Practice, Politics,* both of which appeared in 1996,[7] and Christopher Balme's *Decolonizing the Stage: Theatrical Syncretism and Post-Colonial Drama,* published in 1999.[8] Crow and Banfield's work is closest in approach to previous postcolonial work on nondramatic subjects, exploring the texts of a number of leading postcolonial dramatists, almost all working in parts of the old British Empire—Derek Walcott from the West Indies, August Wilson from the United States, Jack Davis from Australia, Wole Soyinka from Nigeria, Athol Fugard from South Africa, and Bardal Sircar and Girish Karnad from India. Despite its emphasis upon texts, this book gives the least attention of the three to linguistic negotiation, and in particular to heteroglossia, although an important section of the introduction stresses the complexity of the "language issue," noting that postcolonial writers may embrace the colonial language, renounce it, or develop some inflected version of it.[9]

The other two books engage with linguistic choices and practices more directly and in more detail, probably because both move away from a text- and author-based analysis in the direction of performance studies, seeking to view postcolonial drama from a variety of perspectives, both cultural and performative. Although the organization and the focus of these two books is quite different, Gilbert and Tompkins stressing the political and cultural dynamics of postcolonial drama, and Balme seeking to develop a general aesthetics of this type of drama, each includes a chapter on language. Gilbert and Tompkins open this chapter with a statement that recalls the centrality given to imperial language by Ashcroft and his coeditors: "Language is one of the most basic markers of colonial authority."[10] Indeed, language study of the postcolonial theatre, like that of postcolonial culture in general, begins with the colonial project of imposing its own master language upon the colonized subjects in order to gain control over all aspects of their existence—their beliefs and cultural memory, preserved by language, their geography, based upon naming, even their sense of identity and their subjectivity, now interpellated by the colonial discourse.

Equally important to postcolonial studies, however, is the inability in many cases of this linguistic project to be fully installed. As Gilbert and Tompkins observe: "The wide-ranging power of the imperial language has, however, not been entirely successful in its attempt to eradicate local, potentially resistant languages that threaten the borders of imperial authority."[11] Sometimes, particularly in the activities of such linguistically self-conscious agents as writers and dramatists, this resistant use of language is quite conscious, but the project of imposing a stable imperial language upon a colonized people is also compromised at the outset by the natural tendency of language to adjust continually to changing circumstances. A certain continual slippage and negotiation is inevitable in any language, and is obviously more exaggerated when the language is continually exposed to the pressures of possible influence from another language or languages competing for the same population. Out of this slippage comes the whole complex field of accents, dialects, macaronic combinations, and eventually pidgin and creole variations, bringing into being a wide range of linguistic variations that blend into one another so as to make traditional linguistic differentiations almost impossible.

Although I am focusing here upon language, this blending of cultural elements characterizes all aspects of postcolonialism. Ashcroft, Griffiths, and Tiffin suggest that the most "comprehensive comparative models" for the study of postcolonial literatures are those that acknowledge "features such as hybridity or syncreticity" as constitutive elements of all such literatures.[12] Balme, noting the centrality of the term *syncretism* in recent postcolonial theory, announces in the subtitle of his study of post-colonial drama that it is involved with "theatrical syncretism." Within the book he cites as one of the most comprehensive attempts to apply the concept of syncretism to the performing arts the writings of ethnomusi-cologist David Coplan, in studying South African township music and performance. Coplan defines "syncretic" as the "acculturative blending of performance materials and practices from two or more cultural tradi-tions, producing qualitatively new forms."[13]

The quotation from Clifford already cited suggests both *inventive syn-cretism* and *heteroglossia* as terms descriptive of the combining of diverse cultural elements in the contemporary world. The juxtaposition of these two terms stresses an important feature of syncretism as it has been gen-erally used in postcolonial theory: the blending it involves does not result in a homogeneous new monologism, but a continuing heteroglossia, in which discrete voices continue to operate within a single discourse. Thus the Guyanese novelist-essayist Wilson Harris, noting that the "biological hypothesis" of human homogeneity has "become an organ of conquest" through an imposed unity, champions instead a literature of "cultural heterogeneity" in which continued cultural mixing gives rise to a "ceaseless dialogue" that "it inserts between hardened conven-tions."[14] Hybridity, a concept closely related to syncretism, has been par-ticularly important in the writings of cultural theorist Homi Bhabha, who stresses the importance of the continuing play of difference within hybrid or syncretic cultural manifestations. Cultural hybridity, Bhabha asserts, "entertains difference without an assumed or imposed hierar-chy."[15] The confluence of these various syncretic strategies within post-colonial theory is stressed in Marc Maufort's *Transgressive Itineraries: Postcolonial Hybridizations of Dramatic Realism* (2003). "Hybridization," which Maufort derives from Bakhtin, suggests what Maufort argues is a "complementary perspective" between Bakhtin's "heteroglossia" and Bhabha's "hybridity," both useful for analyzing the "mixture of cultural discourses manifest in the postcolonial plays under scrutiny."[16]

This quality of dialogue or difference within syncretic theatre means that languages within the syncretic tradition can be considered as het-eroglossic within themselves, even before they interact in the theatre with other languages, making the operations of heteroglossia within postcolonial theatre particularly complex. In considering the workings of heteroglossia in postcolonial theatre, therefore, I will begin with some observations on the multiple voices of syncretic theatre itself, and then consider ways that syncretic theatre operates within the multilinguistic environment that very commonly surrounds it.

Finding a clear and consistent terminology to discuss the complex and constantly shifting field of language in the postcolonial theatre is very difficult. Gilbert and Tompkins's chapter "The Languages of Resistance" discusses five such "languages," all of which have been utilized in opposition to the attempted monologism of the colonial language, in this case English. In addition to considering silence, song, and music, Gilbert and Tompkins group postcolonial resistant language under three general headings: indigenous languages, indigenized languages, and creole and pidgin. Indigenous languages, they suggest, "can be broadly defined as those which were native to a culture prior to colonization and which have since maintained their original grammatical structures and their basic lexicon."[17] Indigenized languages are colonial languages, such as English, that have been modified in pronunciation as well as lexically and semantically in order to more adequately reflect the concerns and life experiences of the colonized speakers. As Soyinka notes, postcolonial writers are not content with the mere replication of the colonial language. "When we borrow an alien language," he asserts,

> We must begin by co-opting the entire properties of that language as correspondences to properties in our matrix of thought and expression. We must stress such a language, stretch it, impact, and compact, fragment and reassemble it with no apology.[18]

## Pidgin and Creole

Since the resistant voice of the manipulator is central to indigenized languages, a kind of heteroglossia already operates here, but the next languages of resistance, pidgin and creole, are even clearer examples, since they actually incorporate a dialogue between the indigenous languages and the colonial ones, creating complex hybrids involving vocabulary, tonality, rhythm, and grammar. The distinction between pidgin and creole languages is by no means consistent, doubtless reflecting the core instability of the material being studied. Leonard Bloomfield's classic text *Language,* from 1933, used the term *jargon* to refer to pidgin language, a conventionalized corruption of some dominant speech used in both trading and colonial situations. It is "nobody's native language but only a compromise between a foreign speaker's version of a language and a native speaker's version of the foreign speaker's version, and so on." In some cases, however, a subject group gives up its native language in favor of a conventionalized pidgin or jargon, and it becomes a native language. When this happens, according to Bloomfield, it should be called a "creolized language."[19]

Although a number of European scholars began serious studies in the late eighteenth century of the modes of speech that came to be classified as pidgin or creole, more than a century later, when Bloomfield wrote, pidgin and creole were still considered a very minor part of language study, essentially a debased and corrupted sort of slang, lacking even the cultural status of a dialect. In a particularly clear expression of this concern, the Trusteeship Council of the United Nations in 1953 condemned the use of pidgin in the Territory of New Guinea and demanded that it be abolished. Actually, however, this major official attack on pidgin proved a turning point in its respectability. The council ruling raised the concern of the American linguist, Robert A. Hall Jr., who had devoted himself to the study of pidgin and creole languages since the mid-1940s and whose *Haitian Creole* in 1953 was the first major study of francophone Caribbean creole speech. In response to the council ruling, Hall wrote his most famous book, with the pugnacious title challenging the defenders of colonialist linguistic hegemony, *Hands Off Pidgin English.* Its appearance in 1955 brought major attention to the subject of pidgin and creole languages and was the turning point in the general acceptance of their cultural importance.

Since that time the study of the pidgin and creole languages and literatures has steadily grown in amount and sophistication internationally, and not surprisingly, the more such shifting and heteroglossic languages are studied, the greater challenge they present to linguists and cultural analysts attempting to categorize them and to analyze their structures.[20] A useful recent summary can be found in the 2002 *International Encyclopedia of the Social and Behavioral Sciences,* which in general makes a historical distinction between pidgin languages, which it defines as those developed around trade forts or along trade routes, such as on the coast

of West Africa, and creole languages that developed in colonial situations such as sugar cane plantations or rice fields, employing non-Euro-
pean slave labor.[21] Since an important aspect of the colonial project was
the eradication of indigenous languages, this implies a fairly clear distinction, at least in the power valences of the competing languages,
between pidgin and creole. Even among linguists, however, these terms
are by no means so distinct. Indeed, the *Encyclopedia* points out, somewhat despairingly, that a considerable variety of distinctions have been
proposed but still not clearly articulated for the many types of recently
developed languages that are fundamentally heteroglossic, such as pidgin, creole, koine, semicreole, intertwined varieties, foreign workers'
varieties of European languages (such as *Gastarbeiter Deutsch*),[22] and
"indigenized varieties" of European languages.[23]

It might seem that, despite their heteroglossic origins, both pidgin
and creole languages, when utilized for theatre purposes, might operate
like more conventional "standard" languages, especially when they have
become the "native" language for at least the majority of their audiences.
Two qualities or potential strategies of such languages, however, keep
them open to a distinctly heteroglossic development in the theatre:
hybridity and code-switching. David Moody, a specialist in the theatre
of Wole Soyinka and in postcolonial theatre in general, specifically
evokes the concept of hybridity to demonstrate how a Soyinka play like
*The Road* operates in a creative world between languages, preventing a
single voice from subsuming others:

> Soyinka, like other post-colonial writers in English, is producing at
> the margins of the inter-cultural space . . . his plays speak with a lan-
> guage which is neither Yoruba nor English, but which, to use Homi
> Bhabha's term, is a "hybrid" tongue. This "hybrid" tongue is difficult,
> knotty, many-textured; it speaks not just with two discourses, but
> with many.[24]

Code-switching is sometimes combined with hybridity, but involves a
different sort of linguistic mixing. Though found widely in postcolonial
theatre, it has been particularly associated with the Caribbean and with
the linguistic interest in what has come to be known as the "creole continuum." Ashcroft, Griffiths, and Tiffin suggest that postcolonial dis-

course recognizes three main types of linguistic groups, the monoglossic, the diglossic, and the polyglossic. Diglossic communities are those, like Canada and India, where, although multiple languages and dialects exist, bilingualism has become an established, even official practice. Polyglossic communities are not those where a number of distinctly different languages are spoken (those would be "polylingual"), but rather those in which different dialects overlap. Their central example of polyglossic communities are those of the Caribbean, where a multitude of distinguishable forms of language use are creatively combined in ever-changing patterns by speakers with no continuing commitment to any specific established language. The Jamaican writer Jean D'Costa has characterized the situation in these terms:

> The (Caribbean) writer confronts in his own mind the array of possible language forms which arise at the bidding of any single notion he may wish to express. At this partially conscious level he must sift the mental events, emotions, and patterns of association within him such that the ideal balance of meaning may be achieved. This suggests a kind of language competence in which variation, code-switching and minimal shifting form a complete whole rather than clearly separated systems realizing themselves in different surface structures.[25]

The complex and constantly renegotiated pattern of dialects, pidgins, and languages in the Caribbean has come to be referred to among linguists as the *creole continuum*.[26] This term was coined in 1971 by David DeCamp, who suggested that after the relative stabilization of a creole or pidgin language, this language, if continuing to exist in the same cultural situation as the colonial language, would develop into a "post-creole" situation of a continuum, producing a variety of variant tongues lying between the creole and the colonial language but blending into one another so that distinct variations would be difficult if not impossible to define.[27]

The internationally accepted term for the language that provided a creole with its basic vocabulary, such as French or English, is the *superstrate*. This provides one end of a continuum, at the other end of which is the basilect, that form of creole furthest from the superstrate and in some cases essentially an indigenous tongue. The local "standard" form of the creole language is the acrolect, but it in fact shades off into a continuum of various mesolects, which together provide a continuum of language variations between the basilect and the "official" languages of the superstrate and the acrolect. The "lect" combines elements from various major languages and dialects around it, along with features of its own, to mark a functional place on a continuum without ever crystallizing into a discrete dialect.[28] What makes this situation different from more traditional dialect variation is that speakers within a single community are aware of speech variations across a wide range of the continuum, and can shift the level of discourse according to the context in order to give their discourse a particular social or cultural placement. This alteration of "voice" within the discourse of a single speaker is what linguists have called "code-switching," and has proven a particularly effective tool for postcolonial writers to disturb the hegemony of the colonist discourse.[29]

In the previous chapter I introduced a very common variety of code-switching that the linguist Charles A. Ferguson named "diglossia." This differs from the diglossic communities as described by Ashcroft and his coeditors, which involve speakers of two different languages, but is equally relevant to much postcolonial practice. Ferguson's diglossia, it will be remembered, occurs when two or more varieties of the same language are used by the same speakers under different social conditions, most commonly when a local dialect is spoken informally among friends or at home while a more standard dialect is spoken with people from other language communities or in more formal situations. In most cases, particularly in postcolonial linguistic contexts, the "standard" speech provides higher status, has more of what Bourdieu has called "linguistic capital." Speakers of the privileged standard language will commonly denigrate or even deny the existence of the "local" variations. Thus in colonial contexts, the colonial language is naturally championed, while creole or pidgin variations on it are dismissed as corrupt and illegitimate.

Nevertheless, within the operations of diglossia, these variations are simply an alternative means of expression, utilized in particular and almost universally recognized contexts. Since the code-shifting between the colonial language, the indigenous language, and pidgin according to the emotional or cultural situation is a common part of postcolonial linguistic experience, this sort of polyglot speech is often encountered in the postcolonial plays. The so-called pidgin language Cameroon playwrights, such as Victor Musinga, Epie Ngome, or J. T. Menget, for example, all do such code-shifting consciously and strategically. In Musinga's *The Tragedy of Mr. No-Balance,* "the self-conscious, cultivated Bih labours to speak good English in the court scene, but later reverts to pidgin, a language in which he can more freely express himself," and in Ngome's *Not in the Name* the schoolgirls Nlinde and Diengu speak pidgin for relaxing among themselves and faultless English "when engaged in more serious matters." Thus the linguistic shifts allow characters to "speak a language that is appropriate to their status in life and to distinguish and differentiate mood in the same character."[30] Werewere Liking, a leading figure in the Cameroon francophone theatre, does not utilize pidgin, but sprinkles her plays with phrases and words drawn from West African languages.[31]

The practice of placing voices within a linguistic continuum became increasingly common among postcolonial dramatists in the late twentieth century, especially in areas, like the Caribbean, where many varieties of the colonial language were spoken. Robert Yeo, prominent among the new Singapore dramatists of the 1980s, specifically evoked this dynamic, observing that "Singapore English is a speech continuum with upper and lower ends."[32] The most popular Singaporean play of the decade was Stella Kan's *Emily of Emerald Hill* (1985), which carefully mixed different levels of English with short passages of Malay and Tamil. One critical assessment of this play praised it for its accurate reflection of the current mixture of race and culture in Singapore as well as current language use, observing that "Almost all Singapores possess a range of Englishes to meet the range of people and situations, formal and informal, in their lives."[33]

## Arabic Drama

Before continuing with other postcolonial examples, however, I must point out that the workings of code-switching and diglossia are by no means restricted to the postcolonial situation. Two or more varieties of a language utilized in different social settings within the same linguistic community have occurred in many cultures around the world throughout history, and the heteroglossic potentials of this situation have almost invariably been utilized by the theatre of that culture, attuned as it is to the linguistic practices that surround it. I have already mentioned the theatrical heteroglossia that was inspired by the diglossia of Latin and the emerging vernaculars in the early Renaissance and in the competing variations of Italian dialect theatre or of modern Chinese. One further important example should be added, which in part overlaps with post-colonial usage, and that is the Arabic drama.

Elsaid Badawi, one of the leading historians of Arabic drama, has claimed that "in the Arab theatre, perhaps more than any other theater in the world, the problem of language still looms large both for drama-tists and those who care about this language-based art."[34] The leading countries in the development of modern Arabic drama share the colo-nial experience (not coincidentally, since the importation of European-style drama was part of the colonial experience). Nevertheless, the "problem of language" is very different in these than in other postcolo-nial countries, since here the colonial languages, primarily English and French, were imposed not only upon indigenous tribal languages, when they still existed, but upon the intervening language, Arabic, which had already been imposed on these languages during the great era of Islamic expansion from 632 to 750. In a number of North African countries, however, especially in Algeria, a substantial community still exists speaking the local Berber language, Kabyle, and the appearance of play-wrights and performers from this culture at the end of the twentieth century has provided examples unusual in the Arab world of a het-eroglossic theatre mixing Arabic, the colonial language (here French), and the indigenous language (Kabyle). The author-performers Fellag and Sid Ahmed Agoumi and the playwright Aziz Chouaki have all developed forms of this trilingual expression. In a 2003 interview, Chouaki described his motivations and process with particular clarity:

At home, we talked roughly 35 percent Kabyle, 55 percent French, and 10 percent dialectal Arabic, and according to the time of day or the age of the people one was talking to, one spoke this or that lan-guage. Each situation had its register, and one moved naturally from one to another. In other words, there was a Kabyle core surrounded by the French we spoke at school and the dialectal Arabic of the streets. This is the language I am seeking when I write. I try to seize its particular impact. This patchwork, harlequin, bastard language is of an incredible literary modernity. It's pure Joyce. When I am in a writing phase, the four languages of my county [the fourth is literary Arabic] cry out "Here" in my head. Then a subtle play of unconscious protocols takes over that decided that such and such a verb will sound Arabic or such and such an adjective French or Kabyle. It's very strange, very creole; it recalls the language spoken in the Algerian and Mediterranean ports of the eighteenth century. That sort of lingua franca, a mixture of Genoese, Arabic, Maltese, Spanish, was the language of the sailors, of the port. My ideal is to cobble together a writing that would be a sort of linguistic free zone. That is my ideal.[35]

Clearly this is an even more extreme form of heteroglossia than that of normal code-switching, which tends to keep at least phases or sections of speeches in discrete languages, although as Chouaki points out, it results in something rather close to the complex mixtures of historical creole and pidgin languages. At times also, Chouaki, like his fellow multicultural dramatists, uses the more conventional arrangement of having different characters in his play speak distinctly different languages. "All scenes of hybridity fascinate me," he remarks, citing as a "typical example" a scene in his 2002 play *L'Etoile d'Alger* "when Whiba and Moussa make love in a car until they climax, she in Arabic, he in Kabyle."[36]

Although Berber-based performance is growing in North Africa, the heteroglossic Kabyle-influenced theatre of Algeria remains so far a rather special case. It has certain parallels, however, with a growing interest in Egypt with the presentation of Nubian culture on stage. The pioneering work here was the 1999 *Hekayat Nas El-Nahr* (Tales of the river dwellers) based on the writings of the Egyptian Nubian author Jajjaj Hassan Addoul and dealing with the flooding of Nubian lands by the proposed Aswan Dam. Dramaturg Hazem Azmy noted that a goal of the production was clearly heteroglossic: "to allow each voice its moment of realization without favoring any other voices."[37] Thus, although the basic language of the production was Arabic, the Nubian members of the cast also spoke a mixture of the two main Nubian languages, Matoko and Fadeji, along with a few words of Greek, English, and surprisingly, even Hieroglyphic.

The major linguistic tension and site of language negotiation in Arabic theatre, however, exists not, as in the majority of postcolonial drama, between the colonial language, indigenous languages, and the various creoles and pidgins that lie between, but within the Arabic language itself. Long before the colonial period, the language of the Koran, Fusha, had been established as the formal language of the Islamic world. Before the colonial period Fusha was universally recognized as not only the language of Islamic teaching but of poetic expression. When European theatre was introduced to Lebanon, Syria, and Egypt in the mid–nineteenth century, the first assumption was that it too would be written in Fusha, but almost immediately the use of Fusha, never spoken colloquially, to depict the everyday scenes of drama was attacked as unbelievable.

Ya'cub Sannu, one of the founders of modern Arabic theatre, not only broke away from the literary use of Fusha to write in colloquial Arabic, but created truly heteroglossic comedies, using different varieties of spoken Arabic to reflect different cultural and educational backgrounds, including even pidgin Arabic for resident foreigners. This practice was strongly criticized by purist critics who condemned Sannu's work for its lack of dignity.[38] During the early twentieth century, various attempts were made to find a compromise between Fusha and colloquial speech. The best known of all Arab dramatists, Tawfiq al-Hakim, began his career by returning to the heteroglossic method of Sannu, allowing "each of his characters, in plays set in our time, speak in their own specific way."[39] This suiting of language level to the social level of the speaker, with those of education and breeding speaking Fusha and those of the lower classes speaking some form of the colloquial, has been one of the most common ways of creating biglossic drama in the Arabic theatre, although another, related practice has been to use the contrasting language forms to mark different levels of artistic expression within the drama. The Algerian dramatist Bachtarzi Mahiéddine explained the process in a 1932 interview:

> Within the same play we juxtapose literary and spoken Arabic. . . . In scenes of light comedy we have given the preference to colloquial Arabic, but for scenes with more elevated dialogue (love scenes or conversations between characters occupying a certain social position) . . . we have employed literary Arabic.[40]

Although al-Hakim's example inspired a number of other dramatists, strong support for colloquial expression did not develop until the 1960s, when Nasser's pan-Arab socialism gave new dignity to the common people and their speech. During the 1960s drama flourished, especially in Egypt, and heteroglossic expression was an important part of this. A particularly striking political use of biglossic dramatic expression was the *al-Shab'aniin* (The sated) of Ahmed Said, from 1967. The corrupted "sated" of the title, indifferent to the sufferings of the common people, all spoke Fusha. Others spoke colloquial Arabic. The traditional "higher" language "was thus shown as an instrument of subjugation while colloquial Arabic was openly hailed in the play as the tongue of the decent—the workers, peasants, soldiers, and other of society's so-called have-nots."[41]

The decision to write in Fusha, in colloquial Arabic, or in some biglossic combination of the two remains a strongly contested one within the Arab world, although the late twentieth century saw more official recognition of the colloquial languages and thus a tendency, at least in plays set in the present, to represent more accurately the language actually heard on the streets, whether monoglossic or heteroglossic. In 1979 Tunisia took the lead in this direction, according colloquial Arabic official equal status with Fusha. In a directive to all Tunisian theatre artists, the minister of culture declared that the text of a play need only reflect "genuine" usage, and could thus be in "Fusha or colloquial, urban or Bedouin."[42]

## Derek Walcott and Code-Shifting

Such official recognition of colloquial speech, however, has not removed the tension between writing in the privileged Fusha, which is understood throughout the Arab world but removed from the everyday language of almost any individual Arabic speaker, and writing in the vital and natural local variations, which limit the work to the audience of a particular community. Beyond this tension of course lie the competing claims of the local language, such as Berber, claiming yet another community, and the colonial language, especially French, which, if employed, offers the potential of performance and recognition in Europe. Variations of this tension are widely shared by postcolonial dramatists around the world. Derek Walcott, one of the most distinguished of such dramatists, noted in a 1977 interview that he had "not only a duel racial personality but a dual linguistic personality." Although his "real language," and tonally his "basic language," is his native patois, he speaks English and relies upon a basic English for easier audience comprehension.[43] In the 1970 introduction to *Dream on Monkey Mountain and Other Plays,* he suggested that a writer in his position should make "creative use of his schizophrenia, an electric fusion of the old and the new."[44] Thus most of his plays, while dominated by English, suggest the tension created by the suppressed patois through its breaking forth in the form of code-shifting. As early as his second play, *Tri-Jean and His Brothers,* we find the various brothers moving back and forth from English to patois according to the social situation or emotional pressure. This is particularly clear in the case of Mi-Jean, who attempts to impress the colonialist planter with his elegant English: "when you start theorizing that there's an equality of importance in the creatures of this earth, when you animadvertently imbue mere animals with the animus or soul, I have to call you a crooked-minded pantheist." At this point, however, his pompous speech is interrupted by the bleating of a goat, which, suggests the stage direction, sounds like "Hear! Hear!" The somewhat rattled Mi-Jean responds, his English slipping: "Oh, shut up, you can't hear two people talking?" In fact there are two people talking, the "true" Mi-Jean and the affected English-speaking one, as becomes clear almost at once, when, under the goading of the planter and the continued bleating of the goat, Mi-Jean lapses entirely into patois: "On, shut you damn mouth, both o'all you! I ain't care who right who wrong! I talking now! What you ever study? I ain't even finish making my points and all two of you interrupting."[45] Varieties of code-shifting are utilized in all of Walcott's plays. Not surprisingly, the Conteur in *Malcochon, or Six in the Rain* varies his language according to whether he is addressing the audience in straightforward English or various characters in their differing dialects. Lestrade in *Dream on Monkey Mountain* begins with an affected English like that of Mi-Jean in *Tri-Jean and His Brothers,* but as his situation deteriorates his assumed and artificial language does also, moving through a patois into almost inarticulate cries.[46]

Walcott's later *A Branch of the Blue Nile* (1983) provides a particularly rich selection of language varieties. In discussing this play, Stephen P. Breslow has specifically invoked Bakhtin and the concept of heteroglossia, noting the wide variety of "voices" employed, often by the same characters. Within this variety, the major dialogue is between the language of Shakespeare, perhaps the central example of English colonial discourse, and the native dialect of the Trinidadian actors who are rehearsing a production of *Antony and Cleopatra*. Breslow notes not only the operation of hybridity, but its social and cultural import:

> The two realms are inextricably mixed, and their multiple interactions form the central action and meaning of the play. Even on the most minute linguistic level, when Walcott's actors unavoidably interject their Trinidadian accents into Shakespeare's text—when Chris, for example, blurts "Your Lord? No. He gone out"—Trinidadian and Shakespearean "languages" are comically interwoven. This commingling of the performer's national language with the language of the staged text adopts even further import, when we perceive it in extended cultural and political terms: The postcolonial, former slave society struggling to reenact the masterpieces of the colonizer's culture, and the postcolonials chastising each other for not getting the masterpiece "right."[47]

Colonial negotiations with the classic text of the colonizers provide a fertile site for such subversive hybridizations. A particularly complex and interesting example of this was the *Tartuffe* created by the South Indian company Tara in Bristol, which toured in England, Spain, Turkey, Egypt, Australia, and Hong Kong before being presented at the National Theatre in London, the first all-Asian play to be presented at that theatre. The play was based on the actual importation of the play to seventeenth-century India by a French traveler and was performed using Indian popular theatre conventions and a variety of Indian languages, translated in part by two "story-tellers." The dynamics of hybridization dominated this study of a French classic translated into and performed in an acquired colonial English, interspersed with "native" material, which was only translated in part. At one key moment Orgon's children exchanged verses in Urdu from an Indian epic romance, *Heer and Ranjha*. One of the storytellers stepped forward and, the convention having already been established, announced, "Another translation!" But after a brief pause, she announced, "Why bother!" and stepped back amid a burst of laughter from the audience. Director Jatinder Verma comments on the multiple subtexts of this striking moment:

> In some senses it was a defiant validation of a language which has a history of absence on the British stages. In another sense it was simply the recognition by all of the un-translatability of languages; and, paradoxically, the recognition of a common human experience by this fact of difference.[48]

Both of these subtexts, the validation of languages previously silenced in the colonialist theatre tradition and the recognition and acceptance of the fact of difference, are involved around the world in the emergence of heteroglossic postcolonial theatre.

Although the use of different codes by a single character can have a powerful dramatic effect, as can be seen in the constant linguistic shifts in Walcott's *Branch of the Blue Nile,* postcolonial drama more often follows the traditional dramatic practice of having each character employ a fairly distinctive mode of speech throughout, even though all these modes might be located along a pidgin/creole continuum. So the Nigerian play *Katakata for Sofahead* by Segun Oyekunle, cited by Gilbert and Tompkins for its "resistance to the imperial language," establishes "in language a site for anti-colonial activity."[49] Here the imperial superstrate is represented by the basic but functional English of the prison guard, while most of the prisoners speak various mesolects of pidgin, combining distinctly English elements with equally distinctive indigenous ones and blends of the two, as in Okolo's speech:

> You no sabi any ting, Yam Head! Which policeman fit aks for big man in particulars, hinside Mercedez, "King of de Road," for dat matter? Dem nefer born dat police for dis we kontry. Na dat day water go pass im gari.[50]

An additional lectual level is provided by Lateef, a new inmate in the prison, who also speaks pidgin, but with much more English content, marking his greater exposure to a colonial education. Gilbert and Tompkins suggest the multiple functions of this mixture of voices. The use of pidgin "invests the prisoners with a power that their incarceration denies them: the ability to enforce their own linguistic freedom. At the same time, the street pidgin establishes a different social hierarchy, just as the prison context sets up principles which differ from those of the 'outside.'"[51]

## The Polyglottal Stage

Postcolonial writings on language naturally and rightly emphasize the wide variations in the relationships between local and imperial languages, particularly in respect to what the linguistic negotiations between them reveal about power relationships, dominance, and resistance. The literatures and the drama of the postcolonial world, in which language is foregrounded and often highly self-reflexive, has been a rich area for the development of the particular type of heteroglossia that involves such linguistic phenomena as the development of pidgin languages and the so-called creole continuum. Heteroglossia on the postcolonial stage is, however, a phenomenon even more widespread and complex than these cultural negotiations might suggest, since they are themselves often embedded in cultural contexts that are heteroglossic in the more traditional sense that I have discussed elsewhere in this book. As Christopher Balme notes in his study of postcolonial, "syncretic," theatre, the cultural components of such theatre "derive almost without exception from the fact that in most postcolonial countries europhone syncretic theatre is situated in a bi- or multilingual context." Most of the playtexts Balme analyzes in fact make use of more than one language, applying something of the strategy of code-switching not only to dialect levels, but to quite distinct languages. Indeed, Balme asserts, "switching languages in specific contexts and from one mode of expression to another is a feature of syncretic theatre."[52]

Balme's examples of the multiple language theatre he calls "the polyglottal stage" are drawn from sub-Saharan Africa and New Zealand, areas that, like the Caribbean, are rich in postcolonial heteroglossic experimentation. Wole Soyinka's Nigeria is characterized by Balme as a "polyethnic and polylingual state," which is something of an understatement. Nigeria in fact has no less than nine official or national languages: Edo, Efik, Adamawa Fulfulde, Hausa, Idoma, Igbo, Yerwa Kanun, Yoruba, and English, and linguists list an additional 496 living languages spoken there.[53] This provides a particularly difficult challenge for the dramatist who insists upon emancipating himself from the "colonial" language, as, most notably, Kenyan dramatist Ngugi Wa Thiongo has in *Decolonizing the Mind*,[54] since a multiplicity of languages is a common African condition, and while most potential theatregoers will understand several, the colonial language is often the only one understood by all.

The most common dramatic response to this is some variation of syncretism, tempering the colonial language with dialect, patois, pidgin, or even full-blown indigenous languages, a heteroglossia sometimes operating within a single character, sometimes between characters, and sometimes structurally, between different parts of the play (songs in the indigenous language, for example). Although Ola Rotimi is less well known internationally than his countryman Wole Soyinka, his reputation in his native Nigeria is even greater and his experiments with dramatic heteroglossia much more extensive and central to his work. Rotimi's early plays, from the 1960s, rely predominantly upon English. Rotimi himself called this work an attempt at "a domestication of the foreign [English] language," at "handling the English language within the terms of traditional linguistic identity."[55] In a 1987 lecture, "The Trials of African Literature," he elaborated on this position, but suggested a greater role for linguistic mixtures:

As regards the overblown, persistent argument on language, this writer thinks it is such a time-wasting distraction, all thing considered. The real issue should not be *why* an African writer resorts to perpetuating a colonial tongue. Rather, for the debate to be worthwhile, it should bear on *how* the writer uses that tongue to express the conditions and yearnings of his linguistically *diverse* peoples. To ignore the fact of linguistic heterogeneity, is to be hypocritical, because it is the very multi-linguality of the peoples—or to put it more bluntly—it is the very *ethnic* promiscuity in the land that, in the first place, necessitated the adoption of that foreign tongue to serve as a neutral base for communication among a reasonable cross-section of the people.

The incongruity of a foreign language in an African work can further be "tempered" by a sensitive intermingling of the foreign language with some indigenous linguistic representations. This is most feasible in the genre of drama, and recent experiments by this writer along this line have received encouraging response from audiences.[56]

These "recent experiments" were Rotimi's *If* (1979) and *Hopes of the Living Dead* (1985). The former is set in the backyard of a Nigerian apartment block where the speakers use the same variety of languages that one might actually hear in such a situation: Standard English, several local varieties of English, pidgin, and indigenous local languages, such as Kalabari. *Hopes of the Living Dead* takes this experimentation much further. It tells, in highly theatrical terms, the story of the composer Ikoli Harcourt Whyte, who fought with authorities over the closing of a program for the treatment of leprosy in the 1920s. The authorities hoped to exploit the linguistic and cultural diversity among the patients to prevent them from making a unified protest, a strategy the unifying efforts of Harcourt Whyte successfully defeated. Rotimi saw this historical event as offering an important model for developing cross-linguistic and cultural political power in Nigeria today, and so the speaking of a variety of languages within the drama was an essential part of its message. Rotimi noted that over fifteen languages were used in the play, but he also made it clear that his concern was not linguistic verisimilitude, as one might naturally expect, but the overall message of linguistic negotiation and the development of common political goals. This is made clear in Rotimi's foreword to the published text:

> Although specific languages are given to the characters in this play, the producer/director is not bound by these allocations. Any character may be assigned any language, depending on the linguistic varieties which the actors on hand represent. What is important is for the languages spoken to reflect the cultural spread and the linguistic diversity of the nation where it is being produced.[57]

One might expect little heteroglossic activity within the popular folk drama, created for a local audience and based upon their language, but even there the awareness of living in a polyglot culture has its effect on dramatic language. The plays of Yoruba folk dramatist Moses Olaiya are cast in the day-to-day language of his essentially nonliterate audience, yet reflect the complex linguistic world of that audience by shifting from the formal register of Yoruba, Oyo, to dialects like Ijegu or Ekiti, or from these various forms of Yoruba to pidgin.[58] The plays also often contain characters who speak English, almost always improperly, as in the play *Tokunbo,* which employs the classic comic language device of the character improperly using a higher-class language that he does not really understand in order to improve his social status. Here Baba Sala, after a three-week trip to America, attempts to display his new language skills, producing such macaronic displays as the following:

BABA SALA: All. Hawa you re. Wel wel come re. Am alright re, it okay re.[59]

The informal and flexible nature of popular folk theatre also allows for linguistic shifting and adjustment within a particular performance. Moses Olaiya, like many traditional folk entertainers, also takes the leading roles, such as Baba Sala, in his own productions, and thus can orchestrate linguistic shifting within a performance. Olu Obafemi reports:

I have witnessed occasions when Moses Olaiya has, in the middle of a performance, switched from Yoruba to Pidgin English. A ready example was during his performance of *Dayamondi* (Diamond) at the University of Ilorin. He had sensed the dissatisfaction of his multilingual audience with his Yoruba dialogue and changed from Yoruba to pidgin without losing much in terms of providing entertainment.[60]

The other major West African center of drama is Ghana, whose language situation is somewhat less complex than that of Nigeria but only relatively. Only English is recognized as an official language, but nine others are taught in schools and heard on radio and television, and linguists recognize a total of seventy-nine spoken in the nation. Obviously this means that as in Nigeria most theatregoers are multilingual, and one of the earliest examples of theatrical mixing of languages in sub-Saharan Africa is the 1915 study of the effects of colonization on Ghanaian society *The Blinkards* by Kobina Sekyi, which radically blends English and Fanti.[61] Nevertheless, there is a long-standing dichotomy in Ghana between the scripted drama, which strongly favors English, and the nonscripted popular concert party performances, which favor the Ghanaian languages, but which are highly heteroglossic. Catherine Cole, who has published a major study of these performances, reports that they are

> notable for their loquaciousness and unruly amalgamation of disparate languages. While predominantly performed in the Akan dialects of Twi and Fanti, concert parties include English, Hausa, Ga, Yoruba, Pidgin English, Nzema, Zabrama, and Liberian Kru expressions. Such multilingualism is generally not a problem for Ghanaian audiences, since performances are no more polyglot than any open-air market in the country. But foreigners who do not speak any Ghanaian languages are typically mystified by these shows, which are confidently aimed at local rather than international audiences.[62]

Although this sort of linguistic diversity cannot be found in the written Ghanaian drama, it would be quite mistaken to think that although this drama is predominately English, this rules out heteroglossic manipulation. The many varieties of English available allow a distinct differentiation of levels of discourse, which dramatists like Ama Ata Aidoo have used most effectively both to delineate character and to suggest social relationships. Dapo Adelugba, in a study of Aidoo's work, finds six levels of languages operating in *The Dilemma of a Ghost,* from 1964: "the American English of Eulalie Yawson, the educated African English of Ato Yawson, the stylized poetry and prose of the Prelude, the childlike talk of Boy and Girl, the chit-chat in verse of the 1st Woman and the 2nd Woman, and the language of Nana, Akyere, Petu, Mansa, Akroma, and Monka," which, "although 'transcribed' into English by a dexterous dramatist," are clearly recognizable as "a Ghanaian language, probably Fanti."[63]

## South African Experiments

Balme cites South Africa as an African country "offering clear linguistic analogies to Nigeria" in terms of polyglot theatre.[64] Actually, as Ghana and Cameroon suggest, this phenomenon is widespread across a continent that although extremely diverse, provides many examples of "nations" arbitrarily defined by colonialism wherein dramatists must negotiate between the imposed colonial lingua franca and the often numerous indigenous languages that place serious restrictions upon communication. Dramatists in Nigeria and South Africa do not necessarily experience this tension in greater degree than other African dramatists, but the larger and more diverse culture of scripted theatre in these countries has resulted in greater attention to the language of postcolonial theatre than elsewhere in the continent.

Temple Hauptfleisch has been particularly engaged with the question of heteroglossic theatre in South Africa, noting that "language and language variants are part and parcel of our society in South Africa—and have become an inherent part of our theatre. One of the most exciting developments in this regard has been the evolution of a new poetry of the theatre stage, in a language born of the polyglot environment in and around our cities."[65] South Africa has eleven "official" languages—two coming from Europe (English and Afrikaans), four from the Nguni family, headed by Zulu and Xhosa, three from the Sotho family, and two others, Venda and Tsonga. There are also a large number of local language variants and pidgins such as Afrikaner English and South African English. A particularly interesting example is the multilingual "town talk" often called tsotsitaal, which is a kind of pidgin based not upon any particular language, but upon the linguistic melting pot of South African city culture. Originally an Afrikaans dialect primarily used by criminals, it spread through black groups in urban areas and was widely taken up by urban youth, musicians, and other artists.[66] To be complete, one should also include the wide variety of immigrant languages—German, Portuguese, Greek, Dutch, Yiddish, and so on—and their own variants of English and Afrikaans.

Hauptfleisch, summarizing this cultural and social heteroglossia, suggests that it would seem logical to assume that South African writing, and particularly writing for the theatre "would tend to be multilingual texts which—directly or indirectly—mirror the language mix of the society with which they are dealing."[67] In fact, the cultural pressures of apartheid and linguistic separation and the theatrical pressures of seeking to appeal to a presumably homogeneous canonical practice or popular audience, long discouraged (and often continue to discourage) dramatists from addressing the linguistic reality of their culture. South African dramatists have traditionally either created what Hauptfleisch calls "closed" situations, "which ignored the existence of anyone outside the given culture," or else "transliterated" the language of any outsider "into the base language of the given culture." In this latter case, the play is written in a chosen official language, usually English or Afrikaans, and then "'markers' from the character's 'real' language are planted onto the base language to *suggest* that the person is speaking that particular language or dialect."[68] The practice is closely akin to the traditions of stage dialects in Europe and America.

Robert Kavanagh's *Theatre and Cultural Struggle in South Africa* traces the development of socially engaged South African theatre from Athol Fugard's first play, *No-Good Friday* in 1958, and the Union of South African Artists' *King Kong* the following year to works of the black consciousness movement in the early 1970s, such as Mthuli Shezi's *Shanti* and Gibson Kente's *Too Late.* For each of the plays he discusses, Kavanagh provides a detailed linguistic analysis, which clearly demonstrates the accuracy of Hauptfleisch's observation. At most only occasional words of tsotsitaal are used for characters who would clearly be speaking that tongue in real life. More often only vague suggestions of dialects are used, and in some cases dramatists followed the position of the Black Consciousness Movement, which condemned the use of African languages as divisive.[69]

Until the 1970s there was no significant development of what Hauptfleisch calls the "third option" in South African theatre—a truly multilingual theatre that would reflect the actual polyglot character of the surrounding culture. This situation changed markedly, however, during the 1970s and 1980s. During this time South Africa experienced massive antiapartheid dissent, as well as the emergence of a significant alternative theatre movement, much involved in this struggle and much influenced by Brecht and the European and American political theatre and collective creations of the period. Particularly important was the development in the early 1970s of dramas located "in the urban spaces of the oppressed and attempting to represent their experiences,"[70] an interest that was pursued with even more dedication and urgency after the uprising in the black townships and ghettos in 1976–77. New government restrictions and censorship did not stifle but in fact encouraged more devoted and determined political and socially oriented theatre.

A number of university theatres contributed to the new movement, the most important of them being Workshop '71, which gradually evolved from a drama workshop directed by Robert Mshengu Kavanagh (Robert McClaren), a lecturer at Witwatersrand University, into a major professional company. Kavanagh felt that one of the first concerns of the new venture was to "go beyond the impasse concerning the use of language in South African theatre," since the continued use of English "would not be democratic, and it would frustrate its dialogic intention." Thus the workshop, at its very beginning, took what Kavanagh rightly describes as "an important stand on language."

First, it insisted that, at all drama workshops and in all meetings and discussions, members should feel free to express themselves in any of the main South African languages. Second, Workshop '71's first play, *Crossroads,* though still substantially in English, included large sections of action and dialogue in the everyday languages of the majority in the Witwatersrand, and did not restrict the use of these languages to comic effect only. Particularly prominent in this use of majority languages was the serious and substantial use made of authentic tsotsitaal.

As an example of the technique, Kavanagh cites a passage from a street scene near the beginning of *Crossroads:*

(*Seilaneng saunters up to Peter and accosts him saucily*)
SEILANENG: Hello, Loverboy.
PETER (*lowering newspaper slightly*): Hello, Dudu. Go bjang?
SEILANENG: Ke teng. O kae wean?
PETER: Where you from?
SEILANENG: I'm from Diepkloof.
PETER: Jy jol weer in Diepkloof?

SEILANENG: Ya, ke jola le Madubula.
PETER: Moenie jol in Diepkloof. Ouens van da is moegoes.[71]

This heteroglossic approach, along with a resistant political message, characterized most of the offerings of Workshop '71, up to its final and most famous production, *Survival,* in 1976, which was developed out of the life narratives of black male workers in prison, and mixed English and the vernaculars of the prisoners in song, narration, and enactment. It opened at the Space, a major experimental venue in Cape Town, in May 1976 and played in townships on the Witwatersrand in the wake of the Soweto Uprising. Its subject matter and its timing caused it to be received by audiences and the police as part of that uprising,[72] thus insuring it an important place in modern South African political history. The Space in turn was much influenced, as were other experimental theatres of the next decade, by the production approach of Workshop '71 "combining the techniques of workshop, the didactic thrust of Black Consciousness theatre, and elements of township theatre."[73] In terms of heteroglossic production, the township theatre influence was most important, since mixed language performance was an important, if not central part, of that tradition. In his book on township performance, Coplan notes that although the English language dominates this tradition, its dramatists recognize "the widespread use of tsotsitaal and urban dialects of Zulu, Sotho and Xhosa," and thus their scripts are "interlarded with jokes, exclamations, long texts and throwaway lines in a variety of African language and polyglot slang."[74]

The Space, where *Survival* was first performed, was one of the most important of the new experimental theatres of the 1970s. It operated as a club to evade censorship and developed further the reforms associated with Workshop '71, mixing black and white participants and developing collective creations of scripts, such as *Sizwe Banzi Is Dead* (1972), recorded by Athol Fugard, the best known of the artists associated with this theatre. Coplan cites *Survival* and *Sizwe Banzi Is Dead* as leading examples of the blending of the township performance aesthetic with European modes of production. The Space was the first South African theatre to commission a play by a black dramatist, Fatima Dike, whose first two plays, *The Sacrifice of Kreli* (1976) and *The First South African* (1977), were also among the first important heteroglossic South African plays. The first, dealing with a conflict between the British and indigenous people in 1885, allowed each group to utilize its own language, English and Xhosa. The hero of the second is a young man torn between the identities offered by his white father and his Xhosa mother, and is set in the polyglot ghetto where the common language is the colorful tsotsitaal. Afrikaans adds a fourth linguistic component to the naturalistic dialogue of this polyglot script.[75] In 1979 the Space became the People's Space, and specialized in plays about black working people in the cities, such as Matsamela Manaka's *Egoli* (1979), or in rural areas, such as Zakes Mda's *The Hill* (1980).

Johannesburg's Market Theatre opened a few days after the June 1976 uprising and became during the next decade the best-known South African theatre. In many ways it built upon the previous activity of Workshop '71 and the Space, several of whose artists became associated with the new venture, but its claims to be the "only truly national theatre in South Africa" have been questioned by critics such as David Graver and Loren Kruger, who have pointed out that its ties to traditional European-oriented performance and international touring have distanced it more than its predecessors from actual indigenous activity like that of the townships.[76] This orientation is reflected in the Market Theatre's much more cautious treatment of heteroglossic material than was the case with many productions at Workshop '71 or the Space. The first plays presented at the Market were European classics that director Barney Simon believed were relevant to the South African situation: *The Seagull, Marat/Sade, Waiting for Godot,* and Trevor Griffiths's *Comedians.* In 1979 Simon began a series of experimental works more like the collective creations of Workshop '71, with a multiracial cast and collaborative work based on South African situations. Both cast and subject matter here forced the Market to confront the issue of multiple languages. The first work in this series, *Cincinnati,* included scenes in Zulu between an old caretaker and a Zulu call girl, and between the British immigrant Arthur and the Afrikaner boy Pieter, who cannot understand each other's "English."

One of the most famous productions of the Market Theatre was *Woza Albert!* in 1983, another collective piece signed by Percy Mtwa, Mbongeni Ngema, and Barney Simon. The main non-English passages here are songs, but a number of characters speak at least from time to time in other languages, such as the Zulu of Mbongeni (one of the Brechtian devices of a number of Market Theatre productions was that actors played under their own names). The content of these scattered passages is often clearly targeted at the members of the audience who speak that language, not at the majority white audience of the Market Theatre, since the material is often obscene or involved with tribal or intertribal jokes, as Mbongeni's Zulu comment in *Wozu Albert!*: "Yabhodla ingane yenZule ukuba okungu—MSuthu ngabe kudala kuzinyele" [There burps the son of a Zulu; if it was a Sotho he would be shitting].[77] The combination of metatheatrical playfulness and linguistic mixing provides for an interesting variety of language play. In a particularly complex passage Percy, speaking from off stage, provides the "voices" for two other characters, both of whom switch back and forth between English and Afrikaans, for a total of five "voices" provided by a single actor:

> PERCY (As Baas Kun, offstage): Hello? Hello? Lalet Venter? Ja! Now listen here. There's a terrorist here, who's making trouble with my kaffirs. Ek s daar's uitlander hier wat kak maak met my kaffirs. Ja. Hello? Hello? Ag die fuckin' telephone! Bobbejaam! (As Bobbejaan) Ja, Basie? (As Baas Kun) Kom Kom Kom.[78]

*Woza Albert!* marked the high point of Barney Simon's heteroglossic work at the Market. The subsequent *Black Dog* (1984) and *Born in the RSA* (1985) continued to present an image of intercultural and interlinguistic theatre but were more conventional in their use of non-English material, a compromise between Simon's goal of representing the mixed culture of South Africa and communicating effectively with his largely upper-class, largely white, and after *Woza Albert!* potentially international audience. Anne Fuchs, historian of the Market Theatre, describes the situation thus:

> In *Black Dog* language differences were systematized and became part of what Barney himself qualifies as "the different cultures" he attempted to juxtapose on stage. The problem of the Market audience (which was predominantly white) not being able to understand

African languages had by 1984 to be faced by many non-racial or African companies playing there. Barney Simon's solution appears to be the best adapted to the particular circumstances: a minimum token use of African languages which would not hinder communication with a white audience but at the same time entail a certain effort on their part and so constitute a theatrical "sign." . . . Simon was addressing his Market audience not in their own language, but in a deliberately contrived combination of Zulu, Afrikaans and English with the latter serving as a lingua franca.[79]

In short, the true heteroglossia of the culture in fact was turned to essentially monoglossic theatricalization, in the traditional dominant cultural strategy of converting the challenging voice of the Other into a theatrical sign, like a stage dialect.

This does not mean that heteroglossic expression largely disappeared from the Market Theatre during the 1980s, but that its most successful manifestations were presented not by the resident company, but by other groups, more faithful linguistically to the township tradition, that were hosted by the Market during this time. Simon's collaborators on *Woza Albert!*, Percy Mtwa and Mbongeni Ngema, authored plays in 1985 that were more distinctly heteroglossic, a choice closely tied to their social and political commentary. In Ngema's *Asinamali!* (We have no money), five prisoners in a cell relate their stories to each other, stories that often involve shifting language, especially in power relationships. Balme describes a striking sequence in scene 2 where a prisoner is tried and sentenced for a series of unrelated offenses:

A trilingual situation is depicted: the judge speaks Afrikaans, which is rendered into English by the court interpreter; the defendant understands neither language particularly well, and so fragments of these exchanges are translated into Zulu by a Court Orderly. He in turn *selectively* translates the defendant's responses back to the judge. Each rendering results in shifts and slants of meaning until the defendant, Bheki, is struggling like a hapless fish in a net, enmeshed in legal procedures which are everything else but transparent. In performance this linguistic confusion is further underlined by the fact that these exchanges actually gain momentum during the course of the trial until there is almost Babylonian turmoil.[80]

This extremely common use of language as an instrument of oppression, however, is balanced, Balme notes, by many situations "in which multi-lingualism creates an area of freedom in which revenge can be exacted and satirical attacks leveled at white society." Thus in Percy Mtwa's *Bopha!* intertribal jokes are made, "clearly not intended for white consumption," in Zulu and there is much sexually explicit language and humor spoken in an African language "and thus reserved for the African audience." A typical example from *Bopha!* involves a white man who has just been arrested and is discussed by two Zulu policeman. "Pis in die straat," one reports. "An-eke ahamba bonisa umthondo wakhe obomyu yonke indawo" [He was pissing in the street. He cannot expose his red penis all over the place]. The first part of the statement, in Afrikaans, could be understood by the white culprit and the entire audience, but the rest, in Zulu, is directed only to the speakers of that language.[81]

In 1986 the Market Theatre presented what several critics have considered the most comprehensive theatrical statement to date on the linguistic mixing of South Africa, the collective creation *Sophiatown* by the Junction Avenue Theatre Company. The JATC, founded in 1976, specialized in Brechtian documentary pieces dealing with South Africa's recent history. *Sophiatown* was based on the township of that name, destroyed by government edict twenty years before but still remembered and honored as a multiracial center of the emerging urban culture. In addition to offering a variety of characters speaking English, Afrikaans, various African languages, as well as the township "gangster" tongue tsotsitaal, the play also contains many scenes in which language is the central topic of conversation. Thus an entire scene (act 1, scene 4) is conducted almost exclusively in tsotsitaal, involving a language lesson as a visiting Jewish girl, Ruth (who occasionally speaks a bit of Yiddish), attempts to gain an understanding of that tongue to get along in her new surroundings. Later, Ruth speaks a bit of tsotsitaal to the journalist Jakes, who speaks a kind of parody newsroom English, and Mr. Fahfee, who speaks a gambler's slang. They are impressed that a Jewish girl has picked up this language, and Jakes observes approvingly: "She's like us, Fahfee. What am I? The boere want us in separate locations, but what am I? I speak Zulu, Xhosa, Sotho, English, Afrikaans. In moments of weakness I even speak tsotsitaal." Similarly Mingus the gangster shifts easily, even in midspeech, between his basic language, Afrikaans, American slang, and tsotsitaal, as in: "Charlie! Gaan vat daai Delilah and bring her hierso. She's a rubber-neck. Gaan! Speed." Hauptfleisch, who cites these examples from the unpublished playtext, concludes, "By simply allowing the *possibility* of a multilingual conversational convention, this 'mirroring' of reality is, at this level at least, far more 'real' than in most previous plays."[82]

The Junction Avenue Theatre's next major work, *Tooth and Nail* (1989), represented a new direction for the company, assembled out of fragments and strongly influenced by contemporary international experimental companies. Multilingualism is represented here by an interpreter figure that director Malcolm Purkey has called "our most successful realization so far" of the concerns of communication, missed translation, and misunderstanding in a multilinguistic society.[83] The interpreter moves among the fragments of the play, mediating between languages and cultures, translating and sometimes distorting Tswana, Sotho, Zulu, English, and even an artificial "spirit language" invented by the company. Purkey has compared this heteroglossia to normal social experience in South Africa: "If you go to any trade union meeting they will speak in English, then in Zulu, then in Tswama, than in Sotho. So translation is very fundamental to our lives. Mistranslation, misunderstanding, language gaps, language problems are fundamental to South African dilemmas." Within the theatre, as in politics, "It is a game of when which part of the audience hears what. What do they say? Is the translation accurate? Is it a commentary? . . . And then you can play games where you send out messages in one language so the other group can't understand and so on."[84]

## The Trans-Pacific Axis

Aside from the Caribbean and sub-Saharan Africa, the geographic area that has most engaged the attention of students of postcolonial drama has been the Trans-Pacific axis, linking Canada, Australia, and New Zealand. Both Balme and Gilbert and Tompkins devote significant space to examples from this area, and it is the central concern of Marc Maufort's *Transgressive Itineraries,* which, though its concerns are much more general than specific linguistic practice, grounds its usage of hybridizations in the theoretical writing of Bhabha on hybridity and Bakhtin on dialogism and heteroglossia.[85]

The revival of interest in Aboriginal language in Australia has been closely related to heteroglossic study elsewhere, not only because of the alternative this presents to the colonialist language, English, but because, in contrast to the monoglossic claims of the colonial tongue, Aboriginal language is itself conceived as heteroglossic. Hodge and Mishra in their postcolonial analysis of Australian literature, *Dark Side of the Dream,* point out that

> Traditional Aborigines were multilingual, and contemporary Aborigines have their own urgent reason for a fascination for and facility with linguistic pluralism. Aboriginal literature both traditional and modern is characterized by its dialogic qualities, multilingual and multimedia forms that manage diversity by giving it full play in polyphonic genres of text.[86]

The first drama by an Aboriginal author to achieve major recognition was *The Dreamers* (1983), by Jack Davis, whose work, fusing Western and Aboriginal language and aesthetic features, provided a model for subsequent Aboriginal dramatists during the following decades. *The Dreamers* is basically written in English, but it contains characters who sometimes speak in the Aboriginal language Nyungar. A central symbolic figure, the Aboriginal Dancer, who can be seen by the audience but not by the characters in the play, speaks only Nyungar. The climax of the play is a Nyungar chant by the Dancer, in a pool of light. For the non-Nyungar-speaking audience member "this figure is reassuringly recognizable but completely incomprehensible, signifying only Aboriginality . . . and the 'universal' grief appropriate to a moment of death." For Nyungar-speaking audiences, the message is much different: "The white man is evil, evil! My people are dead. Dead, dead dead. The White man kill my people. Kill, kill, kill, kill."[87] Clearly this is another striking example of the use of bilingualism noted by Balme, in which "multilingualism creates an area of freedom in which revenge can be exacted and satirical attacks leveled at white society." Hodge and Mishra, in their study of postcolonial literature in Australia, call such usage an "antilanguage strategy." In the closing chant of *The Dreamers,* they suggest, Nyungar speakers are "separated from the nonNyungars alongside them in the theatre and incorporated into a community with the Dancer." But simultaneously, and equally importantly, a counter-strategy of misdirection is being utilized: "Meanwhile the White audience will have the illusion of having been welcomed without reservation into an inner circle of universal human feelings."[88]

The nostalgic use of Aboriginal speech to signify the colonial destruction of the culture that language represents characterizes the early works of Davis, beginning with his first play, the epic *Kullark* (1979), but gradually he and other heteroglossic Australian playwrights shifted to linguistic mixtures to suggest the complex ongoing linguistic negotiations in that region. Davis's *No Sugar* (1985) offers a wide variety of linguistic variation: academic, professional, and legal English, passages in Nyungar, and local pidgin variants of English, including a significant postcolonial variation known as Kimberly English, described by Stephen Muecke as a pidgin developed by Australian Aboriginal peoples "which in fact made possible their political unification to combat the destructive pressures of White society."[89] The opening of a story told by Billy Kimberly, a black tracker from the north, suggests the polyglot nature of this linguistic mode:

> I bin stop Liveringa station and my brother, he bun run from Oombulgarri [*Holding up four fingers*] That many days. Night time too. He bin tell me 'bout them *gudeeah*. They bin two, three stockman *gudeeah*. Bin stop along that place, Juada Station, and this one *gudeeah* Midha George, he was ridin' and he come to this river and he see these two old womans, *kooris,* there in the water hold. He says, what you doin' here? They say they getting' *gugja*.[90]

Such experimentation grew richer and more complex in plays dealing with Aboriginal life in the 1990s, as may be seen in Nicholas Parsons's *Dead Heart* (1994), which features two Aborigines who refuse to learn

English and speak to each other their native Pintupi and to outsiders pidgin. Helen Gilbert notes the postcolonial subversive significance of this mixture:

> In performance, unlike in the published text where the Pintupi dialogue is glossed, this articulation of linguistic autonomy confirms the agency of Aboriginal languages and their associated lore/law. An extensive use of Pidgin also abrogates the privilege of standard English by hybridizing its grammatical structures and its lexicon to suit the purposes of the colonized group. Even the white "politpalla" is induced to speak Pidgin in an effort to effectively administer his version of law and order, a situation which, paradoxically, undermines his authority in thematic terms and also in terms of the play's performed landscape.[91]

The interest in Aboriginal language and culture that developed in Australia in the late twentieth century and that resulted in a flowing of theatre by Aboriginal authors and dealing with Aboriginal material had its parallel in New Zealand beginning with the political and cultural Maori Renaissance of the 1970s. Within this context appeared what was probably the first play written by a Maori, Harry Dansey's *Te Raukura: The Feathers of the Albatross* (1974). In this historical play, Dansey sought to provide period authenticity by including sung and spoken passages in Maori. As a concession to non-Maori audiences, he established a convention whereby Maori characters would begin an interchange in their own language and then switch to English. In production, however, he discovered to his reported delight that the Maori actors would often in fact shift back into their native language. Balme, who quotes Dansey on this phenomenon, notes that this created a situation encountered in other postcolonial situations, where the bilingualism indicated in the text, but usually mitigated by printed glosses, in performance in fact "creates a divided receptive situation which favors bilingual (Maori) spectators" while it "partially excludes audience members without knowledge of the indigenous language."[92]

Hone Tuwhare's *On Ilkla Moor B'aht'at* (In the wilderness without a hat, 1977) uses Maori much more extensively, and prefigures its more general use in subsequent Maori drama. Maori is spoken by mythologi-

cal ancestral figures, in ritual situations, and by characters from the
North Island, where the language is still commonly heard. Tuwhare,
like Dansey, was concerned about communication with a non-Maori
public, however, and suggested in the text that the longer passages be
translated by a loudspeaker system, anticipating the more common subsequent practice of supertitles.[93]

Both bilingualism and a more regularized bicultural dramatic structure developed from the Maori Renaissance interest in traditional Maori
performances held in the ancestral meeting houses on communal land,
the Marae. In 1990 the Taki Rua company of Wellington began to present what they called Theatre Marae, contemporary productions based
on Maori performance protocols, including a traditional opening chant
(mihi) and summons (karanga) along with embedded formal speeches
(whaikorero) in Maori. Maori is also used in scenes of intimacy, when
characters "are in a heightened state emotionally and English is not adequate to express what they are feeling."[94] The leading Maori dramatist
to develop out of this was Hone Kouka, whose first play, *Mauri Tu*
(1991), a solo performance piece acted by the author, deals directly with
the predicament of the native Other in contemporary society. The audience, moreover, is confronted directly by the question of language,
when a long untranslated speech in Maori is followed by the lines, "So
this is what it's like when a Maori speaks in his own tongue . . . or is it
that you just switch off? . . . Listen here, listen well. This incomprehen-
sion is what it is like for many of us in this world."[95] The distance of this
challenge from the rather apologetic use of Maori by Dansey or
Tuwhare, with their strategies of accommodation, indicates how attitudes toward language usage have changed between the 1970s and
1990s. In the work of Kouka, as in that of postcolonial dramatists
around the world, the empire is not only writing back, but, in more
strikingly theatrical terms, speaking back.

The majority of what has been characterized as postcolonial theatre
has been primarily occupied, in respect to language, with the complex
negotiations between colonial languages and indigenous languages, as
well as with the broad field of communications opened up by the utilization of pidgin and creole forms and the operations of register change
and code-switching. There is yet another sort of postcolonial theatre,
however, in which heteroglossic expression is also central, and which

opens up this practice in quite another direction. The standard model of colonialism, in which a colonial language and culture is imposed upon one or more indigenous languages and cultures, is in most of the world a highly oversimplified one. Australia is a case in point. Traditionally Australia has been considered the product of an Anglo-Celtic culture imposed upon a native Aboriginal population. In fact Australia had West Indians transported as convicts as early as the 1790s, South African blacks as early as the 1820s, Chinese gold miners in the 1850s and by the 1880s substantial populations of Italians, Greeks, Lebanese, Scandinavians, and Germans.[96]

During the closing years of the twentieth century, as the voices of the indigenous population were more and more being heard on postcolonial stages, other voices, of these nonindigenous immigrants, the "Other" Australians, began to be heard as well. Language is frequently both a dramatic device and a central concern in these plays. particularly in dealing with the emigrant experience. An early such work, *Il cabaret dell'emigrante* (The emigrant cabaret, 1984) utilized a kind of pidgin Italo-Australian dialect as one part of "the four-tiered bilingual texture . . . which switched from Italian to Sicilian, Veneto or Calabrese dialects and from English to *emigrante,* sometimes within the same scene."[97] Tes Lyssiotis has authored a series of dramas dealing with the Greek diaspora in Australia. The group Doppio Teatro began producing bilingual Italian/English theatre in Australia in 1988. Their opening production, *A White Sports Coat,* was a kind of extended dramatic monologue in which the "daughter" describes her coming of age as a woman in a hybrid cultural situation.[98] Marc Maufort has commented that "The play's hybridity derives partly from its prolific use of Greek," and that "The preservation of linguistic identity can be decoded as a sign of resistance against an unwanted assimilation into mainstream Australia,"[99] a point to which I will return later. Dina Panozzo's *Varda che Bruta . . . Poretta* (Look how ugly she is . . . poor thing, 1992), involves both the complexity of Italian dialects and the negotiations of Italian as an immigrant language in Australia. When the heroine returns from Australia to her family's native Venice, she finds that the Italian she learned in Australia, derived from Venetian, is not only so different from other dialects that she cannot get work as an actress in Italy, but even in Venice the dialects have so diverged within a generation that she can scarcely understand her own relatives. Within the play, as within her career, "several forms of Italian compete with English."[100]

In an even more complex manner, Noëlle Janaczewska's *Cold Harvest* (1998) depicts two young women whose parents were immigrants, one family from Poland, the other from Korea, who struggle between the language and culture of their disparate ancestors and that of their present home. Both Mi-Kyong and Kasia have adopted the same "Australian" name, "Kathy," but as they grow up they also feel the need to maintain a connection with their "first" culture. In the central metaphor of the play, they sing about the construction of their "Australian" wedding cakes, which combine food elements, cultural elements, and linguistic elements in a heteroglossic fantasy. Typical is the song sung by the young women suggesting decorations for the cakes, which contains such lines as

MI-KYONG: Chicken/chestnuts/fruits/traditional/Korean
KASIA: Kolacz/chooks/pigs/leaves/birds/kangaroos[101]

Joanne Tompkins, to whom I am indebted for these examples, suggests that the term *multicultural,* commonly applied to plays of this sort, might usefully be replaced by *polynational,* which lacks the totalizing suggestion of the former term and its appeal to a particular kind of authenticity. The latter, on the other hand, "would not pretend to unite disparate groups that have hitherto resisted nationalist stereotypes; instead it would reconsider relationships in contested space, as well as reconsidering the ways in which literatures are categorized, funded, distributed, and marketed in national and specific communities."[102] This redirection of emphasis would also be useful, I believe, in the discussion of contemporary heteroglossic drama, which obviously has close connections with the resistance of nationalist stereotypes remarked upon by Maufort and which also characterizes Tompkins's "polynationalism."

Maufort's *Transgressive Itineraries* even more directly and at more length than Tompkins challenges the concept of multicultural democratic equality. Here modern political and theatrical discourse often attempts to assimilate the heteroglossia created by the increasing importance of ethnic voices in theatre cultures around the world. Maufort illustrates this dynamic in the case of Canada by providing a number of alternative voices that challenge the traditional bilingual model of a French- and English-speaking population (with a mostly suppressed indigenous Indian below the colonial overlay). The linguistic range of this heteroglossic ethnic minority writing in Canada today is impressive; *Canadian Theatre Review* has devoted several special issues to such theatre, including one on Italian Canadian theatre and one on Chinese Canadian theatre.[103] In both *Come Good Rain* (1992) by Ugandan Canadian George Seremba and *Noran Bang. The Yellow Room* (1998) by Korean Canadian Myung Jin Kang, songs in the "other" language provide an important alternative linguistic voice. Hindi phrases and references to the legends of the *Mahabharata* fill the text of Indian Canadian playwright Padma Viswanathan's *House of Sacred Cows* (1997). In some cases, as in polylinguistic theatre elsewhere in the world, more than one alternative language is offered, further complicating the linguistic mix. Chinese Canadian Betty Quin's *Mother Tongue* (1995) offers a complex linguistic mosaic, in which the immigrant mother speaks Cantonese, her daughter Mimi speaks English, while Mimi's deaf brother, Stevie, uses American Sign Language (the contemporary use of signing I will address later).

Even more complex are the language webs in the work of one of best-known contemporary Quebec dramatists, Marco Micone. In a 1984 interview Micone discussed the problems of writing dramas concerning a population that was placed between French, standard Italian, and home Italian dialects. He opted for a consciously hybrid speech that represents his idea of "the street language which Italians will speak in about twenty years from now in Quebec."[104] In fact, his plays present an even more complication linguistic world, and one much closer to that of his contemporary society. In his aptly named one-act *Babele* (1989), characters speak standard Italian, the Molisan Italian dialect, Quebecois French, and English,[105] while in the *Addolorata* (1984) the heroine Lolita has different names and different identities in each of the play's various languages. Her comment on her linguistic experience suggests that of many in today's polyglot world (like the earlier mentioned polyglot Algerian dramatist Aziz Chouaki):

I can speak English with my friends, French with my neighbours, Italian with the machos and Spanish with certain customers. With my four languages I never get bored. With my four languages, I can watch soaps in English, read the French TV Guide and the Italian fotoromanzi and sing "Guantanamera."[106]

Similarly, Mario in Micone's *Voiceless People* (1984) remarks, "I speak Calabrese with my parents, French with my sister and my girlfriend, and English with my buddies."[107]

The various "voices" of Lolita suggest another kind of heteroglossic theatre that has become particularly popular in recent North American performance, that performed by a single actor playing a variety of Others. Jennifer Harvie and Richard Paul Knowles discuss this practice in a 1994 article in *Theatre Research in Canada* that appropriately and unconventionally is written in the form of a dialogue.[108] The authors apply Bakhtin's concepts of dialogism and heteroglossia to a number of contemporary Canadian dramatic monologues, suggesting that current monologue artists often utilize dialogism to destabilize unitary notions of gender, race, and sexuality. A central example of this phenomenon is the work of Argentine Canadian Guillermo Verdecchia, which has been examined by a number of scholars as a leading example of postcolonial multicultural expression, the destabilization of identity, and dialogic "border" performance.[109] Verdecchia sought in his best-known work, *Fronteras Americanas/American Borders* (1993), the kind of linguistic and cultural challenge to fixed borders that Guillermo Gomez-Peña has undertaken in the United States. Indeed, Verdecchia's character "Wideload" sounds much like Gomez-Pena's "Border Brujo": "Ay! Ayayayyay! Aja. Bienvenidos. Yo soy el mesonero aca en La Casa de la Frontera. Soy el guia. A su servicio . . . I am a direct descendant of Tupac Amaru, Pancho Villa, Dona Flor, Pedro Navaja, Sor Juana and Speedy Gonzalez."[110] Richard Paul Knowles calls attention to the features that this work shares with most of the monodramas under discussion, including "its 'linguistic carnival' (Spanish and some French as well as various modes of spoken English)" and "its disruptions of subjectivity."[111]

All of the Harvie and Knowles examples involve aspects of a single character, the different cultural "voices" speaking in "border" identities like that of Guillermo Verdecchia. They specifically exclude from their consideration multicharacter monodramas, arguing that these "remain predominantly monologic—at least from the point of view of the audience—in that the virtuosity of role switching produces the illusion of dialogue among discrete characters for whom the need to create distinct, unitary voices is felt, for reasons of clarity, to be particularly urgent."[112] Helen Gilbert and Jacqueline Lo take issue with this exclusion, arguing that the very form of monodrama necessarily constructs such characters as overlapping "precisely because they converge in and on a single performing body." This shift in focus is in part reflected in the conceptual structures of their two articles, the one by Gilbert and Lo devoted to the separation of "dialogism" and one by Lo to the overlapping of "hybridity." They point out that in Margo Kane's 1992 *Moonlodge,* one of the central examples used by Harvie and Knowles, the central figure Agnes "meets, and embodies for the audience, men and women from different races and backgrounds, many of them also marginalized from the mainstream white society." Since each of these figures has left its mark upon Agnes, they can be claimed as contributing to an "ongoing process of hybrid subject formation."[113]

Gilbert and Lo present other examples of monodramatic presentations of the "hybridized and unstable post-colonial body" from recent performance in Singapore. Emily in Stella Kon's *Emily of Emerald Hill* (1985) "is adept at changing not only her personality but also her language, both verbal (from Standard English to colloquial Singaporean English to the Peranakan Patois) and gestural."[114] Even more striking is the role differentiation of the protagonist in Chin Woon Ping's 1992 *Details Cannot Body Wants.* In a sequence from the "Cannot" section, the actress has painted half of her face black and half white, and shifts back and forth to provide the "voices" of varied characters and roles (an ancient comedic device that we have already noted in the work of Lolli more than two centuries earlier):

> (*In a deep husky voice, with black profile to the audience*)
> Hello Doll. Where are you from? I'll bet you're lonesome, aren't you?
> I bet I know what you want. I know *all* about you. How about some
>     hunky chunk company. How about it, lovey dove?
> And you're supposed to reply,
> (*In docile, "Oriental" voice and posture, with while profile to audience.*)

Hai. Watashi karimatsu. Arigato gozaimas. Me China Doll. Me
Inscrutable Doll., me sexy Miss Saigon, me so horny, so so horny,
me so horny / me love you long time (*etc. from 2-Live rap song*).
(*The chorus pick up the beat and song.*)
BUT WHAT YOU REALLY WANT TO SAY IS,
(*Using loud, sassy Black mannerisms and tone, with black profile to audi-
ence.*)
Hey Muthafukka. Quit messin' round with me and mah sistahs you
hear?
We don't want yo jive talk and you bullshittin. You know what yo
problem? You ain't got no RESPECT, that's yo problem.[115]

In addition to the various English dialects, the text utilizes Cantonese,
Mandarin, Bhasa Indonesian, and French.

These examples, although they broaden the concerns of Harvie and
Knowles to include the performance of voices of other ethnicities and
genders, still ground them in the hybrid formation of a single, if heteroglossic, identity. I would argue, however, that a consideration of
recent heteroglossic monodrama would also have to include solo multivoiced performers who do not seek to illuminate the heteroglossia
within the multicultural individual, but that within the modern multicultural society. The outstanding example in America is surely Anna
Deavere Smith, whose *Fires in the Mirror* (1992) and *Twilight: Los Angeles* (1993) offered what has been widely hailed as a radical new mode of
theatrical representation.[116] Deavere's innovative technique in these
works consisted of holding extensive taped interviews with persons of
differing perspectives on current social crises and then skillfully repro-
ducing segments of these interviews with an exact re-creation of every
detail of vocal and gestural inflection. As Lyons and Lyons note: "These
performances are polyphonic, both in the sense of representing multiple
voices and in their refusal to synthesize difference in any intervening
personal statement, any *authorial* commentary." The absence of such an
authorial voice "puts the emphasis upon the polyphonic display of
voices."[117] The dynamic here seems to me almost identical to that proposed by Gilbert and Lo for the performance of hybridity in postcolonial
monodrama, in which a tension is created between clearly differentiated

characters and the fact that they overlap through the medium of a single performing body. Richard Schechner has called Smith's portrayal of other personae an "incorporation," comparing it to the operations of the ritual shaman, who becomes possessed by the voice of another without wholly becoming that other.[118]

Although the particular strategy of reproduction of interviews is closely associated with Smith, the monodramatic presentation of other voices, and particularly of other minority voices, is an important part of much recent performance in America. Such performance almost invariably shares the characteristics of polyphony noted by Lyons and Lyons, that is, the representation of multiple voices and the refusal to synthesize difference through intervening authorial commentary or presence. An excellent example of such work is *Bridge and Tunnel* by Sarah Jones (2004). The production is in the form of an evening of immigrants telling bits of their history or performing pieces they have presumably created. The various presentations are introduced by a kind of variety show emcee, who is far from an authorial presence, but another minority "voice," a Paki/American created by Jones. He introduces the various "border" voices that make up the evening, a Polish/American, Vietnamese/American, Jamaican/American, Dominican/American, Australian/American, Jordanian/American, AfroAmerican, Chinese/American, Russian/American, and Haitian/American. The various dialects and creoles employed suggest the heteroglossia of a contemporary world city like New York and give a playfully ironic edge to the emcee's naively enthusiastic comment, "God Bless the English for the language we all speak." English, or rather the multiple Englishes of postcolonialism, indeed make up the bulk of the production, though other languages occasionally add to the mix. In one charming passage the Jordanian woman reads a love poem she composed in Arabic, then translates it to reveal that it in fact is the words to the Beatles' "I Want to Hold Your Hand," another testimony to the interrelatedness of the world's cultural production today.

Clearly the dynamics of modern immigration and of the emergence of immigrant voices, bicultural or multicultural, have vastly increased the heteroglossia of the contemporary stage, and give strong support to Tompkins's suggestion that the term *multicultural,* with its assimilationist overtones, might be better replaced by some such term as *polyna-*

*tional,* if that is more helpful in suggesting the truly mixed nature of much contemporary expression. In terms of theatrical language, *postcolonial* seems to me also inadequate. Focusing as it does upon the interplay of colonial and indigenous discourse, it either excludes the increasingly important voices of other cultures, especially immigrant populations, that have a different relationship to the cultural dynamic, or else it tends, like *multiculturalism,* to blend all minority voices into a generalized "other," thus seriously misrepresenting the actual variations they introduce into contemporary theatrical discourse. The developing practice of dramatic discourse at the end of the twentieth century clearly showed that the central negotiations between the colonial languages and their various pidgin and creole forms have been made much more complex by the emergence of indigenous languages on the one side and alternative immigrant languages on the other. The forces that have brought about this cultural and linguistic mixing are becoming ever more pronounced with the increased mobility of peoples in the new century. There is every indication that the polyglot theatre represented by these culturally hybrid artists of modern global communities will become a prominent feature of world theatre in the coming century.

# 4 *Postmodern Language Play*

In the preceding chapters, a very wide variety of linguistic mixing, historically and geographically, has been examined, utilized for a very wide variety of reasons. It has been used for comic and serious purposes, for consolidation or subversion of current cultural practice. Almost always it has in some measure reflected the political dimensions of language analyzed by Bourdieu, drawing upon the linguistic capital of language use in the surrounding society, as manifested in the operations of the whole spectrum of linguistic differentiation, from dialects through pidgin and creoles to distinctly different languages. This reflection of the linguistic capital of various speech options in the surrounding society means that in most of the examples of heteroglossia so far discussed, different language options have in large measure marked different cultural groups, insiders and outsides, colonizers and colonized, dominant and dominated, just as they do in the everyday world the theatre takes as its ground. Very often the dynamic driving the dramatist to heteroglossic usage is that traditional concern of the theatre, verisimilitude. Dramatists living in a heteroglossic culture, writing for a heteroglossic audience, as is the situation in much of the world today, are more and more resisting the strongly monoglossic tendencies of much traditional European (and American) theatre, with its strong ties to modern nationalism.

As I have noted, particularly in the previous chapter on heteroglossia in the postcolonial theatre, this interest in linguistic mixing became increasingly common in the closing years of the last century. During the same general period, a quite different sort of heteroglossic experimentation also steadily increased, especially in the European experimental theatre, which operated in a way largely different from most of the heteroglossic theatre so far discussed. Its basis was not, or not primarily,

verisimilitude. Although its presumed audiences might v
number of languages, such productions did not seek to refl
language practice or experience of those audiences, nor atte..._
manner of realism to fit languages to characters who would normally
speak them, with whatever cultural implications that might involve.
Multiple languages were used instead, in an almost decorative manner,
as abstract formal elements in the theatrical composition, as one might
mix colors or musical tones or passages. Such linguistic passages are not,
of course, devoid of meaning; they are simply separated from the traditional realistic connection with a character who is speaking a language
that he or she might use in "real life." The function of such language
passages, even though normally spoken by an actor, is less like the traditional dramatic speech revealing character than like a piece of background music, a recognizable quotation from Wagner, Mozart, or a
recent rock song, which is not realistically motivated, but which adds
importantly to the texture of the performance.

It is not coincidental, I believe, that this kind of heteroglossic performance has become far more common at the same time that the concept
of postmodernism has come to circulate widely in contemporary culture
and criticism, since in a very direct way postmodernism itself can been
seen as a heteroglossic attitude. One of the most fundamental differences between modernism and postmodernism, especially in the arts,
has been the emphasis within modernism on the unity of the work, upon
simplicity, directness, and clarity, the striving for a minimalist essence of
each art form. One of the first attempts to articulate a postmodern aesthetic was Ihab Hassan's *The Dismemberment of Orpheus: Towards a
Postmodern Literature* (1971).[1] In a subsequent essay, Hassan suggested
that postmodernism "veers toward open, playful, optative, disjunctive,
displaced, or indeterminate forms, a discourse of fragments, an ideology
of fracture, a will to unmaking."[2] Although Hassan and other major
early theorists of postmodernism did not use the term *heteroglossic*
(Linda Hutcheon perhaps comes closest with her stress upon the importance in postmodern art of parody and pastiche,[3] both strategies cited by
Bakhtin as key examples of heteroglossic practice in literature), clearly
postmodernism's modes of operation are heteroglossic, just as those of
high modernism were monoglossic.

## The Spanish Tragedy

Before considering some of the recent examples of heteroglossia in a postmodern performative mode, I would like to look back to a famous example of such usage long before the emergence of postmodernism. This is important for several reasons. One of these is to demonstrate that striking examples can be found in earlier periods of dramatic works that used a mixture of languages in a distinctly postmodern way, that is, as a device based on formal or thematic concerns rather than upon the much more common concern with verisimilitude. Another, however, is to show that as such works have been reexamined in recent years, their use of heteroglossia, subordinated, ignored, or even denied by critics working in the modernist monoglossic tradition, has been given new value and importance, both in critical writing and in the theatre, by a postmodern recognition of heteroglossia's potential artistic power and value.

My example, one of the best-known examples of dramatic heteroglossia after the works of Shakespeare, also comes, not surprisingly, from the Renaissance, a period of great fascination with language variety, as I have noted earlier. The first great popular success of the English Renaissance theatre, Thomas Kyd's *The Spanish Tragedy* (ca. 1590), provides as its climactic scene a heteroglossic play-within-the-play that offers as strange and surprising a linguistic potpourri as almost anything encountered in the modern repertoire. The central character, Hieronimo, in preparing the play, explains the device:

> Each one of us must act his part
> In unknown languages,
> That it may breed the more variety.
> As you, my lord, in Latin, I in Greek,
> You in Italian, and for because I know
> That Bel-imperia hath practiced the French,
> In courtly French shall all her phrases be.[4]

Within the single surviving edition of the play, printed in 1592, the lines for Hieronimo's play are in fact given in English, but they are preceded by an unusual, and seemingly unambiguous interpolation by the printer:

Gentlemen, this play of HIERONIMO in sundry languages, was thought
good to be set down in English more largely, for the easier understanding of every public reader.[5]

Up until very recently, commentators on the play, working within
the tradition of essentially monoglossic theatre, and finding the idea of a
key passage presented in languages inaccessible to all or most of the presumed audience, provided an ingenious variety of ways of reading the
fairly clear indications of both the play and the printer so that they did
not really mean what they apparently meant. P. W. Biesterfeldt, one of
the first major modern interpreters of Kyd, suggested in his 1935 study
that the scene was "apparently done in pantomime with very short fragments of text that only faintly suggested foreign speech and could be
partially understood by the audience,"[6] an interpretation that nothing
whatever in the existing text supports. Philip Edwards, editor of the
1568 Revels edition of the text, suggests a variation of the Biesterfeldt
argument, based upon the incontrovertible fact that Elizabethan plays
were often cut and adjusted in performance:

I take it that Kyd originally intended the play to be in English, but
that, when abridgement of an over-long play was required, a mime
was substituted, a mime accompanied, for the sake of "drama," with
a few well-chosen lines in gibberish or "sundry languages," and references to these languages were inserted before and after the mime.[7]

One might ask, to begin with, why Edwards "takes it" that Kyd's original intention was monoglossic, again in defiance of the clear statements
in the text, and why like Biesterfeldt (whom Edwards quotes approvingly) Edwards is willing to create a totally hypothetical mime and gra-
tuitously and inaccurately gloss "sundry languages" as "gibberish" on
the basis of no supporting evidence other than his own imagination and
fear of heteroglossia (the condescending quotes around "drama" give
further evidence, if any were needed, of the traditional literary bias of
this approach).

Muriel Bradbrook, one of the most distinguished of early-twentieth-
century scholars of Elizabethan drama, at least recognized how wide-

spread the practice of language mixing was in the drama of this period, suggesting, "The groundlings might not be able to understand them, but they were interested to hear the sound of a strange language." For this reason she is more willing than most of her contemporaries to entertain the possibility that Kyd's play-within-the-play "may really have been given in the 'sundry languages' on the stage," although in her final analysis she concludes with the now traditional wisdom that "considering Kyd's reputation, it would be unlikely."[8]

More recent scholarship takes a quite different view of the staging of heteroglossia in *The Spanish Tragedy,* a shift marked by the appearance in 1962 of S. F. Johnson's seminal essay *"The Spanish Tragedy,* or Babylon Revisited." As the title suggests, Johnson argues not only that the "sundry languages" Kyd calls for were actually spoken in the original performance, but that the "Tower of Babel" evoked by this pivotal scene is in fact central to the play's concerns with communication, discord, and punishment for overweening pride and display of power.[9] Subsequent critical discussion of this play has tended to focus more particularly upon performance practice and upon linguistic usage. It has normally begun with an assumption of the play's heteroglossia, and attempted to understand its possible effects. Thus Michael Hattaway's *Elizabethan Popular Theatre: Plays in Performance* (1982) finds the heteroglossia of Kyd's play-within-a-play crucial to the drama's "architectonic design," fully revealed only in performance. "One of Kyd's great fascinations," notes Hattaway, "was for memorable speech-rhythms and cadence and it is possible that he was trying to see whether he could employ a theatre language that would, to the unlettered at least, communicate by pure sound." Thus the heteroglossic section at least in performance can be seen as

> the culmination of a movement from the pronounced narrative elements of the opening of the play, through the manifest dramatic conflicts and on-stage violent action of the middle, towards a species of music that suggest that the action includes more than merely the characters, that it creates its own mythic order.[10]

Janette Dillon, whose excellent work concerning language on the medieval and Renaissance English stage I have already cited in my opening chapter, also insists that doubts about the playing in multiple languages in Kyd's play arise from the critics, not from the text itself, which is quite clear on the matter. Like Hattaway, she sees the device as potentially of great effect in performance, but in emblematic and evocative, rather than in directly discursive terms: "The confusion of languages, as sound effect, functions as jarring music might do in film at the moment of killing, freezing the event as image in order to compel the spectator into a deep engagement with its horror."[11]

An important theatrical confirmation of this shift in critical opinion was provided by a major revival of *The Spanish Tragedy* at London's National Theatre in 1982, the same year that Hattaway's book appeared. Director Michael Bogdanov's decision to perform the climactic sequence "in sundry languages" was widely praised, a device, in the words of one critic, "brilliantly and wittily carried out."[12] Another called it "a direct hit" and provided some interesting details of how individual language choices reinforced overall production values. Patti Love as Bel-Imperia, speaking in French alexandrines, suggested "a French tragic queen." Michael Frenner as "Soliman, in bushy beard and fluent Latin" achieved "a new comic seriousness and expansiveness." Greg Hicks as Lorenzo revealed "all the vanity and self-centredness of the bad amateur actor as the play invites him to show off in public the Italian into which he so often and easily falls in the earlier, more intimate scenes." Against these renditions, Hieronimo's (i.e., Michael Bryant's) "brisk delivery of his Greek lines as the Bashaw projects a grimly comic anticipation of his play's true catastrophe."[13]

This description of an actual successful modern revival of this classic heteroglossic scene suggests how even the performance-oriented and sympathetic speculations of critics like Dillon and Hattaway fail to take into account the complex communicative operations of theatre. Both are still oriented toward the text, and see the heteroglossia as resulting in a kind of abstract sound effect, which both, interestingly, compare to music. Hattaway even specifically situates this effect beyond the individual characters. Certainly heteroglossia in the postmodern theatre can work that way, as some of my subsequent examples will demonstrate, but the Bogdanov revival also showed clearly the importance of remembering the importance of the actor's body and voice, not to mention the texture and associations of the individual languages involved, in providing audiences with something much more detailed and complex than either the impression of a Tower of Babel or some totalizing "mythic order."

## Karen Beier and Peter Brook

A number of European experimental productions in the final years of the twentieth century demonstrated how the kind of heteroglossic performance suggested by Kyd and staged with such success by Bogdanov could be extended from a single sequence to an entire evening. One of the most complex as well as one of the most successful recent attempts at creating a production utilizing artists from different language groups each speaking his or her own language was a production of Shakespeare's *Midsummer Night's Dream* staged in Düsseldorf in December 1995 by the innovative Karen Beier. Although Beier has been closely associated with Shakespeare throughout her career, this production was equally inspired by the increasing internationalization of the European theatre toward the end of the twentieth century. In 1990 Giorgio Strehler, long associated with this concern, organized and became the first president of the Union of European Theatres, dedicated to cooperative work among fourteen of the most prestigious theatres in Europe. In 1995, under the auspices of the union, and with the cooperation of Strehler, Ingmar Bergman, and Andrey Wajda, Beier organized a series of workshops, out of which grew her idea of a "European Shakespeare," utilizing actors from different countries all speaking their own language.

In August 1995 Beier assembled a company of fourteen actors from nine countries with no common language to create collectively a production *A Midsummer Night's Dream.* Beier made no attempt to impose some overarching style of her own upon this disparate company. Rather she accepted the differences in style, the certainty of communication problems among the cast and between cast and audience, the inevitable misunderstandings and surprising and unexpected communications, and wove all of this into a production that both illuminated Shakespeare's own comedy of confusion and misunderstanding, and spoke fascinatingly to today's multicultural world. What may have seemed a formula for confusion and frustration in fact produced an experience of astonishing richness and clarity, a solid demonstration of the artistic and communicative viability of this sort of experiment. The production won high praise from public and critics and was invited to the annual Berlin Theatertreffen as one of the outstanding German-language productions of the year. Traditional and current linguistic and national rivalries added extra depth to confrontations, and allowed interesting connections to be made, as when Peter Quince and Hippolytus/Oberon (played by the same actor) not only both spoke Italian, but exhibited certain similar qualities suggesting the traditional Italian maestro attempting to orchestrate the unruly company under his supervision. Lysander (Michael Teplisky from Tel Aviv) recognized almost at once that Hermia (Penny Needler from London) could not understand him, and he ingeniously acted out lines to her, which she enthusiastically translated into English. Helena (Giorgia Senesi from Milan), suspecting that Hermia's ability in English is the secret of her attractiveness, tried to challenge her by reciting a heavily accented "Shall I compare thee to a summer's day?" in that language. When Lysander and Demetrius (Gergö Kaszás from Budapest) fight, their conflict took on a chilling contemporary and metatheatrical turn as they exchanged half-muttered taunts of "gypsy" and "fucking Jew."

A central reference point for the linguistic and theatrical variety of this production could be found in the rehearsal and performance of the Rude Mechanicals, who, like the actors in the larger performance, brought to their work quite varied traditions—Anastasia Bousyguina, from the Moscow Art Theatre (Starvling), cited Stanislavsky and gave the audience an emotional speech in that director's style, ending with a tearful "V Moskva, V Moskva" at the footlights. She was interrupted by Bottom (Jacek Poniedzialek from the Stary Theatre in Kracòw, Poland), who insisted on the superiority of Grotowskian techniques and demonstrated with a hilarious parody of those techniques, ending with a kind of seizure flat on his back. Jost Grix (Flute), the only German in the production, naturally championed Brecht, and suggested playing Thisbe with his sweater pulled over his head, as an "alienating device." Snug (Mladen Vasary from Paris) offered a balletic turn, insisting that the production needed more "delicatesse," and so on.[14] The audience's delight in recognizing the intercultural play of these different acting styles added enormously to the fun of the whole and also reminded us that in addition to Shakespeare and to whatever "universals" of rhythm and balance may exist in any theatrical creation, the international theatre community also shares a complex tradition of performance experience that can be cited and built upon for this sort of intercultural theatre.

Beier returned to multilanguage production in 1997 with *The Tempest,* subtitled "A European Shakespeare," which again assembled an international company speaking a variety of languages. This production was even more elaborately heteroglossic than her *Midsummer Night's Dream,* however, since characters often spoke in a variety of languages within a single speech. The tone was set by the opening sequence, newly created for this production, in which Alonso and his party, all with a distinct mafioso edge, are addressing an international congress of tomato producers and championing the unity of the new Europe. A part of Alonso's opening speech will give an idea of the technique.

> This is un historic moment. Mes chers collègues, ladies and gentlemen, I am extremely glücklich to welcome you all to this grandioso conferenza di famiglia di nazioni. Meine Damen und Herren, I feel that the goldene Zeit lies not behind us but before us . . . I am extremely heureux das Instrument zu sein which sans doute will lead us to the one unified geistige Einheit of the famiglia delli nazioni.[15]

Such elaborate heteroglossia has not been repeated in Beier's subsequent work, although she continues to produce macaronic productions, mixing Italian- and German-speaking actors, for example in her 1999 production of Tankred Dorst's *Merlin* and her 2000 production of Pirandello's *Tonight We Improvise.*

The shifting in a great deal of European experimental theatre from a modernist monoglossic model to the sort of heteroglossic production admirably illustrated by the Beier *Midsummer Night's Dream* can be traced in the changing performance practices within a single company that certainly stands among the most important and influential in late-twentieth-century Europe. This is Peter Brook's Centre International de Recherche Théâtrale (CIRT), established in Paris in November 1970. The center, like Beier's production twenty-five years later, had its roots in the Théâtre des Nations, headed in the late 1960s by Jean-Louis Barrault. Barrault invited Brook to Paris for the spring 1968 season of the Théâtre des Nations to run a workshop for actors visiting the festival, but Brook proposed instead an ongoing group of actors from different countries, to which Barrault agreed. The political unrest of May 1968 caused a delay in the project, so that it was not actually launched until 1970, but the concept remained the same. The original 1968 company was almost twice as large as Beier's, numbering twenty-seven, but it included four directors and a designer. The actors came from the United States, England, France, and Japan. The actual starting company, in 1970, resembled Beier's much more closely, with fifteen actors from seven countries representing five languages (English, French, Spanish, Portuguese, and Japanese). The mixture came even closer to that of Beier in the following months when actors were added from Iran, Mali, Cameroon, and Greece.[16]

Although both Brook in 1970 and Beier in 1995 began with the assembling of actors from strikingly different linguistic and theatrical backgrounds, their work with these actors makes clear the difference between the high modernist search for some kind of precultural "essence" and the postmodernist acceptance of, indeed glorification of, difference and discontinuity. Although Brook regularly denied that he was attempting to synthesize different cultural theatre techniques into a sort of "dramatic Esperanto" or indeed create a new linguistic Esperanto in the artificial language Orghast, developed by Ted Hughes out of the work of the CIRT.[17] Brook's explanations of his work clearly suggest that he was in fact seeking a universal communicative mode that would function as a sort of ur-language. The bringing together of actors from different cultures, he suggested, could set up a "difficult friction" so that "each one's culture slightly eroded the other's until something more natural and human appeared." The goal was to eliminate the "artificial mannerisms" and "accreted ethnic tics" that "propagate national culture" and to reveal beneath them "a level where forms aren't fixed."[18] At this precultural level a new communal work of art can be created out of impulses and materials common to all, thus creating an expressive mode that would have essentially the same artistic "meaning" to artists from different cultures and also, potentially, to audiences from quite different cultural backgrounds. As Brook explained in Shiraz in 1971:

I brought together an international group so that different human fibers, the different human materials shaped and worked over by all possible cultural factors, could come together on the simplest level. If one can find forms which are shared in the group and if the purpose of the group is always to perform the grand exercise—in other words, to make its relationship with the audience—then the forms shared by a very variegated group should make sense to a very variegated audience.

The language for this "grand exercise," like its physical embodiment, should be composed of "shared but nonceptualized—or hardly conceptualized references. And that is where we found Orghast, a language that in a sense has always existed and needed only to be created."[19] Indeed, Brook and Hughes were always resistant to attempts to categorize the artificial speech system Orghast as a "language," but rather wanted it considered as an expressive product of company research into this deeper level. Significantly, both artists frequently spoke of it as operating more like music than language, carrying on the romantic and symbolist view of music as a more "universal" expressive form, relatively uncontaminated, as language was, by the accidental and artificial qualities of spoken or written discourse.

Brook's vision of an intercultural theatre that could draw upon a precultural grounding to avoid the accidents and specificity of various cultural expressions can still be found in significant experimental theatre work, such as, for example, the research into "theatre anthropology" by Eugenio Barba, but this sort of universalist concept has been replaced in much postmodern experimental theatre by an openness to heteroglossic expression, both in language and in performance style, as is illustrated by the difference between Brook's 1971 *Orghast* and Beier's 1995 *Midsummer Night's Dream*. In fact, this particular shift from modernist monoglossia to postmodern heteroglossia can be traced within the work of Brook himself, who continued through the rest of the twentieth century to explore the expressive possibilities of theatre in his CIRT. Surely the most famous of his productions after *Orghast* was *The Mahabharata* in 1985, a production that toured the world, in French and English productions, during the late 1980s. The production was widely praised as one of the most important international dramatic events of the decade, but it also aroused significant controversy. At a time when the emerging theories of postmodernism were challenging the totalizing orientation of high modernism on artistic grounds, the emerging concerns of postcolonialism were challenging this orientation on political grounds. In this context, Brook's search for a totalizing transcultural theatrical expression seemed more and more problematic. One of the strongest expressions of this shift was the strong criticism of Brook's "orientalism" by Gautam Dasgupta in the *Performing Arts Journal* in 1987. Dasgupta granted that the totalizing "syncretic cultural universe" posited by Brook was "a grand and perhaps even noble vision," but one that, by denying or eliding cultural difference "inevitably raises the problematic spectre of what Edward Said has termed 'Orientalism,'"[20] that is, a dynamic by which a Western writer replaces and silences the voice of the Other.

Probably the best-known actor of Brook's permanent company and one of the clearest examples of Brook's interest in drawing upon disparate theatrical traditions is the Japanese artist Yoshi Oida, who was trained in Noh, Kabuki, and experimental theatre before joining Brook's CIRT, of which he was one of the founding members. In a 1985 interview concerning the preparations for *The Mahabharata* he made an interesting observation about the use of language by the heteroglossic company: "When we came to the text, initially some scenes were approached in the individual mother tongues to free certain actors from the difficulties of the French language."[21] Although this strategy was seemingly employed in the service not of heteroglossia, but of Brook's continuing search for a more basic expressive mode that the "difficulties" of French would hinder, it is worth noting that a very similar strategy has been employed by a number of postcolonial dramatists, who write material first in the indigenous language and then translate it into English, not to avoid the "difficulties" of English and thus achieve a more "universal" expression, but on the contrary, to introduce into English the "resistance" of another language and thus encourage an impression of heteroglossia. Several African dramatists have used this technique to introduce a subterranean alternative voice, as has Maori dramatist Harry Dansey, who mentions it in the preface to his pioneering 1974 play *Te Raukura:*

It might be of interest to note that many parts of the play were written first in Maori and then recast in English. Thus here and there I
like to think that something of the feel of the Maori situation has
remained like an echo among the English words.[22]

The next project at Brook's CIRT after *The Mahabharata* continued
to move, albeit guardedly, in a heteroglossic direction. The French government declared 1989, the bicentennial of the French Revolution, to be
"The Year of the Rights of Man and of Freedom," and Brook, arguing
that the current struggle for liberty closest to that of Revolutionary
France existed at that moment in South Africa, offered a program of
music and theatre from that country. This program, seeking to "represent" South Africa in Paris, was the most heteroglossic yet offered at
Brook's theatre. Brook was well aware of the work of the leading multicultural theatres of South Africa in the 1980s. In 1986 he visited the Market Theatre in Johannesburg and traveled to Cape Town to see a performance of the Junction Avenue Theatre Company's *Sophiatown.*[23] In
1989 he returned again to arrange for South African productions for his
own theatre. Despite his professed interest in politically resistant drama,
however, he did not present anything either so radical or so heteroglossic
as *Sophiatown.* His program consisted of six concerts of traditional South
African music in the languages Venda, Pedi, and Xhosa, and of two
plays, both of which had already achieved a considerable international
success in English-speaking countries, *Woza Albert!* and *Sarafina!* Both
were distinctly more monoglossic than their English language versions.
For *Woza Albert!,* which Brook directed, Jean-Claude Carrière, who had
created the text for Brook's *Mahabharata,* replaced the Afrikaans, English, and Zulu of the original with a purely French text, reducing the
three actors of the original to two, Bakary Sangaré and Mamdou
Bioumé, both African, but also both speakers of French, one from the
former French colony of Senegal, the other from Mali. *Sarafina!* was presented with its original song lyrics intact, but author Mgongeni Ngema
allowed Brook to build into the production two actors who provided
commentaries in French, written again by Carrière.[24]

Thus Brook's South African festival, although developed out of
strongly heteroglossic materials, retained much of the cultural diversity
of music, dance, and movement of the original works, but when it came

to language itself, the theatrical portion of the program c⸢
strongly monoglossic tradition of CIRT and indeed of the
atre in general. The heterogeneity represented by this materi
may well have left its mark on the evolving aesthetic of Bro
mentation, or it at any rate supplemented a turn toward heteroglossia in
that experimentation, as Brook's theatre itself seemingly turned, along
with much significant experimental European and American theatre,
from the high modernism of the 1960s and 1970s to the postmodernism
of the end of the century. One might locate the turn in Brook's work
with the production that opened the final decade of the century, the 1990
offering of Shakespeare's *The Tempest,* a production that looked backward to Brook's earlier utilization of a wide variety of cultural styles and
elements and forward to more radical mixtures of these elements with
less concern for reducing their heteroglossia, their otherness. Interestingly, David Williams specifically evokes postmodernist aesthetics in
describing the approach of *The Tempest,* speaking of Brook's "syncretism" and "hybridization," terms we have found common to discussions of heteroglossia in postcolonial writing, The "multi- and intertex-
tuality" of the work marks it, Williams argues, as postmodern, as does its
"plurality of voices, accents, conventions, styles," by which the production "joyfully celebrates the ludic aspect of theatricality."[25]

The reference to plurality of voices in general and accents specifically
evokes the dynamics of heteroglossia, and unquestionably that effect
was part of the aesthetic of *The Tempest.* Literally, however, the production remained determinedly monoglossic, in the elegant French of
Brook's faithful translator, Jean-Claude Carrière. Only when the production toured to English-speaking countries did a kind a natural heteroglossia occur rather in the manner of postcolonial translations
through which the indigenous original shines. Michael Coveney, of the
*Observer,* noted this effect in his review of the production in Glasgow:
"Jean-Claude Carrière's beautiful translation into French gives a British
audience a chance both to hear the play through a refreshing, transparent film, and to enjoy the overlapping assonances."[26]

Thus, despite the natural pressures toward truly heteroglossic expression arising from the international company assembled at its founding,
Brook's theatre remained essentially committed to French (though spoken, naturally, with a variety of accents) until 1995, when it offered a new

version of *Hamlet* called *Qui est là?,* which was as strikingly heteroglossic as Beier's *Midsummer Night's Dream.* It seems unlikely that Brook was aware of Beier's production, which opened the same month as his own, but other more immediate influences may have contributed. It may possibly have been Brook's awareness of and sponsoring of the heteroglossic South African theatre productions that turned his interest in this direction, but an even more immediate suggestion may have been provided by the London-based Théâtre de Complicité (founded in 1983) that Brook hosted earlier in 1995, thus introducing this important experimental company to France. Heteroglossic production has been an important part of the Complicité aesthetic throughout their work; indeed, their name itself suggests a multicultural orientation. *The Three Lives of Lucie Cabrol* (1994), which Brook presented, allowed the actors, coming from a variety of linguistic backgrounds, to speak a substantial number of lines in their native speech, most of it dialects of French and German. This approach called attention to the varied cultural backgrounds of the artists who came together to create this work, a concern with obvious potential relevance to Brook's own international company,[27] but beyond that it also reflected an interest in heteroglossia itself that the company has regularly utilized in ways not related to their individual linguistic backgrounds. *The Street of Crocodiles* (1992), for example, contained material in English, French, German, Latin, and Spanish.[28]

Gerhard Preußler, reporting on Beier's *Midsummer Night's Dream* in the German magazine *Theater Heute,* was not yet aware of the parallel Brook experiment that opened this same month. Even so he credited Brook with initiating the line of experimentation that Beier was continuing by first bringing together an international company with no common language and creating the first "mixed language production though a synthetic myth mixture with the title Orghast."[29] The two 1995 productions, though very different in tonality, were remarkably similar in their use of heteroglossia, since both made extensive use not only of different languages, often the native languages of the actors involved, but also of physical "citations" from the dramatic tradition. Perhaps most strikingly, both productions offered extended multicultural internal discussions among their actors about the theatre and especially about different approaches to the art of acting.

Just as Beier, in her brilliant "Pyramus and Thisbe" sequence utilized not only different spoken languages, but (often closely related) different performance languages, such as Stanislavskian realism (done by a Russian speaker), Brechtian epic style (done by a German speaker), Grotowskian stylization (done by a Polish speaker), commedia dell'arte (done by an Italian speaker), and so on, so Brook offered quotations, often in appropriate languages, from a variety of theatre theorists—Craig, Brecht, Meyerhold, Zeami, Stanislavsky, Artaud—some the same as those used by Beier.[30] Although French was utilized in Brook's production, not one of his seven actors was in fact French, and most spoke at least part of the time, like Beier's actors, in their native tongue: Yoshi Oida (Caudius) in Japanese, Bruce Meyers (Polonius) and Anne Bennet (Gertrude) in English. One of the most memorable sequences was the confrontation between Hamlet (Bakary Sangaré) and the Ghost (Mamdou Bioumé), in which these two long-standing central members of Brook's company for the first time in his theatre conversed not in French, but in Barbara, the Mande language spoken in both their home countries of Mali and Senegal.[31] The Ghost also spoke only in Bambara when he appeared in Gertrude's chamber.

Andy Lavender, in his study of three recent experimental *Hamlets,* quotes Brook to the effect that Bioumé's use of Bambara, like Oida's quotations from Zeami in Japanese, was seen less as a strategy of postmodern cultural mixing than as a strategy for achieving a deeper authenticity, a goal much more in keeping with the theatrical essentialism that has marked so much of Brook's work. "The African, in this instance, is used to signify something especially pure," says Lavender. "The African language works here as a guarantee of that simplicity, relocating the scene to the site of the actor's birthplace." Since language operates as "a basic signifier of cultural identity," "the conversation in Bambara marks the Ghost as being especially 'authentic,' not so much supernatural as super-natural."[32] Similarly, when Yoshi Oida as the First Player is asked by Hamlet to present the speech about the death of Priam, he presents it solemnly and elegantly, but in Japanese. The speech was transposed into Japanese, Brook commented, so that Oida "could play it as well as possible, with the greatest intensity, in his own language."[33]

The production's other source of heteroglossia was the extensive quotations from Craig, Meyerhold, and other theorists that opened the evening and that occurred at other key moments, such as the arrival of the Players. Strikingly, however, these historical "voices" were stripped of any part of the authenticating "presence" that Brook sought in the use of Bambara or Japanese. These quotation sequences, notes Lavender, presented "statements but not characters. Meyerhold and Stanislavsky are not played as individuals. Their words are voiced by actors, with no sign of characterization, or role-playing."[34] And, significantly, the quotations were not in their original languages, except, of course, those from Artaud. In fact, the "voices" of the variety of theorists utilized by Brook were brought into a totalizing aesthetic, not only linguistically, but philosophically. As Lavender observes, "the writings of Brecht, *et al.* have been usefully distilled by Brook and his team. In fact they have been ruthlessly interpreted—*synthesized*—in order to present a coherent aesthetic." Various phrases, "taken out of context . . . truncated and transplanted" present "the problematics of theatre as a single field, to be resolved practically and philosophically through the agency of the super-skilled (rational-and-intuitive) practitioner. Who other than Brook himself?"[35] Given this totalizing process, the question naturally arises of whether Brook's work, even so apparently a heteroglossic work as *Qui est là?,* can really be considered, as David Williams and others have suggested, postmodern. Certainly Brook effectively, even brilliantly utilized in his works toward the end of the century many of the devices of postmodernism, supporting Shomit Mitter's characterization of him as a brilliant theatrical magpie.[36] Nevertheless, the apparent heteroglossia of these works remained in the service of the distinctly monoglossic vision of Brook himself. Patrice Pavis clearly has pointed out this dynamic, calling Brook "only superficially postmodern."

> Fundamentally he isn't a postmodernist at all, in spite of certain stylistic approaches and ingredients [such as language mixing or quotation of other "voices"] which often constitute a kind of "postmodern" dressing. Brook is the last of the humanists. His discourse is "profound" on the level of his persistent return to an essentialist vision of humanity, to a belief in the possibility of "meeting" the Other, to a particular positioning of humanity in the universe.[37]

As Pavis suggests, Brook's experiments of the late twentieth century, despite their occasional postmodern gloss, continued to look backward to high modernism, giving even his experiments with heteroglossia a monoglossic orientation. Whether Brook was literally the last major director to subscribe to this high modernist essentialism might be debated, but by 1995 it was clear that the great majority of experimental work with heteroglossic expression was more like the postmodern, nonessentialist approach of Beier. A clear example of this was a new international organization founded this same year and clearly inspired by the earlier Théâtre des Nations, out of whom the Beier multilingual Shakespeares developed. While Giorgio Strehler, the major architect of the Théâtre des Nations, primarily looked northward to Europe, another Italian director, Giovanna Marinelli, looked southward, to the countries of the Mediterranean. The theatrical organization headed by Marinelli, the ETI (Ente Teatrale Italiano) has been since the 1940s a major presence in Italy, controlling major theatres in Rome, Florence, and Bologna. In 1995 the ETI organized the Porti del Mediterraneo (Mediterranean Gateways), which was dedicated to organizing international productions much in the manner of the Beier *Midsummer Night's Dream.* The Porti del Mediterraneo likewise brought together actors from different theatres in different countries, speaking different languages, in order to create multilinguistic projects that would then tour to various participating countries. The most successful production of this collaboration was the 1999 *Sacrifice,* conceived by the Italian director Marco Baliani. The action was based on the biblical story of the sacrifice of Isaac and the mythological story of the sacrifice of Iphigenia, and drew parallels between these ancient narrations and the sacrifices of innocent victims of recent ideological conflicts. The general production style suggested a Greek tragedy, with chorus members drawn from Italy, Tunisia, Morocco, France, Lebanon, and Albania, all speaking their own language. In the powerful conclusion, Agamemnon fails in his attempts to communicate with the troubled and confused chorus members as behind him the curtain rises on a burning city, an all too familiar contemporary image that transcends linguistic barriers.[38]

## Festivals and Touring

The burgeoning of international theatre festivals at the end of the twentieth century provided a particularly fertile ground for intercultural performances of this sort, since these brought together in a regular and highly publicized manner artists, critics, and a public from a wide variety of cultural and linguistic backgrounds. In the summer of 1998, for example, attending a theatre festival in Pula, Croatia, I was struck by the number of productions bringing together actors in heteroglossic productions. The linguistic complexity of the former Yugoslavia has made this an area particularly interested in such experimentation. As early as the 1980s Yugoslavian companies such as KPGY, directed by Ljubisa Ristic, regularly presented productions mixing the various official languages of that country. The breakup of Yugoslavia, with all its divisive pressures, has not destroyed such experiments, but has on the contrary given them a particular urgency and relevance, since their aim has shifted from a fairly complacent celebration of the multiculturalism of the Yugoslavian state to a rather desperate reaffirmation of that multiculturalism in the face of the frightful cultural conflicts that so tortured Yugoslavia's successor states. I was particularly impressed at Pula by the production *Cezar,* directed by Branko Brezovec, one of the region's best-known experimental directors. This production combined a Slovenian play from the 1920s with a contemporary play from Macedonia and material from Brecht and Shakespeare in a performance utilizing actors from Slovenia, Croatia, Macedonia, and Bosnia, sometimes speaking their own languages, sometimes each other's, and sometimes bits of English and German in a very contemporary meditation on politics, tyranny, and current cultural tensions.

As these examples suggest, Europe was a fertile area for heteroglossic performance in the final years of the twentieth century, but the bringing together of actors from different linguistic backgrounds to create productions utilizing their varied languages was a worldwide phenomenon, and closely related to the aesthetics of postmodernism. In Japan, as in Western Europe, an important inspiration for this work was provided by a highly influential experimental director who, like Peter Brook, bore an ambiguous relationship to late-twentieth-century intercultural theatre, drawing together artists, subject matter, and formal techniques from widely separated cultural traditions, but still on the whole subjecting them to a totalizing aesthetic much more like that of high modernism than of postmodern expression. Suzuki Tadashi, surely the best-known Japanese theatre director of this period, began his career in the 1960s applying rigorous instruction in classic Japanese modes to contemporary themes and to classic Western, especially Greek, material. Despite the intercultural nature of such work, it remained entirely in Japanese until 1982, when he combined American actors from the University of Wisconsin with his Japanese troupe to create a bilingual version of Euripides' *Bacchae* that was performed in both the United States and Japan. William Beeston, in analyzing this production, likened it to works in the classical theatre traditions of South and Southeast Asia "where elevated characters speak one kind of language, and low characters another," since the different characters in the *Bacchae* spoke different languages "to some extent because they exist on different planes of reality."[39] This *Bacchae* production provided a model for subsequent bilingual experimentation in Japan, but Suzuki himself tended to work more in the manner of Peter Brook. Like Brook, he developed an international training and performing company, SCOT (Suzuki Company at Toga), where he gathered an international company of actors to do research in performance techniques. Despite the heteroglossic background of the performers themselves and the fact that like Brook's company, they often worked with both Eastern and Western material (in Suzuki's case with Western classics like the Greeks or Shakespeare and with Japanese forms like the Noh and Kabuki) Suzuki's approach, like Brook's, did not seek to stress the different voices involved in this work, but on the contrary to find beneath the heteroglossia a single language of "universal" postures and movements.[40] Thus Suzuki, like Brook, may be considered a director who has utilized postmodern material, with its proclivity for heteroglossia, in a monoglossic high modernist aesthetic.

During the 1990s, however, other theatre artists in Japan would draw upon the potentially heteroglossic work of Suzuki, as a number of Europeans drew upon that of Brook, to create much more distinctly multivoiced experiments. The shift from the monoglossic theatre of Suzuki to a clearly heteroglossic one is clearly illustrated in the work of two of Suzuki's leading actors at Toga, Kenji Suzuki (no relation to Tadashi) and Ayako Watanabe. These two actors left SCOT in 1986 to found their own company, TAO, which in 1996 changed to ETI (the Evolutional Theatre Institute). Its first major production was a bilingual one, *Opium,* in 1997, which, according to its dramaturg, Stephen Weeks, "reflected the commitment of all concerned to the careful development of an experimental work whose inflections were both postmodern and intercultural."[41] Every effort was made to avoid the traditional single controlling voice, whether that of the author, the director, or even the theatrical culture. Three American actors and three Japanese actors developed the work alongside an American playwright-compiler, J. Steven Pearson from the University of Washington School of Drama, and a Japanese director, Kenji Suzuki. Central to the production concept was its heteroglossic commitment, as Weeks explains:

> Throughout the process, both in rehearsal and in performance, the collaborators worked and thought in binary terms: two languages, two traditions, two audiences, two geographies. Accordingly, there was no single presiding artistic consciousness working from a single cultural context.[42]

Surely the most elaborate international heteroglossic project of the late twentieth century was the *Undesirable Elements* of the Chinese-American experimental artist Ping Chong. The project began in 1992 specifically as an experiment with a work in multiple languages dealing with people who, like Ping Chong himself, were children in one culture and then moved into another. The ongoing project had by 2004 been staged in more than twenty different versions, across the United States and in a number of foreign countries, including Germany, Japan, and the Netherlands. For each production Ping Chong assembles an international cast of six young persons (the first versions used eight), but unlike the international companies of Brook or Suzuki, these performers are not professional actors, nor do they appear in more than one version of the piece. The cultural backgrounds they bring to the production are thus not theatrical, but social, political, and linguistic. The overall form of the evening is the same, though the content is based on material provided by the performers. Each begins with a purely heteroglossic passage, as the participants introduce themselves in their native languages. These will be different in each production, but no version has more than one speaker of each language. In the 1995 production in Seattle, Washington, for example, the performers spoke English (an African-American), Icelandic, Indonesian, Inupiaq, Iranian, Japanese,

Latvian, and Palestinian (this was while the production  
eight participants), while in New York in 2002 the perfor.  
English (from the Philippines), Filipino, Swahili, Arabic, Jap.  
Tongan.[43] Subsequent sections grow out of discussions about ti  
ing of each participant's name, about recent world history as se  
the different cultural perspectives, and about associations, as whe.. each  
participant asks the others, "What do you think of when you hear the  
word Lebanon (or Tonga, or Iceland, whatever the place of origin)?" In  
Ping Chong's *Undesirable Elements,* involving hundreds of participants  
from dozens of cultures and presented before both national and interna-  
tional audiences, the heteroglossic potential of the intercultural casts  
assembled by the experimental directors of the late twentieth century  
has received its fullest realization to date.

*Undesirable Elements* also offers an elaborate example of the blending  
of heteroglossic expression with another important part of postmodern  
theatrical experimentation, the emergence of the self as the subject of the  
theatrical event. During the 1970s, autobiographical performance  
became a central part of American performance art, especially by  
women, seeking to gain a "voice" for their concerns and experiences in  
the traditionally male-dominated theatre. In the following decades  
other silenced voices, gays and lesbians and members of ethnic minori-  
ties, also utilized autobiographical performance to articulate their con-  
cerns.[44] Within the theatrical culture as a whole, such performances  
obviously created a new heteroglossia, but clearly each individual per-  
formance made a kind of monoglossic claim. Even that monoglossia  
began to break down in the later years of the twentieth century, how-  
ever, as a number of performance artists began to recognize, and per-  
form, the multiple "identities" that exist within each individual, and  
particularly strikingly within individuals with multiple cultural back-  
grounds. So we find, for example, such mixed identity performers as the  
already mentioned Guillermo Verdecchia in Canada, or Guillermo  
Gomez-Peña, who emphasizes "multiple identities" in his perfor-  
mances, explaining, "Depending on the context I am Chicano, Mexican,  
Latin American, or American in the wider sense of the term. The Mex-  
ican Other and the Chicano Other are constantly fighting to appropriate  
me or reject me."[45]

There is clearly a considerable difference between the internalized heteroglossia of a Gomez-Peña and the multiple individualized "voices" of the *Undesirable Elements* project, just as there is between the presentation of non-role-playing but linguistically diverse "selves" in *Undesirable Elements* and the role-playing, linguistically diverse performers in Beier's *Midsummer Night's Dream* or *Qui est là?* Lavender may be right in his contention that the use of Bambara in the latter "returns the scene to the actor's birthplace," but this process is still heavily conditioned by the mimetic conditions that place the actor in the context of the ramparts of Elsinore Castle and the narrative of Hamlet, a situation very different from the evocation of birthplace in the essentially nonmimetic *Undesirable Elements*. Despite these distinct differences in the dramatic and performance strategies, however, all of these heteroglossic experiments make a similar claim to Brook's "authenticity," in that each is tied to or grounded in the speaker. The "native language" and the heteroglossia in such productions is one of the most important markers of the heterogeneous cultural backgrounds of those bodies assembled to create the performance.

## Linguistic Collage

This sort of theatrical heteroglossia became prominent in the late twentieth century because of its close and obvious ties to the intercultural companies that became an important part of the experimental theatre of this period. Almost as important, however, and even more distinctly representative of postmodernism, with its suspicion of any claims of authenticity and grounding, was another type of theatrical heteroglossia, in which multiple languages are utilized not for the traditional motives of verisimilitude or humor, nor in recognition of varying linguistic backgrounds within the company or the public, nor even for political or social commentary, but rather out of an interest in linguistic mixing for its own sake, as one might mix elements of various decorative, historical, or theatrical traditions in the sort of open, decentered experimentalism that characterizes much postmodernist art. Cultural collage is a common postmodern creative strategy, and it should not be surprising that language fragments, like other cultural fragments, have begun to be worked into theatrical collage.

This sort of postmodern linguistic mixing has become widely

employed by leading experimental directors and companies around the world. Italy's Societas Raffaello Sanzio, a leading attraction in recent years at Avignon and other major European festivals, is primarily known for its bold, hallucinatory images, but along with these its free-wheeling theatrical collages also typically include scraps of various languages. One of Montreal's best-known experimental groups, Carbone Quatorze, led by Gilles Maheu, not only mixes French and English in its productions, as one might expect, but also regularly includes other languages as well: Italian in the recent production, *Le Dortoir* (1988), and German in the previous *Le Rail* (1983), essentially for formal or even decorative rather than realistic purposes. Ciulli's Turkish/German *In the Jungle of Cities* also included, mostly in asides to the audience, a variety of much less clearly motivated language fragments—some Spanish, some French, some English. A much more surrealistic and oneiric exploration of similar concerns is offered by the linguistically dazzling monologue *Don't Blame the Bedouins,* by Canadian René-Daniel Dubois, which mixes speakers of various dialects of French, English, Italian, German, Russian, and Chinese in an apocalyptic vision of an ultimate fusion of culture and technology. In the 1991 *Chant du Bouc* of the French Théâtre du Radeau, the dialogue of the performance was composed entirely of a sequence of sound patterns from different languages, ancient Greek, French, Italian, and German.

Few theorists and practitioners have been more influential in the development of a postmodern aesthetic than John Cage, both for his interest in the introduction of chance to the artistic process and for his attention to expanding the concept of potential artistic sound from the highly structured art of music to any acoustical phenomenon. Cage's attention to nonmusical sound opened the way, particularly in late-twentieth-century dance, first to nonmusical sound accompaniment, then to language, both on and off stage, and then to multiple language experimentation, with language as a formal element in the composition, like gesture and movement. Alexander Bakshi's environmental performances in Russia from the mid-1990s onward show this progression in a nondance environment. Early works, such as *A Hotel Room in the Town of N* (1994) surrounded their audience with a complex environment of musical and nonmusical sounds, performed on traditional and newly created instruments. Gradually, vocal material was added, and with it a commitment to heteroglossic expression. The aptly named *Polyphony of the World,* created for the International Theatre Olympics of 2001, collected sixty artists plus choruses from around the world who provided both sounds and languages from a wide variety of cultures. Bakshi described it in terms that precisely capture a widespread attitude toward heteroglossic expression at the beginning of the new century:

> This will be a spectacle about the equality of voices from various cultures. I believe the age-old ideal of harmonious unification has given way to the notion of polyphony. I do not mean that in a political sense where the equality of all voices represents the equality of all before God. I mean the equal significance of diverse voices from all cultures. They are all different and they are all equal.[46]

The use of language fragments as a formal element is often found in the work of those experimental dance companies that work along the boundary between theatre and dance. After John Cage's attention to nonmusical sound opened the way for dance to utilize a variety of sound, the development of German Tanztheater, a form midway between dance and theatre, opened the way for the use of language as well. In its original form (advanced by Gerhard Bohner in 1972) Tanztheater used the human body not as a formal object in space but as an instrument to explore emotions or express ideas. Early Tanztheater's use of language was thus largely functional and mimetic, but with the coming of postmodernism it began to be fragmented and manipulated in the kind of collage construction often found in postmodern performance.[47] One may follow this trajectory of experimentation quite clearly in the late-twentieth-century productions of one of the most important creators of the modern Tanztheater, Anne Teresa De Keersmaeker. In her early signature piece, *Rosas danst Rosas* (1983), five women explored simple actions such as standing, sitting, and walking, but with strong intimations of character in a theatrical sense. *Elena's Aria* (1984) added spoken text, as different dancers at different points moved a chair downstage, turned on a light, sat, and read passages from Dostoyevsky, Tolstoy, and Brecht. During the late 1990s De Keersmaeker created a series of pieces specially exploring relationships between movement and text, culminating in *I Said I* (1999), in which the performers developed a meditation upon identity based on the speaking pieces of Peter Handke but articulated through verbal fragments of English, Japanese, German, Dutch, and French.[48]

Similarly complex heteroglossic experimentation can be found in a number of the Europe's leading experimental dance companies. Michael Laub, a Belgian who directs an experimental company in Sweden, Remote Control Productions, provides a particularly striking example of such linguistic collage. In works like *Fast Forward/Bad Air und So* (1991), with its macaronic title, he mixes texts in English, German, French, Dutch, and Swedish to create a fragmented multiple text operating on several linguistic and theatrical channels simultaneously.

Needcompany, an internationally acclaimed experimental dance company based in Brussels, regularly mixes languages in its distinctly postmodern performances. In its 2001 adaptation of *King Lear,* for example, although the basic language of the production was Flemish, there was a constant mixing in of other languages (and indeed material from other Shakespearian plays and elsewhere, in the manner of much modern German experimental theatre). In what must be meant as a postmodern linguistic joke, the King of France in fact speaks English throughout and his English wife, Cordelia, French. Both of Cordelia's sisters and their husbands sometimes speak English and sometimes Flemish. Edmund's bastard monologue is given entirely in English, and the Fool often breaks into English for his jokes and sometimes into songs from other plays, such as "The Rain It Raineth Every Day" during the tempest scene.

This sort of casual mixing of languages not on grounds of dramatic verisimilitude, but for particular theatrical effects, seems particularly marked in the recent German theatre, perhaps due in part to the significant late-twentieth-century tradition in Germany of directors taking liberties with texts that would be unusual in most other countries of Western Europe and unthinkable in any major theatre of England or the United States. Leading contemporary directors such as Frank Castorf almost invariably insert into both classic and contemporary plays material from other sources—from other plays, from pop culture, from sports, from the surrounding world of politics. Not infrequently this interpolated material comes in its original language. In his 1998 production of Sartre's *Dirty Hands,* for example, in addition to passages in English (almost always utilized in a Castorf production) and French (some from Sartre's original, some from other sources) the production included many passages in Serbo-Croatian as Castorf developed parallels between Sartre's troubled protagonist Hoederer and Bosnian war criminal Radovan Karadzic. Hoederer in several places actually quotes Karadzic's speeches and writings, but other Serbo-Croatian passages come from Tito and others. In one complex sequence Hugo, arguing with Hoederer in Serbo-Croatian, quotes a story about Serbian atrocities from a collection by Senada Marjazovic of children's recollections. Another character, Jessica, begins translating their speeches for other characters on the stage and then walks out of the theatrical frame to tell the story directly to the audience.[49] Similar examples of intertextual and interlinguistic mixing, along with the disruption of theatrical illusion, could be cited from any Castorf production. This sort of heteroglossic collage construction, in many different forms, can be found among the work of most of the leading experimental directors in contemporary Germany, especially those associated with Castorf and his theatre, the Berlin Volksbühne, such as Christoph Marthaler or René Pollesch.

My final example of postmodern heteroglossia is of a rather different kind, an extreme example of linguistic syncretism in which two languages are not merely placed side by side, but so interpenetrated that they alternate almost word to word. This was the linguistic strategy in a major part of the epic production *Schlachten!*, one of the great successes of the European theatre in 1999. *Schlachten!* was created in Belgium (as *Ten Oorlog*) by the well-known Flemish author Tom Lanoye and the even better-known Flemish theatre director Luk Perceval. This twelve-hour cycle of the Shakespearian history plays from *Richard II* to *Richard III* created such a stir in Belgium that it was invited to participate in the Salzburg Festival that spring. It then traveled to Hamburg and eventually to the Theatertreffen in Berlin, a festival of the outstanding productions of the previous year in German-speaking countries. One might naturally assume that the Flemish author Lanoye would have rendered Shakespeare's play into his own language for his Flemish public and that this production, sent on tour to international festivals, would follow the normal practice today of such touring productions, being offered to foreign audiences in its native language, but supplemented by supertitles.

I will consider some of the practices and implications of supertitles, an important new addition to theatrical language, in the next chapter, but in fact this common aid was not used either in Salzburg or in Berlin. A new version of the text was created, which replaced the Flemish with German but which left intact the most distinctive linguistic feature of the production, which was that it was thoroughly macaronic, mixing the local language significantly with English, and moreover with English of a particular style. The audience member who attended, for example, the *Richard III* section of this production in Salzburg, Hamburg, or Berlin was offered a version of Richard's famous opening speech "Now is the winter of our discontent . . ." quite recognizable, but still far removed from traditional renderings of that speech in any of the three national or linguistic traditions involved: Flemish, German, or English. Here are the opening lines:

Now is the fokking winter unseres Würgens
Befreit vom Eis zu einem heißen Sommer
Dank Kronprinz Eddy, dieser "Sonne Yorks"!
And clouds of doom that hung above our heads,
Sind in des Ozeans feuchtem Loch begraben;
In unserm Haar klebt Glitter und Konfetti,
Und müßig rost' die Rüstung an der Wand!
Our speech of war schlägt um in trunknes Lallen
Our proud parade in schlappen Schwof . . . Und Bruder Eddy,
Der Schlachtengott, wird fett and smiles like Buddha . . .
'Tis not his horse, dem er die Sporen gibt,
To terminate his furious opponents:
Er galloppiert durch tausend Weiberzimmer,
Und bringt den Frauen die Flötentöne bei.[50]

The creation of this modern macaronic dramatic vocabulary grew out of an attempt by the adaptor and director to create a parallel between the movement from the medieval world of *Richard II* to the suggestion of a modern gangster mentality in *Richard III,* and to play this out in changing styles of language, somewhat parallel to the James Joyce's famous parody evocation of the evolution of English literature in *Ulysses.* In the original version of *Schlachten!,* adapter Lanoye based the language of

*Richard II* on old Flemish and French, gradually moving to a more contemporary idiom until the penultimate play, *Eddy the King,* in which the sons of the Duke of York, who dominate this play and the next, moved into what Lanoye himself described as a linguistic atmosphere of "Tarantino, Elmore Leonard, American Slang, Motown-quotations, and so on."[51] The German adaptation followed a similar pattern, beginning with high classical German sprinkled with French, and evolving into the macaronic speech of the York/Tarantino brothers.

I must admit that my own reaction to this project was to see Lanoye's linguistic experiment as suggesting a distinct current social commentary. The dynamic of the production, beginning with elegant and stately opening sequences, and descending to the ruthless and degenerate intrigues of Dirty Rich and his confederates, seemed to me strongly to suggest a parallel decline and corruption in the language itself, from the pure classical German of the opening scenes to the corrupt, debased speech of American gangster films and advertising, all too familiar in contemporary German culture. Lanoye, however, in an interview about the genesis of the project, suggested no such social implication. He spoke of his goals only in formal and morally neutral terms, drawing upon a parallel from the world of the plastic arts:

> What I was trying to do in literary terms may be thought of as similar to going to an art museum when one leaves the classical section (the world of *Richard II*) and then finds himself in a room in which a quite different aesthetic challenges him, a room in which an inverted urinal hangs on one wall and in the corner pieces of driftwood are scattered about, where half of the visitors say, "Yes, but is this just everyday driftwood?" And the critics say, "No, no, this is art!" That is just the sort of effect I was seeking in language. The English at the end of the play had for me less the connotations of real English, but rather of the confusion of languages that totally surround us today. All we have to do is turn on the TV or the radio. We live in a speech aquarium, which seems, depending on how you view it, extremely rich and varied or extremely polluted. I used this aquarium to create a speech of existential anguish and destructiveness around the figure of Dirty Rich, who is the most modern of all the kings.[52]

Quite aside from the inspiration or the effects of this particular production, both of the images evoked by Lanoye—that of the modern museum, with its eclectic collection and display of found objects, natural and artificial, and the speech aquarium, with its richly mixed (some would say polluted) display of difference—are highly suggestive of the complex role that language is now playing in theatres around the world. In country after country dramatists and directors are experimenting with the realization that the language pool as well as the cultural pool in which they swim is no longer, if it ever was, the kind of uniform and stagnant carp pond that forms such a powerful central image in Ibsen's *Lady from the Sea,* but a postmodern aquarium, in which the oddest and most surprising encounters have become commonplace.

So-called intercultural theatre up until late in the twentieth century normally either took material from one culture and appropriated it for work in another, in the manner of Mnouchkine's use of Kathakali makeup and costumes in *Les Atrides,* or wove it into a modernist totalizing unity in the name of a kind of transcultural theatre in the manner of Brook's *Mahabharata.* The more recent experiments of artists and groups like Carbone 14, Beier, Castorf, Lanoye, and many of the leading figures in the modern Tanztheater point in quite a different direction, one that allows material, including language, from different cultures to play against material from other cultures, without necessarily privileging any particular cultural material, even that most familiar to a presumed majority of the audience. As the communicative network of the modern world becomes more complex and more intertwined, linguistic collages of this sort are becoming more and more common in the theatre. Unquestionably these present new challenges and will demand new strategies for reception, but they nevertheless reflect, as the theatre has always reflected, current cultural consciousness and concerns. The alien outsider whose voice appeared only in a few grotesque fragments in the Greek theatre has today become one of a fugal chorus of voices, in some cases with none of them claiming linguistic primacy, weaving new theatrical mixtures for the audiences of a new multicultural society.

# 5  *The Heteroglossia of Side Texts*

THE PREVIOUS MATERIAL IN this study has concerned the type of heteroglossia that has been most widespread in the theatre throughout its history, considering the various strategies and various results involved when actors have utilized a mixture of languages and dialects on historical and contemporary stages. I will conclude with a dimension of theatrical heteroglossia quite different from that discussed in the rest of the book, a dimension that has really emerged only in recent years but that is very rapidly growing in importance in theatres around the world. This is a heteroglossia that presents simultaneously on the stage different languages, but involves both languages that are spoken and others that are not.

When we use the term *language* in the theatre, we normally think only of spoken language, but the rise of modern semiotic theory encourages us to apply this term more broadly. Drawing upon linguistic analysis, the first modern theatre semioticians often spoke of the various "languages" utilized in the theatre, as in the title of one of the first major books on the subject, Patrice Pavis's *Languages of the Stage*.[1] Since semiotic theory was concerned with the communicative process of the total theatre experience, these "languages" included the language of costume, of gesture, of scenery, of lighting, and so on. In this study I have so far considered language in its more conventional sense, in the form of words spoken by the actors on stage, what is usually referred to as the dramatic dialogue. Without broadening the idea of language as semiotics has done, to include all potential communicative systems on stage, however, I wish in this section to consider another way that language, more narrowly defined, is utilized in the theatre and, more importantly for my present concern, has come to contribute directly to the play of languages on the modern stage. I am here speaking of language that operates not orally but visually.

The most common visual appearance of language on stage is that of the written text, from various printed signs in previous eras to the modern supertitle. Less obvious, but also important to the theme of this study, is another visual language that has grown steadily in importance in recent years, sign language. Each of these alternative language processes, beginning as simple translation devices, has recently grown beyond that function to enter more directly into the aesthetic frame of the theatrical production and thus into the play of language that is the subject of this book. Before addressing this more recent development, however, let us consider the framework in which these processes first appeared, that of translation, a framework that is almost always involved whenever the theatre utilizes more than one language.

## On-Stage Translation

Whenever a language or dialect appears in a production that is not likely to be understood by a majority of the audience, it requires some sort of performance adjustment if full or general communication is desired. We have already seen a variety of strategies utilized at different periods for dealing with this problem, ranging from the straightforward presentation of alien languages that the audience is not expected to understand, as in David Edgar's *Pentecost,* to the almost total, if inauthentic transparency of conventional stage dialects and accents, simply used as markers of an alien speech. In modern times, technological change has provided a variety of other means of assisting communication, most notably by simultaneous translations, either aural, normally by the use of earphones, or visual, in the form of supertitles. The use of such technical devices, and of other translation aids as well, has important effects upon theatrical reception, which will be one concern of this chapter, but another concern, perhaps less obvious, results from the fact that the modern stage, especially the experimental stage, is often highly self-conscious of its means of production and process of reception. Thus, as various mediating translation devices have become more familiar parts of the theatrical experience, these devices have themselves been consciously brought into the theatrical frame, adding what are in effect additional languages to the modern heteroglossic stage. The play of language in the modern theatre has broadened to include not only the encounter of diverse languages, but the mechanics by which this encounter is negotiated and their own effect upon reception, thus bringing this sort of theatrical experimentation directly into the domain of language play that is the central interest of this book.

In the simplest terms, when a human or mechanical "translator" is interposed between one language and other, it produces a third speech that is a compromise between the original content and the new form. Thus the device for negotiating heteroglossia adds another "voice" to the mixture. This fact, although basic to translation theory, tends to be hidden under the popular myth of "transparent" translation, even though there are many well-known examples of translations that are recognized as important independent creations, such as the Schlegel Shakespeare or the Chapman Homer. In the modern theatre, this "new voice" of the translator or medium of translation has received particular attention *as* an independent voice. That contribution to theatrical heteroglossia will be the central concern of this chapter.

The function now most frequently served in the theatre by the projected translation in the form of a supertitle was of course for centuries carried out by individual humans, who had some knowledge of languages other than their own and could serve as translators for their fellows. An example is the Boy pressed into the service of translation by Pistol in *Henry V:*

> PISTOL: Come hither, boy: ask me this slave in French What is his name.
> BOY: Écoutez: comment êtes-vous appelé?
> FRENCH SOLDIER: Monsieur le Fer.
> BOY: He says his name is Master Fer.
> PISTOL: Master Fer! I'll fer him, and firk him, and ferret him: discuss the same in French to him.
> BOY: I do not know the French for fer, and ferret, and firk.

Already we see the emergence of a third "voice," the boy's, which must adjust to his own understanding of both languages. Nor is this merely a matter of diminishment, for later we find him equally ready to embellish, adding in another way a new voice to the exchange:

PISTOL: Tell him my fury shall abate, and I
The crowns will take.
FRENCH SOLDIER: Petit Monsieur, que dit'il?
BOY: Encore qu'il est contre con jurement de pardoner aucun pris-
    onnier, néanmoins, pour les écus que vous avez promis, il est con-
    tent de vous donner la liberté, le franchisement. [Further, that it is
    against his better judgment to pardon any prisoner, but neverthe-
    less, considering the crowns that you have promised, he is satisfied
    to give you your liberty and freedom.][2]

Here is clearly another "voice," that of the translator, not only more elegant than Pistol's, but in fact providing substantial new information.

It is doubtless a mark of the growing preoccupation with the functions of language and also of the more frequent and complex linguistic
encounters in modern times that characters serving as translators are
more often encountered on contemporary than on historical stages.
Even more significant, from the point of view of this study, is the attention often given to the operations of translation, to its inadequacies, its
compromises, and thus to its functioning as yet another voice in the play.
The guide-translator Khwaya is a major figure in Tony Kushner's
*Homebody/Kabul.* He is a man of many languages (within the play he
speaks Dari, Pashtun, English, French, and Esperanto) and many
voices. One of the many subthemes of the play, for which Khwaya serves
as a focus, is the idea that different languages, even when spoken by the
same person, are in fact different "voices," expressing different world-
views. As a poet, Khwaya works in Esperanto, claiming that it is a language without history, and therefore without a history of oppression.
He finds it a language "not universally at home, rather homeless, state-
less, a global refugee patois,"[3] and thus a most useful language for contemporary displaced populations.

Perhaps the most interesting "translation" passage in the play is the
final scene of the second act, where Pricilla meets the former librarian,
Mahala. I have already mentioned this scene as an example of macaronic
theatre, but here wish to stress its commentary on language and its
demonstration of the process by which translation itself adds yet another
"voice" to the discourse. Khwaya during the scene provides translations

that are approximately correct, but often truncated and sometimes changed in content, either because he does not know the best word or because he wishes to avoid unpleasant material. Significantly, this process only occurs in the translations in this part of the play, when he is translating from French, the foreign language of the play most likely to be understood by Kushner's audiences, who can thus also understand the changes occurring in the translation. The opening of this scene contains both observations on the relationships between different cultures and their language as well as examples of the slippage of translation:

> MAHALA: Ces gens parlent Pashto, ces etrangers, ces occupants, ces Talibani; Kabul speak Dari. Vous le saviez? De sont des nettoyeurs ethniques. [These people speak Pasto, these strangers, these occupiers, these Taliban; Kabul speaks Dari. Do you know this? They are ethnic cleansers.]
> KHWAJA (Translating haltingly, a few words behind Mahala, starting after "parlent Pashto"): These peoples speak Pasto, these, um … Strangers, these occupiers, these Taliban. They are … ah … (In French, to Mahala) Nettoyeurs ethniques?
> MAHALA: They seek to … destroy all who are not Pashtun.[4]

French-speaking audience members will recognize the phrase "ethnic cleansers," but it is not part of Khwaya's French vocabulary nor of Mahala's English, and so it is in their voices converted into a phrase with similar meaning but a very different resonance.

The slippage of translation and the emergence of a new "translator's" language as a result of this slippage is even more openly addressed in Robert Lepage's *The Seven Streams of the River Ota,* a major modern heteroglossic work. Here also a translator appears on stage, but not as a character, as in Shakespeare or Kushner, but as a more neutral, if living, dramatic device. In three different scenes, a "Translator" enters an onstage booth, switches on a light, and provides simultaneous translation. The impression of a "neutral" voice is at first created by the fact that the translator is appearing in the booth separated from the action, is not identified as a character, and translates the voice of both speakers on stage in each scene. In the third scene, however, the independent voice of the translator is foregrounded:

HANAKO/TRANSLATOR: . . . Cet après-midi, je travaillais sur des texts d'Arthur Rimbaud. C'est mon poète favori. Il a cessé d'écrire il avait dix-sept ans. Je trouve ça triste qu'il soit tu si jeune. [This afternoon, I'm working on texts by Arthur Rimbaud. He's my favorite poet. He stopped writing when he was seventeen. I think it's very sad that he killed himself so young.] (Or, at least, this is how the translator interprets Hanako's last statement. Hanako speaks now to the Translator.)

HANAKO: C'est pas ce que j'ai voulu dire. [That's not what I wanted to say.]

TRANSLATOR (in English): Pardon me.

HANAKO (in English): That is not what I wanted to say. (In French) J'ai pas dit: qu'il se soit tué, j'ai dit: qu'il se soit tu. [I didn't say he killed himself, I said he went silent.]

TRANSLATOR (in English): I find it sad that he went silent so young.

HANAKO: Traduttore, traditore.[5]

The switch into Italian to end this interchange allows an extra linguistic joke, but the familiar quotation ("Translator, traitor," or "To translate is to betray") is perfectly appropriate, and once again calls attention to the independent "voice" of translation.

Not only the heteroglossic text, but the heteroglossic production history of *The Seven Streams of the River Ota* makes it a rich example of linguistic play in the contemporary theatre. The first version of the play opened at the Edinburgh Festival in 1994 and toured that fall to other venues in England, Scotland, and France. The following year, an expanded version toured the world, playing in Austria, Germany, Italy, Spain, Switzerland, Denmark, Japan, and Canada. A third version opened in Quebec in May 1996 and then played at the Vienna Festwochen in a somewhat altered form. This version is the one published by Methuen. Later in 1996 it continued to tour, to Germany, Denmark, England, France, and the United States.[6] Moving so heteroglossic a production among so heteroglossic an audience obviously provided a major challenge to communication, and Lepage employed a variety of devices to address this matter, though they are by no means totally consistent in their usage.

As the examples from Kushner and Lepage suggest, the onstage translator can relate to the surrounding action in a variety of ways. Traditionally, as in *Henry V* or *Homebody/Kabul,* he is embedded within the dramatic world of the play, a character among characters, a voice among voices, and the fact that he may provide a necessary communication aid to the audience is hidden within the convention of dramatic illusion, like a drama's necessary exposition. The translators in *Seven Streams* occupy a much more ambiguous position, literally on the margins of the action, in their own booths, and openly serving as informants to the audience. They do, however, interact with the characters, who indicate that they overhear the translations, so they remain partly embedded in the play.

*Side Texts*

For most of the scenes in *Seven Streams* that involve translation, Lepage uses a device that remains entirely outside the dramatic action, and one that has become far more standard than an embedded translator in the contemporary theatre for the performance of alien languages. This is the supertitle, an aid to communication in heteroglossic drama that has moved within a relatively short period of time from a feature of the experimental stage and occasionally of the opera to a major feature of international performance. The supertitle is the most familiar performance example of what I will refer to as a *side text,* a term borrowed from Roman Ingarden but used in a different and expanded way.

Ingarden's term appears amid his discussion of how the same object is presented in different ways in different modes of representation, especially when different relationships of the "narrating" subject are involved. He notes, but does not develop, the difference between the dramatic text and the stage realization of it, which was from the beginning one of the fundamental concerns of theatre semiotics, focusing instead upon how a playtext as a mode of representation differs from a novel or lyric poem:

What is most conspicuous in a "written" drama is the existence, side by side, of two different texts: the "side text" or stage directions—i.e. information with regard to where, at what time, etc., the given represented story takes place, who exactly is speaking, and perhaps also what he is doing at a given moment, etc.—and the main text itself.[7]

Ingarden's distinction, as I have noted, was widely employed by most early semiotic analysts of the theatre, who based their discussions on the conventional model of a playscript consisting of essentially three elements: the stage directions or didascalia, the character name attributions of the lines to be spoken (these two together comprising Ingarden's side text) and the lines actually spoken by the actors. According to the almost invariable model both of conventional production and semiotic analysis, each of these three elements undergoes a different transformation in the movement from page to stage. The stage directions serve as performance guides to actors on their movements and their reading of lines, to designers on the scenic environment of the action, and occasionally to directors on the overall visual composition (most famously perhaps by Diderot in his evocation of specific paintings). Just how faithful actors, directors, and designers are to be in converting the stage directions into the operations of their various arts was a matter of considerable controversy and disagreement during the twentieth century,[8] but there was general agreement that such directions, if followed at all, were to be converted into the various "languages" of the stage itself, those of costume, lighting, gesture, scenic design, makeup, and so on.[9] The only general exception was the normally very short indication of the time and place of action, which alone retained its written form, moving from the printed text to the theatre program. The second element, line attributions, disappeared entirely, except as a guide to the assigning of lines to the actors, a guide that was upon occasion not followed but that on the whole was accorded much more widespread respect than the other side-text material of scenic description and suggested line interpretations. The third element, the actual "lines" of the actors, the privileged part of the playtext (though susceptible to cutting in lengthy scripts) moved from page to stage by changing from uninflected printed text (except for the comparatively crude suggested inflections of the occasional stage directions) to the richly inflected verbal interpretation of the individual actors.

In the printed versions of many nineteenth- and twentieth-century plays, more elaborate side-text material became common. The extended prefaces and novelistic stage directions of Bernard Shaw are the best-known example of this, but long before Shaw, various supplementary background material, especially in the case of historical plays, was sometimes added to the other side text of the published drama, material presented for the reader, but not, like the lines, actually spoken on stage. Interestingly, some of the first such material was the translation, for the reader, of foreign language passages in heteroglossic plays. So, as early as Pixérécourt's *Christopher Columbus* (1815), translations of the Guana-hani language used in the play are provided in footnotes, along with other information the author wished to provide the reader, even though these translations were not available to spectators in the theatre. Contemporary heteroglossic dramas like those of Kushner and Lepage generally follow some variation of this practice, as David Edgar notes in the introduction to his *Pentecost:*

> All characters speak in the languages they know, whether their own or indeed English For information, I have identified the languages and given English translations of the Non-English speeches (printed in square brackets and not intended to be spoken).[10]

To assume, as Ingarden and traditional theatre semioticians have done, that the side text simply disappears, or is replaced by nonwritten equivalents in production, however, is to take an overly simple view of its operations. Evidence suggests that, from the Renaissance onward, at least some of the side text was carried over into the physical productions. Early Renaissance manuscripts of Terence suggest that identifying signs may have appeared over doorways on these early stages, and even if these images spring from the fantasy of early engravers, there is much clearer evidence that the Elizabethan theatre at least occasionally used printed signs to indicate scenes (Sidney remarks on a sign placed above a stage door designating it as "Thebes").[11] This custom continued during the nineteenth and twentieth centuries, if not in the realistic theatre, at least on more presentational and variety performances, where signs at the sides of the stage might introduce acts or locate scenes. Even more importantly, during the twentieth century, the epic and documentary theatre tradition, especially as developed by Piscator and Brecht, often utilized printed, painted, and projected written material to supplement and comment upon the action.

Another important intervention of side-text material into the actual experience of a production in the theatre is provided by such devices as the theatre program, which has been a standard part of the Western theatre experience for more than a century. The strict performance focus suggested by Barthes (whose theatrical "cybernetic machine" begins to emit its signals only when the curtain opens) would seem to exclude written material from the program from contributing to the actual performance experience,[12] but even the casual glance of a spectator at the program to see how much imaginary time has elapsed between acts brings a small bit of the side text, despite its written form, directly into the performance experience.

The occasional casual glance at the written information in a program might perhaps be dismissed as not a significant part of the actual performance experience, but there are also examples from theatre history in both the East and West of much more extended, indeed almost continuous simultaneous experience of written and performed texts. A clear example in the Western theatre was the common practice of many of the great international stars of the late nineteenth century when on their frequent tours. When such artists as Sarah Bernhardt, Tomasso Salvini, and Helena Modjeska traveled far beyond their native language communities, one of the common devices used to make them more accessible was printed translations in the local language, so that audiences not familiar with the star's language could follow along during the performance. In many cases almost every audience member utilized this printed "simultaneous translation," to the extent that reviews of Salvini's tours in America sometimes complained of the distraction of hundreds of pages being simultaneously turned in the auditorium by attentive readers.[13] In the Eastern theatre a similar phenomenon can still be observed in the Noh theatre, where faithful audience members traditionally follow the printed text of the performance's arcane language while the performance is going on, and one may still occasionally see in operatic performance a devotee following the score with the aid of a penlight, despite the potential distraction to his neighbors.

During the latter part of the twentieth century, two developments in international production produced important changes in the frequency and the phenomenology of this sort of extra written text that could be experienced simultaneously with its performed variation. First, in the course of the century, the ever-increasing ease of international transportation caused the international star to be gradually replaced by a much more complex system of international theatrical production in general. International tours of entire companies and productions became increasingly common, as did international festivals attracting both productions and audiences with extremely varied linguistic backgrounds. Under these circumstances the problem of language accessibility assumed proportions far greater than anything encountered by audiences or performers in earlier centuries. Second, the growth of technology provided much more sophisticated methods than the old printed libretti for providing audiences with simultaneous linguistic access to performances in languages not their own. Basically these methods have been of two types, each offering stimulating challenges for the semiotic analysis of theatrical reception. On the one hand, there are the simultaneous translations provided for audience members through headphones, and on the other, some form of projected printed translation, most commonly supertitles above the proscenium opening, but also sometimes seen on screens at either side of the stage or occasionally, as at the Metropolitan Opera in New York, as a kind of subtitle, presented on small individual screens mounted on the back of each seat for the patron behind. These different approaches to translation have their obvious parallels in the film, which provided a model for theatre in dealing with this problem.

Clearly in either case we are dealing here with a quite different kind of multiple language experience in the theatre than was available in the premodern age. Traditionally theatre audiences essentially experienced the play of languages only aurally, and these languages blended or clashed in the speech of the performers. Today nonactor channels can provide other sorts of linguistic mixing, either aural, when a language heard through earphones supplements a different language being simultaneously produced on the stage, or both aural and visual, when an audience member can hear one language being spoken by the actors and see a translation of that language in the projected form of a supertitle.

Since these supplementary language texts are literally produced alongside and simultaneously with the performance itself, I propose to refer to them as side texts, recognizing that this application extends Ingarden's term considerably beyond his own usage. While it is in fact the case that in some productions (I will present some examples later) supertitles have actually been used to make present in the theatre the written side text of, for example, stage directions that traditionally disappear in performance, the much more common use of these techniques is to provide an ongoing translation equivalent not of Ingarden's side text but of his "main text." It is not however, a main text that, as Ingarden defines it, is "really spoken" but one that doubles that text—a main text, as it were, that serves on the side of another main text.

## Supertitles and Simultaneous Translations

In discussing the heteroglossic implications of this supplementary performance text, I will devote my primary attention to the projected translation or supertitle, since it is at present the most favored of these technological alternatives, and since it has been the object of the most interesting and innovative developments as an alternative "voice" in the theatre. Before discussing the supertitle, however, it might be well to consider, if more briefly, some of the reception implications of its major alternative, the simultaneous translation, which offers rather different challenges and concerns. Both kinds of translation of course became fairly familiar to twentieth-century audiences for films well before they became widely established during the 1980s in the performance of opera. The filmic subtitle in fact doubtless provided the model for the theatrical subtitle and more common supertitle.[14] The simultaneous translation has a more complicated background. While subtitles are primarily associated with the film, simultaneous translation has become familiar in a far wider range of contexts, being the standard mode of communication in all sorts of international gatherings, political, commercial, professional, and social. Indeed the particular form it takes in the theatre, the wearing of earphones through which one hears a live translator, has its parallel only in the world of government and commerce, not in the film, where the nearest equivalent effect is achieved in a quite different way, by dubbing, which replaces the film's vocal sound track with recordings of other voices, synchronized as well as possible with the movement of the actors' lips in the filmic image.

   Although both are based upon the principle of simultaneous translation, the dubbing in film and the translation through earphones in the
theatre result in quite different reception experiences. While watching a
well-dubbed film, it is almost impossible to resist the illusion that the
heard voices are actually those of the actors whose images are being
shown. The nearest theatrical equivalent to film dubbing is in fact not
simultaneous translation but lip-synched performances. These, however, are created by a process exactly opposite to that of the dubbed film,
since here the silent actor attempts to fit his facial and bodily movements
to an already existing auditory text instead of vice versa. Still, both
dubbed films and lip-synched live performances depend for their success upon the illusion of a blend between a voice and an image that the
audience knows are not naturally united. Despite the rather different
attitudes of audiences toward these types of presentation, where a certain amount of the pleasure in seeing a lip-synched performer is in the
skill of the lip-synching itself, while the audience for a dubbed film normally would consider an awareness of the dubbing a distraction, generally speaking these two processes, which are in fact both heteroglossic,
are produced, presented, and experienced as univocal.
   The reception process involved in simultaneous translation is quite
different. Most obviously, the physical fact of wearing the earphones
denaturalizes the received voice and serves as a constant reminder that it
is not in fact being produced by the actor simultaneously visible on stage
but by someone else in an unseen "elsewhere." Moreover, while dubbing
and lip-synching seek as precise a coordination of sight and sound as is
technically possible, such coordination is not sought, nor indeed is it
really possible in simultaneous translation. In both dubbing and lip-
synching one side of the voice-body dualism is fixed by previous recording, so that the other, the live part, can be carefully adjusted for an
extremely close fit. In simultaneous translation, where both the actor on
stage and the translator off stage are live and therefore subject to continual variation, such close coordination is virtually impossible. Normally
the translator is situated so that he or she can observe the actor and speak
at approximately the same time, but the fit can really never be as close as
in dubbed films, and an audience member is therefore continually aware
of a disjuncture between the physical delivery of lines on the stage and
the aural delivery of them through earphones. This would be true even

if the earphones prevented any sound leakage whatever from the action on stage, but there is almost invariably some such leakage, so in fact the spectator hears the voice of the actor as a kind of ongoing background to the voice of the translator. Nor is this necessarily a negative or confusing effect. I know many spectators who, when attending productions with simultaneous translations, purposely run their translations at a barely audible level, or even listen to them in only one ear, precisely so that they can also gain some idea of the vocal inflections and emphases of the actor's delivery, blending in their own mind the features of this delivery with the content provided by the translator. This is most easily done when the translation remains as close as possible, line to line and phrase to phrase, to the stage delivery, but is itself presented in a fairly flat and neutral tone. Another alternative to this process, the simultaneous projection of a translation over loudspeakers, was suggested by Maori dramatist Hone Tuwhare, but has to the best of my knowledge never been utilized with any success.[15]

A curious and quite radical variation on these practices was provided by one of the most memorable and challenging sequences in the 2004 production *Poor Theater* by the Wooster Group, a sequence that offered an effect situated somewhere between that of lip-synching, where an actor appropriates an alien voice, and simultaneous translation, where an audience member can hear two voices at the same time. The Wooster Group, America's best-known experimental company, and for many critics one of the central examples of a postmodern approach,[16] has throughout its career been involved in heteroglossic experimentation, separating voices from bodies and dividing and fragmenting voices by various electronic means. Often video or film projections or recorded sounds have added extra "voices" to the complex textures of their productions. In a central sequence of *Poor Theater,* however, they take this layering in a new direction, related to dubbing, but driving a wedge between the normally convergent voices. The title of the production comes from the well-known book by the seminal Polish experimental director Jerzy Grotowski, and during a part of *Poor Theater* a section of Grotowski's best-known production, *Akropolis,* is shown on a video monitor while members of the Wooster Group perform a simultaneous reproduction of the sequence, speaking Polish, as in the original, and with an uncannily exact reproduction of the timing and precise vocal inflection (often a highly stylized one) of each line. The effect has some relation to lip-synching, but radically breaks apart the hopefully seamless blend that is central to lip-synching, both because the original source of the voice is electronically visible and because the live artists are in fact producing a voice that now doubles the original. The doubling pushes the sequence in the direction of simultaneous translation, but the effect sought, and largely gained, is not that of a translation but of an uncanny double, a new voice that is both the same and not the same as the original. This remarkable sequence, as in much Wooster Group work, combines physical and technical means to open up challenging new perspectives both upon the theatrical tradition and upon the processes of production and reception in the theatre.

The Wooster Group moves in a new direction by offering a kind of simultaneous translation that is in the conventional sense not a translation at all but a new voice that is a simulacrum of the original (the work is significantly subtitled "Simulations"). As such it seeks to reproduce not just the original words, but also the specific tone and inflection in the physical delivery of those words. This second aspect of language is traditionally absent both from supertitles and from simultaneous translation, in the former case by necessity, in the latter by artistic choice. Erika Fischer-Lichte notes a fundamental distinction between the printed and performed theatrical text, and thus also between the kind of written side text a supertitle creates and the text being simultaneously presented on stage:

> Books and typeface function as media which convey the drama's literary text and have no impact on the constitution of the meaning. . . . By contrast, actor and stage space comprise media which always introduce certain signifying qualities into the process of conveying meaning and thus cannot be used to convey meaning without altering the meaning.[17]

This distinction is highly important in pursuing the reception implications of written and performed texts, but the read simultaneous translation occupies an uneasy ground between the two. Clearly, we enter the realm of heteroglossia when we consider simultaneous translation, although the new "voice" consciously works against the heteroglossic effect by seeking to minimize its independence. Goethe, who in his later years became more and more suspicious of the signifying power of theatrical performance, suggested that the most effective performance of Shakespeare was an essentially unmediated one, in which a trained but neutral voice simply read the lines without adding the distractions of physical staging. Goethe thought that such a "completely transparent" delivery would give the imagination complete freedom to work, without having any specific meaning suggested to it.[18]

There is, however, much disagreement among theatre producers and translators about whether this is in fact the best way to manage simultaneous translation, or indeed whether such transparency is even possible. It seems clear that for the spectator who is attempting to make his own blend of translation and performance, a totally neutral tone is best, since a translator who attempts his own interpretation adds another interpretive level to the performance. This is by no means an easy matter to negotiate, however, since a totally flat reading without any inflection whatsoever is both difficult and wearing for translator and spectator alike. We are accustomed to developing our own meanings out of the neutrality of written texts, but in the theatre we are equally accustomed to listening for clues to meaning in the inflections of spoken language, and any attempt to avoid them seems odd and artificial.

Nor do all spectators desire this sort of neutral reading, even to the extent that it can be achieved. For many, who find the language on stage too alien or too difficult to provide any aural clue for its interpretation, a highly inflected reading by a translator provides a much more satisfying experience than a fairly neutral one. The more the simultaneous translation attempts to provide an inflected interpretation, however, the greater becomes another problem, the voice of the translator. For a fairly neutral inflection a single voice can be adequate, although it is common for a male and female translator to read the appropriate gender lines, for clarity, variety, and to provide the translators with some relief. One could imagine, however, although I have never experienced this, a simultaneous translation in which each character had their own translator's "voice," as in a dubbed film, which would be the logical extension of the thoroughly inflected translation. This would, however, be well on the way of creating the translation equivalent of a radio play, the coordination of which with the activities of a completely different cast simultaneously on stage would surely be a recipe for spectatorial confusion. The *Akropolis* sequence in *Poor Theater* provides another alternative, an actual reproduction of both words and inflections, but of course this moves outside the realm of translation entirely and raises the very complex question of what sort of voices in what relationship can in fact be considered heteroglossic.

In comparison with the welter of phenomenological questions involved with the multiple uses of translated voices on stage, the projection of supertitles seems a fairly straightforward matter, and this is doubtless one of the reasons for the growing dominance of this alternative. The supertitle, however, is also a device that is potentially much more complicated than it might at first appear, and it is developing in some surprising and unexpected directions that open intriguing new performance possibilities and new areas for the exploration of the use of language in the theatre.

Returning to Fischer-Lichte's distinction between printed and staged media, and to the comparative interpretive neutrality of print, the projected supertitle may seem to solve the tension potentially introduced into the reception process by the operations of the translator's voice, since the supertitle remains unambiguously in the realm of print. Its relationship to the performance that it accompanies, however, is as problematic as that of the simultaneous translation, if for different reasons. One very serious problem is distraction. Wherever supertitles are actually placed, they create a center of attention outside the conventional proscenium frame and thus force audiences to divide their attention between the titles and the ongoing action. There is no question that the widespread use of supertitles has increased the accessibility of opera for many, but a significant part of the audience sees them as intrusive. The strong division between operatic audiences on this matter has inspired the ingenious arrangement at the Metropolitan Opera in New York, where the titles are electronically shown on the back of each chair, screened so that those who do not wish to see them do not even glimpse those seen by their neighbors in adjoining seats.

I am not aware of any such controversy surrounding the use of supertitles in the spoken theatre, even though one could make an even stronger case there for their tendency to distract. Simultaneous translations, whatever their problems, at least overlay the same sensual channel that they are designed to replace, the auditory, leaving the sight free to concentrate on the acting, scenery, costume, lighting, composition, and so on. Supertitles, forcing spectators to shift their focus, even if momentarily, away from the stage, are much more actively disruptive, since they are directly competing with other stimuli to the visual channel, leaving unimpeded the auditory channel. This is not nearly so serious a problem in opera (where the auditory contribution of the music is central) as in theatre, where the unimpeded auditory channel is essentially receiving only the language that presumably cannot be understood. Thus in the spoken theatre the supertitle leaves open the reception channel it is designed to replace and blocks the major one not involved in the problem it seeks to solve.

Nor is visual distraction the only problem presented by supertitles. Even more serious is their necessary selectivity. Unlike simultaneous translations, supertitles cannot provide running translations of virtually every word spoken on stage because few audience members can read that rapidly, or if they could, they would have to pay almost constant attention to the supertitles with little opportunity to watch the performance itself. Therefore supertitles provide a much abbreviated version of what is being spoken. Short phrases and exclamations present little problem, but longer speeches or rapid interchanges require selective presentation. Even spectators with no knowledge of the language being spoken on stage are often frustrated by extended verbal passages on stage that are provided with only a few translated phrases or no translation whatever in the supertitles, and anyone who has ever attended a production knowing both the stage language and the supertitles will inevitably have been struck by the continual inaccuracies, seemingly arbitrary substitutions, and outright omissions that characterize the latter. I recently had the unusual but informative opportunity to see productions of *Hamlet* on two successive nights in Paris, the first by Peter Brook, a radically abbreviated production performed in English with supertitles in French, and the second a much praised Vienna production by Peter Zadek, a more complete version performed in German again with French supertitles. The first night I was struck by how banal, reductive, and occasionally incorrect the French supertitles were and the second night not only by how much was lost but by how different the translations were, even of identical scenes. This experience emphasized to me the inadequacy of the common assumption that supertitles, like simultaneous translations, are a basically transparent aid to communication, a presumably neutral device not actually part of the production. They in fact present a text that is by no means the straightforward, presumably neutral equivalent sought (if never precisely achieved) by simultaneous translation, but a heavily edited selection of material that might very easily totally erase even some of the performers' key lines for those audience members (presumably a significant percentage of them) relying primarily upon this channel for the discursive text of the production. Any alert audience member, however, even if he or she does not understand a word of the performed text, will soon realize that it is significantly different from the projected one. An awareness of the extent of the disjuncture obviously increases for audience members who have knowledge of both the performed and projected languages.

## Experimental Supertitles

So far I have been speaking only of the most traditional use of supertitles in the theatre. Most American audiences, accustomed to a largely monolinguistic theatre, may be tempted to make what seems an obvious assumption, that when a theatre uses supertitles, it is only and always because the actors are speaking a language that almost no one in the audience understands, and for whom they therefore provide a necessary if minimal translation. This assumption is, however, no longer necessarily true in many parts of the world, where theatre audiences are increasingly international and multilinguistic. Although international theatre festivals today usually offer supertitles in their national language, it is with a full awareness that much of their audience will be familiar with several other languages as well, and even in the more nationalistic theatre world of a city like Paris, I found it clear, from audience reactions, that a significant portion of the audience for the Peter Brook *Hamlet* was following the English of the actors perfectly well, even without the French supertitles, as was a significant portion of the audience for the German of the Peter Zadek production. In circumstances like these, by no means uncommon in the growing internationalization of theatre productions and audiences, the printed words of the supertitles may remain primarily an aid to understanding for a part of the audience, but for many will operate instead as simply another element in the multi-channeled reception experience offered by theatre. It is truly simply another "voice," and thus a potential contributor to the heteroglossia of performance. Although it is often, as I have suggested, a somewhat muted or truncated voice, it does not have to be so. I have seen, for example, French or German productions of Shakespeare, which used actual Shakespearian lines in the supertitles, so one could hardly accuse this projected "voice" of any innate inferiority to those on stage.

Another development that I have observed in recent European production, however, acknowledges the fact that the supertitle, since it operates as a channel of communication, an additional "voice," especially in the case of multilanguage audiences, can use its inevitable difference from the spoken text in more original and powerful ways, for the production of additional meanings. One early model is suggested by the experiments of Piscator and Brecht in the early twentieth century with supplementary projected written material. Although normally much less closely tied to the dramatic text than the supertitles, these devices shared the same potential problem of dispersing audience focus but compensated by creating a dialectic among the various channels offered. According to C. D. Innes, the multiple focus areas of the Piscator-Bühne, with a screen above the stage and smaller screens on either side or dropped in from the flies for multiple projection of images, films, statistics, captions, or quotations, created "various poles within a production which could be played off against one another. . . . The placard and the written word could, for example, present a different level of reality to both the celluloid and the acted scene."[19] Although Brecht certainly used projected texts as ironic counterpoint to the stage action, he was much more concerned than Piscator with the phenomenological effect of the texts themselves. What critics of supertitles have seen as their redundancy and tendency to distract from the illusion were precisely for Brecht the advantages of such devices. In his notes to the *Threepenny Opera* he explains:

The orthodox playwright's objection to the titles is that the dramatist ought to say everything that has to be said in the action, that the text must express everything within its own confines. The corresponding attitude for the spectator is that he should not think about a subject, but within the confines of the subject. But this way of subordinating everything to a single idea, this passion for propelling the spectator along a single track where he can look neither right nor left, up nor down, is something that the new school of play-writing must reject. . . . Some exercise in complex seeing is needed—though it is perhaps more important to be able to think above the stream than to think in the stream. Moreover the use of screens imposes and facilitates a new style of acting. This style is the epic style. As he reads the projections on the screen the spectator adopts an attitude of smoking-and-watching.[20]

Although supertitles, with their distinctly utilitarian background, may seem at first glance to have little in common in terms of reception affect with the calculatedly disruptive and ironic projected titles, statistics, and quotations of Piscator and Brecht, their status as an alternative communicative channel operating outside of the illusory world of the stage places them precisely in the position described in this key passage. Indeed, perhaps even more than Brechtian titles, running supertitles provide a constant reminder to the audience of the constructedness of the event they are watching, and their alternative "reading" of the lines provides what also might be seen as a continual Brechtian reinforcement of the possibility of an alternative line of thought and expression.

Whatever its initial defamiliarizing effect, however, the supertitle, like any theatrical convention that is regularly repeated, gradually becomes naturalized, absorbed into the horizon of expectations of the audience and thus less available to reception usages other than serving as the almost unacknowledged bearer of a text that is assumed equivalent to that being spoken on stage. To keep an audience conscious of its extradimensionality, the supertitle itself must be subjected to a kind of defamiliarization, encouraging spectators to recognize it as something other than an accepted convention, and a transparent conveyer of meanings identical to those expressed in another language by the actors.

A number of recent productions in both European and, to a lesser extent, in America offer provocative examples of supertitles as a more independent stage language, not simply a device for duplicating the spoken text, but a separate communicative channel in the theatrical experience. Frank Castorf at the Berlin Volksbühne has long been interested,

like Piscator, in creating multiple and often ironically juxtaposed channels of communication on stage, mixing live action with film, recorded
music, still images, and projected texts. He has also, unlike Piscator, but
like many other contemporary German directors, included extensive
passages of English and other languages in his basically German texts.
These two concerns have not surprisingly led him recently to begin utilizing supertitles, but almost never in a conventional manner, rather
with a specific interest in opening up another, often contradictory channel of communication. In his 2001 adaptation of Tennessee Williams's
*Streetcar Named Desire,* called (in part due to conflicts with the Williams
estate) *Endstation Amerika,* the production begins with a setting (typical
for Castorf) having almost nothing to do with the traditional setting
described by Williams. However, this disjunction is foregrounded, even
for audiences unfamiliar with Williams's play, by the simultaneous projection of Williams's stage directions describing his idea of the setting.
Here Ingarden's literary side-text actually reappears as a literal theatrical side-text in the form of a supertitle.

In this surprising, even shocking opening, Castorf both extends and
subverts the mandate of supertitles. In terms of textual grounding, what
has distinguished modern supertitles from the projected texts of Piscator (or of some of Castorf's earlier productions) is that supertitle texts are
not drawn from "found" material outside the grounding drama, but
come directly from that grounding drama, or a translation of it. In this
respect, Castorf's supertitles are solidly within the tradition of this technique. In two other fundamental respects, however, he undermines this
technique. First, traditional supertitles are devoted only to that part of
the text which is normally presented on stage, that is, the spoken lines of
the characters, not to the side text of stage directions and other authorial
indications, which in traditional theatrical productions are ignored,
altered, or converted into visual or aural equivalents. Castorf simultaneously ignores and reinscribes this normally hidden textual channel by
displaying it as a supertitle. Second, traditional supertitles, at least in
theory, are supposed to provide a reasonably accurate equivalent of the
lines spoken by the actors. Far from providing such a printed equivalent, Williams's projected stage description is so clearly at odds with
what is seen on stage that the disjuncture itself becomes the major point
of the projection. Even in the more conventional use of the supertitle to

present lines from the text, Castorf often drives a wedge between the "voice" of the supertitle and those of the actors as, for example, when Stanley in scene 7 reveals to Stella what he has discovered about Blanche's past. In Castorf's production Stanley does not speak these lines. Rather they are projected in "zipper" form, like a breaking news story, on the supertitle screen, and Stanley pulls Stella and the other actors downstage to watch this "news" as Blanche tries in vain to distract them. The projection takes on its own "voice" to which all the onstage characters react.

An even more extreme example of the production manipulation of supertitles as an independent channel of communication was offered by the 2000 production of *King Lear* by the Needcompany of Belgium, a prominent European experimental company strongly influenced by the American Wooster Group. Although their basic language is Flemish, Needcompany, like Castorf and many other European experimental directors and groups, normally utilizes a variety of languages in its productions. Although they use dance extensively, their productions are deeply involved with language experimentation, and since they tour widely in Europe, this experimentation has not surprisingly extended to their use of supertitles. When I saw them on tour in Berlin in May 2001, the supertitles were almost entirely in German (with occasional bits of English), while the majority of the actors spoke Flemish (with occasional English passages) and some spoke entirely in English or French.

As in Castorf's *Endstation Amerika,* the Needcompany *King Lear* confronted its audiences from the opening moments with supertitles operating in a clearly unconventional manner. The actor playing Gloucester sat downstage in a comfortable chair (as he did throughout the first four acts). Kent stood beside him, but neither of them spoke their opening lines. Instead they, like the audience, watched these opening lines that appeared only as supertitles (complete with the character attribution of each line, another part of the traditional side-text) above their heads. To these projected lines they reacted with nudges and gestures. Thus, from the opening moments, supertitles were established as a channel of communication separate from the voices of the actors, in this instance (as in the Castorf *Endstation Amerika*) representing the normally silent voice of the hidden "author-god." Often, in the course of the production, the supertitles performed their conventional function of providing German equivalents of at least some of the Flemish lines (French and English passages were provided with no translation). Even so, spectators were continually reminded that the supertitles, even when parallel to the lines and actions on the stage, were separate from them and independently generated.

An example of this in the fourth act also involved another important semiotic feature of this production. Many of the referential performance elements normally seamlessly joined together (actor and character, voice and body) were separated, as the supertitle texts were separated from the actual voices and bodies of the actors. Similarly, as is often the case in Wooster Group productions, the bodies of actors were separated from specific characters. So, for example, the same actor played Kent and the Fool, and the same actor both Albany and Cornwall, usually with a reversible placard hung around his neck (another printed sign) with "Albany" on one side and "Cornwall" on the other, to keep the identities straight (a convention in turn subverted when the actor sometimes neglected to turn the sign, or remembered and turned it in the middle of a speech). Such shifting and unstable significations could be confusing to the audience and clearly were meant to be so. There were even occasions when they were presented as equally confusing to the actors. Thus in the fourth act, when the Messenger enters with the key line, "O, my good lord, the Duke of Cornwall's dead," the actor began the line boldly, but stopped after "Duke of" apparently unable to remember which one he was speaking about. Fortunately he recalled a handy aid available to him, and so glanced quickly but obviously up to the supertitle to read there the proper name and thus correctly complete the line.

Metatheatrical playfulness of this sort occurred throughout the production, but reached its peak in the final act, when in parallel to the growing disorder of Lear's kingdom, the production itself, and all its signifying systems, careened more and more wildly out of control. In this calculated chaos, the supertitles played a major role. The act began with the stage empty and Kent appearing speaking into a handheld microphone and announcing (in English): "Act 5, scene 1. I'll need a table and three chairs center stage for this." When these were produced, he sat on a chair at one end of the table and began to read the text from pages he brought in with him. He read, however, only those parts of the text normally omitted from the stage performance, that is, the side text of the stage directions and the names of the characters before each line. Just as this device converted into spoken language the side text that normally remains only in the written version, what is normally spoken on stage was here presented only as written. That is, as Kent read the name of each speaker, that person's line was not spoken, but appeared only above the stage, as a supertitle. As he read the name of each character, the line presumably spoken by that character appeared only as a supertitle above him. As he continued, the play's concluding turbulent battles swirled around him, in an increasingly chaotic visual and aural field. Sound effects, music, smoke effects, flashes of light mixed with rapidly moving and struggling bodies. Gloucester wandered about the stage laughing into an open mike. Battens hung with operating lighting equipment descended from the flies. As the visual and aural frenzy on stage increased, the supertitles contributed to this disintegration. Kent read the names of speakers more and more rapidly, and their lines flashed by so quickly that they could not possibly be read by the audience. Finally the supertitles themselves degenerated, like the visual field as a whole, into confused, almost random elements, trailing off into a repeated line of "helphelphelphelp . . ." and then going to complete darkness. The final lines of Lear, Kent, Edgar, and Albany were read quietly, with minimal inflection, from handheld scripts by actors gathered around the table, a final emphasis of the separation of actor and character. This sequence was done in work lights. All the normal technical means of the stage were gone, including the supertitles, whose screen hung blank and silent over the stage.

This kind of postmodern deconstruction of a classic text and traditional stage practices, while common enough in continental Europe, is far removed from the normal practice of the modern Anglo-Saxon theatre, yet there too one finds increasingly, even in mainstream theatre, a willingness to regard supertitles not simply as a transparent duplication of the spoken text on stage, but as another separate dramatic voice. The well-established convention of supertitles in operatic performance has encouraged the directors and designers of musical comedy to begin to explore the expressive possibilities of the supertitle as a separate design element, in a less radical way certainly than in the work of Castorf or Needcompany, but still allowing the supertitle to emerge as its own distinct voice or voices in the production. The supertitles in Baz Luhrmann's visually extravagant *La Bohème* on Broadway in 2002 provided a striking example, using different styles of lettering to suit the different characters (crude lettering for the lines of Schaunard, elegant script for Rodolfo), and then moving on to the conventions of cartooning to suggest profanity by nonlettered symbols (such as "f??!!#+") for profanity, or moving outside spoken language entirely for the cartoon-derived "Wham! Pow! Ka-boom!" to accompany the fight in the last act.

Several sequences in Richard Morris and Dick Scanlan's *Thoroughly Modern Millie,* playing on Broadway at the same time, provided someone different, but even more complex examples of the supertitle taking on a dramatic life of its own and contributing another distinct voice to the scene. Millie's opening number, "Not for the Life of Me," is sung as a reprise in the Priscilla Hotel laundry room by Ching Ho and Bun Foo, Asian characters played by Asian-American actors Ken Leung and Francis Jue. They sing the verses in Mandarin Chinese, translated into English in supertitles. This is of course a quite conventional use of the "transparent" supertitle glossing a speech in a foreign language. Later in the scene, however, Ching Ho and Bun Foo are joined by their aunt, Mrs. Meers, a villainous character played in yellowface by a Caucasian actress, Harriet Harris. Pleading with Mrs. Meers to provide money for their mother to immigrate from China, the two young men sing (in Mandarin) the song "Muquin" ("Mammy"), which they perform with the attitudes and gestures traditionally associated with the blackface performance of Al Jolson. Mrs. Meers next joins the song, singing in English, while the supertitles join in the increasingly complex ethnic and gender confusion by translating her words into English with a Jolson blackface dialect. Finally, the two young men switch into English with a strong Chinese accent, which the supertitles (moving from a horizontal to a vertical display) now translate into Mandarin. In this delightfully postmodern play upon racial and ethnic display on the stage, the supertitles provide their own contribution, as important as the spoken dialect, the stage makeup, or the references to previous performance traditions.

In both of these examples, the actors on stage do not directly interact with supertitles, as in the examples from Castorf and Needcompany, but even that more extreme acknowledgment of the supertitle side text as interactive participant can be occasionally seen in contemporary American productions. In the 2004 *Silent Laughter,* an amusing live takeoff on silent film comedy at the Lamb's Club, supertitles were used in a manner suggesting the inserted text replacing stage directions and dialogue in early silent films. Occasionally, however, an actor would bring a postmodern consciousness to this early modern technique by stepping downstage, like the characters in the Needcompany *Lear,* to observe what the supertitle was saying. In one striking sequence, the supertitle was projected (in apparent error) upside down and the character miming the projected line could not make himself understood. After several unsuccessful attempts, he went downstage, discovered the source of the problem, and then returned to his position and spoke the line standing on his head. The title now appeared right side up and order was restored. In addition to its effectiveness as a visual joke, this sequence suggests a profound change in the status of the supertitle. No longer merely a parasitic derivative of another text, it now controls the stage action, taking on the primary control of the sequence and making the stage action derivative from it.

The 2005 production *Boozy,* a multimedia comic meditation on the dreams and careers of planners Le Corbusier and Robert Moses by one of New York's most innovative young experimental companies, the Les Freres Corbusier, made the playful metatheatrical use of supertitles an important part of their depiction of the figure from whom they derive their name. The actor playing Le Corbusier in the early part of the production spoke generally accurate but nonsense French, of the *les pommes frites de mon grand-père sont sur la plume de ma tante* variety. These meaningless French phrases were then solemnly rendered into rather pretentious philosophical statements about architecture and Le Corbusier's mission in the English supertitles, much to the amusement of the off-Broadway audience, who clearly understood enough French to get the joke. Since Le Corbusier's lady friend either could speak no French or could extract no meaning from the nonsense French Le Corbusier was speaking, she, like the audience, had to read the supertitles to understand what he was saying. When they finally broke up, she cited as among the major failings of their relationship the fact that she was tired of reading his subtitles. Clearly this once presumably transparent device had become a semi-independent "voice" among voices.

*Sign Language*

Traditionally, of course, it is in the nature of the printed side-text to disappear when the script is moved to the stage, but the use of supertitles provides an opportunity for written elements of the script, normally accessible only to the reader, to become accessible to the theatrical viewer as well. In this case they become, even more literally than Ingarden suggested, an actual side text, existing alongside the visual text of the performance, but not actually a part of it. This is also true of another sort of performance side text, also fundamentally involved with heteroglossia, less familiar and widely employed than the now common supertitles, but also more closely tied to the traditional theatrical experience, since it is generated by the performing body rather than by a written and projected text. This physical side text involves the use of sign language, a type of language that in recent years has become an increasingly important part of theatrical performance, especially in the United States.

Although not nearly so common as the supertitle, the signed "side text" performs a similar basic function, although in this case often directed not at the majority of the audience, but at a particular minority. Hilary U. Cohen describes this "most widely known technique for making performances accessible to the deaf in the U.S." thus:

> Through the placement of interpreters either at the side of the stage or within the performance space, deaf audience members are presented with a simultaneous signed/visual translation of the words of speaking actors. In this method, hearing actors and hearing interpreters placement include deaf spectators in performances that are largely created for the hearing.[21]

In this model a live interpreter performs essentially the same function as the supertitle, but, as a visible presence, is phenomenologically much closer to the live "translators" at the side of the stage in *Seven Streams*. In this position, the interpreter, like the translator, provides a simultaneous parallel text for audience members who cannot directly access what is being spoken. It is important to recognize, however, that as theatre utilizing sign language has developed in the United States, this simple model no longer has much to do with the increasingly elaborate inter-play of sign language and other languages on stage. Central to the change has been the political choice made early in the history of deaf theatre in the United States to develop a theatre not just by and for the deaf, but one that would offer a satisfactory theatrical experience to deaf and hearing audiences alike.

A key figure in this experimentation has been David Hays, who began his career as a highly successful scenic designer, best known for the Eugene O'Neill revivals of the 1950s. He became interested in the theatrical possibilities of sign language as a result of his connection with William Gibson's *The Miracle Worker,* the breakthrough play that first gave serious theatrical attention to sign language. Both leading actress Anne Bancroft and designer Hays were energized by this production to explore and encourage the development of deaf theatre expression. A number of developments in the early 1960s supported their interest, pri-marily involving Gallaudet University, the leading American center of higher education concerned primarily with the deaf. The 1960 book *Sign Language Structure,* by William C. Stokoe Jr., head of the Gallaudet Department of English, was the first to recognize American Sign Lan-guage (ASL) as a language in its own right, opening acceptance of this language in academic, public, and theatre circles. That same year another member of the Gallaudet English department, Leonard Siger, published a groundbreaking article in the *Johns Hopkins Magazine* con-cerning the theatrical potential of sign language:

> Of course, the sign language of casual conversation is not appropriate to the stage, but sign language properly learned and properly used can be a vehicle of considerable power and beauty, better suited to the expression of emotion, in some respects, than any spoken language.[22]

A highly successful production of Thornton Wilder's *Our Town* at Gallaudet in 1961, attended by both Bancroft and Hays, provided fresh evidence of the theatrical possibilities of sign language. Hays continued to champion a theatre that would explore these possibilities and was finally given the opportunity to established such a venture in 1966, when the Eugene O'Neill Center was established in Connecticut by George C. White, who was excited by the idea of creating there a National Theatre of the Deaf, with Hays as its managing director. Under his leadership it has been ever since a model and leading force for theatre utilizing sign language in America. Although there has been a debate from the beginning over whether deaf performers should develop a theatre "for the deaf" (that is, primarily for signing audiences) or "of the deaf" (for both signing and nonsigning audiences), the success and visibility of the NDT has tipped the balance, at least in America, toward the latter, and thereby opened the possibility for sign language to be developed as another means of theatrical expression for a general public.[23] Interestingly, Hays has specifically invoked both semiotic theory (seeing sign language as one of the "multiple languages" potentially contributing to a total theatrical experience) and filmic subtitles in speaking of sign language, which he called "pictures in the air": "Watch the language in the air and you will find a suddenly sharper, clearer understanding of the spoken word. It's akin to the phenomenon of your memory of a captioned foreign film."[24]

This aesthetic took the National Theatre of the Deaf from the outset in a strikingly different direction than that pursued at Gallaudet, and one that brought multiple voices on stage from the very beginning. At Gallaudet, speaking actors, called "readers," were always off stage, out of sight of the audience, reading the text over microphones as they watched the performers on stage. From the very beginning at NTD Hays brought all actors, including readers, on stage, and worked on a continual interplay and theatrical fusion of these different elements. An early NTD poster suggested the effect sought. A reader-actress, Linda Bove (later to become Linda the Librarian on *Sesame Street*), was shown using a finger rabbit sign, with a hearing rabbit, indicated by her left hand, listening to the voice actor, while her right hand represented a deaf rabbit that is watching the deft signer, Joseph Sarpy, "thus creating a unique oneness of voice and sign that the audience can *see* and *hear*."[25] During its first decade, the NTD staged almost as many poems as plays, developing a style that could both develop the aesthetic potential of American Sign Language and integrate it successfully with the verbal presentation of the text, as in one of the company's first major successes, *Songs from Milk Wood* (1969), based on the work of Dylan Thomas.[26] From the beginning NTD was devoted to touring nationally and, soon after, internationally, where rather than rely upon a simplistic model of cross-cultural "language of gesture," they often stressed their work's multiplicity of languages. In their 1986 tour to the People's Republic of China, for example, they offered performances that mixed ASL, English, and Mandarin.[27]

The success of the NTD called attention to the potential of utilizing deaf actors to open up the stage to new dimensions of communication, a potential that was subsequently explored by some of America's leading experimental directors. Peter Sellars cast a deaf actor, Howie Seago, in *Ajax* and *The Persians,* and collaborated with deaf playwright Shanny Mow in a 1981 NTD production, *The Ghost of Chastity Past.*[28] Sellars observed that deaf actors "who are aware of the miracle of getting an idea across," brought "an extra dimension" to theatrical performance.[29] Robert Wilson drew upon the abilities of deaf actor Raymond Andrews in *The King of Spain* and *Deafman Glance,* remarking that often individuals who have been restricted in their use of verbal language "have compensated for this by developing awarenesses and sensitivities to nonverbal channels of communication that go unnoticed by people who use verbal language regularly."[30] The theatre, however, provides an ideal means for foregrounding such channels of communication and making them a part of the overall theatrical effect.

NTD naturally served also as an inspiration for other deaf theatre groups, the most important of which has been the Deaf West Theatre Company, formed in Los Angeles in 1991 by Edward Waterstreet, a graduate of Gallaudet University, a founding member of the NTD, and a director there for fifteen years before he moved to California. After almost a decade of development, based on the aesthetic of the NTD, Deaf West gained wide visibility on the cultural scene with two major productions in 2000, *A Streetcar Named Desire* and its first musical, *Oliver!* In such productions, Deaf West made extensive use of what Waterstreet significantly called a "third language," combining expressive signing and inventive voicing.[31] They also developed the complex use of deafness and hearing, in that the fact that certain actors spoke and others did not continuously operated on several levels. At the simplest level, Blanche was a hearing and speaking actor, Stanley a deaf, signing one, which provided an extra, social dimension to Blanche's regard of Stanley as crude and ignorant. At the same time, other stage figures provided signing for Blanche's lines and spoken lines for Stanley, so that each always operated with a doubled speech. Finally the actors themselves occasionally blurred these boundaries. In one of the most memorable moments of the production, the deaf actor playing Stanley (Troy Kotsur) stood signing beneath a balcony on which a speaking actor delivered his lines. However, Kotsur had laboriously taught himself to produce the sound "Stella" and his sudden production of this single cry, which he himself could not hear, electrified the hearing members of the audience.

*Oliver!* presented an entirely new set of challenges, since few deaf actors had ever worked with music and nondeaf actors were suspicious of trying out for what was advertised as a deaf musical. Eventually, however, a largely new vocabulary of singing, signing, and movement was developed that brought new fame and success to the theatre. As a result of this, the *Oliver!* production team of Waterstreet, producing director and composer Bill O'Brien, and director-choreographer Jeff Calhoun, undertook an even more ambitious project, *Big River,* a musical based on Mark Twain's *Huckleberry Finn.* A major attraction of this story for them was the culture clash between young Huck and his black friend Jim, which division they could emphasize, as in the earlier *Streetcar,* by casting a deaf (Huck) and hearing (Jim) actor on each side of the divide. Unlike *Streetcar,* however, the major dynamic of *Big River* would be the bond that is established despite this division.

*Big River* went on to become the most significant and widely praised production of theatre involving deaf actors since the watershed *Miracle Worker.* A huge success at its own theatre, it moved in November 2002 to the mainstream Mark Taper Forum in downtown Los Angeles, and the following summer to the American Airlines Theatre on Broadway, where it enjoyed a very successful run. On both coasts audiences were dazzled by the richness and variety of expression opened up by the multiple "voices," silent and speaking, on the stage. *Big River* went much further than earlier experiments in introducing different ways of expressing this multiplicity. Most commonly, it employed the now-standard device of having a costumed speaking actor, placed in a somewhat less prominent position, providing the "voice" for a deaf actor, but many ingenious variations were developed. In *Oliver!* Charles Dickens had appeared as narrator, and this device was utilized again in *Big River* with the actor Daniel Jenkins narrating the story as Mark Twain and also providing the voice of deaf actor Tyrone Giordano as Huck. One of the most amusing "doubled" characters was Finn's Pap, delightfully played by speaking actor Lyle Kanouse and silent actor Troy Kotrun. Although often the costumed speaking actor was placed in a less conspicuous position, the two Paps performed like a comedy duo. Of contrasting physical types, one heavy and one tall and thin, they were costumed in similar rags and with shaggy unkempt hair and beards. Inseparable, they shared physical reactions, gestures (one would take a deep drink from a whisky jug and the other wipe his sleeve across his mouth) and, most interestingly, signs. This technique of actors making signs together was one of the most powerful in the production, and centrally tied to its theme. Key to this were the two duets of Huck and Jim (speaking actor Michael McElroy), "Muddy Water" and "Worlds Apart." Both offer a fascinating and complex laying of "voices," the sung duet of McElroy and Jenkins (standing near the proscenium), and the signed duet of Giordano and McElroy, who present simultaneous signs that are mirror images of each other, and then create signs together, each forming a part of the visual communication. In this, as in the powerful company chorus number, "Waitin' for the Light to Shine," the repetition of words and phrases natural to musical presentation allows the hearing audience to learn and recognize certain repeated signs and thus to understand and appreciate this extra "voice" added to the staging. As director Calhoun remarked: "We're asking people to *see* music, so you get *more* of the musical experience."[32]

Writing on *Big River* for *American Theatre,* Karen Wada suggested that in this sort of experiment "the challenge for actors and directors, whether they can hear or not, and the payoff for the rest of us, is confronting a different set of questions than we're used to: What does love or suspense, Lorca or Shepard, *look* like?"[33] The moving of the signed side text from the wings to center stage, like the movement of the written supertitle to a similar central position, indeed involves more than adding another "voice" to the heteroglossia of theatre; it also demands a broader comprehension and acceptance of the available means of communication, and thus a potentially richer, more complex, and more nuanced theatrical experience.

Bert States, in *Great Reckonings in Little Rooms,* spoke of the continual process in the theatre of omnivorously devouring the reality around it and converting it into theatre.[34] Nothing in its surrounding culture has escaped this process, and that includes the operations of theatre itself. From the very beginning theatre has taken a strong interest in its own procedures and devices, giving rise to the long tradition of metatheatrical expression. It was thus inevitable, once heteroglossic theatre became sufficiently common to inspire various translation strategies and devices for its operation, that these strategies and devices would themselves be converted by practitioners into new material for metatheatrical experimentation. It is not surprising that the most popular of such experimentation in America has appeared in the musical theatre, which has always been less committed to illusionistic realism and more open to metatheatrical playfulness than the main tradition of spoken theatre. Nevertheless, the success of the performance of heteroglossia in such major commercial Broadway successes as *Big River, Thoroughly Modern Millie,* and *La Bohème* provides clear evidence that the play of language has entered the theatrical mainstream, both in the form of specific linguistic mixing, and by extension, in the theatrical manipulation of the mediating devices that support this mixing. This mainstream theatre, especially in the United States, does not yet reflect the increasingly heteroglossic community that surrounds it, as theatres in many other parts of the world are doing, but the mainstream attention to such heteroglossic dramatists as Tony Kushner or Robert Lepage and the growing heteroglossic practice in both large and small theatres suggest that the voices of others will in the years to come increasingly be heard even on the most traditional monolinguistic stages.

# Notes

*Introduction*

   1. Noam Chomsky, *Aspects of the Theory of Syntax* (Cambridge: MIT Press, 1965), 3.

   2. See *Introduction to Integrational Linguistics,* ed. Roy Harris, and *Integrational Linguistics: A First Reader,* ed. Roy Harris and George Wolf (both Oxford: Pergamon, 1998).

   3. Roy Harris, *The Language Myth* (New York: St. Martin's Press, 1981), 167.

   4. See Marvin Carlson, "Nationalism and the Romantic Drama in Europe," in *Romantic Drama,* ed. Gerald Gillespie (Philadelphia: John Benjamins, 1994), 139–52; Loren Kruger, *The National Stage: Theatre and Cultural Legitimation in England, France, and America* (Chicago: University of Chicago Press, 1992).

   5. Mikhail Bakhtin, *Problems of Dostoevsky's Poetics,* ed. and trans. Caryl Emerson (Minneapolis: University of Minnesota Press, 1984), 17.

   6. Marvin Carlson, "Theatre and Dialogism," in *Critical Theory and Performance,* ed. Janelle G. Reinelt and Joseph R. Roach (Ann Arbor: University of Michigan Press, 1992), 313–23.

   7. James Clifford, *The Predicament of Culture: Twentieth Century Ethnography, Literature, and Art* (Cambridge: Harvard University Press, 1988), 50.

   8. Ibid., 23 and 23n.

   9. Patrice Pavis, *Languages of the Stage: Essays in the Semiology of Theatre* (New York: Performing Arts Journal, 1982).

   10. Harris, *The Language Myth,* 167.

   11. David Crystal, *A Dictionary of Linguistics and Phonetics,* 3rd ed. (Oxford: Blackwell, 1991), 193.

   12. Ibid., 102–3; capitalization to indicate cross-references omitted.

   13. John McWhorter, *Word on the Street* (Cambridge, Mass.: Perseus, 1998), 35.

   14. See, for example, McWhorter, *Word on the Street,* or Anthony Arletto, *Introduction to Historical Linguistics* (Washington, D.C.: University Press of America, 1981). A classic in the field is Robert A. Hall, *Leave Your Language Alone* (Ithaca: Linguistica, 1950).

   15. These dynamics have been perhaps most thoroughly explored by Bourdieu, whose writings on the subject have been collected in the English volume

*Language and Symbolic Action,* ed. and trans. John B. Thompson (Cambridge: Harvard University Press, 1991).

16. See Roy Harris, "The Dialect Myth," in Harris, *Introduction to Integrational Linguistics,* 83–85.

17. *The Iliad of Homer,* 2.867, trans. W. C. Green (London: Longmans, 1884), 101.

18. *The Geography of Strabo,* book 14, chap. 2., trans. Horace Leonard Jones (Cambridge: Harvard University Press, 1923), 303–7.

19. Crystal, *Dictionary,* 2.

20. Jerry Blunt, *Stage Dialects* (New York: Harper and Row, 1967), 1.

21. Angela C. Pao, "False Accents: Embodied Dialects and the Characterization of Ethnicity and Nationality," *Theatre Topics* 14, no. 1 (2004): 353–72.

22. Pao, "False Accents," 355.

23. Marvin Carlson, "The Iconic Stage," *Journal of Dramatic Theory and Criticism* 3 (spring 1989): 3–18.

24. Bert O. States, *Great Reckonings in Little Rooms* (Berkeley and Los Angeles: University of California Press, 1985), 36–39.

25. Celeste Olaquiaga, "From Pastiche to Macaroni," in *Performing Hybridity,* ed. May Joseph and Jennifer Natalya Fink (Minneapolis: University of Minnesota Press, 1999), 171, 173.

26. Tom Lanoye and Jozef de Vos, "Ein Spiel mit der Sprache," in Lanoye and Luk Perceval, *Schlachten!* (Frankfurt am Main: Verlag der Autoren, 1999), xlvi.

*Chapter 1*

1. Victor Hugo, "Preface to Cromwell," in Barrett H. Clark, *European Theories of the Drama* (New York: Crown, 1965), 369.

2. Ibid., 370.

3. Guilbert de Pixérécourt, "Christopher Columbus," in *Four Melodramas,* trans. and ed. Daniel Gerould and Marvin Carlson (New York: Martin E. Segal Theatre Center, 2002), 146.

4. See "Style and Language," in *Aeschylus' Persians,* ed. Edith Hall (Warminster: Aris and Phillips, 1996), 22–23.

5. W. J. M. Starkie, *The Archarnians of Aristophanes* (London: Macmillan, 1966), 245. Pickard Cambridge has identified a "barbarian" character in a vase painting of the fourth century by the mock Persian word he is speaking. *Dramatic Festivals of Athens* (Oxford: Clarendon, 1968), 217 and fig. 105.

6. Walt Wolfram and Natalie Schilling-Estes, *American English,* no. 24 in the series Language in Society (London: Blackwell, 1998), 33.

7. William Labov, *The Social Stratification of English in New York City* (Washington, D.C.: Center for Applied Linguistics, 1966).

8. Pierre Bourdieu, *Ce que parler veut dire: L'économie des échanges linguistiques* (Paris: Librairie Arthème Fayard, 1982), trans. as *Language and Symbolic Action.*

9. J. Stephen Lansing, "The Aesthetics of the Sounding of the Past," in *A Range of Discourses Toward an Ethnopoetics,* ed. Jerome Rothenberg and Diane Rothenberg (Berkeley and Los Angeles: University of California Press, 1983), 241–56.

10. A. L. Becker, "Text-Building, Epistemology, and Aesthetics in Javanese Shadow Theatre," in *The Imagination of Reality,* ed. A. L. Becker and A. Yengoyan (Norwood, N.J.: Ablex, 1990), 45.

11. Lansing, "Aesthetics," 248.

12. Linda Conner, "Corpse Abuse and Trance in Bali: The Cultural Mediation of Aggression," *Mankind* 12 (1979): 113.

13. Lansing, "Aesthetics," 249.

14. Mary Sabina Zurbuchen, *The Language of Balinese Shadow Theatre* (Princeton: Princeton University Press, 1981), 31, 125.

15. Matthew Boyd Goldie, "Audiences for Language-Play in Middle English Drama," in *Traditions and Transformations in Late Medieval England,* ed. Douglas Biggs, Sharon D. Michalove, and Compton Reeves (Leiden: Brill, 2002), 191.

16. William Tydeman, *The Theatre in the Middle Ages* (Cambridge: Cambridge University Press, 1978), 124.

17. See, for example, Gail McMurray Gibson, *The Theatre of Devotion: East Anglican Drama and Society in the Late Middle Ages* (Chicago: University of Chicago Press, 1989); Martin Stevens, *Four Middle English Mystery Cycles: Textual and Critical Interpretations* (Princeton: Princeton University Press, 1987); Peter Meredith, "Scribes, Texts, and Performance," in *Aspects of Early English Drama,* ed. Paula Neuss (Totowa, N.J.: Barnes and Noble, 1983).

18. Tydeman, *Theatre in Middle Ages,* 124.

19. Janette Dillon, *Language and Stage in Medieval and Renaissance England* (Cambridge: Cambridge University Press, 1998), 37.

20. E. Catherine Dunn, "The Literary Style of the Towneley Plays," *American Benedictine Review* 20, no. 4 (1969): 483.

21. *The N-Town Play,* ed. Stephen Spector, 2 vols. (Oxford: Oxford University Press, 1991), 1:165–66.

22. Dillon, *Language and Stage,* 41.

23. David Mills, ed., *The Chester Mystery Cycle* (East Lansing, Mich.: Colleagues Press, 1992), 140–41.

24. This point was first developed by Joanna Dutka, in her 1972 doctoral dissertation at the University of Toronto, "The Use of Music in the English Mystery Plays," cited in A. C. Cawley, *The Wakefield Pageants in the Towneley Cycle* (Manchester: Manchester University Press, 1958), 111.

25. Stevens, *Middle English Mystery Cycles,* 162.

26. Dillon, *Language and Stage,* 46.

27. Sarah Beckwith, *Christ's Body: Identity, Culture, and Society in Late Medieval Writings* (London: Routledge, 1993), 38.

28. Ibid., 39.

29. Mikhail Bakhtin, *The Dialogic Imagination,* ed. Michael Holquist, trans.

Caryl Emerson and Michael Holquist (Austin: University of Texas Press, 1981), 68.

30. François Rabelais, *The Histories of Gargantua and Pantagruel,* trans. J. M. Cohen (Baltimore: Penguin, 1955), book 2, chap. 9, 197–201.

31. Ibid., book 2, chap. 6, 184–85.

32. Andrea Calmo, "Prefazione" to *Il Travaglia* (Venice: Alessi, 1556), 2v.

33. Henri Bergson, "Laughter," in *Comedy,* ed. Wylie Sypher (Garden City: Doubleday Anchor, 1956), 92–93.

34. Luigi Riccoboni, *An Historical and Critical Account of the Theatres in Europe* (London: T. Waller, 1741), 68.

35. M. Lea, *Italian Popular Comedy* (New York: Russell and Russell, 1962) 125–26.

36. M. C. Bradbrook, *Themes and Conventions of Elizabethan Tragedy* (Cambridge: Cambridge University Press, 1960), 83–84.

37. Dillon, *Language and Stage,* 154.

38. Ibid., 155.

39. *The Lamentable Tragedy of Locrine,* ed. Jane Lytton Gooch (New York: Garland, 1981).

40. Thomas Lodge, *The Wounds of Civil War,* 5.5.300–306, ed. John W. Houppert (Lincoln: University of Nebraska Press, 1969), 95.

41. *Dido, Queen of Carthage,* 4.1.136–40, in *The Complete Works of Christopher Marlowe,* ed. Fredson Bowers, 2 vols. (Cambridge: Cambridge University Press, 1981), 1:53.

42. John Marston, *Antonio and Mellida,* 4.1.181–224, in *Selected Plays of John Marston,* ed. Macdonald P. Jackson and Michael Neill, 2 vols. (Cambridge: Cambridge University Press, 1986), 1:70–71.

43. Dillon, *Language and Stage,* 136; Robert Greene, *Orlando Furioso,* 2.1.685–92, in *The Life and Complete Works of Robert Greene,* ed. Alexander B. Grosart, 15 vols. (London: Hazell, Watson and Viney, 1881–86), 12:150. The lines quoted are from Ariosto's *Orlando Furioso,* canto 27, stanzas 117 and 121.

44. Canto 20, stanza 131.

45. Canto 10, 15.

46. "Dicito (inquam) lingua maternal: nos enim omnes belle intelligimus, quamis Anglice loqui dedignamur," *An Edition of Robert Wilson's Three Ladies of London and Three Lords and Three Ladies of London,* ed. H. S. D. Mithal (New York: Garland, 1988), 91.

47. Ibid., 92.

48. *Henry V,* act 3, scene 4.

49. Lisa Jardine, *Reading Shakespeare Historically* (London: Routledge, 1996), 11.

50. David Mason Greene, "The Welsh Characters in *Patient Grissil,*" *Boston University Studies in English* 4, no. 3 (1960): 171–80.

51. Edward Albee, *Who's Afraid of Virginia Woolf?* (London: Jonathan Cape, 1964), 220–27.

52. George Villiers, *The Rehearsal,* act 2, scene 2, in *Burlesque Plays of the Eighteenth Century,* ed. Simon Trussler (Oxford: Oxford University Press, 1969), 19.

53. Carlo Goldoni, *Una delle Ultime Sere di Carnovale,* in *Tutte le Opere di Carlo Goldoni,* 14 vols. (Rome: Arnoldo Mondadori, 1948), vol. 5.

54. Ibid., act 5, 13, 5:292.

55. Jerzy Limon, *Gentlemen of a Company: English Players in Central and Eastern Europe, 1590–1600* (Princeton: Princeton University Press, 1979), 1.

56. E. K. Chambers, *The Elizabethan Stage,* 4 vols. (Oxford: Clarendon Press, 1923), 2:262.

57. Virginia Scott, *The Commedia dell'Arte in Paris, 1644–1697* (Charlottesville: University Press of Virginia, 1990), 193. Chapter 9 of Scott's book gives a detailed account of the development of French in the Italian repertoire.

58. Thomas-Simon Guellette, "Traduction du scenario de Joseph Dominique Biancolelli, dit Arlequin," 329–31, quoted in Scott, *Commedia dell'Arte in Paris,* 199–200.

59. Marvin Carlson, *The Italian Shakespearians* (Washington, D.C.: Folger Books, 1985), 152.

60. My colleague Daniel Gerould recalls seeing the production entirely in Russian in Moscow in the late 1960s and with Polish sequences later in Warsaw.

61. Robert Kavanagh, *Theatre and Cultural Struggle in South Africa* (Totowa, N.J.: Zed Books, 1985), 214.

62. Charles F. Hockett, *A Course in Modern Linguistics* (New York: Macmillan, 1958), 585.

63. Blake Green, "Curtains Going Up," *New York Newsday,* September 3, 2001, 6.

64. Tony Kushner, *Homebody/Kabul* (New York: Theatre Communications Group, 2002), 45.

65. My information on both *The Phoenix Trees are Rising* and Li Guoxiu's *Play Hard* comes from the detailed discussion in John B. Weinstein, "Multilingual Theatre in Contemporary Taiwan," *Asian Theatre Journal* 17, no. 2 (2000): 269–81.

66. Quoted in ibid., 274.

67. Ibid., 275.

68. Dan Urian, "Israeli Drama: A Sociological Perspective," *Contemporary Theatre Review* 12, no. 3 (2002): 86–87.

69. Dan Urian, *The Arab in Israeli Drama and Theatre* (Amsterdam: Harwood, 1997), 28–34.

70. B. Evron, "Bravo! Yediot Aharonot," in Shoshana Weitz, "Mr Godot Will Not Come Today," in *The Play Out of Context: Transferring Plays from Culture to Culture,* ed. Hanna Scolnicov and Peter Holland (New York: Cambridge University Press, 1989), 186–98. Most of my information on the Ronen production comes from this article.

71. Weitz, "Mr. Godot," 194.

72. As I write, ongoing tensions in Israel make this seem less likely, but there was a production of the play in 1994 in Jerusalem codirected by Arab and Jewish director and with an Arab actor as Romeo (Halifa Natur) and a Jewish actress as Juliet (Orna Katz). See Urian, *Arab in Israeli Drama,* 65.

## Chapter 2

1. Crystal, *Dictionary,* 102–3; capitalization to indicate cross-references omitted.

2. A more detailed discussion of this unusual production may be found in Marvin Carlson, "The Berlin Theatertreffen, Spring 2000," *Western European Stages* 12, no. 3 (2000): 23–26.

3. "Dialettale, Teatro," in *Encyclopedia dello Spettacolo* (Rome: Le Maschere, 1954–68), 4:627.

4. Ludovico Ariosto, *The Comedies of Ariosto,* trans. and ed. Edmond M. Beame and Leonard G. Sbrocchi (Chicago: University of Chicago Press, 1975), 3.

5. Niccolò Machiavelli, *Discorso intorno all nostra lingua,* ed. Paolo Trovato (Padua: Antenore, 1982), 59ff., ed. and trans. J. R. Hale in *The Literary Works of Machiavelli* (London: Oxford University Press, 1961), 188.

6. Giovan Batista Gelli, *Opere,* ed. Amelia Corona Alesina (Naples: Fulvio Rossi, 1969), 415.

7. Ariosto, *Comedies,* 103n.

8. Richard Andrews, *Scripts and Scenarios: The Performance of Comedy in Renaissance Italy* (Cambridge: Cambridge University Press, 1993), 22.

9. Although dialect humor was particularly highly developed in Venice, it has always been an important part of folk entertainment. The most famous of the late medieval French farces, *Pathelin,* created in Paris in the late 1400s, contains a scene in which the rogue Pathelin confounds his victim by refusing to speak their actual common dialect, assaulting him instead with corrupted passages of Latin and of various French dialects: Limousin, Picard, Flemish, Norman, and Breton (scene 8).

10. Andrews, *Scripts,* 121–22.

11. On the problems of translating Ruzante's dialects into English, see Ronnie Ferguson's introduction to Angelo Beolco (Ruzante), *The Veteran and Weasel: Two One-Act Renaissance Plays* (New York: Peter Lang, 1995), 61–66.

12. Ruzante, *Teatro,* ed. Ludovico Zorzi (Turin: Giulio Einaudi, 1967), 152.

13. Ibid., 726.

14. Ibid., 1110.

15. Andrews, *Scripts and Scenarios,* 144.

16. Calmo, "Prefazione," 2v.

17. The document is reproduced in Ferdinando Taviani and Mirella Schino, *Il segreto della Commedia dell'Arte* (Florence: Casa Usher, 1982), 186.

18. Of course there were exceptions to this general trend, especially in cosmopolitan centers like Rome and Venice with an extremely varied linguistic population and a relatively weak central source of literary authority. The comedy *Diversi linguaggi,* published in 1609 by "Sig. Vergilio Verucci, a Roman gentle-

man," introduces in its prologue its ten characters, each one speaking a different language, in defiance of all rules of decorum or verisimilitude. The merchant Pantalone appears, speaking his traditional Venetian, but his wife speaks Tuscan and his son Roman. Their two servants speak Bolognese and Bergamask. The son is in love with a young woman speaking the dialect of Perugina, though her father speaks French and her serving maid Amatrician. The cast is rounded out by a Sicilian pedant and a Neapolitan captain. Luciano Mariti, *Comici di professione, dilettanti, editori teatrale nel Seicento. Storia e testi* (Rome: Bulzano, 1978), clxxiv.

19. Ferruccio Marotti and Giovanna Romei, *La Commedia dell'Arte e la società barocca: La professione del teatro* (Rome: Bulzano, 1991), 22.

20. Gianrenzo P. Clivio, "The Languages of the Commedia Dell'arte," in *The Science of Buffoonery: Theory and History of the Commedia dell'Arte,* ed. Domenico Pietropaolo (Toronto: Doverhouse Editions, 1989), 209–37.

21. Ibid., 228.

22. Andrea Perrucci, *Dell'arte rappresentative premeditata ed all'improvviso,* ed. Anton Giulio Bragagalia (Florence: Sansoni, 1961), 163.

23. Ibid., 195.

24. See Francesco Coco, *Il dialetto di Bologna. Fonetica storica e analisi strutturale* (Bologna: Il Mulino, 1970), 21.

25. Perrucci, *Dell'arte rappresentative,* 198.

26. Ibid., 210.

27. Ibid., 215.

28. Ibid., 224.

29. Riccoboni, *Historical and Critical Account,* 68.

30. Dante Isella, "Introduzione" to C. M. Maggi, *Il teatro Milanese* (Turin: Edizioni dell'Orso, 1964), 36.

31. Carlo Goldoni, *Mémoires,* ed. Paul de Roux (Paris: Mercure, 1965), 265–66.

32. Gianfranco Folena, "L'esperienza linguistica di Carlo Goldoni," in Folena, *L'Italiano in Euopa: Esperienze linguistiche del Settecento* (Turin: Einaudi, 1983), 91.

33. Carlo Goldoni, *Tutte le Opere,* ed. Giuseppe Ortolani, 14 vols. (Verona: Mondadori, 1956), 14:465.

34. Carlo Gozzi, *Opere,* ed. Giuseppe Petronio (Milan: Rizzoli, 1962), 977.

35. Carlo Gozzi, *Scritture consestative al taglio della Tartana,* quoted in Gerard Lucinai, *Carlo Gozzi (1720–1806): L'Homme et l'oeuvre,* 2 vols. (Lille: Honore Champion, 1977), 1:106.

36. Giovan Cresimbeni, *Istoria della volgar poesia,* quoted in Robert Freeman, "Opera without Drama," Ph.D. diss., Princeton University, 1967, 21–22.

37. Giuseppe Baretti, *Opere scelte,* 2 vols. (Turin: Unione tipgrafico-editrice torinese, 1972), 1:243.

38. Bruno Migliorini, *Storia della lingua italiana,* new ed. (Florence: Sansoni, 1987), 95.

39. Alessandro Manzoni, *Tutte le Lettere,* ed. Cesare Arieti, 3 vols. (Milan: Adelphi, 1986), 1:158.

40. Ibid., 1:246.

41. Quoted (with translation) in Hermann W. Haller, *The Other Italy: The Literary Canon in Dialect* (Toronto: University of Toronto, 1999), 44–45.

42. Ibid., 80.

43. Thomas Goddard Bergin, *Giovanni Verga* (New Haven: Yale University Press, 1931), 107.

44. Giovanni Cecchetti, *Giovanni Verga* (Boston: Twayne, 1978), 150.

45. Quoted in Olga Ragusa, "Early Drama," in *Luigi Pirandello: Modern Critical Views,* ed. Harold Bloom (New York: Chelsea House, 1989), 104.

46. The best study of this movement is Giuseppe Tamburello, *Sull'aia: Fonografie realmontane* (Naples: Chiurazzi, 1899).

47. Charles A. Ferguson, "Diglossia," *Word* 15, no. 2 (1959): 325.

48. Tullio De Mauro, *Storia linguistica dell'Italia unita* (Bari: Edittore Laterza, 1986), 105–6.

49. Antonio Scuderi, "Code Interaction in Nino Martoglio's *I Civitoti in Pretura,*" *Italica* 29, no. 1 (1992): 62–63.

50. Luigi Pirandello, *Saggi, poesi e scritte vari,* ed. M. La Vecchio Musti (Milan: Mondadori, 1973), 1206.

51. Ibid., 1208.

52. Leonardo Bragaglia, *Interpreti pirandelliani* (Rome: Trevi, 1969), 14.

53. Antonio Gramsci, "Angelo Musco," *Avanti,* March 29, 1919, quoted in Haller, *The Other Italy,* 45.

54. Luigi Pirandello, *Luigi Pirandello in the Theatre: A Documentary Record,* ed. Susan Bassnett and Jennifer Lorch (Chur, Switzerland: Harwood, 1993), 39.

55. Antonio Gramsci, *Selections from Cultural Writings,* ed. David Forgacs and Geoffrey Nowell-Smith, trans William Boelhower (Cambridge: Harvard University Press, 1985), 140.

56. Haller, *The Other Italy,* 252.

57. Gramsci, *Selections from Cultural Writings,* 183–84.

58. Pier Paolo Pasolini, "Manifesto per un nuovo teatro," *Nuovi argomenti* 9 (January–March 1968): 13.

59. See Lorenzo Coveri, ed., *Parole in musica: Lingua e poesia ella canzone d'autore italiana. Saggi critici e antologia di testi* (Novara: Interlinea, 1996).

60. Eric Bentley, *In Search of Theatre* (New York: Vintage, 1954), 290.

61. Lanfranco Bino, *Dario Fo* (Rome: Il Castoro, 1977), 52.

62. Antonio Scuderi, "Updating Antiquity," in *Dario Fo: Stage, Text, and Tradition,* ed. Joseph Farrell and Antonio Scuderi (Carbondale: Southern Illinois University Press, 2000), 54.

63. Quoted in Tony Mitchell, *Dario Fo: People's Court Jester* (London: Methuen, 1984), 12.

## Chapter 3

1. Bill Ashcroft, Gareth Griffiths, and Helen Tiffin, eds., *The Post-Colonial Studies Reader* (London: Routledge, 1994), 283.

2. Goldie, "Audiences for Language-Play," 191.

3. Frantz Fanon, *Black Skin, White Masks,* trans. Charles Lam Markmann (New York: Grove Press, 1967), 18, 38.

4. Ibid., 25.

5. Bill Ashcroft, Gareth Griffiths, and Helen Tiffin, *The Empire Writes Back* (London: Routledge, 1989), 9.

6. Clifford, *The Predicament of Culture,* 23.

7. Brian Crow and Chris Banfield, *An Introduction to Post-Colonial Theatre* (Cambridge: Cambridge University Press, 1996); Helen Gilbert and Joanne Tompkins, *Post-Colonial Drama: Theory, Practice, Politics* (London: Routledge, 1996).

8. Christopher Balme, *Decolonizing the Stage: Theatrical Syncretism and Post-Colonial Drama* (Oxford: Oxford University Press, 1999).

9. Crow and Banfield, *Introduction to Post-Colonial Theatre,* 8.

10. Gilbert and Tompkins, *Post-Colonial Drama,* 106.

11. Ibid., 165.

12. Ashcroft, Griffiths, and Tiffin, *The Empire Writes Back,* 15.

13. David B. Coplan, *In Township Tonight! South Africa's Black City Music and Theatre* (London: Longman, 1985), vii.

14. Wilson Harris, *The Womb of Space: The Cross-Cultural Imagination* (Westport, Conn.: Greenwood, 1983), xviii.

15. Homi K. Bhabha, *The Location of Culture* (London: Routledge, 1994), 4.

16. Marc Maufort, *Transgressive Itineraries: Postcolonial Hybridizations of Dramatic Realism* (New York: Peter Lang, 2003), 21.

17. Gilbert and Tompkins, *Post-Colonial Drama,* 169.

18. Wole Soyinka, "Artistic Illusion: Prescriptions for the Suicide of Poetry," *Third Press Review* 1, no. 1 (1975): 67.

19. Leonard Bloomfield, *Language* (New York: Holt, Rinehart and Winston, 1933), 473–74.

20. Gilbert and Tompkins (*Post-Colonial Drama,* 184–85) distinguish between *pidgin* and *creole* on essentially heteroglossic terms, *pidgin* referring "to linguistic forms which have arisen from the blending of one imperial language with an indigenous language," whereas *creole* often points to the input of several source languages. I have not found this particular distinction elsewhere, and there are certainly many so-called creole languages that derive from a single colonial source.

21. Neil J. Smelser and Paul B. Baltes, eds., *International Encyclopedia of the Social and Behavioral Sciences,* 26 vols. (Oxford: Elsevier, 2002), 17:11441.

22. Although Berlin has since 1983 possessed a Turkish theatre, presenting plays in their native language for the Turkish *Gastarbeiter,* a popular Turkish-German cabaret also evolved during the 1980s, presenting plays in Turkish-inflected German by Turkish actors. In 1987 the Turkish-German Kabarett Knobi-Bonbon was awarded the German Kabarett Prize. An all-woman Turkish-German cabaret, Die Bodenkosmetikerinnen, was formed in 1992. Advertis-

ing for their 2004 program *Arabesk* notes: "We are German Turkish women—in us dwells the powers of two cultures and two languages."

23. Smelser and Baltes, *Encyclopedia of Social Sciences,* 17:11442.

24. David Moody, "The Steeple and the Palm-Wine Shack: Wole Soyinka and Crossing the Inter-Cultural Fence," *Kunapipi* 11, no. 3 (1989): 99.

25. Jean D'Costa, "The West Indian Novelist and Language: A Search for a Literary Medium," in *Studies in Caribbean Language,* ed. Laurence Carrington (St. Augustine, Trinidad: University of the West Indies, 1983), 253.

26. Ashcroft, Griffiths, and Tiffin, *The Empire Writes Back,* 44–47.

27. David DeCamp, "Toward a Generative Analysis of a Post-Creole Speech Continuum," in *Pidginization and Creolization of Languages,* ed. Dell Hymes (Cambridge: Cambridge University Press, 1971), 349–70.

28. See Derek Bickerton, "The Nature of a Creole Continuum," *Language* 49, no. 3 (1973): 642.

29. Ashcroft, Griffiths, and Tiffin, *The Empire Writes Back,* 46.

30. Asheri Kilo, "The Language of Anglophone Cameroon Drama," in *The Performance Arts in Africa,* ed. Frances Harding (London: Routledge, 2002), 205.

31. Judith G. Miller, "Translator's Note" to Werewere Liking, *Singuè Mura: Considérant que la femme. . . , TheatreForum* 19 (Summer–Fall 2001): 16.

32. Robert Yeo, "The Use of Varieties of English in Singaporean Writing," *Southeast Asian Review of English* 9 (December 1984): 55.

33. J. Rajah and S. Tay, "From Second Tongue to Mother Tongue: A Look at the Use of English in Singapore English Drama from the 1960s to the Present," in *Perceiving Other Worlds,* ed. E. Thumboo (Singapore: Times Academic Press, 1991), 408.

34. Elsaid Badawi, "The Continuing Debate," in *The World Encyclopedia of Contemporary Theatre,* ed. Don Rubin, 6 vols. (New York: Routledge, 1994–2000), vol. 4, *The Arab World,* 24.

35. Aziz Chouaki, "L'Humour c'est la maquis suprême," in "Théâtres d'Algerie," special issue of *UBU: Scènes d'Europe* 27–28 (2003): 46–47.

36. Ibid., 50.

37. Azmy's notes, along with critical reviews of the production by the leading Egyptian critic Nehad Selaiha and others may be found on the production's website, the first attempt to use the Internet to document and publicize an Egyptian production: http://nilescape.theartzone.net.

38. Matti Moosa, "Ya'Qûb Sanû and the Rise of Arab Drama in Egypt," *International Journal of Middle East Studies* 5 (1974): 417–18.

39. Pierre Cachia, "The Use of the Colloquial in Modern Arab Literature," *Journal of the American Oriental Society* 87, no. 1 (1967): 12.

40. Bachtarzi Mahiéddine, interview in *Oran-Matin,* May 28, 1932, quoted in Arlette Roth, *Le Théâtre Algérien de Langue Dialectale, 1926–1954* (Paris: François Maspero, 1967), 46.

41. Badawi, "The Continuing Debate," 21.

42. Omar Binsalim, *al-Rastid al-Masrahi Biwazaarat al-Thaqaafah* (Tunis: Centre for Sociological and Economic Studies, 1993), 259.

43. Robert Hamner, "Conversation with Derek Walcott," *World Literature Written in English* 16 (November 1977): 417.

44. Derek Walcott, "What the Twilight Says: An Overture," in *Dream on Monkey Mountain and Other Plays* (New York: Farrar, Straus and Giroux, 1976), 17.

45. Derek Walcott, *Ti-Jean and His Brothers,* in *Dream on Monkey Mountain,* 128–30.

46. See Susan Beckmann, "The Mulatto of Style: Language in Derek Walcott's Drama," *Canadian Drama* 6, no. 1 (1980): 71–89.

47. Stephen P. Breslow, "Trinidadian Heteroglossia: A Bakhtinian View of Derek Walcott's Play *A Branch of the Blue Nile,*" in *Critical Perspectives on Derek Walcott,* ed. Robert D. Hamner (Boulder, Colo.: Lynne Rienner, 1997), 390.

48. Jatinder Verma, "Cultural Transformations," *TheatreForum* 3 (April 1993): 39.

49. Gilbert and Tompkins, *Post-Colonial Drama,* 187.

50. 'Segun Oyekunle, *Katakata for Sofahead* (London: Macmillan, 1983), 26, quoted in Gilbert and Tompkins, *Post-Colonial Drama,* 187.

51. Gilbert and Tompkins, *Post-Colonial Drama,* 188.

52. Balme, *Decolonizing the Stage,* 107.

53. John Bendor-Samuel, *The Niger-Congo Languages: A Classification and Description of Africa's Largest Language Family* (Washington, D.C.: University Press of America, 1989).

54. Ngugi Wa Thiongo, *Decolonizing the Mind: The Politics of Language in African Literature* (London: Heinemann, 1986).

55. Ola Rotimi, interview by Dapo Adelugba, 1984, quoted in Martin Banham, "Ola Rotimi: Humanity as My Tribesmen," *Modern Drama* 33, no. 1 (1990): 68.

56. Ola Rotimi, "The Trials of African Literature," lecture delivered at the opening of the English and Literature Students Association Week of the University of Benin, Bendel State, Nigeria, Monday, May 4, 1987, quoted in Banham, "Ola Rotimi," 75–76.

57. Ola Rotimi, *Hopes of the Living Dead: A Drama of Struggle* (Ibadan: Spectrum Books, 1988), vi.

58. Olu Obafemi, "Theatre of Farce: The Yèyé Tradition in Moses Olaiya's Plays," *Odu* 26 (July 1984): 79.

59. Quoted in ibid., 81.

60. Ibid., 83 n. 15.

61. Kobina Sekyi, *The Blinkards* (London: Heinemann, 1974).

62. Catherine M. Cole, *Ghana's Concert Party Theatre* (Bloomington: Indiana University Press, 2001), 8.

63. Dapo Adlugba, "Language and Drama: Ama Ata Aidoo," in *African Literature Today,* vol. 8, ed. Eldred Durosimi Jones (London: Heinemann, 1976), 72–73.

64. Balme, *Decolonizing the Stage,* 115.

65. Temple Hauptfleisch, "Citytalk, Theatretalk: Dialect, Dialogue and Multilingual Theatre in South Africa," *English in Africa* 16, no. 1 (1989): 77.

66. Kavanagh, *Theatre and Struggle,* 41. See also Robert McLaren, "'Two Many Individual Wills.' From *Crossroads* to *Survival:* The Work of Experimental Theatre Workshop '71," in *Theatre and Change in South Africa,* ed. Geoffrey V. Davis and Anne Fuchs (Amsterdam: Harwood, 1996), 25–48.

67. Hauptfleisch, "Multilingual Theatre and Apartheid Society (1970–1987)," in *Proceedings of the XIIth Congress of the International Comparative Literature Association* (Munich: Iudicium verlag, 1990), 103–4.

68. Hauptfleisch, "Multilingual Theatre," 104.

69. Kavanagh, *Theatre and Struggle,* 192. The specific sections on theatrical language are found on pp. 78–83, 101–4, 139–43, and 192–95.

70. Martin Orkin, *Drama and the South African State* (Manchester: Manchester University Press, 1991), 148.

71. Kavanagh, *Theatre and Struggle,* 213.

72. Loren Kruger, *The Drama of South Africa: Plays, Pageants and Publics since 1910* (London: Routledge, 1999), 164.

73. Orkin, *Drama,* 177.

74. Coplan, *In Township Tonight,* 213.

75. Fatima Dike, *The First South African* (Johannesburg: Raven, 1977).

76. David Graver and Loren Kruger, "South Africa's National Theatre: The Market or the Street?" *New Theatre Quarterly* 5, no. 19 (1989): 272–81.

77. Percy Mtwa, Mbongeni Ngema, and Barry Simon, *Woza Albert!* (London: Methuen, 1983), 50.

78. Ibid., 51.

79. Anne Fuchs, *Playing the Market: The Market Theatre Johannesburg, 1976–1986* (Chur, Switzerland: Harwood, 1990), 70.

80. Christopher Balme, "The Performance Aesthetics of Township Theatre: Frames and Codes," in Davis and Fuchs, *Theatre and Change,* 78–79.

81. Ibid., 79.

82. Quoted in Hauptfleisch, "Multilingual Theatre," 107.

83. Malcolm Purkey, "*Tooth and Nail:* Rethinking Form for the South African Theatre," in Davis and Fuchs, *Theatre and Change,* 171.

84. Interview with Malcolm Purkey, quoted in Balme, *Decolonizing the Stage,* 121.

85. Maufort, *Transgressive Itineraries,* 20–22.

86. Bob Hodge and Vijay Mishra, *Dark Side of the Dream: Australian Literature and the Post-Colonial Mind* (North Sydney, NSW: Allen and Unwin, 1991), 107–8.

87. Ibid., 110.

88. Ibid., 208.

89. Stephen Muecke, "Ideology Reiterated: The Uses of Aboriginal Oral Narrative," *Southern Review* 16 (1983): 97.

90. Jack Davis, *No Sugar,* in *New Australian Drama* (London: Nick Hern Books, 1989), 233.

91. Helen Gilbert, "Reconciliation? Aboriginality and Australian Theatre in the 1990s," in *Our Australian Theatre in the 1990s,* ed. Veronica Kelly (Amsterdam: Rodopi, 1998), 82.

92. Balme, *Decolonizing the Stage,* 123.

93. Ibid., 124. Balme notes, however, that Tuwhare's suggestion has never been put into practice since the play's first performance in 1985, a demonstration of the success of the broadly based Maori Renaissance between 1977 and 1985.

94. William Peterson, "Reclaiming the Past, Building a Future: Maori Identity in the Plays of Hone Kouka," in *Theatre Research International* 26, no. 1 (2001): 19.

95. Hone Kouka, *Mauri Tu* (Auckland: Aoraki Press, 1992), 21.

96. Joanne Tompkins, "Inter-referentiality: Interrogating Multicultural Australian Drama," in Kelly, *Our Australian Theatre,* 117–18.

97. Tony Mitchell, "Maintaining Cultural Integrity: Teresa Crea, Doppio Teatro, Italo-Australian Theatre and Critical Multiculturalism," in Kelly, *Our Australian Theatre,* 134. See also "New Forms, New Relationship: An Interview with Teresa Crea," *New Theatre Quarterly* 8, no. 29 (1978): 75–80.

98. Tony Mitchell, "Going to the Source: Tes Lyssiotis Talks to Tony Mitchell," *Australian Drama Studies* 23 (1980): 147–60.

99. Maufort, *Transgressive Itineraries,* 122.

100. Ibid., 123–24.

101. Ibid., 129.

102. Ibid., 131 n. 7.

103. Italian Canadian theatre, *Canadian Theatre Review* (Winter 2001); Chinese Canadian theatre, *Canadian Theatre Review* (Spring 2002).

104. Fulvio Caccia, "Marco Micone: Le travail sur la langue," *Vice Versa* 1, no. 3 (1983–84): 4–5.

105. Marco Micone, *Babele,* in *Vice Versa* 26 (1989): 30–32.

106. Micone, *Two Plays* (Montreal: Guernica, 1984), 137.

107. Ibid., 51.

108. Jennifer Harvie and Richard Paul Knowles, "Dialogic Monologue: A Dialogue," *Theatre Research in Canada* 15, no. 2 (1994): 136–63.

109. See Maufort, *Transgressive Itineraries,* 86–93; Ann Wilson, "Border Crossing: The Technologies of Identity in *Fronteras Americanas,*" *Australasian Drama Studies* 29 (October 1996): 7–15; Mayte Gomez, "Healing the Border Wound: *Fronteras Americanas* and the Future of Canadian Multiculturalism," *Theatre Research in Canada* 16, nos. 1–2 (1995): 26–39.

110. Guillermo Verdecchia, *Fronteras Americanas/American Borders* (Toronto: Coach House Press, 1993), 22–23.

111. Harvie and Knowles, "Dialogic Monologue," 149–50.

112. Ibid., 141.

113. Helen Gilbert and Jacqueline Lo, "Performing Hybridity in Post-Colonial Monodrama," *Journal of Commonwealth Literature* 32, no. 1 (1997): 8. The article by Lo is "Disorientations: Contemporary Asian-Australian Theatre," in Kelly, *Our Australian Theatre,* 53–70.

114. Ibid., 12.

115. Chin Woon Ping, *Details Cannot Body Wants,* in *The Naturalization of Camellia Song and Details Cannot Body Wants* (Singapore: Time Books International, 1993), 106–7.

116. Charles R. Lyons and James C. Lyons, "Anna Deavere Smith: Perspectives on her Performance within the Context of Critical Theory," *Journal of Dramatic Theory and Criticism* 9, no. 1 (1994): 43.

117. Ibid., 45.

118. Richard Schechner, "Anna Deavere Smith: Acting as Incorporation," *Drama Review* 37, no. 4 (1993): 63.

*Chapter 4*

1. Ihab Hassan, *The Dismemberment of Orpheus: Towards a Postmodern Literature* (Madison: University of Wisconsin Press, 1971).

2. Hassan, "The Question of Postmodernism," in "Romanticism, Modernism, Postmodernism," ed. Harry R. Garvin, special issue of *Bucknell Review* 25 (1980): 125.

3. Linda Hutcheon, *A Poetics of Postmodernism* (London: Routledge, 1988).

4. Thomas Kyd, *The Spanish Tragedy,* act 4, scene 1, ed. Philip Edwards (Cambridge: Harvard University Press, 1959), 107.

5. Ibid., act 4, scene 4, 112.

6. P. W. Biesterfeldt, *Die dramatische Technik Thomas Kyds. Studien zur inneren Struktur und szenischen Form des Elisabethanischen Dramas* (Halle, Salle: M. Neimeyer, 1935), 45.

7. Philip Edwards, introduction to Kyd, *The Spanish Tragedy,* xxxvii.

8. Bradbrook, *Themes and Conventions,* 83–84.

9. S. F. Johnson, "*The Spanish Tragedy,* or Babylon Revisited," in *Essays on Shakespeare and Elizabeth Drama in Honor of Hardin Craig,* ed. Richard Hosley (Columbia: University of Missouri Press, 1962), 23–36.

10. Michael Hattaway, *Elizabethan Popular Theatre: Plays in Performance* (London: Routledge and Kegan Paul, 1982), 110.

11. Dillon, *Language and Stage,* 184–85.

12. Elizabeth Maslan, "The Dynamics of Kyd's 'Spanish Tragedy,'" *English* 32, no. 143 (1983): 112.

13. Richard Proudfoot, "Kyd's *Spanish Tragedy,*" *Critical Inquiry* 25, no. 1 (1983): 74.

14. Marvin Carlson, "Karen Beier's *Midsummer Night's Dream* and *The Chairs,*" *Western European Stages* 7, no. 3 (1995–96): 71–73.

15. Transcribed from the ZDF videotape of the performance.

16. A. C. H. Smith, *Orghast at Persepolis* (New York: Viking, 1972), 23, 30–31.

17. In a 1791 interview at Shiraz, Brook observed flatly, "I don't give a fuck about ritual, about myth, about universal language." Peter Brook and Erika Munk, "Looking for a New Language," *Performance* 1, no. 1 (1971): 74. Smith, in *Orghast at Persepolis,* reproduces this quote as "I don't give a damn about . . ." (239).

18. Peter Brook, quoted in David Williams, *Peter Brook: A Theatrical Casebook* (London: Methuen, 1991, 170–71.

19. Brook and Munk, "Looking for New Language," 75.

20. Gautam Dasgupta, "Peter Brook's 'Orientalism,'" *Performing Arts Journal* 10, no. 3 (1987): 9–16.

21. Martine Millon, "An Interview with Yoshi Oida," *Alternatives Théâtrales* 14 (May 1985), trans. David Williams, in Williams, *Peter Brook*, 381–82.

22. Harry Dansey, *Te Raukura: The Feathers of the Albatross*, x, quoted in Balme, *Decolonizing the Stage*, 122.

23. Fuchs, *Playing the Market*, 137.

24. Véronique Hotte, "'Theatre and the Rights of Man,' Extract from an Interview by Peter Brook," in Williams, *Peter Brook*, 403–4.

25. Williams, *Peter Brook*, 416–17.

26. Michael Coveney, "Brook Revels in his Brave New World," *Observer*, November 4, 1990.

27. The group's more recent *Mnemonic,* dealing again with origins, memory, and the common humanity beneath our diversity, provides several sections in other languages, with Kostas Philippoglou, for example, presenting several sequences in Greek that evoke his own Greek origins as well as those of the character he is playing. Scene 34 provides extensive multilanguage humor as delegates speaking Greek, French, Swiss German, and English quarrel at an international conference.

28. Rush Rehm, "Lives of Resistance," *TheatreForum* 7 (Winter–Spring 1995): 94.

29. Gerhard Preußler, "Viele Sprachen des Begehrens," *Theater Heute,* January 1, 1996, 51.

30. This postmodern device of inserting fragments of other texts, in this case fragments of both theatrical techniques along with their associated language, appeared in an even more extreme and extended form in the 2004 production *Poor Theatre* by the Wooster Group, America's best-known postmodern experimental company. This production contains one extended sequence in which the American actors re-create, in exact detail, the physical gestures, expressions, intonations, and language (Polish) of a scene from Jerzy Grotowski's production *Akropolis.*

31. Michael Coveney, "Can't Make a Hamlet without Breaking Heads," *Observer,* January 14, 1996.

32. Andy Lavender, *Hamlet in Pieces* (New York: Continuum, 2001), 57.

33. Quoted in ibid., 81.

34. Ibid., 70.

35. Ibid., 90.

36. Shomit Mitter, *Systems of Rehearsal: Stanislavsky, Brecht, Grotowski, and Brook* (London: Routledge, 1992), 5.

37. Patrice Pavis, ed., *The Intercultural Performance Reader* (London: Routledge, 1996), 67.

38. "Il sacrificio di Isacco rivive a Kabul," *Etinforma di Valle,* December–January 2000, 6, no. 1.

39. William O. Beeman, "Tadashi Suzuki's Universal Vision," *Performing Arts Journal* 6, no. 2 (1982): 83.

40. James R. Brandon, "Contemporary Japanese Theatre: Interculturalism and Intraculturalism," in *The Dramatic Touch of Difference: Theatre, Own and Foreign,* ed. Erika Fischer-Lichte, Josephine Riley, and Michael Gissenwehrer (Tübingen: Gunter Narr Verlag, 1990), 92.

41. Stephen Weeks, "Opium: Intercultural Performance in Seattle and Tokyo." *TheatreForum* 17 (Summer–Fall 2000): 33.

42. Ibid., 34.

43. Philippa Wehle, "What's Fiction When You Have Real Life," *Theatre-Forum* 21 (2002): 40.

44. See Marvin Carlson, "Performing the Self," *Modern Drama* 39 (1996): 599–608.

45. Quoted in C. Carr, *On Edge: Performance at the End of the Twentieth Century* (Middletown, Conn.: Wesleyan University Press, 1994), 197.

46. John Freedman, "Alexander Bakshi and His Mythological Theatre of Sound," *TheatreForum* 19 (Summer–Fall 2001): 8.

47. Although most theorists agree, in general, on the decentered and fragmentary nature of postmodern expression, there has never developed any clear consensus on what constitutes either postmodern theatre or postmodern dance. For a summary discussion of this subject see Marvin Carlson, *Performance: A Critical Introduction* (London: Routledge, 1996), 123–43.

48. Royd Climenhaga, "Anne Teresa De Keersmaeker: Dance Becomes Theatre," *TheatreForum* 25 (Summer–Fall 2004): 60–63.

49. John Rouse, "Frank Castorf's Deconstructive Storytelling," *TheatreForum* 17 (Summer–Fall 2000): 89.

50. Lanoye and Perceval, *Schlachten!* 251.

51. Lanoye and de Vos, "Ein Spiel met der Sprache," xliv.

52. Ibid., xlvi.

*Chapter 5*

1. Pavis, *Languages of the Stage.*

2. Shakespeare, *Henry V,* 4.4.21–30, 45–51.

3. Kushner, *Homebody/Kabul,* 65.

4. Ibid., 81.

5. Robert Lepage, *The Seven Streams of the River Ota* (London: Methuen, 1996), 98–99.

6. Ibid., viii.

7. Roman Ingarden, *The Literary Work of Art,* trans. George G. Grabowicz (Evanston, Ill.: Northwestern University Press, 1973), 208. In the original, Ingarden's term for "side text" is *Nebentext,* as opposed to the main text, the *Hauptext.* See *Das literarische Kunstwerk,* 2nd ed. (Tübingen: Max Niemeyer Verlag, 1960), 220.

8. See my essay "The Status of Stage Directions," *Studies in the Literary Imagination* 22, no. 2 (Fall 1991): 37–47.

9. Roland Barthes, *Critical Essays,* trans. Richard Howard (Evanston, Ill.: Northwestern University Press, 1972), 261.

10. David Edgar, *Pentecost* (London: Nick Hern Books, 1995), xx.

11. Sir Philip Sidney, *Defense of Poetry,* ed. Lewis Soens (Lincoln: University of Nebraska Press, 1970), 36.

12. Barthes, *Critical Essays,* 261–62.

13. Carlson, *The Italian Shakespearians,* 52.

14. This is the genealogy offered by Christina Alves in her doctoral dissertation, "The Use of Supertitles by American Opera Companies," Louisiana State University, 1991. This dissertation is, so far as I know, the only study yet made of this significant (and at least in opera rather controversial) phenomenon. It offers almost no theoretical consideration of this practice, but provides information on the technology itself and an analysis of three audience surveys concerning this practice.

15. See Balme, *Decolonizing the Stage,* 124.

16. See my discussion in Marvin Carlson, *The Haunted Stage* (Ann Arbor: University of Michigan Press, 2001), 169–73.

17. Erika Fischer-Lichte, *The Semiotics of Theatre,* trans. Jeremy Gaines and Doris L. Jones (Bloomington: Indiana University Press, 1983), 192.

18. Johann Wolfgang von Goethe, "Shakespeare ad Infinitum," trans. Randolph S. Borne in *Shakespeare in Europe,* ed. Oswald LeWinter (Cleveland: Meridian, 1963), 58–59.

19. C. D. Innes, *Erwin Piscator's Political Theatre* (Cambridge: Cambridge University, 1972), 104.

20. Bertolt Brecht, *Brecht on Theatre,* ed. and trans. John Willett (New York: Hill and Wang, 1978), 44.

21. Hilary U. Cohen, "Theatre By and For the Deaf," *TDR* 33, no. 1 (1989): 68.

22. Leonard Siger, "The Silent Stage," *Johns Hopkins Magazine,* October 1960, 12.

23. This has not generally been the case elsewhere in the world, as Hilary Cohen notes in her report on deaf performance from a wide variety of countries at the Tenth Congress of the World Federation of the Deaf in Helsinki in July 1987 ("Theatre By the Deaf," 68–78). According to Cohen, the main thrust in the United States has been "to gain acceptance for sign language and deaf performance by the mainstream," while European and Asian performances, designed for largely deaf audiences, offered "no integration of hearing and deaf actors and no spoken text" (69).

24. Quoted in Lester Brooks, "Sculptures in the Air," *Sky Magazine,* July 1986, 34.

25. Stephen C. Baldwin, *Pictures in the Air: The Story of the National Theatre of the Deaf* (Washington, D.C.: Gallaudet University Press, 1993), 33.

26. Ibid., 103.

27. Ibid.

28. Mow provided a useful survey of the state of Deaf theatre in America at the opening of the new century in his "Away from Invisibility, Toward Invinci-

bility: Issues with Deaf Theatre Artists in America," in *Deaf World: A Historical Reader and Primary Sourcebook,* ed. Lois Bragg (New York: New York University Press, 2001), 51–67.

29. Peter Sellars, quoted in Alvin P. Sanoff, "The Power of Unspoken Words," *U.S. News and World Report* 101 (1986): 83.

30. Jerrold A. Phillips, "Strategies of Communication in Recent Experimental Theatre," *Proceedings of Speech Communication Association in Convention, 4 November 1978, Minneapolis, Minnesota,* ERIC fiche ED 165212, grid 15.

31. Karen Wada, "A Show of Hands," *American Theatre* 20, no. 7 (2003): 25.

32. Jeff Calhoun, panel on *Big River* sponsored by the American Theatre Wing, CUNY Graduate Center, September 18, 2003.

33. Wada, "A Show of Hands," 25.

34. States, *Great Reckonings,* 36–39.

# Bibliography

Adlugba, Dapo. "Language and Drama: Ama Ata Aidoo." *African Literature Today* 8 (1976): 72–84.

Albee, Edward. *Who's Afraid of Virginia Woolf?* London: Jonathan Cape, 1964.

Andrews, Richard. *Scripts and Scenarios: The Performance of Comedy in Renaissance Italy.* Cambridge: Cambridge University Press, 1993.

Ariosto, Ludovico. *The Comedies of Ariosto.* Trans. and ed. Edmond M. Beame and Leonard G. Sbrocchi. Chicago: University of Chicago Press, 1975.

Arletto, Anthony Arletto. *Introduction to Historical Linguistics.* Washington, D.C.: University Press of America, 1981.

Ashcroft, Bill, Gareth Griffiths, and Helen Tiffin, eds. *The Empire Writes Back.* London: Routledge, 1989.

———, eds. *The Post-Colonial Studies Reader.* London: Routledge, 1994.

Badawi, Elsaid. "The Continuing Debate." In *The World Encyclopedia of Contemporary Theatre,* ed. Don Rubin, 6 vols., vol. 4, *The Arab World,* 19–24. New York: Routledge, 1994–2000.

Bakhtin, Mikhail. *The Dialogic Imagination.* Ed. Michael Holquist, trans. Caryl Emerson and Michael Holquist. Austin: University of Texas Press, 1981.

———. *Problems of Dostoevsky's Poetics.* Ed. and trans. Caryl Emerson. Minneapolis: University of Minnesota Press, 1984.

Baldwin, Stephen C. *Pictures in the Air: The Story of the National Theatre of the Deaf.* Washington, D.C.: Gallaudet University Press, 1993.

Balme, Christopher. "The Aboriginal Theatre of Jack Davis: Prolegomena to a Theory of Syncretic Theatre." In *Crisis and Conflict in the New Literatures in English,* ed. Geoffrey V. Davis and Hena Maes-Jelenik, 401–17. Amsterdam: Rodopi, 1989.

———. *Decolonizing the Stage: Theatrical Syncretism and Post-Colonial Drama.* Oxford: Oxford University Press, 1999.

———. "New Maori Theatre in New Zealand." *Australasian Drama Studies* 15–16 (1989–90): 149–66.

———. "The Performance Aesthetics of Township Theatre: Frames and Codes." In *Theatre and Change in South Africa,* ed. Geoffrey V. Davis and Anne Fuchs, 65–84. Amsterdam: Harwood, 1996.

Banham, Martin. "Ola Rotimi: Humanity as My Tribesmen." *Modern Drama* 33, no. 1 (1990): 67–81.

Baretti, Giuseppe. *Opere scelte.* 2 vols. Turin: Unione tipgrafico-editrice torinese, 1972.

Barthes, Roland. *Critical Essays.* Trans. Richard Howard. Evanston, Ill.: Northwestern University Press, 1972.

Becker, A. L. "Text-Building, Epistemology, and Aesthetics in Javanese Shadow Theatre." In *The Imagination of Reality,* ed. A. L. Becker and A. Yengoyan, 71–91. Norwood, N.J.: Ablex, 1990.

Becker, A. L., and A. Yengoyan, eds. *The Imagination of Reality.* Norwood, N.J.: Ablex, 1990.

Beckmann, Susan. "The Mulatto of Style: Language in Derek Walcott's Drama." *Canadian Drama* 6, no. 1 (1980): 71–89.

Beckwith, Sarah Beckwith. *Christ's Body: Identity, Culture, and Society in Late Medieval Writings.* London: Routledge, 1993.

Beeman, William O. "Tadashi Suzuki's Universal Vision." *Performing Arts Journal* 6, no. 2 (1982): 77–87.

Bendor-Samuel, John. *The Niger-Congo Languages: A Classification and Description of Africa's Largest Language Family.* Washington, D.C.: University Press of America, 1989.

Bentley, Eric. *In Search of Theatre.* New York: Vintage, 1954.

Beolco, Angelo (Ruzante). *Teatro.* Ed. Ludovico Zorzi. Turin: Giulio Einaudi, 1967.

Bergin, Thomas Goddard. *Giovanni Verga.* New Haven: Yale University Press, 1931.

Bergson, Henri. "Laughter." In *Comedy,* ed. Wylie Sypher, 61–192. Garden City: Doubleday Anchor, 1956

Bhabha, Homi K. *The Location of Culture.* London: Routledge, 1994.

Bickerton, Derek. "The Nature of a Creole Continuum." *Language* 49, no. 3 (1973): 640–59.

Biesterfeldt, P. W. *Die dramatische Technik Thomas Kyds. Studien zur inneren Struktur und szenischen Form des Elisabethanischen Dramas.* Halle: M. Neimeyer, 1936.

Bino, Lanfranco. *Dario Fo.* Rome: Il Castoro, 1977.

Binsalim, Omar. *Al-Rastid al-Masrahi Biwazaarat al-Thaqaafah.* Tunis: Centre for Sociological and Economic Studies, 1993.

Bloomfield, Leonard. *Language.* New York: Holt, Rinehart and Winston, 1933.

Blunt, Jerry. *Stage Dialects.* New York: Harper and Row, 1967.

Bourdieu, Pierre. *Ce que parler veut dire: L'économie des échanges linguistiques.* Paris: Librairie Arthème Fayard, 1982. Ed. and trans. John B. Thompson as *Language and Symbolic Action* (Cambridge: Harvard University Press, 1991).

Bradbrook, M. C. *Themes and Conventions of Elizabethan Tragedy.* Cambridge: Cambridge University Press, 1960.

Bragaglia, Leonardo. *Interpreti pirandelliani.* Rome: Trevi, 1969.

Brandon, James R. "Contemporary Japanese Theatre: Interculturalism and Intraculturalism." In *The Dramatic Touch of Difference: Theatre, Own and For-*

*eign,* ed. Erika Fischer-Lichte, Josephine Riley, and Michael Gissenwehrer, 89–99. Tübingen: Gunter Narr Verlag, 1990.

Brecht, Bertolt. *Brecht on Theatre.* Ed. and trans. John Willett. New York: Hill and Wang, 1978.

Breslow, Stephen P. "Trinidadian Heteroglossia: A Bakhtinian View of Derek Walcott's Play *A Branch of the Blue Nile.*" In *Critical Perspectives on Derek Walcott,* ed. Robert D. Hamner, 388–93. Boulder, Colo.: Lynne Rienner, 1997.

Brook, Peter, and Erika Munk. "Looking for a New Language." *Performance* 1, no. 1 (1971): 72–75.

Brooks, Lester. "Sculptures in the Air." *Sky Magazine,* July 1986, 32–39.

Caccia, Fulvio. "Marco Micone: Le travail sur la langue." *Vice Versa* 1, no. 3 (1983–84): 4–5.

Cachia, Pierre. "The Use of the Colloquial in Modern Arab Literature." *Journal of the American Oriental Society* 87, no. 1 (1967): 12–21.

Calmo, Andrea. "Prefazione" to *Il Travaglia.* Venice: Alessi, 1556.

Carlson, Marvin. "The Berlin Theatertreffen, Spring 2000." *Western European Stages* 12, no. 3 (2000): 21–26.

———. *The Haunted Stage.* Ann Arbor: University of Michigan Press, 2001.

———. "Karen Beier's *Midsummer Night's Dream* and *The Chairs.*" *Western European Stages* 7, no. 3 (1995–96): 71–73.

———. "The Iconic Stage." *Journal of Dramatic Theory and Criticism* 3 (Spring 1989): 3–18.

———. *The Italian Shakespearians.* Washington, D.C.: Folger Books, 1985.

———. "Nationalism and the Romantic Drama in Europe." In *Romantic Drama,* ed. Gerald Gillespie, 139–52. Philadelphia: John Benjamins, 1994.

———. *Performance: A Critical Introduction.* London: Routledge, 1996.

———. "Performing the Self." *Modern Drama* 39 (1996): 599–608.

———. "The Status of Stage Directions." *Studies in the Literary Imagination* 22, no. 2 (Fall 1991): 37–47.

———. "Theatre and Dialogism." In *Critical Theory and Performance,* ed. Janelle G. Reinelt and Joseph R. Roach, 313–23. Ann Arbor: University of Michigan Press, 1992.

Carr, C. *On Edge: Performance at the End of the Twentieth Century.* Middletown, Conn.: Wesleyan University Press, 1994.

Carrington, Laurence, ed. *Studies in Caribbean Language.* St. Augustine, Trinidad: University of the West Indies, 1983.

Cawley, A. C. *The Wakefield Pageants in the Towneley Cycle.* Manchester: Manchester University Press, 1958.

Cecchetti, Giovanni Cecchetti. *Giovanni Verga.* Boston: Twayne, 1978.

Chambers, E. K. *The Elizabethan Stage.* 4 vols. Oxford: Clarendon Press, 1923.

Chomsky, Noam. *Aspects of the Theory of Syntax.* Cambridge: MIT Press, 1965.

Chouaki, Aziz. "L'Humour c'est la maquis suprême." In "Théâtres d'Algerie," special issue of *UBU: Scènes d'Europe* 27–28 (June 2003): 43–51.

Clifford, James. *The Predicament of Culture: Twentieth Century Ethnography, Literature, and Art.* Cambridge: Harvard University Press, 1988.

Climenhaga, Royd. "Anne Teresa De Keersmaeker: Dance Becomes Theatre." *TheatreForum* 25 (Summer–Fall 2004): 59–66.

Clivio, Gianrenzo P. "The Languages of the Commedia Dell'arte." In *The Science of Buffoonery,* ed. Domenico Pietropaolo, 209–37. Toronto: Doverhouse Editions, 1989.

Coco, Francesco. *Il dialetto di Bologna. Fonetica storica e analisi strutturale.* Bologna: Il Mulino, 1970.

Cohen, Hilary U. "Theatre By and For the Deaf." *TDR* 33, no. 1 (1989): 68–78.

Cole, Catherine M. *Ghana's Concert Party Theatre.* Bloomington: Indiana University Press, 2001.

Conner, Linda. "Corpse Abuse and Trance in Bali: The Cultural Mediation of Aggression." *Mankind* 12 (1979): 56–68.

Coplan, David B. *In Township Tonight! South Africa's Black City Music and Theatre.* London: Longman, 1985.

Coveney, Michael. "Brook Revels in his Brave New World." *Observer,* November 4, 1990.

———. "Can't Make a Hamlet without Breaking Heads." *Observer,* January 14, 1996.

Coveri, Lorenzo, ed. *Parole in musica: Lingua e poesia ella canzone d'autore italiana. Saggi critici e antologia di testi.* Novara: Interlinea, 1996.

Crow, Brian, and Chris Banfield. *An Introduction to Post-Colonial Theatre.* Cambridge: Cambridge University Press, 1996.

Crystal, David. *A Dictionary of Linguistics and Phonetics.* 4th ed. Oxford: Basil Blackwell, 1991.

Dasgupta, Gautam. "Peter Brook's 'Orientalism.'" *Performing Arts Journal* 10, no. 3 (1987): 9–16.

Davis, Geoffrey V., and Anne Fuchs, eds. *Theatre and Change in South Africa.* Amsterdam: Harwood, 1996.

Davis, Geoffrey V., and Hena Maes-Jelinek, eds. *Crisis and Conflict in the New Literatures in English.* Amsterdam: Rodopi, 1989.

Davis, Jack. *No Sugar.* In *New Australian Drama.* London: Nick Hern Books, 1989.

D'Costa, Jean. "The West Indian Novelist and Language: A Search for a Literary Medium." In *Studies in Caribbean Language,* ed. Laurence Carrington, 66–83. St. Augustine, Trinidad: University of the West Indies, 1983.

DeCamp, David. "Toward a Generative Analysis of a Post-Creole Speech Continuum." In *Pidginization and Creolization of Languages,* ed. Dell Hymes, 349–70. Cambridge: Cambridge University Press, 1971.

De Mauro, Tullio. *Storia linguistica dell'Italia unita.* Bari: Edittore Laterza, 1986.

Dike, Fatima. *The First South African.* Johannesburg: Raven, 1977.

Dillon, Janette. *Language and Stage in Medieval and Renaissance England.* Cambridge: Cambridge University Press, 1998.

Dunn, E. Catherine. "The Literary Style of the Towneley Plays." *American Bene-dictine Review* 20, no. 4 (1969): 481–504.

Edgar, David. *Pentecost.* London: Nick Hern Books, 1995.

*Encyclopedia dello Spettacolo,* ed. Sandro d'Amico. Rome: Le Maschere, 1954–68.

Fanon, Frantz. *Black Skin, White Masks.* Trans. Charles Lam Markmann. New York: Grove Press, 1967.

Farrell, Joseph, and Antonio Scuderi, eds. *Dario Fo: Stage, Text, and Tradition.* Carbondale: Southern Illinois University Press, 2000.

Ferguson, Charles A. "Diglossia." *Word* 15, no. 2 (1959): 325–40.

Ferguson, Ronnie. Introduction to *The Veteran and Weasel: Two One-Act Renaissance Plays,* by Angelo Beolco (Ruzante). New York: Peter Lang, 1995.

Fischer-Lichte, Erika. *The Semiotics of Theatre.* Trans. Jeremy Gaines and Doris L. Jones. Bloomington: Indiana University Press, 1983.

Fischer-Lichte, Erika, Josephine Riley, and Michael Gissenwehrer, eds. *The Dramatic Touch of Difference: Theatre, Own and Foreign.* Tübingen: Gunter Narr Verlag, 1990.

Folena, Gianfranco. *L'Italiano in Euopa: Esperienze linguistiche del Settecento.* Turin: Einaudi, 1983.

Freedman, John. "Alexander Bakshi and His Mythological Theatre of Sound." *TheaterForum* 19 (Summer–Fall, 2001): 3–15.

Freeman, Robert. "Opera Without Drama." Ph.D. diss., Princeton University, 1967.

Fuchs, Anne. *Playing the Market: The Market Theare Johannesburg, 1976–1986.* Chur, Switzerland: Harwood, 1990.

Gelli, Giovan Batista. *Opere.* Ed. Amelia Corona Alesina. Naples: Fulvio Rossi, 1969.

Gibson, Gail McMurray. *The Theatre of Devotion: East Anglican Drama and Society in the Late Middle Ages.* Chicago: University of Chicago Press, 1989.

Gilbert, Helen. "Reconciliation? Aboriginality and Australian Theatre in the 1990s." In *Our Australian Theatre in the 1990s,* ed. Veronica Kelly, 71–88. Amsterdam: Rodopi, 1998.

———, ed. *Postcolonial Plays: An Anthology.* London: Routledge, 2001.

Gilbert, Helen, and Jacqueline Lo. "Performing Hybridity in Post-Colonial Monodrama." *Journal of Commonwealth Literature* 32, no. 1 (1997): 5–39.

Gilbert, Helen, and Joanne Tompkins. *Post-Colonial Drama: Theory, Practice, Politics.* London: Routledge, 1996.

Gillespie, Gerald, ed. *Romantic Drama.* Philadelphia: John Benjamins, 1994.

Goethe, Johann Wolfgang von. "Shakespeare ad Infinitum." Trans. Randolph S. Borne in *Shakespeare in Europe,* ed. Oswald LeWinter. Cleveland: Meridian, 1963.

Goldie, Matthew Boyd. "Audiences for Language-Play in Middle English Drama." In *Traditions and Transformations in Late Medieval England,* ed. Douglas Biggs, Sharon D. Michalove, and Compton Reeves, 110–26. Leiden: Brill, 2002.

Goldoni, Carlo. *Mémoires.* Ed. Paul de Roux. Paris: Mercure, 1965.

——. *Una delle Ultime Sere di Carnovale.* In *Tutte le Opere di Carlo Goldoni.* 14 vols. Rome: Arnoldo Mondadori, 1948.

——. *Tutte le Opere.* Ed. Giuseppe Ortolani. 14 vols. Verona: Mondadori, 1956.

Gomez, Mayte. "Healing the Border Wound: *Fronteras Americanas* and the Future of Canadian Multiculturalism." *Theatre Research in Canada* 16, nos. 1–2 (1995): 26–39.

Gooch, Jane Lytton, ed. *The Lamentable Tragedy of Locrine.* New York: Garland, 1981.

Gozzi, Carlo. *Opere,* ed. Giuseppe Petronio. Milan: Rizzoli, 1962.

Gramsci, Antonio. *Selections from Cultural Writings.* Ed. David Forgacs and Geoffrey Nowell-Smith, trans. William Boelhower. Cambridge: Harvard University Press, 1985.

Graver, David, and Loren Kruger. "South Africa's National Theatre: The Market or the Street?" *New Theatre Quarterly* 5, no. 19 (1989): 272–81.

Green, Blake. "Curtains Going Up." *New York Newsday,* September 3, 2001.

Greene, David Mason. "The Welsh Characters in *Patient Grissil.*" *Boston University Studies in English* 4, no. 3 (1960): 171–80.

Greene, Robert. *Orlando Furioso.* In *The Life and Complete Works of Robert Greene,* ed. Alexander B. Grosart, 15 vols. London: Hazell, Watson and Viney, 1881–86.

Hall, Edith, ed. *Aeschylus' Persians.* Warminster: Aris and Phillips, 1996.

Hall, Robert A. *Leave Your Language Alone.* Ithaca: Linguistica, 1950.

Haller, Hermann W. *The Other Italy: The Literary Canon in Dialect.* Toronto: University of Toronto Press, 1999.

Hamner, Robert D. "Conversation with Derek Walcott." *World Literature Written in English* 16 (November 1977): 417.

Harris, Roy. *The Language Myth.* New York: St. Martin's Press, 1981.

——, ed. *Introduction to Integrational Linguistics.* Oxford: Pergamon, 1998.

Harris, Roy, and George Wolf, eds. *Integrational Linguistics: A First Reader.* Oxford: Pergamon, 1998.

Harris, Wilson. *The Womb of Space: The Cross-Cultural Imagination.* Westport, Conn.: Greenwood, 1983.

Harvie, Jennifer, and Richard Paul Knowles. "Dialogic Monologue: A Dialogue." *Theatre Research in Canada* 15, no. 2 (1994): 136–63.

Hassan, Ihab. *The Dismemberment of Orpheus: Towards a Postmodern Literature.* Madison: University of Wisconsin Press, 1971.

——. "The Question of Postmodernism." *Bucknell Review* 25 (1980): 117–26.

Hattaway, Michael. *Elizabethan Popular Theatre: Plays in Performance.* London: Routledge & Kegan Paul, 1982.

Kyd, Thomas. *The Spanish Tragedy.* Ed. Philip Edwards. Cambridge: Harvard University Press, 1959.

Hauptfleisch, Temple. "Citytalk, Theatretalk: Dialect, Dialogue and Multilingual Theatre in South Africa." *English in Africa* 16, no. 1 (1989): 71–92.

———. "Multilingual Theatre and Apartheid Society (1970–1987)." In *Proceedings of the XIIth Congress of the International Comparative Literature Association,* 103–9. Munich: Iudicium verlag, 1990.

Hockett, Charles F. *A Course in Modern Linguistics.* New York: Macmillan, 1958.

Hodge, Bob, and Vijay Mishra. *Dark Side of the Dream Australian Literature and the Post-Colonial Mind.* North Sydney, NSW: Allen and Unwin, 1991.

Homer. *The Iliad.* Trans. W. C. Green. London: Longmans, 1884.

Hugo, Victor. "Preface to Cromwell." In Barrett H. Clark, *European Theories of the Drama.* New York: Crown, 1965.

Hutcheon, Linda. *A Poetics of Postmodernism.* London: Routledge, 1988.

Hymes, Dell, ed. *Pidginization and Creolization of Languages.* Cambridge: Cambridge University Press, 1971.

Ingarden, Roman. *The Literary Work of Art.* Trans. George G. Grabowicz. Evanston, Ill.: Northwestern University Press, 1973.

Innes, C. D. *Erwin Piscator's Political Theatre.* Cambridge: Cambridge University Press, 1972.

Isella, Dante. "Introduzione" to Carlo Maria Maggi, *Il teatro Milanese.* Turin: Einaudi, 1964.

Jardine, Lisa. *Reading Shakespeare Historically.* London: Routledge, 1996, 11.

Johnson, S. F. *"The Spanish Tragedy,* or Babylon Revisited." In *Essays on Shakespeare and Elizabeth Drama in Honor of Hardin Craig,* ed. Richard Hosley, 23–36. Columbia: University of Missouri Press, 1962.

Jones, Eldred Durosimi, ed. *African Literature Today.* Vol. 8. London: Heinemann, 1976.

Joseph, May, and Jennifer Natalya Fink, eds. *Performing Hybridity.* Minneapolis: University of Minnesota Press, 1999.

Kavanagh, Robert. *Theatre and Struggle in South Africa.* Towata: Zed Books, 1985.

Kelly, Veronica, ed. *Our Australian Theatre in the 1990s.* Amsterdam: Rodopi, 1998.

Kilo, Asheri, "The Language of Anglophone Cameroon Drama." In *The Performance Arts in Africa,* ed. Frances Harding, 198–207. London: Routledge, 2002.

Kouka, Honi. *Mauri Tu.* Auckland: Aoraki Press, 1992

Kruger, Loren. *The Drama of South Africa: Plays, Pageants and Publics since 1910.* London: Routledge, 1999.

———. *The National Stage: Theatre and Cultural Legitimation in England, France, and America.* Chicago: University of Chicago Press, 1992.

Kushner, Tony. *Homebody/Kabul.* New York: Theatre Communications Group, 2002.

Kyd, Thomas. *The Spanish Tragedy.* Ed. Philip Edwards. Cambridge: Harvard University Press, 1959.

Labov, William. *The Social Stratification of English in New York City.* Washington, D.C.: Center for Applied Linguistics, 1966.

Lanoye, Tom, and Luk Perceval. *Schlachten!* Frankfurt am Main: Verlag der Autoren, 1999.

Lansing, J. Stephen. "The Aesthetics of the Sounding of the Past." In *A Range of Discourses: Toward an Ethnopoetics,* ed. Jerome Rothenberg and Diane Rothenberg, 241–56. Berkeley and Los Angeles: University of California Press, 1983.

Lavender, Andy. *Hamlet in Pieces.* New York: Continuum, 2001.

Lea, M. *Italian Popular Comedy.* New York: Russell and Russell, 1962.

Lepage, Robert. *The Seven Streams of the River Ota.* London: Methuen, 1996.

Liking, Werewere. *Singuè Mura: Considérant que la femme . . . TheatreForum* 19 (Summer–Fall 2001): 16–32.

Limon, Jerzy. *Gentlemen of a Company: English Players in Central and Eastern Europe, 1590–1600.* Princeton: Princeton University Press, 1979.

Lo, Jacqueline. "Disorientations: Contemporary Asian-Australian Theatre." In *Our Australian Theatre in the 1990s,* ed. Veronica Kelly, 53–70. Amsterdam: Rodopi, 1998.

Lodge, Thomas. *The Wounds of Civil War.* Ed. John W. Houppert. Lincoln: University of Nebraska Press, 1969.

Lucinai, Gerard. *Carlo Gozzi (1720–1806): L'Homme et l'oeuvre.* 2 vols. Lille: Honore Champion, 1977.

Lyons, Charles R., and James C. Lyons. "Anna Deavere Smith: Perspectives on her Performance within the Context of Critical Theory." *Journal of Dramatic Theory and Criticism* 9, no. 1 (1994): 43–66.

Machiavelli, Niccolò. *The Literary Works of Machiavelli.* Ed. and trans. J. R. Hale. London: Oxford University Press, 1961.

Manzoni, Alessandro. *Tutte le Lettere.* Ed. Cesare Arieti. 3 vols. Milan: Adelphi, 1986.

Mariti, Luciano. *Comici di professione, dilettanti, editori teatrale nel Seicento. Storia e testi.* Rome: Bulzoni, 1978.

Marlowe, Christopher. *Dido, Queen of Carthage.* In *The Complete Works of Christopher Marlowe,* ed. Fredson Bowers. 2 vols. Cambridge: Cambridge University Press, 1981.

Marotti, Ferruccio, and Giovanna Romei. *La Commedia dell'Arte e la società barocca: La professione del teatro.* Rome: Bulzoni, 1991.

Marston, John. *Antonio and Mellida.* In *Selected Plays of John Marston,* ed. Macdonald P. Jackson and Michael Neill. 2 vols. Cambridge: Cambridge University Press, 1986.

Maslan, Elizabeth. "The Dynamics of Kyd's 'Spanish Tragedy.'" *English* 32, no. 143 (1983): 111–25.

Maufort, Marc. *Transgressive Itineraries: Postcolonial Hybridizations of Dramatic Realism.* New York: Peter Lang, 2003.

McLaren, Robert. "'Two Many Individual Wills.' From *Crossroads* to *Survival:* The Work of Experimental Theatre Workshop '71." In *Theatre and Change in South Africa,* ed. Geoffrey V. Davis and Anne Fuchs, 25–48. Amsterdam: Harwood, 1996.

McWhorter, John. *Word on the Street,* Cambridge, Mass.: Perseus, 1998.

Meredith, Peter. "Scribes, Texts, and Performance." In *Aspects of Early English Drama,* ed. Paula Neuss, 13–29. Towata, N.J.: Barnes and Noble, 1983.

Micone, Marco. *Addolorata.* Montreal: Guernica, 1984.

———. *Babele. Vice Versa* 26 (1989): 30–32.

———. *Two Plays.* Montreal: Guernica, 1984.

Migliorini, Bruno. *Storia della lingua italiana.* New ed. Florence: Sansoni, 1987.

Mills, David, ed. *The Chester Mystery Cycle.* East Lansing, Mich.: Colleagues Press, 1992.

Mitchell, Tony. *Dario Fo: People's Court Jester.* London: Methuen, 1984.

———. "'Going to the Source': Tes Lyssiotis Talks to Tony Mitchell." *Australian Studies* 23 (1980): 147–60.

———. "Maintaining Cultural Integrity: Teresa Crea, Doppio Teatro, Italo-Australian Theatre and Critical Multiculturalism." In *Our Australian Theatre in the 1990s,* ed. Veronica Kelly, 130–39. Amsterdam: Rodopi, 1998.

———. "New Forms, New Relationship: An Interview with Teresa Crea." *New Theatre Quarterly* 8, no. 29 (1978): 75–80.

Mitter, Shomit. *Systems of Rehearsal: Stanislavsky, Brecht, Grotowski and Brook.* London: Routledge, 1992.

Moody, David. "The Steeple and the Palm-Wine Shack: Wole Soyinka and Crossing the Inter-Cultural Fence." *Kunapipi* 11, no. 3 (1989): 98–107.

Moosa, Matti. "Ya'Qûb Sanû and the Rise of Arab Drama in Egypt." *International Journal of Middle East Studies* 5 (1974): 401–33.

Mow, Shanny. "Away from Invisibility, Toward Invincibility: Issues with Deaf Theatre Artists in America." In *Deaf World: A Historical Reader and Primary Sourcebook,* ed. Lois Bragg, 51–67. New York: New York University Press, 2001.

Mtwa, Percy, Mbongeni Ngema, and Barry Simon. *Woza Albert!* London: Methuen, 1983.

Muecke, Stephen. "Ideology Reiterated: The Uses of Aboriginal Oral Narrative." *Southern Review* 16 (1983): 86–101.

Obafemi, Olu. "Theatre of Farce: The Yèyé Tradition in Moses Olaiya's Plays." *Odu* 26 (July 1984): 68–83.

Olaquiaga, Celeste. "From Pastiche to Macaroni." In *Performing Hybridity,* ed. May Joseph and Jennifer Natalya Fink, 171–76. Minneapolis: University of Minnesota Press, 1999.

Orkin, Martin. *Drama and the South African State.* Manchester: Manchester University Press, 1991.

Pao, Angela C. "False Accents: Embodied Dialects and the Characterization of Ethnicity and Nationality." *Theatre Topics* 14, no. 1 (2004): 353–72.

Pasolini, Pier Paolo. "Manifesto per un numovo teatro." *Nuovi argomenti* 9 (January–March 1968): 13–14.

Pavis, Patrice, ed. *The Intercultural Performance Reader.* London: Routledge, 1996.

————. *Languages of the Stage: Essays in the Semiology of Theatre.* New York: Performing Arts Journal Publications, 1982.

Perrucci, Andrea. *Dell'arte rappresentative premeditata ed all'improvviso.* Ed. Anton Giulio Bragagalia. Florence: Sansoni, 1961.

Peterson, William. "Reclaiming the Past, Building a Future: Maori Identity in the Plays of Hone Kouka." *Theatre Research International* 26, no. 1 (2001): 15–24.

Phillips, Jerrold A. "Strategies of Communication in Recent Experimental Theatre." *Proceedings of Speech Communication Association in Convention, 4 November 1978, Minneapolis, Minnesota.* ERIC fiche ED 165212, grid 15.

Pickard-Cambridge, W. A. *Dramatic Festivals of Athens.* Oxford: Clarendon, 1968.

Pietropaolo, Domenico, ed. *The Science of Buffoonery: Theory and History of the Commedia dell'Arte.* Toronto: Doverhouse Editions, 1989.

Ping, Chin Woon. *The Naturalization of Camellia Song and Details Cannot Body Wants.* Singapore: Time Books International, 1993.

Pirandello, Luigi. *Luigi Pirandello in the Theatre: A Documentary Record.* Ed. Susan Bassnett and Jennifer Lorch. Chur, Switzerland: Harwood, 1993.

————. *Saggi, poesi e scritte vari.* Ed. M. La Vecchio Musti. Milan: Mondadori, 1973.

Pixérécourt, Guilbert de. *Four Melodramas.* Trans. and ed. Daniel Gerould and Marvin Carlson. New York: Martin E. Segal Theatre Center, 2002.

Preußler, Gerhard. "Viele Sprachen des Begehrens." *Theater Heute,* January 1, 1996, 51.

Proudfoot, Richard. "Kyd's *Spanish Tragedy.*" *Critical Inquiry* 25, no. 1 (1983): 71–76.

Purkey, Malcolm. "*Tooth and Nail:* Rethinking Form for the South African Theatre." In *Theatre and Change in South Africa,* ed. Geoffrey V. Davis and Anne Fuchs, 155–72. Amsterdam: Harwood, 1996.

Rabelais, François. *The Histories of Gargantua and Pantagruel.* Trans. J. M. Cohen. Baltimore: Penguin, 1955.

Ragusa, Olga. "Early Drama." In *Luigi Pirandello: Modern Critical Views,* ed. Harold Bloom, 129–32. New York: Chelsea House, 1989.

Rajah, J., and S. Tay. "From Second Tongue to Mother Tongue: A Look at the Use of English in Singapore English Drama from the 1960s to the Present." In *Perceiving Other Worlds,* ed. E. Thumboo, 400–412. Singapore: Times Academic Press, 1991.

Rehm, Rush. "Lives of Resistance." *TheatreForum* 7 (Winter–Spring 1995): 88–96.

Reinelt, Janelle G., and Joseph R. Roach, eds. *Critical Theory and Performance.* Ann Arbor: University of Michigan Press, 1992.

Riccoboni, Luigi. *An Historical and Critical Account of the Theatres in Europe.* London: T. Waller, 1741.

Roth, Arlette. *Le Théâtre Algérien de Langue Dialectale, 1926–1954.* Paris: François Maspero, 1967.

Rotimi, Ola. *Hopes of the Living Dead: A Drama of Struggle.* Ibadan: Spectrum Books, 1988.

Rouse, John. "Frank Castorf's Deconstructive Storytelling." *TheatreForum* 17 (Summer–Fall 2000): 82–92.

Schechner, Richard. "Anna Deavere Smith: Acting as Incorporation." *Drama Review* 37, no. 4 (1993): 63–64.

Scolnicov, Hanna, and Peter Holland, eds. *The Play Out of Context: Transferring Plays from Culture to Culture.* New York: Cambridge University Press, 1989.

Scott, Virginia. *The Commedia dell'Arte in Paris, 1644–1697.* Charlottesville: University Press of Virginia, 1990.

Scuderi, Antonio. "Code Interaction in Nino Martoglio's *I Civitoti in Pretura.*" *Italica* 29, no. 1 (1992): 61–71.

———. "Updating Antiquity." In *Dario Fo: Stage, Text, and Tradition,* ed. Joseph Farrell and Antonio Scuderi, 39–64. Carbondale: Southern Illinois University Press, 2000.

Sekyi, Kobina. *The Blinkards.* London: Heinemann, 1974.

Sidney, Sir Philip. *Defense of Poetry.* Ed. Lewis Soens. Lincoln: University of Nebraska Press, 1970.

Siger, Leonard. "The Silent Stage." *Johns Hopkins Magazine,* October 1960, 12: 63–72.

Smelser, Neil J., and Paul B. Baltes, eds. *International Encyclopedia of the Social and Behavioral Sciences.* 26 vols. Oxford: Elsevier, 2002.

Smith, A. C. H. *Orghast at Persepolis.* New York: Viking Press, 1972.

Soyinka, Wole. "Artistic Illusion: Prescriptions for the Suicide of Poetry." *Third Press Review* 1, no. 1 (1975): 45–56.

Spector, Stephen, ed. *The N-Town Play.* 2 vols. Oxford: Oxford University Press: 1991.

Starkie, W. J. M. *The Archarnians of Aristophanes.* London: Macmillan, 1966.

States, Bert O. *Great Reckonings in Little Rooms.* Berkeley and Los Angeles: University of California Press, 1985.

Stevens, Martin. *Four English Mystery Cycles: Textual, Contextual, and Critical Interpretations.* Princeton: Princeton University Press, 1987.

Strabo. *Geography of Strabo.* Trans. Horace Leonard Jones. Cambridge: Harvard University Press, 1923.

Sypher, Wylie, ed. *Comedy.* Garden City: Doubleday Anchor, 1956.

Tamburello, Giuseppe. *Sull'aia: Fonografie realmontane.* Naples: Chiurazzi, 1899.

Taviani, Ferdinando, and Mirella Schino. *Il segreto della Commedia dell'Arte.* Florence: Casa Usher, 1982.

Thiongo, Ngugi Wa. *Decolonizing the Mind: The Politics of Language in African Literature.* London: Heinemann, 1986.

Tompkins, Joanne. "Inter-referentiality: Interrogating Multicultural Australian Drama." In *Our Australian Theatre in the 1990s,* ed. Veronica Kelly, 117–31. Amsterdam: Rodopi, 1998.

Tydeman, William. *The Theatre in the Middle Ages.* Cambridge: Cambridge University Press, 1978.

Urian, Dan. *The Arab in Israeli Drama and Theatre.* Trans. Naomi Paz. Amsterdam: Harwood, 1997.

———. "Israeli Drama: A Sociological Perspective." *Contemporary Theatre Review* 12, no. 3 (2002): 67–96.

Verdecchia, Guillermo. *Fronteras Americanas/American Borders.* Toronto: Coach House Press, 1993.

Verma, Jatinder. "Cultural Transformations." *TheatreForum* 3 (April 1993): 36–40.

Villiers, George. *The Rehearsal.* In *Burlesque Plays of the Eighteenth Century,* ed. Simon Trussler. Oxford: Oxford University Press, 1969.

Wada, Karen. "A Show of Hands." *American Theatre* 20, no. 7 (2003): 7–15.

Walcott, Derek. *Dream on Monkey Mountain and Other Plays.* New York: Farrar, Straus and Giroux, 1976.

Weeks, Stephen. "Opium: Intercultural Performance in Seattle and Tokyo." *TheatreForum* 17 (Summer–Fall 2000): 33–39.

Wehle, Philippa. "What's Fiction When You Have Real Life." *TheatreForum* 21 (Summer–Fall 2002): 37–42.

Weinstein, John B. "Multilingual Theatre in Contemporary Taiwan." *Asian Theatre Journal* 17, no. 2 (2000): 269–83.

Weitz, Shoshana. "Mr Godot Will Not Come Today." In *The Play Out of Context: Transferring Plays from Culture to Culture,* ed. Hanna Scolnicov and Peter Holland, 186–98. New York: Cambridge University Press, 1989.

Williams, David. *Peter Brook: A Theatrical Casebook.* London: Methuen, 1991.

Wilson, Ann. "Border Crossing: The Technologies of Identity in *Fronteras Americanas.*" *Australasian Drama Studies* 29 (October 1996): 7–15;

Wilson, Robert. *An Edition of Robert Wilson's Three Ladies of London and Three Lords and Three Ladies of London.* Ed. H. S. D. Mithal. New York: Garland, 1988.

Wolfram, Walt, and Natalie Schilling-Estes. *American English.* No. 24 in the series Language in Society. London: Blackwell, 1998

Yeo, Robert. "The Use of Varieties of English in Singaporean Writing." *Southeast Asian Review of English* 9 (December 1984): 53–66.

Zurbuchen, Mary Sabina. *The Language of Balinese Shadow Theatre.* Princeton: Princeton University Press, 1981.

# Index

# Index of Languages and Dialects